Patricia Yager Delagrange

Moon Over Alcatraz

a novel

ALAMEDA, CALIFORNIA

Printed in the U.S.A.

Digital ISBN: 9781954395053
Print ISBN: 9781954395046

Dedication

I'd like to dedicate this book to my mom and dad who never lived long enough to know I became an author, and to James, Dylan, and Allessandra, the loves of my life, and to my sister Kathy who makes my life complete.

Chapter 1

"Breathe, Brandy, breathe."

Weston's voice came from the side of the hospital bed where I lay propped up, knees bent to accommodate Dr. Farney checking to see how far my cervix had dilated.

Gritting my teeth, eyes shut, I inhaled through my nose. The pungent odor of sweat wafted through my nostrils. I imagined the crest of a deep-blue wave curling over, white foam churning, crashing down, wave after wave speeding toward the edge of a sandy beach.

But I couldn't take in a full breath. I opened my mouth, tried sucking in air, lungs on fire, the pain like a serrated knife to my belly, hands flailing, slapping the sides of the bed to get Weston's attention.

"She can't breathe." I could hear the panic in his voice. He was scared. So was I. *Is this how a first delivery is supposed to go?*

Dr. Farney's voice tore through the delivery room. "The baby's heart rate is slowing."

A plastic mask lowered over my mouth and nose, and a steady flow of oxygen began pouring through. I shifted my gaze to the right. Weston's eyes were riveted on my lower body, his brows dipped down, mouth set in a tight line.

"What's wrong?" I shouted, my voice muffled beneath the mask.

Weston leaned down, his body blocking the glare of the overhead lights. "Take deep breaths. They're using forceps to get the baby out." He gripped my hand and squeezed then edged toward the foot of the bed. "Doctor, is the baby okay?"

"Umbilical cord's wrapped around her neck. She's twisted in the birth canal." Dr. Farney's voice sounded achingly calm.

Wrapped around her neck… twisted in the birth canal… My baby girl had been due in early June, but she was being born three weeks early. However, Dr. Farney had urged us not to worry.

The pain was beyond bad. It was excruciating. Suddenly the pressure in my groin subsided. I inhaled one deep breath, then another, and my lower body deflated like a leaky tire.

"The baby's not… She's not breathing," Weston whispered.

A deafening silence splintered through the room.

I tugged on Weston's hand. He twisted his head in my direction, tears glistening along his lower lashes.

My mind registered the screams, but my ears heard only the wild thumping of my heart as flecks of black clouded my vision.

* * * *

Weston opened the front door of our house on Lauren Drive just a few blocks away from the hospital and I stepped through the threshold. Every chair, each pillow in the front room looked as if it had been reupholstered in drab, lifeless material. Walls, knickknacks, rugs took on an alien quality. I was seeing them for the first time with a new pair of eyes, filtered through a veil of tragedy and disappointment.

I sat on the couch, squinting out the window. Tiny sparrows flitted between the branches of the oak trees in our front yard. The warmer than average May weather had wilted the white petunias and pink geraniums cascading over the sides of the hanging baskets on the front porch. I'd have to water them soon.

Maybe if I closed my eyes when I awakened all of this would not have happened. Resting my hands on my stomach, I felt the place where she'd lived for nine months. Now only a small bulge remained which would be gone in a month or two. There was no baby inside of me. There was no baby outside of me. There was no baby, period.

Unable to give birth to a healthy baby, I couldn't give my husband the child we'd been waiting for, for nine long months. On the other side of the room my mother's gilt-edged mirror reflected an image—a woman with an empty womb, a black void for a uterus. My body had betrayed me.

Weston sat next to me and I reached out and grasped his wrist. "Remember the night she was conceived?"

He bent his head, shaking it from side to side. "Don't do this, Brandy."

"We were living in San Francisco. We made love on the deck.

You could see the full moon—like a huge medallion, hanging by an invisible chain over Alcatraz."

"Never saw it look that way before," he whispered then walked over to the window and stood, his back facing me.

"I thought it was a sign… a good sign… like an omen, you know?"

He turned back around, his lips set in a tight line. "I'll get you some breakfast."

He walked into the hallway, his steps sluggish. He brought in a tray with dry toast, juice and coffee and placed it on the table in front of the couch then sat down next to me. "I know you're devastated you lost the baby, honey, but we can—"

My knee caught the edge of the breakfast tray as I stood up, food toppling onto the floor. Gritting my teeth so hard my temples throbbed, I glared down at him. "Don't you dare."

His jaw dropped open, eyes wide. "What the… ? What do you mean?"

"You know damn well what I mean." My bottom lip quivered, tears coursed down my cheeks. "You were going to tell me we can have another baby, weren't you?" His silence was my answer but I needed to hear the words. "Weren't you?" I yelled, droplets of spit flying from my lips.

He glanced down at his hands then up at me. "Yes," he muttered, his face a mask of hurt and pain. "Does that make me some kind of monster?"

In my heart, the truth was just the opposite. *I* was the monster. My body had given birth to a dead baby. Something inside *me* had killed her. Weston had done nothing wrong. But I had. Sometime during my pregnancy I'd messed up, and now I'd have to live with that knowledge. Forever.

Desperate for sleep, I trudged up the stairs, hoping to wake up and discover my world hadn't come crashing down around me. But at three a.m. my mind stirred. Cradling my abdomen with both hands, I missed the feel of Christine's nighttime punches and kicks. Slumping down under the comforter, I turned onto my side and prayed slumber would overtake me. A single star appeared behind my closed eyelids and I mouthed a wish that I'd never wake up.

But I *did* wake up, and lay staring at the window, mesmerized by the sun's rays that highlighted thousands of tiny dust motes fluttering near the curtains. Nothing mattered. I couldn't imagine making the effort to leave my bed, get dressed, walk downstairs, fix a meal. They all seemed like unimaginably complex and exhausting tasks.

At some point, Weston entered the bedroom and laid a hand on my shoulder. "Honey, would you listen to me for a second?"

I turned onto my back and stared at him, knowing if I opened my mouth I'd cry a ceaseless ocean of wasted emotion. Not one tear, or a million tears, would bring her back.

"We *both* lost Christine, honey, and I'm sad too. You've got to get up, take a walk, start writing again, whatever." He knelt beside the bed and covered my hand with his. "Do this for yourself, Brandy. Or do it for me."

Scenes in the hospital played over and over, my mind spinning like a DVD player. If I said anything, it would have to be about my daughter dying before I had a chance to hold her.

"I'm sorry for getting angry with you," I mumbled. Weston's face shimmered back at me, tears veiling my vision. "It's just… my heart's been ripped out, and what do I have to replace it? What am I going to do?"

He lay down on the bed, facing me. "We lost our daughter. You have every right to break down, fall apart, do whatever you need to, babe." He wrapped a stray piece of hair around my ear and gently rubbed the back of his hand down my cheek. "I'm here for you, whenever you need me."

I sat up and leaned back against the pillows, staring at the far wall. "I have a follow-up appointment with the doctor in a month. I'll talk to her about it."

He sat up, gave me a chaste kiss then wrapped me in his arms. "It'll take time. We'll never forget what happened and we'll always remember Christine. She won't be here with us, but we can be happy again."

I squinched my eyes shut tight, trying to turn off the never-ending videotape of the recent past. He'd never know what it felt like to lose a child that had lived inside your body all those months. Maybe we'd both feel better soon. I just prayed what I'd feel someday would be an emotion other than loss.

Chapter 2

The following morning at the breakfast table Weston's barely audible voice broke the silence in the kitchen. "Brandy?"

I glanced at him over the mug cradled in my hands. "Uh-huh?"

"I talked with the funeral director yesterday. I told him I'd call him back about our plans—"

"Christine's burial," I said, my voice barely more than a whisper.

He nodded. "Your parents passed away. My mom's in the care facility in Chicago. We don't have any close relatives. There's our friends in San Francisco, and a few in the neighborhood like Cecilia and Perry, some guys at work but... I don't know. How do you feel about a private service. Just you and me."

I closed my eyes, rubbed my forehead with my fingertips, tried to wrap my head around the inevitable. I'd pushed this subject to the back of my mind, not wanting to ever deal with it. "I want our baby to have a home where I can visit her. That's the most important thing. The rest of it"—I waved my hand—"the funeral service with guests, a reception afterward... I couldn't handle it, Weston." My chest tightened. It felt as if a bag of stones had been laid on top of my stomach. I couldn't imagine ever feeling unemotional when it came to talking about the death of my child.

Weston walked around to my side of the table and put his arms around my shoulders, bringing me in close. I laid my head on his solid chest. "Whatever you want, Brandy. I can't imagine being social right now either. If people ask, we'll tell them we decided to keep it just for you and me. They can send a card instead... or make a donation."

I nodded, rubbing my face against the soft flannel of his shirt, feeling raw inside. Talking about the burial of my baby was like poking a stiletto into my heart.

He rubbed my back with his splayed hand, his warmth seeping

through me, relaxing the muscles running down the sides of my spine. "I'll call Mr. Peralta," he said. "He owns the funeral home over on Everett Street. You know the one I'm talking about."

I pulled back and looked up at him. "You'll take care of it then?"

"I'll handle it," he said then kissed my forehead.

Three days later we were standing at the edge of a hole in the ground at Holy Sepulcher Cemetery in Hayward, the silence so thick, the insides of my ears buzzed like a distant swarm of angry bees. Mr. Peralta and another gentleman stood off to the side while Weston and I held hands next to a tiny casket.

Weston had chosen a simple mahogany box with gold handles, a bouquet of white lilies graced the top of the small box. I knelt down and laid a kiss on the smooth wood then wiped off the tears that had fallen on top. Weston joined me, placing a single red rose in the middle of the lilies.

He helped me up and we stood side-by-side in silence, my guilt over her death like a stone in my empty belly. I missed everything I'd dreamed would be happening right now, yearned for all that could have been.

Weston nodded at the man standing next to Mr. Peralta and our baby was slowly lowered into the gaping maw. She reached the bottom, and a bird landed on the rich brown dirt piled next to the grave. It pecked around, chirping a little song then flew off—as if saying goodbye. My heart squeezed inside my chest.

I picked up a small handful of soft dirt. "Goodbye, Christine," I whispered, throwing it on top of her casket.

Weston wrapped his arm around my waist and pulled me in close to his side. Why her? Why my baby? Was this supposed to make sense? And, if so, to whom?

We drove home in silence. No words existed to express my grief.

* * * *

Weston had time off under the Family and Medical Leave Act but by Sunday, I could tell he was bored. I opened my MacBook to the novel I was writing, hoping to take my mind off the relentless thoughts of the funeral. I glanced over at Weston but the newspaper hid his face. One foot lay crossed over his knee and it jittered up and down.

"I think you should call your supervisor, West. Tell him you'll return to work."

He lowered the paper, his eyebrows arched. "The new bridge span will get built whether I'm there or not, Brandy. You shouldn't worry about it."

"I'm not worried about the San Francisco Bay Bridge, West," I said, shaking my head. "You've only had this job since January. That's six months. I know legally you can take off six weeks but I don't need you to stay home with me."

He folded the newspaper back to its perfectly creased square and laid it on the table. "I talked to Cecilia and Perry. She said to call her if you need anything."

I smiled. "She's right next door and since she works from home, she's always there. And I'm getting back into the groove of writing. There's no need for you to sit at home and watch me type, West."

He got out of his chair and sat down next to me on the couch. "If you're absolutely sure," he said, tilting his head, his deep brown eyes meeting mine. "What about your appointment with Dr. Farney?"

"I'm perfectly capable of driving myself. Really," I insisted.

He crooked one eyebrow upward and I could tell he wasn't buying it. I smiled to reassure him I wasn't lying—at least not completely anyway. Physically, I was getting better every day, but I was having a tough time concentrating on writing—a bad sign. Writing had always been my great escape, but now... not so much.

However, Weston was battling his own depression over our loss, and didn't need to add me to his plate of sorrow and worry. What he needed was to get back on the job to take his mind off the death of our baby.

So, at the end of May, two weeks after we laid Christine to rest, Weston returned to work, and I went back to my novel. I'd just sat down with my MacBook, opened to the same page I'd been looking at since last weekend, when the phone rang.

"Hi, Brandy." It was Cecilia. "Can I bring over some hot blueberry muffins? They're right out of the oven and taste great with coffee. *And* they go perfectly with a friend who cares about you."

I still felt raw from losing the baby, more comfortable cocooning in my own little world inside the house. But Cecilia had offered me her friendship, and I suddenly realized how much I needed that closeness.

"Sounds great," I answered. "I'll make us both a latte."

Within minutes, the doorbell chimed. Cecilia stood on the front doorstep, a basket draped with a red-checkered napkin cradled in her arms. "Hey, you." She smiled. "How're you doing, hon?"

I gestured her inside, leading the way into the kitchen where she pulled out a chair at the table and swept back her long black hair as she sat down. Her bright, emerald eyes glanced out the window to the back yard. A wet April had brought a profusion of flowers in May with budding roses, and the lawn was lush and green.

"You look tired, Brandy," she said, frowning. "And you've lost a lot of weight."

Setting our coffees down on the table, I pulled up a chair across from her. "Well, yeah, I'm not pregnant anymore."

She reached across the table, taking my hand in hers. "How are you *really* doing?"

I stared into my coffee cup. "Truth?"

"Of course I want the truth, Bran."

I glanced up at her through the curtain of my bangs. "I'm a mess. I can't sleep. I barely eat anything."

She squeezed my hand gently. "Don't expect too much too soon. You've just lost your child. Your first baby."

"If I tell you something, promise me you'll—"

"There's nothing you can't tell me, sweetie. I promise not to reveal what you say to anyone."

"Something's wrong with me." I bit my lower lip, felt the pain of my teeth digging into the tender skin.

Her eyebrows dipped down into a vee. "You mean something physical?"

"No, nothing like that. It's just… I don't even know how to explain this, to myself or anyone else."

She smiled, tentatively. "I won't judge you."

"I'm having these… weird feelings. I get pregnant, carry my baby to *almost* full-term and she dies. But Dr. Farney had told us not to worry about giving birth a few weeks short of her due date. Now all that hope and emotion and love. For what? She's dead before I have a chance to experience her." I pounded my fist on the table. "I did everything right, Cecilia. I ate the right foods, I exercised, I wasn't stressed out, the baby appeared perfectly developed…"

Cecilia leaned back in her chair. "Of course you'll be depressed, Brandy."

"I'm not finished." I took a deep breath, felt the tears sliding over the edges of my eyelids, down my cheeks. "I guess I blame myself for her death… no, make that I *definitely* blame myself for her death. Something went wrong inside *me*, in *my* body that caused this to happen. Weston and I don't have our child because of me!"

Her lips set in a tight line. "Have you talked to Dr. Farney about this?"

"My appointment is scheduled for one month after… after delivery, in a couple of weeks," I stumbled.

"Have you told Weston?"

"I mentioned it one time in the hospital. He didn't agree with me, but what did I expect? 'Yeah, Bran, I blame you for our daughter's death and I think you're a terrible person for allowing this to happen.' I know he feels that way, but he'll never admit it." I swiped the tears from my cheeks with my fingertips.

"I don't believe that for a second." She covered my hand with hers. "I doubt he blames you for your daughter's death."

I looked at her sheepishly. "That's not the only thing going on."

Her eyebrows flicked up, her lips puckered as she chewed the inside of her lip, waiting for my explanation.

"Every time he touches me I have this…" I searched for the right words, needing her to understand.

"You have this what?" she said, her voice barely above a whisper.

"I'd call it a vision but I never actually saw it happen, so—"

She squinted at me, looking confused.

After one deep, shuddering breath, having never said the actual words to anyone before, I muttered, "In my mind I see a baby… my baby, her face swollen and purple. She's struggling to breathe and I can't help her." I covered my face with my hands. "Weston's been very patient and understanding but—"

"He doesn't expect you to have sex already, does he?"

"Well, Dr. Farney said as soon as the bleeding or spotting ceases we can make love. And it has… But these pictures I see in my mind, Cecilia…"

"Did you talk to a grief counselor before you left the hospital?"

I looked over at her, my face wet from crying. "A woman stopped by before I was discharged but I didn't want to talk about it. And Weston has that typical macho attitude, he'd never spill his guts to a counselor."

"But what about you? If Weston won't go, that doesn't mean you can't."

"I read the pamphlet—the stages of grief and all that? Fits me to a tee. I'm angry and depressed. But most women have a baby to show for their pain. God, I'm so confused right now. I just wish I didn't feel this way. I'm hoping it'll pass. Weston deserves better than a wife who can't give him the baby he so desperately wants, who doesn't want him to get near her because she has visions of her baby dying every time he touches her."

"You should at least talk to Dr. Farney about this."

I dabbed at my eyes with a napkin then grabbed a muffin from the basket and placed it on my plate. "I will... at my next appointment. I'll discuss it with her then. Maybe I'm a candidate for drug therapy. You know, for postpartum depression?" I shrugged. "One suggestion was exercise."

"You used to jog. You could try that again."

"Endorphins, right? I saw something about that on the Dr. Oz show." I paused, contemplated taking a bite of muffin, then decided I couldn't swallow anything right now. "I can't go on like this, Cecilia. I'm determined to wrench myself out of this."

"At least you're not accepting it as the status quo," she said, patting my arm. "You've decided to do something about it. Give yourself points for trying."

"Thanks for bringing these over, Cece. The way to a friend's heart is through her stomach ya know."

"I've gotta go." She smiled and tilted her head. "Will you be all right here alone?"

"I'm writing again but I get so distracted, thinking about what might have been." My eyes started watering, emotion overtaking me again. "I have to be so disciplined when I'm working. No one will write my book for me. I've got to get back into a routine."

She stood up, leaned over, and gave me a hug. "Hey, you've got a plan, Brandy. You'll talk to the doctor, start running again. I bet pretty soon you'll be feeling back to normal."

I gave her a weak smile. "I hope so," I said then walked her to the door.

"If you need *anything*," she insisted then gave me a wave and walked next door.

What I *needed* was to get back to work. I refused to wallow in despair. Life really did go on. And I had to learn to accept that.

Chapter 3

After Dr. Farney examined me, she tore off the sanitary gloves, and leaned back against the counter. "I'm sorry about your baby, Brandy." I nodded with a grimace for a smile. "How are you doing?"

"I'm a writer, Doctor. I spend the majority of my time alone in the house, and I'm haunted day and night with thoughts about my baby's death. It's overwhelming."

She rolled the stool over and sat down, her brows furrowed. "Are you getting out of the house, at least for a little while each day?"

"I planned to start jogging but I wanted to see you first. If you say it's okay—" She nodded. "I read the pamphlets the social worker gave me about losing a child and also those from your office on postpartum depression."

"Did you see a counselor?"

I shook my head. "I don't want to rehash the whole experience over and over again, Dr. Farney. According to what I read, I'm following the grief timeline—first denial then anger, bargaining, depression and finally acceptance. I'm trying to accept it. That's the last stage."

"Have you had any suicidal thoughts?"

I shook my head. "No, never."

"Trouble concentrating?"

I shrugged. "I just started writing again. I suppose it'll take a while, though."

"I wouldn't expect you to be feeling completely well, Brandy. It's been," she looked at my chart, "about four weeks. That's not a lot of time. Your depression won't disappear overnight." She paused. "How about Weston? How's he doing?"

"He's okay. I think he's dealing with it the only way he knows how. He doesn't like to talk about it but I can see it in his eyes. He gets this blank look. He tries to be supportive and loving but—" I stared down at my folded hands, feeling a hot blush crawl up my neck to my face.

"But what?" she urged.

"I don't want him to touch me," I mumbled. "Every time he holds me or kisses me I get these visions of my dead baby." I took a trembling breath and continued, "I'm scared for him to touch me because the visions are so realistic, it frightens me." Tears edged toward my eyelids and I tried blinking them away. I didn't want her pity. I needed her advice.

I glanced at her, trying not to cry, but it was useless. The tears dripped onto the blue paper gown laid across my lap.

She placed her hand over mine and looked in my eyes. "We could try antidepressants, Brandy, but I'm hesitant to do that given the fact what you're experiencing right now is to be expected. You lost your baby. And you carried her almost to full term. That's devastating for any woman. And being intimate in any way will naturally bring up thoughts of procreation, and thus the fears surrounding her death." She tapped her chin with her pen. "Let's hold off for right now. See how you're doing in a few weeks. Make an appointment and we'll talk then. Perhaps you'll feel differently about talking to a counselor."

She patted my shoulder and left the room.

I dreaded going home, knowing what awaited me—an empty house, my laptop with a partially completed manuscript, and a fully decorated nursery awaiting an infant. I'd have to put everything in boxes and store them in the attic. I could ask Weston to do it but I felt so guilty about losing Christine I could barely look him in the eye.

He'd arrive home for dinner soon, we'd sit together on the couch and watch a little television, and inevitably our holding hands would lead to a few kisses which would segue into another of my explanations. I could not continue shunning his advances forever.

At the same time, I felt the tug of my novel. I hadn't written but a few pages since coming home from the hospital and I wanted more of the story completed before the inevitable call from my agent.

So I drove home and had just settled on the couch with my MacBook when the doorbell rang. I peeked through the curtains and saw a truck, sides plastered with pictures of flowers of all types, sizes, and colors.

When I opened the front door, I could barely see the person cradling a large bouquet of pink roses. A young man bent his head around to the side and held the flowers out in front of him.

"Brandy Chambers?"

"That would be me."

"Lucky lady." He handed me the bouquet.

I thanked him and he took off running down the pathway toward his truck. I set the vase on top of the coffee table in the front room. A card jutted out of the top of the bouquet and I thumbed it open. It was Weston's handwriting: "We'll both feel better soon. Hope these make you smile. Think of me when you look at them. I love you."

I fondled the pink petals with my fingers, wishing I'd feel *something* besides guilt and grief. I certainly didn't feel romantic. But this was a temporary state. Worrying about 'when' instead of 'if' my depression would disappear was a better way to view my mental status.

After completing one chapter of my book, I smiled to myself, closed my laptop, and went to the kitchen to start dinner before Weston got home from work. I'd just put a casserole in the oven when he phoned, telling me he and James were in a meeting with the "big boys" and he'd be home after it ended. I was watching TV when he returned at ten o'clock.

I grabbed the remote and pushed the mute button. "How did the meeting go?"

He stood in the foyer a second before joining me and my eyes took in the full picture. He was a handsome man, full dark mustache gracing a wide mouth, straight even teeth, a tiny strip of hair ran from the middle of his bottom lip downward toward a sexy cleft in his chin, thick straight eyebrows hovered above chocolate brown eyes, slim nose, high cheekbones. And his smile was "to die for" lighting up his entire face with a grin that used to melt my heart. In the past, just looking at him would turn me on. But now I felt nothing and wondered for the hundredth time when I would feel normal again.

And no matter what clothes he wore, he always filled them out like a bodybuilder, full chest muscles, thick biceps, steel thighs. He loved working out at the gym, and it showed in how physically fit he was. He was a big guy. When he walked into a room, it filled with his presence.

Sitting down beside me, he took a deep breath. "They want me to travel to the East Coast to help with the initial building phase on a bridge in the New York area. There aren't a lot of people who know how to run a job this size. I told 'em I'd have to talk to you first, but they need an answer as soon as possible."

"Do you want to go?"

"It'll mean a huge raise while I'm there, and they promised to pay me the same after I come back."

"How long would you be gone?"

His eyebrows dipped down, his lips set in a straight line. "That's what bothers me. I'd be gone for four or five months. I don't feel right leaving you here all alone. It may not be the best idea." He paused and then slapped his knee with the palm of his hand. "I forgot. How did your appointment go with the doctor?"

"She said it's too early to treat my depression with drugs, that it's natural to feel this way after losing a child at birth, and I shouldn't expect too much too soon. She wants to see me in a few weeks to re-evaluate."

He shook his head and leaned back on the couch. "I shouldn't leave you, Brandy. It's too early."

"I could go with you."

"You probably could, honey, but you'd be sitting in a hotel room all day. They said I should expect to work pretty long hours. Six in the morning until seven at night. You hate hotels."

"You're right." I paused, thinking. "I'd feel more comfortable staying home where I can do my own thing. I really want to finish this draft and hand it over to Brent. He's given me a lot of latitude already because of… everything."

He shook his head. "Still. I'm not sure it's wise, Brandy, you being alone for months after what you've just gone through. And I wanted to… you know… get the nursery taken care of, put everything in the attic."

"I'll do it, West." I knew in my heart it would mean closure after I accomplished that feat. "I need to do it."

He put his arm around my shoulders, bringing me toward his chest. Leaning down, he kissed me tentatively, slowly widening the kiss, his hand roving under my shirt, searching for my breast.

I could sense what he wanted and pulled back, turning away from him. "I can't do this."

Shoving himself off the couch, he stood, facing me. "I've been really patient, Brandy, but this is getting to be too much. It's June. We lost the baby in early May. You told me you've healed already so what's your excuse this time?"

He was frustrated, and I understood if he was leaving for several months there wouldn't be many opportunities left for us to have sex. "I wasn't making excuses. I've been too depressed to have sex." Tears dripped down my cheeks—again. "Maybe it's the price I have to pay for giving birth to a dead baby."

He sat back down, turning me toward him. "I'm sorry I used the word excuse, Brandy. It was thoughtless. What I should have said is, do you think we could make love?" He smiled, engaging me with his eyes.

I shook my head. "There's nothing wrong with making love, but I just can't do it… yet."

"I'm not sexually appealing to you anymore? Did the doctor say this is part of the postpartum depression thing going on here? How long am I supposed to wait?"

"Oh, West." I sighed, aching inside, wishing there was a way I could explain what refused to be explained. It was easier to simply let him make his own assumptions than tell him the truth about my horrifying visions, the feelings of failure, the guilt. I had to believe I'd work my way through this in time, with or without a counselor's help.

"It's like we're roommates. We share the same house but that's about all. Every time I come to bed and try to cuddle, you mumble something about not feeling well or you're exhausted or you're too sad."

I was caught in a web of my own deception. I couldn't tell him *again* about blaming myself for our baby's death. He'd already said he disagreed with me. "I was talking to Cecilia about this and…"

"You talked to Cecilia?" His voice echoed off the front room walls. "Great! You can share the most intimate details of our… non-existent sex life with our next-door neighbor but not with me. That's just crazy, Brandy!"

"It wasn't like that. We were having coffee one morning. I wanted to run it by her, woman to woman, get her opinion about whether it was normal or not, you know? Was that so wrong?"

He stood up again, walked to the front room window and stared out the glass. "The fact you confided in your girlfriend before you talked to me about it makes me feel pretty left out."

I got up and stood next to him. "I'm sorry, West."

He turned to look at me. "I forgive you, Brandy, but can't you at least try?" He took me in his arms. "Let me make love to you, show you how good it can be again—like it was before."

The warmth of his breath along my neck made me shiver. Leaning back, I closed my eyes and tried desperately to melt into the physical feelings of his kisses, his solid arms around my back.

"Oh, Weston, I just—"

"Shhh," he interrupted. "Don't think about anything. I'll take care of you. Just let everything go."

I let my thoughts drift, making my mind a screen filled with images of waves meandering toward the shore. Weston lifted me in his arms, placing me gently on the couch, then covered me with his warm body. I forced myself to relax into his closeness while his hands slid along my stomach, pushing away my shirt, his tongue stroking the skin around my navel, up to my breasts, suckling my nipples. I tried to focus on the physical experience of his lovemaking and my insides loosened.

I'd always been an active partner in bed, giving as good as I got. But I felt different now; my mind and body were two separate entities that wouldn't converge toward my sexual fulfillment. But I was a partner in this union. Everything wasn't all about me.

I focused on making Weston happy. I could fake it, couldn't I? I couldn't continue rejecting him, expecting him to return again and again to give it his best shot. There'd come a time when he would give up entirely, perhaps look for solace elsewhere.

"I love you so much, Brandy." He was breathing hard now, his voice edged rough by desire.

"And I love you," I whispered.

He pulled back, staring down at me, eyes half-closed, one hand cradling my head in his palm while he guided my pants past my knees. Finding the zipper's tag on his jeans, I tore it down to the end, widening the gap in his pants enough for me to feel his erection beneath the tight briefs. I gently pulled downwards along the edge of the soft cotton where he stood full and erect, waiting for my attentive hands.

Strobe-like images flared behind my eyelids, a baby's face purple and swollen, arms punching the air with each stunted breath. My hands went limp, and I turned my head to the side, struggling to gain my mental balance. I gasped for air, unable to breathe, hyperventilating.

"What is it? Are you okay?"

I sat up, cradling my head in my hands, and tried to slow my breathing. "I… saw… a…" I paused, not wanting to add this night to all the others when I'd shunned him sexually.

"You saw what?" He grasped my wrists and slowly guided them down to my lap.

"Nothing. I'm having a problem focusing." My eyes met his. "I'm sorry, West. It's not you. It's me. I just need more time."

He pushed himself up off the couch, turned his back, and zipped up his pants while walking to the study. Seconds later, I could hear him talking on the phone and assumed he'd called James regarding the job in New York.

Moments later he returned and stood in front of the couch where I was sitting, kneading my temples. "I told James I'll take the job. I'm leaving after the Fourth of July sometime. I'll know the exact date soon enough."

I looked up at him. "When you come back I'm sure I'll be my old self again."

"Hope so," he mumbled, and then turned and walked up the stairs.

Several months apart would give me the time I needed to overcome my depression. I prayed these frightening feelings would fade then go away entirely while he was away. I longed to recapture the emotions I'd always felt toward him.

During the next several weeks, I didn't see Weston until he pulled back the covers at night to get into bed. He was busy preparing to leave and had a great deal to accomplish before his departure. Each night he'd quietly seek me out, moving to my side of the bed, softly caressing my shoulders, rubbing my back.

Every touch brought back memories of being in the hospital and the pain of losing Christine, poisoning my libido, inhibiting any sexual response. The thoughts wouldn't go away, and I couldn't reach out to him for solace either.

In mid-July I drove him to the airport. He was flying out of San Francisco, and the traffic was horrible early in the morning. When I pulled up to the appropriate airline drop-off, he quickly kissed me goodbye and told me he'd call that evening then ran toward the gate to catch his plane. An odd sense of relief washed over me.

Not only did I have to deal with my physical reactions toward him, I felt guilty for feeling this way in the first place. What a vicious circle. And I didn't know the way out, but I was hoping I'd work my way through this over the next several months. Otherwise I couldn't see a reason for him to stay married to me. I used to be his wife, his lover, and his friend. Right now I was a failure in the lovemaking arena, and I couldn't expect him to stick around forever if my behavior didn't change.

Chapter 4

Every day I exercised whether I felt like it or not, hoping the endorphins would lift my mood. On my good days, I believed I could recapture the sexual attraction I'd always experienced with Weston. At other times, fear overwhelmed me that losing our baby had rendered me incapable of ever having a sexual relationship. However, I tried to *act* like everything was normal in hopes I'd start to *feel* normal again. My appointment with Dr. Farney was scheduled in a few weeks and if I wasn't better by then I planned to ask her to refer me to a psychologist.

I jogged along the streets of Alameda, to and from Peet's coffeehouse, taking a longer route each day to increase my stamina and raise my heart rate—a woman on a mission to win back her husband.

Weston called every night at nine o'clock my time, midnight on the East Coast. It was a warm August night when the phone on my nightstand let out its distinctive Fur d'Elyse ringtone. I turned over, patting the top of the bedside table, still ensconced in a dream that came to me repeatedly—a baby was crying somewhere in the house and I searched every room but couldn't find her.

My sweaty hand finally made contact with the cordless phone, grabbing it off the base. "Hullo?"

"Brandy?"

"Weston? What time is it?" He'd already phoned before I went to sleep. What had prompted this second call?

"Search me." He burst out laughing then howled as if he'd just heard the funniest joke in the world.

I sat up in bed and turned on the lamp on the night stand. "You're drunk, West. Where are you? You won't drive anywhere, will you?"

He burped into the phone then chuckled. "Sorry 'bout that. Had a wee bit too much to drink. And no, not driving. In my hotel room. But I'm alone, sweetie, don't worry."

I frowned. "Well, of course you're alone. Who else would be in your hotel room with you at—" I looked over at the clock. It read two in the morning. "At five in the morning?"

"I miss you, Brandy. I wanna make love but *you* don't. You still feel that way 'bout me?"

He was smashed, and this was completely out of character for him. I'd seen him tipsy perhaps two or three times, only because he hadn't eaten after drinking a few too many beers or more than a couple of glasses of wine. He was a big guy, weighed over two hundred pounds, and could hold the liquor he drank without anyone noticing.

"You've obviously had too much to drink and this isn't the time for a conversation about our sex life."

"What sex life?" His voice had risen several octaves and I pulled the phone away from my ear. "Do you ssstill luvme?" he slurred.

"Yes, I love you. That hasn't changed. But can we please hang up now? Why don't you call me tomorrow... I mean tonight when you get off work?"

"You don't luffme then, do you Bran?"

"Honey, I *do* love you. But I'm hanging up now. Go sleep this off. I imagine you have to go to work in a couple of hours. I'll talk with you tonight." I placed the phone back on the side table and shut off the light.

What a bizarre conversation! I closed my eyes and tried to get back to sleep, but Weston's words kept replaying in my head: "I'm alone... don't worry."

Those four words festered in the back of my mind like an unclean wound.

He didn't phone me that night or the following night, so the next day I called him on his cell phone because he was out in the field the majority of the day. But every time his voice mail recording chimed in. I left a message telling him I loved him, missed hearing from him, and asked him to call me back when he returned to his hotel that evening.

He was probably busier than he'd ever imagined so I tried not to make his drunken rambling into anything more than it was. Instead of obsessing and worrying about him, I decided to clean out the nursery—if only to prove to myself I'd made at least a smidgen of emotional progress. I could do this.

Laying my head against the nursery door, I closed my eyes, knowing what I'd find inside. I grasped the door handle and turned it slowly, heard the distinctive creak of the hinges. Weston had said he would fix it before I brought the baby home. We'd even joked about it in the birthing room.

The pink walls and white furniture, the rocker in the corner, the crib with a mobile hanging over the side… I could picture it in my mind's eye before I even opened the door.

I imagined my baby lying on her stomach in the crib, butt in the air, sucking on her fingers. I'd dreamed of rocking back and forth in the rocking chair, her body tucked in my arms, tiny lips sucking on my breast while she nursed.

Seeing the inside of her room for the first time since coming home from the hospital was a different story.

I opened the top drawer of the dresser and looked down at the teensy undershirts, pink booties, velvety pajamas, and reached out to fondle them. My heart twisted in my chest like a dying animal. Tears streamed down my cheeks.

I left the drawer open and ran out of the room, slamming the door behind me, sliding my back down the front of the door until I was sitting on the floor. My breathing hitched in my throat. Why my baby? Why?

* * * *

By the third night, I still hadn't heard from Weston. His supervisor in New York, or James here in the Bay Area, would have phoned me if something had happened to him. He was either returning to his hotel room later than usual and it was too late to call me, or he was intentionally not phoning because he was angry with me about our last conversation. I'd left messages on his cell phone and his voice mail at the hotel and still hadn't heard from him.

I was doing the best I could to work through my emotional problems since our baby's death. Did he expect me to do an about-face in so little time? We'd been married for seven years, and up until now we'd had a solid marriage. We could get through this rough patch. All married couples had their ups and downs. But we had to work it out together. Pulling away from me completely was different than giving me the space I needed to figure things out.

It had been seven days since I'd heard from him when the phone rang at one in the morning East Coast time. I fumbled for the handset, pressing it to my ear. I could hear Weston crying on the other end, repeating my name over and over.

"Weston, what's wrong? Are you hurt?" A thousand different images scattered through my brain. Had he been in an accident? Had he been fired?

"I'm sorry. I love you, Brandy." I could barely understand him. He was drunk. Again. However, I'd never heard him this upset before. I'd never seen him cry until the morning in the hospital after Christine died. It terrified me to think something equally upsetting could have happened to him while he was so far away from me.

"I love you too, West. But what are you sorry for?" I asked, my voice ragged with panic. "Oh, God. What's going on?"

The dial tone broke in over his sobbing.

I immediately called him back on his cell, but it went straight to voice mail. I didn't leave a message. My mind raced. What now? I phoned the hotel and reached his room's voice mail. At least I knew he was alive. But why all this drinking? Was he apologizing for that… or for something worse? I left a terse message for him to call me then sank back onto the bed.

I didn't want to list the possibilities. The obvious. I would not sit back and let my marriage fall apart. I was doing all I could on my end during his absence, getting stronger, doing some serious thinking about my attitude concerning our child's death. What was he doing in New York? Getting drunk every night? Doing things he had a reason to regret and feel guilty for?

I never fell back to sleep, rehashing everything over and over in my mind, reviewing my actions since our baby's death and what I knew of Weston's behavior after he arrived in New York.

In the morning, I was able to get the direct number for Weston's supervisor in New York and called him immediately, but he was away from his desk. I explained to his secretary I needed to speak with Weston Chambers right away. She transferred my call to Weston's personal secretary. *Since when did Weston have a personal secretary?* After several rings a woman's voice answered.

"Mr. Weston Chamber's office. This is Carol Smith speaking. May I help you?"

"Yes, this is Mr. Chamber's wife. May I speak with him?"

There was a slight pause. "Weston is out in the field at the moment. Is there something I can help you with?"

"Could you get an urgent message to him, Ms. Smith?"

Another pause. "It's *Miss* Smith and yes, I can try phoning him on his Nextel but he's made it clear it's only for emergencies. Is this an emergency?"

So, whoever this woman was, she wanted to make it known she wasn't married. That came through loud and clear. "No, this isn't an emergency, but could you please ask him to call me this evening when he returns to his hotel room, no matter the hour?"

Another pregnant pause, which I felt was purposeful. "I'll give him the message, Mrs. Chambers. Is there anything else I can do for you?"

"Just make sure he sees the message when he returns to the office, please."

I heard her give a short laugh. "*If* he returns to the office, I'll give him the message."

It had been over a week since the first drunken phone call then there had been last night's insane call. I was determined to get to the bottom of this, even if I was afraid of discovering the truth.

"Miss Smith, is there a possibility he won't be returning to the office today?"

"I can't say, Mrs.—"

"I'm assuming you must have *some* knowledge of his daily schedule."

"Of course."

"And if he's not coming back he'd do you the courtesy of phoning."

"Yes, he's very good about—"

"Then when he phones would you make absolutely sure he knows I want him to phone me tonight from his hotel room. It's very important I speak with him. Today."

I could hear her let out an irritated breath of air. "I understand. Thank you for calling." The line immediately went dead. She'd hung up on me. The bitch.

I was so angry I wanted to jump on a plane to New York today. But maybe I was just overreacting to a rude employee. Maybe whatever was going on could be cleared up by talking to Weston in a few hours.

I'd just have to wait and see.

Chapter 5

Around nine o'clock I went to bed, snuggling under the covers with a new book I'd purchased at the local Borders. I'd just settled back into the down pillows when the phone rang. Reaching over to grab it, I answered before the second ring.

"Brandy, it's me."

Weston.

Not sure whether to be confrontational and accusing, or confused and wanting clarification, I hesitated for a moment. This conversation had to go smoothly, so I tamped down my anger. "How are you? I was so worried about you."

"I'm all right."

"What's going on with you, West? I'm confused."

"About what, besides whether you love me or not."

Sighing inwardly, I reined in my frustration. "Last time we talked I told you how much I love you, West, but you were too drunk to remember." I paused, drew in a deep breath. "I couldn't have a rational conversation with you, or discuss our marriage when you were slurring every word. But I love you so much, honey. How many times do you want me to say it?"

"Whatever… Carol said you demanded I call you tonight. Or else."

"That's not true," I said, a little too loudly. "I simply asked her to make sure you got the message. She acted as if she didn't know whether you were returning to the office. If she's your secretary I'm sure she knows exactly where you are and can get in touch with you at a moment's notice. Yet she was acting totally ignorant about—"

"She's not ignorant, Brandy."

"Let's not argue about your secretary, Weston. She had an attitude, okay? And I didn't appreciate it. I'm your *wife*! But maybe she didn't know you were married."

"I don't know whether I mentioned it or not. What's that got to do with anything?" His voice was a perfect example of boredom.

"You don't know whether you *mentioned* it or not," I said, exasperated. "I guess I'm not important enough to—"

"Like I'm so important to you? You can't even show me you love me," he countered, his voice harsh and louder than before. "Hell, I guess I had the answer when you told me you couldn't make love to me anymore."

"That's not what I said. You're taking our conversation out of context, and you know it." I paused, shaking my head. "I'm going through a tough time. I lost my child. I'm confused about how I feel about everything right now and—"

"You act like you're the *only* one who lost their child, Brandy. And I feel like I've lost my wife too. What the hell does losing a baby have to do with your feelings about me?"

"I know I'm not the only one hurting, West. You're just more stoic about it, I guess. Can't you see I may feel differently about it than you? I carried her to full term, for Gods' sake." I stopped. Should I just go ahead and say what I'd been hiding for months? "Every time you touched me I saw this image of…" How could I tell him? I dropped my head into my palm and squeezed my eyes shut on the pain.

"You see images of what?" he asked, his voice tinged with irritation.

"Of a baby taking her last dying breath, okay? I've finally said it. Are you happy now?"

I could hear him let out a sigh. It took him a moment to respond, and now his voice sounded subdued. "Of course I'm not happy. Why didn't you tell me about this before?"

"I didn't want you to think I was crazy. I'm trying *so* hard to pull myself out of this depression, I really am. You just don't know how difficult it's been. And I love you, West. That's never been the issue. I was having trouble with the sexual part of our relationship. Nothing else has changed."

"We could have saved ourselves a lot of grief if you'd shared your feelings with me right from the beginning," he muttered. "I thought you didn't love me anymore."

"You make it sound like it's too late or something." Silence blared so loudly between us, I was afraid he'd hung up on me. "Is it too late?" I whispered, holding my breath for his answer.

"You're telling me you saw this image, or whatever you call it, only when I touched you? Why? I'm totally lost here."

This was so damn frustrating. I wasn't sure how much to reveal to him about my blaming myself for Christine's death, and I surely wouldn't confide such a devastating secret when he was across the country, thousands of miles away. I wanted to look him in the eyes when I described my overwhelming guilt. "I hate having this type of conversation over the phone. When you called me the other night you seemed to be apologizing for something. You said you were sorry then you hung up. What was that all about?"

"I had too much to drink. I don't remember. Just forget about it, all right?" I could tell he wouldn't open up to me. We were already beyond the point of having a decent conversation.

I rubbed my temples, holding the phone in the crook of my neck, a small drum pounding inside my head. "You're never drunk, West. What's going on with you? I'm worried."

"You won't let me get near you for months and don't tell me why. Then you tell me you have visions of our child dying every time I touch you. Isn't that enough to upset a man, Brandy?" He sounded hostile, angry, his attitude defensive and confrontational.

"You've taken everything I shared with you about my depression over Christine and not being intimate, and turned it into something it's not," I said, feeling myself getting angrier as this discussion dissolved. "This time away from each other was supposed to give me a chance to sort things through, figure out what's going on in my head.

"*You've* used this time apart to purposely misconstrue what I told you, giving you an excuse to behave out of character, getting drunk all the time, maybe doing things that would cause you to call me and apologize for them. Then you have the gall to pretend you don't know what you were talking about, blaming it on the alcohol."

"Why don't you just come right out and say what you're thinking."

"I didn't know you had a personal secretary. Does she figure into this equation?"

"She's my secretary. She works for me. That's it."

"Just because she's your secretary doesn't automatically take her out of the equation. You're being purposefully obtuse, Weston. She had an attitude when I called today and behaved possessively about my contacting you. Is she rude to all your callers or was she reacting to the fact I'm your wife?"

"This conversation is getting us nowhere, Brandy. Let's call it a night. I'm tired. You're tired. It's late."

"You're right. Why don't you give me a call when you can see beyond your anger and hostility toward me. And perhaps you should explain who I am to *Miss* Smith." I slammed the phone down on the handset, turned off the light and stared out the bedroom window, my heart pounding.

I hated it when conversations deteriorated to this degree. Certain subjects needed to be dealt with face to face, and the telephone was not the venue for discussing marital problems.

But what was going on with him? He'd been so drunk when he asked me if I still loved him that he didn't remember I'd reassured him several times I loved him very much. And didn't he understand why I wouldn't want to talk to him when he was in such a stupor?

Thoughts and worries whirled around my brain like mosquitoes on a windowpane the entire night. At five a.m. I pulled back the comforter and climbed out of bed, lethargic from lack of rest and weary from worry. Making a conscious effort to put aside my concerns, I decided to wait until he called me. Labor Day was approaching. Maybe he could fly home for the weekend, giving us time to sort out our problems and talk one-on-one.

Chapter 6

With that hopeful plan in mind, I put on shorts and running shoes and jogged along the beach on my way to Peet's. A typical August morning for Alameda, fog hugged the coast, occasional breaks in the clouds allowing a bit of sun to shine through, sixty-four degrees. The refreshing wind along the shoreline cooled me as my feet pounded the sand. Turning up Park Street, I slowed to a quick walk until I reached the coffee shop.

The baristas were busy this morning, the waiting line extending all the way to the front door. I took the opportunity to buy a copy of the town newspaper, the *Alameda Times Star,* reading while my place in line slowly inched toward the front counter. Latte in hand, I noticed a young woman and her toddler getting ready to leave, giving me the rare chance to sit at one of the window seats where I could watch people walking along the busy street.

While sipping my coffee, a gentleman dressed in an impeccable dark grey suit, red tie and baby-blue shirt approached my table.

"This is the only unoccupied chair. Do you mind?"

I looked over at the empty seat and nodded. "Go ahead," I mumbled then continued reading. I turned the page and noticed his hand reach across the small round table, handing me my keys.

"Oh, my God! I must have dropped them. Thank—" I looked up at his face. "Edward? Edward Barnes?" My eyes widened. "Is that really you?"

He pulled out the chair and sat down, his blue eyes snagging me with an intense stare. "Brandy Donovan?"

"Brandy Chambers now. I don't think I've seen you since high school graduation."

"I left for NYU two days later and—"

"Law school, right?"

"You remembered." He smiled, revealing beautiful straight teeth. "Then I came back here and I've been practicing law ever since."

"What type of law?"

"Criminal. What about you, Mrs. Chambers?" he teased.

"Well, I married Weston after I graduated from Cal. He works as a structural engineer on the San Francisco Bay Bridge project."

"And you? A mom? Two point five kids?"

I looked down into my paper coffee cup, fiddled with the top. "No, no kids yet." Feeling too raw to discuss it now, I changed the subject. "Do you work here in Alameda?"

"Yeah, I do." He glanced down at his wrist watch. "I'd love to continue our discussion but I've got a meeting in ten minutes. How about lunch soon? Remember how I was planning on becoming a chef some day?"

I laughed, recalling his regaling me with the list of applications he'd received for culinary institutes all over the world. "I remember all right. And you were always demanding I taste your latest creation, asking if I thought it needed more spice or a little less olive oil."

He stood, pushing the chair back toward the table. "I'll have to cook for you one of these days. Sometimes I think I'm a better chef than I am a lawyer."

"Well, most of the time you were a fantastic chef."

He grinned mischievously. "And you were always a bad liar. Some of the dishes I served you should never have made it onto the plate."

I laughed again. He'd always been nice looking but now he was older, he'd matured, no longer a gangly teenager. He'd filled out but was still slender with long legs and he appeared to be at least six foot five inches tall. He turned to leave.

"Wait!" Grabbing the corner of his sleeve, I smiled up at him. "It was nice seeing you again, Edward."

He looked right through me with that blue-eyed stare. "It certainly was, Brandy. You take care now." He tipped his head once in acknowledgement then wended his way through the crowd toward the door.

"Edward Barnes," I whispered to myself. "I'll be darned."

I threw my cup in the recycling can and speed-walked out of Peet's, jogging home in less than ten minutes. What a surprise, meeting Edward after so many years. I plopped down on the front room couch and gazed up at the ceiling.

Edward Barnes in the flesh, I reflected. He looked so different than when we'd known each other in high school. He'd become a strikingly handsome man, a perfectly shaped nose widened a bit at the bottom, a dark mustache hovered over his now-straightened teeth, an impressively square jaw, crescent-shaped eyebrows, and the bluest eyes I'd ever seen without contact lenses.

He reminded me of the guy who played a private detective in Magnum, P.I.—Tom Selleck—in his younger days! And he'd always had a fantastic personality, funnier than hell, joked around a lot. I'd enjoyed hanging around him in the classes we shared at St. Joseph's Notre Dame High School. It would be fun to catch up on old times, along with playing guinea pig to one of his homemade meals.

I shoved these thoughts to the back of my mind and got on with my day, keeping busy with chores, working on my current novel, blogging on my personal website to promote my first book—a comfortable routine, giving me a sense of solidity. These days I wasn't so mentally scattered, obsessing about my loss or my feelings toward Weston every moment. I was getting better, just as I'd hoped.

* * * *

Curled up in the corner of the front room couch one morning, absorbed in revising a scene in the first chapter, the phone jangled my thoughts away from the intense concentration.

"How's the writing going?" It was Brent.

My agent rarely called me on a whim to ask me how I was doing. I surmised he had an agenda he'd reveal soon enough. "It's coming along, Brent. I'm on my hundredth revision. I've taken your suggestions to heart, making Annabella much more likable. I agree with you, readers will put the book down if she's a complete bitch. There's gotta be something appealing to her. I'm finding it really difficult, though, changing her from a self-centered diva to a devoted wife."

I could hear him chuckle. "You want to sell your book, Brandy, you'll listen to me. You know that by now. Wasn't I right about your first book?"

Brent was a superb agent. He'd bent over backwards from the day I'd received "the call" when he agreed to represent me, and he was correct now in the revisions necessary for my second novel to sell. I could hear him inhale his twentieth cigarette of the day and shook my head. He knew the business inside and out though he was a bit rough around the edges. After reading the first draft, he was certain he could find a publisher for my current book.

"Yeah, Brent, you were right about the first book." I laughed. He loved to be right and I didn't mind telling him. "Why did you call?"

"Can't I call one of my favorite authors just to see how she's doing?"

I closed my eyes, anticipating any number of avenues this conversation might take. Perhaps someone wanted changes to the plot or the ending. I braced myself for the bad news.

"There's been some discussion about a sequel to your second book."

This was a surprise. I'd never given any thought to writing a sequel. In fact, right at the moment I couldn't imagine how I'd change the ending to my current draft so my characters' lives could continue into the future.

"You do recall my protagonist dies, don't you?"

"Of course I know she dies at the end. You can change that."

I took a deep breath, letting it out slowly, along with the inevitable frustration this conversation had already created. "I'll think about it."

A pregnant pause interrupted our conversation. "Carmichael wants an answer right away."

My stomach clenched, along with my teeth. This put me in a difficult situation because I really wanted to work with this publishing house. "So, I either say I'll let my heroine live and write a sequel or my entire book's dead in the water. Is that what you're saying?"

"In a nutshell." His voice held no emotion—an even keel of authority.

"I don't want to lose this opportunity to have them publish my book, Brent. You know that."

"My hands are tied." He paused. "But if you're not in a hurry, and I don't think you are, then I can keep shopping around. I didn't think you'd want to write a sequel but I had to put it on the table, Brandy."

I tried to imagine writing the book with a completely different ending, changing my characters' lives and loves and emotions, everything I'd worked on for months. I'd dedicated my heart and soul to my current manuscript, through the trauma of losing Christine and my strained relationship with Weston. And they wanted me to change it to meet some nebulous plan to make more money by producing a sequel?

"You said Carmichael wants to know right away. When do I have to decide?" My heart lodged in my throat where my stomach had already risen.

A few seconds of silence passed. "They have to know today."

He knew me pretty well by now, through the revision process of my first book, the death of my baby, and a little about my problems with Weston. He and I had spoken about how I'd used those experiences to flesh out my characters, making the novel what it was today.

"I'd say take your time, but I can't, Bran."

"I have to say no. I just can't do it. I know signing a deal for this manuscript and a sequel would mean major bucks for me and for you but… I have to go with my gut. And it's telling me not to do it."

I could hear him cough then take a long drag from the perennial cigarette, no doubt dangling out of the side of his mouth, as always. So easy to picture him, so classic for Brent Martin. "Okay then. I'll call you back after I've talked to another editor I've worked with before. I think he might like your book as much as I do."

"Thanks, Brent. I'm sorry but I know you understand."

He coughed again then drew in another drag on his cigarette. "Gotta go. I'll pitch the book as a single title. No sequel." Long pause. "I'll call you."

I slowly placed the phone down on the table. We'd come so close to getting an offer. This was really disappointing. But I trusted Brent. He'd been my agent for several years now, took me on when no one else had faith my first novel would sell. And money had never been the main focus for why I'd become a writer. I poured my emotions and feelings into my books, hoping readers would find an outlet for theirs while reading my novel. The almighty dollar was not the ruler of my world.

And I wasn't in a hurry either. I'd leave the hard part for Brent and, in the meantime, I'd continue writing and revising my second book while promoting my first novel on the internet, working on keeping my marriage intact, and fighting against the insidious depression. Did I feel up to the task? Hell yes!

What other choice did I have?

Chapter 7

When I needed a break from writing, I researched the Romance Writers of America website for conferences I might attend in the future. Writing was such a solitary endeavor. Days went by when I never left the house other than my daily run to Peet's Coffee. One afternoon the phone rang, and I was surprised to hear Weston's voice. I hadn't heard from him in several days.

"You don't usually call at this time. How are you doing?" I was in a better mood, albeit busier than I'd ever imagined, blogging on my website and revising my book to be as perfect as I could make it. Keeping busy and focused, as well as jogging, was doing wonders for my mental health.

"I'm fine," he replied. "I apologize for the argument we had the other night. I…"

"I'm sorry too, West. Listen, I was thinking… is there a chance you could fly home for Labor Day weekend?"

Silence greeted my question, then he answered with a sigh, "I can't, Brandy."

"Why not? This would be a perfect opportunity for us to hang out for the three-day holiday and I thought—"

"It's impossible. A fifty-thousand-ton piece of bridge is on its way from China and is supposed to arrive sometime over that weekend. I'm supervising the project and I'll be working 24/7."

I blew out a puff of air in exasperation. It seemed the Fates were against us at every turn. "I understand."

"Anyway, I'm surprised you'd want to be with me after what you said the other night. You know, about having horrifying visions every time I touch you and—"

"Saying I'm having trouble making love isn't the same as saying I don't love you, Weston," I interrupted, feeling overwhelmingly annoyed at having to repeat myself. "Don't you understand there's a difference or can you only think with your dick?"

Crude, but it was the only thing that made sense right now.

"I guess thinking is the only thing I can do with it since I can't use it at home, right?"

"Then use it in New York, or have you already done that?" By this time I was shouting, frustration getting the best of me.

"You're referring to my secretary?"

"If the shoe fits," I replied, gritting my teeth. Maybe there was some truth to my implications. Perhaps I wasn't fabricating the feelings of jealousy I'd felt from *Miss* Smith.

"We're getting nowhere again, Brandy… Labor Day's out of the question. I'll talk to Frank, see when I can get away for a few days, all right?"

"Whatever." Our conversation hadn't gone the way I'd hoped and I was deeply disappointed and hurt. "I'll talk to you soon."

I put the phone down. I'd been hoping we could spend some quality time together, sooner rather than later. And it didn't look like that would happen. I could feel myself getting depressed again and wished someone was here to give me a hug.

But that wasn't going to happen either. Closing my MacBook, I rushed upstairs and changed my shoes. Maybe a jog along the beach would pick up my spirits. I could only wish it were that easy.

I was out the door within minutes, hair up in a ponytail, my faithful running shoes on my feet. Another beautiful day in Alameda, never too hot and the wind along the beach sweet with the scent of ocean and seaweed.

I reached the end of the boardwalk in twenty minutes and turned up Park Street, headed for Peet's. A cold frappuccino sounded heavenly, and I deserved one after the conversation I'd just had with Weston. I felt so alone right now. The only person on my side these days was my friend Cecilia.

The coffee house was far less crowded this time of day. An empty seat facing the window greeted me where I could watch people passing by, the occasional dog leading its owner by the leash.

Sipping my ice-cold drink, gazing toward the sidewalk, I sensed a figure approaching my table. "We meet again, Mrs. Chambers." It was Edward.

I smiled and motioned for him to sit down. "Please join me, Mr. Barnes."

He pulled out the chair across from me and sat down with his coffee, staring at me with those big blue eyes. "You're looking well, Brandy. I didn't ask you when I saw you last time, do you have flexible work hours or do you run a business out of your home or what?"

I stared down at my cup and took a sip, savoring the thick whipped blend of coffee and cream.

"Sorry," he interrupted my thoughts. "I wasn't prying. It's none of my business anyway." He turned his wrist inward, looked at his watch. "I should really go. It was nice—"

I placed my hand on his arm, stalling his departure. "Don't go, Edward." He placed his cup back down on the table. "I lost my baby a few months ago. I'm still messed up."

Lowering his hand over mine, he rubbed my wrist. "I'm so sorry, Brandy. I've never had a child of my own though I'd love to some day. That must have been terrible for you and your husband… ?"

I looked up at him. "Weston… And thank you for saying that. It's been a bad time for me. And him, too, of course."

"At least you have him to lean on. You're lucky."

I glanced out the cafe window, biting my lower lip, then turned toward him. His warm palm over mine was the hug I needed today. I wanted to share this with someone other than my girlfriend Cecilia. "Weston's been out of town for more than a month now. It's been, uh, difficult for both of us, being apart."

His eyes widened. "He left you so soon after losing your child?"

I shook my head. "It wasn't like that. He was offered a fantastic opportunity in New York. I didn't think he should pass it up. Plus it gives me some much needed time to get my head together. You know, postpartum depression and all that."

"Sounds like you could use a little TLC, Brandy. I make an incredible Quiche Lorraine. You'd love it."

I laughed out loud. "The last one you made for me, the eggs were all runny. Totally gross."

He tapped his finger to his temple. "I've learned a lot more about cooking since I last saw you. Took several top-notch classes." He grinned. "Different day, different quiche, Brandy… You up for it?"

He could always make me smile. "I'd love to."

"Tomorrow night, my place, eight o'clock?"

Nodding, I answered right away, "Sounds perfect."

He got up to leave.

"Edward?" I called after him.

He glanced back at me. "Yes?"

"Your address?"

Shaking his head, he looked down at the floor. "Sorry. I'm not thinking straight." He grinned sheepishly. "You always had that effect on me, Brandy… 7177 San Antonio Avenue." He turned and walked out the door.

I covered my mouth with my hand, smiling, remembering how shy he used to be back in high school. Maybe getting together with him would lift my spirits, especially after my last conversation with Weston. I was looking forward to spending time with my old high school buddy.

The next day I went through my closet, looking for something appropriate to wear for dinner at Edward's house. I tried on three different outfits before deciding on my favorite white stretchy top, jean skirt, and black tennis shoes. I didn't want to get dressed up as if I was going on a date—which this wasn't—but I didn't want to wear sweatpants and a t-shirt and look like a slob either. At 7:50 p.m. I grabbed my purse and drove to his house. I parked, checked my lipstick in the rear view mirror, and then walked up the pathway to the door.

He answered, wearing jeans and a white shirt open at the neck. He was so movie-star handsome, it took me a second to adjust to the fact this man was the same teenager who had been my best friend in high school.

"Hello, Brandy. Come in, come in." He gestured to the foyer.

I followed him into a large front room. A couch covered with oversized pillows sat in front of a flat-screen television hung above the fireplace. He motioned for me to sit down.

"Would you like a drink?"

I sat at one end of the couch, leaning back against the huge pillows. "I'd love a Coke or a Pepsi, please."

He nodded. "I have both, but as I recall you always drank Coke, right?"

"I can't believe you remembered," I said, laughing.

"There's a lot you may not believe, Brandy," he replied, laughing along with me.

"What do you mean?"

"Hold on a sec. I'll get your Coke. Over ice?" He raised his eyebrows and I nodded with a smile. Did this guy have an incredible memory or what?

When he returned from the kitchen, he handed me my drink, sat down at the other end of the couch, and turned toward me. Leaning over, he stretched out his hand holding his glass and I held out mine. Our glasses clinked together.

"To memories and old times together," he toasted.

"To both of us now, wiser and a little bit older," I replied seriously.

I leaned further back into the puffy pillows, the atmosphere of the house both warm and comfortable. "You said there were other things I wouldn't believe, Edward. What were you referring to?"

His eyes met mine. "Did you know I had a crush on you throughout our four years of high school?"

My mouth dropped half-open. It took a few seconds to find my voice. "You're not serious."

Shaking his head, he added, "I was too shy to actually say anything to you. I remember feeling I'd die of embarrassment if I asked you out and you turned me down. So I never said anything, never broached the subject."

"I'm flattered." He chuckled. "No, I'm serious. I didn't know you thought about me that way."

"I thought about you a lot, believe me. In ways that would turn both our faces red as a beet." He took another sip of his drink then placed it on the table.

I felt awkward, didn't know what to say. So I kept quiet, looking down at the couch, fiddling with a stray thread in the cushion. Edward and I had been close during high school but we'd lost touch when we departed for our respective colleges. A lot of time had passed since we'd been friends.

In high school, he was kind, funny, had a great personality, and I'd always felt comfortable and safe when we hung out together. I recalled how he'd come to my rescue many times, saving me from unwanted advances from some of the more aggressive guys who frequented our school.

Looking up, I could see the longing in his eyes, his gaze fixed on mine, pupils dilated, the silence between us palpable. He reached out his hand and took my drink, placed it on the table next to his then covered my hand with his warm palm. I turned mine upward and grasped his fingers.

The tug on my hand was barely perceptible but there nonetheless. I moved toward him several inches and he stretched out his other arm, pulling me into his embrace. His lips were warm, the caress of his tongue on mine hot. I shivered. His arms around me were like a security blanket, holding me close to his chest. Tingling sensations zipped through my body.

He slowly pressed me back onto the seat of the couch, angling his body to the side of me, engaging my mouth in long, lazy caresses with his tongue. I settled my hand over the zipper of his jeans, rubbing in slow pressured circles. His mouth found my nipple protruding through the material of my shirt and he suckled the nub gently. Zinging currents ripped through my groin.

I hadn't felt any of these sensations since before that awful day in the hospital and I succumbed to how good it felt, burning sexual desire saturating my body. Not thinking of the past or the future, my mind floated in the inexplicable present, my only awareness the physical heat spreading through every part of me.

Kissing a path up my neck toward my lips, his mouth met mine in a frenzied array of deep kisses interspersed with my nibbling on the sweet flesh of his full lips. Weaving my hands through his thick hair, I moved my hips inward, pressing against the bulge in his pants, further enhancing his growing passion.

He moaned, pulling away from me. "Are you sure about this?" he whispered.

I shook my head, never breaking our gaze. "No, I'm not sure. But I don't want you to stop."

He reached under my skirt, pushing it up to my waist, sliding my underpants off my legs. I unzipped his jeans, forcing his hardness between my thighs, pushing him inside. I was enjoying this more than I could have imagined, needing the feel of him within me. I couldn't get enough of this man and I didn't want this to end. Reaching my apex, I screamed his name, he grasped my hips, forcing himself deeper, a loud moan escaped his lips and I felt his whole body shudder.

Our labored breathing cut through the silence. Moving to the side of the couch, he draped his arm across my waist. His breathing slowed, his eyes closed, time passed. He was asleep. And the reality of what I'd done crawled into my consciousness like a snake. I rolled over onto the floor, grabbed my shoes in one hand and my purse in the other, stood, adjusted my clothes and then ran out the door.

What had just happened?

I jumped in my car and, oddly enough, pressed the automatic door lock. I shook my head, my mind swirling. Couldn't think clearly. Turning the key in the ignition, slamming my foot down on the accelerator, I peeled away from the curb, my head pounding. What was wrong with me?

Within moments, I'd reached home, raced into the driveway, ran inside, and headed straight for the shower, as if I could wash away all traces of our coupling. Leaning my head back in the steamy spray, I closed my eyes. What had I done? Why had I acted that way?

It had been a sex scene to rival any you'd see in the theater! Except for one thing. What I'd done was not part of a movie script. It had been a scene from my real life.

Chapter 8

Physically and emotionally exhausted, I fell into a deep sleep within moments, and woke up the following morning sick with guilt. I played the scene over and over in my head, a film in which I was a mere observer and not a participant. I didn't know what to do next. Should I go back to my usual routine? Make myself a latte and sit down and write my novel? Call Weston and ask him how the weather was in New York?

My infidelity tinged every action and my day metamorphosed into the surreal. Nothing was normal anymore, least of all me. I searched for something to grab onto, to make me feel my life wasn't tilted precariously on the edge of an abyss. But it was like trying to grasp fog. I couldn't make any solid sense of last night's foray into adultery.

And I dreaded Weston's next call. What would I say? I tried my best to write but couldn't type a single word I didn't delete. After several hours, I closed my Mac, disgusted with myself. That evening after fixing a salad, I sat in front of the TV to watch a movie but couldn't eat a bite. I expected the phone to ring any moment. But would it be Weston or Edward?

After revisiting my promiscuous scene over and over throughout the day, I fell into bed early, mentally exhausted. Did I plan to lie to Weston when we next talked, wait until he returned home to drop my bombshell? I lay in bed staring out the window watching the stars, wishing on each of them for guidance.

When the phone rang my heart sped up, matching the rhythm of my pulse. I sat up, staring at the jangling object on the nightstand, questioning my sanity if I answered it. Counting the rings, after ten piercing rounds of irritating tones, I grabbed it off the base, dropping it on the floor as it slipped out of my sweaty hand.

I scooped it up, my insides cringing. "Hello?"

"Brandy? Are you all right?" West asked in a rush of words.

"Yes, I just dropped the phone. I was hoping you'd call tonight."

"I wanted to talk to you too. I got a flight out for Labor Day."

I held my breath, stunned speechless.

"Brandy? You there?"

I cleared my throat. "Yeah, sure. Just surprised. I thought you had to work."

"There's been a delay involving the ship from China."

"Well, that's great. Umm, let me get a piece of paper."

After writing down the pertinent flight details we agreed we'd see each other in a few days. I lay back on the pillows but slept for mere minutes at a time, waking up every hour to look at the clock, hoping to have the luxury of realizing my evening with Edward had been a bad dream. That I hadn't acted like an unmarried woman with no attachments, free to do what I pleased with whomever I pleased because my libido had felt the urge. I'd made mad and passionate love to another man.

And I hadn't had any visions of Christine!

Needless to say, I wouldn't be stopping by Peet's every morning. Instead, I jogged along the beach boardwalk, ending my journey without my favorite latte, exercising my way to forgetting or perhaps to forgiving myself. If I ran faster and harder and longer than ever before, maybe I could quell the constant replay of that night.

Weston's flight was scheduled to arrive on Friday night before the Labor Day weekend. My concerns I'd never be attracted to *any* male were obviously not true. Sexual desire was no longer an impossible dream. But what about when I got together with Weston? Would I be able to make love to my husband without seeing frightening images of my dying baby? Had those visions completely dissipated since my interlude with Edward?

An idea popped into my head. I'd drive to Nordstrom's in San Francisco, buy something sexy for our first night together. I loved my husband. Maybe now I could "make" love to him. I was willing to try. I didn't know whether this was guilt talking but something inside me had turned a corner after my night with Edward. I felt more alive and attractive and looked forward to giving myself sexually to Weston, anticipating I'd enjoy the experience with him.

On the one hand, I was grateful for this opportunity to prove to him we could have an active sex life, while on the other hand, what had precipitated this change was my unexpected sexual interlude with Edward. But I *would* admit my one-night stand. I just wasn't sure when the best time for that admission should be.

I'd have to deal with the ramifications of telling Weston about Edward, and, hopefully he'd understand. Though if I couldn't make sense of it, why should I expect he would? I continued my shopping spree in a haze of confused thoughts about the how and why of the return of the old "me," but decided to give up trying to figure out the puzzle right now. I put that dilemma on the back burner and drove back to Alameda with just enough time to take a bath, do my hair and make-up, and get dressed.

I left early enough to allow time for parking and reaching the gate to greet Weston when his flight arrived, nervous but grateful for the positive way I was feeling. My mind was a whirlwind of emotions—guilt for sleeping with Edward, excitement over the possibility the scary visions of my unborn child were gone, fear of Weston's reaction to my infidelity, and confusion of when would be best to tell him.

When the timing was right, I'd know and decided not to worry about it. I didn't want the anticipation of my confession to ruin our little vacation, wanting to make the most of the limited hours we'd have together over Labor Day weekend.

The possibility popped in my mind Edward might call to ask why I'd left so suddenly. However, my unexplained and immediate departure after having sex with him would be answer enough to whether I wanted to continue our relationship. In my mind, the least of my worries was what Edward would think about my running away without a word.

Weston walked through the gateway and my heart did a skipitty rhythm; I ran to him as fast as my heels and dress would allow. He seemed not to recognize me at first, and did a double take then jogged in my direction, a huge smile gracing his handsome face.

The only clothing he'd seen me wear before he left for New York was sweat pants, an old favorite t-shirt, and tennis shoes. Apparently, he wasn't expecting me to be dressed up, and the look on his face was worth the time and effort I'd taken with my appearance. And I was sure he realized I'd done it for him.

He stopped about a foot from me, obviously not sure whether he should give me a hug, kiss me, or what.

"Brandy, you look beautiful," he whispered. "I love it when you let your hair down." He fingered a long strand of my dark auburn hair.

Placing my hands along the sides of his face, I smiled. "Thank you… I'm happy you're home." Pulling him down toward me, I gave him a gentle kiss, pressing up against his hard, warm body.

His arousal was evident. Slowly widening our kiss, he hugged me tightly against him and his breathing deepened into a low groan. "I love you, Brandy. And I've missed you so much."

I looked longingly into his deep chocolate brown eyes, hoping he'd see how much I'd missed him, my arms wrapped closely around his neck. Pulling him back for another kiss, I caressed his lips with my tongue, letting him know I wanted this as much as he did.

He smiled, took my hand then grabbed his carry-on case from the floor, leading me to the parking garage.

"How was the flight?" I asked as we took the elevator to the floor where I'd parked.

"Too long… And I didn't know what to expect when I arrived." He looked at me with knitted brows. "Our conversations haven't exactly been—"

"Let's not rehash our misunderstandings and accusations, West. We'll start fresh. Take it from today and go from here."

He smiled. "Being apart wasn't such a good idea. I was worried I shouldn't leave."

"I'm feeling much better now." I put my arm around his waist and snuggled closer to his side. "Much."

He stopped in the middle of the parking lot and turned me toward him. "You're feeling better about… you know—"

"Making love to you?" He nodded. "Yeah, I am. In fact, you always drive over the speed limit, so I'll ride shotgun on the way home."

He bent down, engaging my mouth in a deep, exploring kiss, his erection pressed against my pelvis. I pushed against him with my lower body, relishing his arousal.

There was minimal traffic across the Bay Bridge, and we made it home in less than half an hour. Pulling into the driveway, he shut off the ignition and silence enveloped us like a cloak. He turned to me with a confused look on his face.

"Are you sure you're okay with this? I think I've taken all the rejection I can handle when I was home last."

I placed my hand on top of his lap, caressing him. He grinned, grasped the door handle, and jumped out of the car, rushing to my side to put his arm around my shoulders. We entered the foyer, and he guided me upstairs to our bedroom. We reached for each other, falling back onto the down comforter, my body pinned underneath his.

"I've missed this, Brandy. I want to make tonight special for both of us."

I rolled over on top of him and sat up, straddling him. "Let me take it from here."

I leaned over him, my hair forming a waterfall around us, and began at his stubbled chin, working my way down while unbuttoning his shirt, massaging his chest muscles, licking my way around his belly toward the top of his zipper. His stomach muscles flinched with each tongued caress and the sound of the zipper pulling downwards sang through the silence.

My hand found his swollen member, my lips met the beaded tip, his moans escalated, he intertwined his fingers in my hair. I'd almost brought him to climax when he bent forward, pulling me up to the top of the bed, hovering above me in all his hard masculinity.

Pushing up my dress, he pulled down my underpants, massaging my clitoris with his thumb. I was already floating toward delirium, wanting the release my body craved. With wide-open eyes, I met his stare, grabbed the sides of his shirt, pulling him down to kiss me. I opened my legs, anticipating his entrance.

My renewed passion thrilled and surprised us both. I arched my back and he slid inside and upwards, taking me higher with each increasing thrust. I cried out his name, he buried his face in the side of my neck, his body shuddering to stillness.

We slept on and off through the night, in between lovemaking. Our world shifted back to the past, how we'd been before our lost child.

Labor Day passed in a whirlwind of walking along the beach, eating, resting, and making love at every opportunity. Sunday night arrived in what seemed like minutes, and I found myself once again driving him to the airport for his flight to New York. We kissed and hugged until the time came for his departure, silently acknowledging we were back together again and on the same wavelength.

I'd thought of telling him about Edward over the short weekend, but was afraid of ruining what little time we had together. I didn't know whether he would forgive me for my transgression. Our relationship had been shaky at the time I met Edward. That didn't excuse my behavior but I didn't want to admit to what I'd done right before telling him goodbye before he flew off to New York. We wouldn't be able to work on our relationship from a distance. We'd already experienced what could happen when so many miles separated us from daily contact, the constant arguing and misunderstandings.

I drove back to Alameda contemplating when would be best to confess my one-night stand. It was like walking a balance beam. If I told him over the phone while he was in New York, I'd run the risk of our never having the opportunity to salvage our marriage. And if I kept it from him much longer, he'd wonder if my waiting couldn't be construed as devious and deceptive and our marriage would be damned.

But after my journey to the edge of the planet, I was on my trip back home. I felt right again, smiling, remembering our short time together over the holiday. And I was already looking forward to his returning home for Christmas vacation, happy I'd reconnected with my husband after months of shunning him. I guess I wouldn't need a referral to a counselor after all!

I surmised the best time to reveal my indiscretion would be when Weston returned permanently from New York, after the New Year. Then we could deal with our issues together, not over the phone, with no time constraints. And I was prepared to live with the ramifications of my actions whatever they might be.

Chapter 9

I continued revising my novel, about a young woman whose husband dies and she finds love and a new life after settling in a fictional town in California. Brent had connected with the editor he'd told me about last time we'd spoken and Brent had sent him a copy of the first several chapters of my manuscript.

Brent and I spent a good deal of time on the phone haggling over character behavior, the use of slang, plot. We argued over everything, but it was an infusion of lifeblood for me. I loved the process almost as much as writing the book, knowing it was never easy getting your novel published and a spine of steel was always necessary. And I was happy I wouldn't have to write a sequel. Brent had made that clear to the editor upfront.

Every now and again I'd think of Edward and our one night of passion; but not too often anymore. I called his law firm from a public telephone once, just to see whether he was still in town; he'd mentioned the possibility of a transfer. I was told he'd moved to Washington State where their newest satellite office had opened.

Now I could return to Peet's for my daily caffeine fix, but I hadn't been adhering to my jogging routine. I'd been tired and strung out, worried about what the editor would say about my book, on edge about how Weston would react to my indiscretion.

I was caught in a Catch-22 with not enough energy to exercise which exacerbated my exhaustion and I felt more tired than ever. The tension continued to build up inside me with no release. No exercise, no sex, just sitting on the phone with Brent about my manuscript or typing on my computer, editing and revising. It was physically and mentally fatiguing.

Weston and I talked on the phone several times a week. The bridge span project was coming to fruition and would be finished in

January. Having made the decision to wait until he returned home for good to tell him about Edward, I was excited about the upcoming holiday. We'd have plenty of time to talk in January, and I was sure we could work it out then. The "me" Weston knew and loved would never have had a one night stand and I trusted he'd forgive me for my aberrant behavior.

Cecilia was preparing the account books for her husband's company, Saxton Inc., which reduced our time together to snippets of talk on the phone every now and again. Between my book and her accounting, we didn't get an opportunity to see each other often.

Weston was scheduled to arrive on December eighteenth for a week's vacation. I managed to squeeze in some shopping, knowing our time together once he came home would be filled with visiting friends, Christmas parties, and just relaxing together.

The night before his arrival, I'd awakened during the night with a bad case of vertigo, the room going round like a carousel. I fell back to sleep and when I woke up again at seven a.m. I felt a little better. I had a piece of toast for breakfast and felt almost like myself again. However, knowing I could have a spell of dizziness while driving made me uncomfortable, so I called Cecilia to ask her a favor.

"Do you think you could pick up Weston at the airport this afternoon? I think I have a touch of the flu or something and don't feel myself."

"What are your symptoms?"

"It was as if I'd just gotten off the TiltaWhirl at Santa Cruz! The room was spinning and my stomach felt weird. I'm fine now but I'm afraid to drive in case I have another dizzy episode."

"Don't think anything of it. I'll pick him up," she insisted. "Anything to take me away from these damn numbers and columns. I'm going crazy stuck at this computer all day. Just take care of yourself. I'll come by for the flight info in a little while."

She was a lifesaver, going out of her way to help me out and a great friend, always there when I needed her. By the time she dropped Weston off later that day I was feeling better, ready to enjoy the holiday with him. That evening we both fell asleep early. He was jet-lagged and I wasn't completely back to normal after the previous night's episode of vertigo.

The next day Weston planned to Christmas shop. I was overly

tired and couldn't shake it, no matter how much I tried to ignore it. I didn't understand why I felt under the weather, but underneath it all, the stress from everything that had happened in my life had taken its toll.

Losing my child, my subsequent spiral into depression, the one night with Edward—all these had happened in such a short time, wreaking emotional havoc on my body. I surmised I was experiencing some sort of post-traumatic stress disorder. My periods had always been erratic and since losing Christine they'd become more irregular so I called Dr. Farney to ask her about it. She agreed my menstrual history coupled with the emotional toll of losing Christine and postpartum depression would explain my not menstruating on any set schedule.

When she asked if I could be pregnant, I paused, recalling Weston's return home for Labor Day weekend and our nights of passion. We'd made love more times than I could count. I hadn't used protection, hadn't given it a moment of thought, and wasn't thinking clearly at the time. Was there a possibility I could be pregnant? It would explain my missed periods, the vertigo, and the exhaustion I'd been experiencing.

Suddenly I *had* to know. I jogged to the pharmacy around the corner to buy a home pregnancy kit but when I returned, I came down with a bad case of "cold feet," put the kit in my bottom drawer, and decided if I woke up on Christmas morning and felt funky, I'd use it.

Weston and I stayed up late on Christmas Eve, catching up on each other's stories, the New York bridge project, my novel. We watched *Miracle on 34th Street* for the zillionth time, falling asleep on the couch by ten o'clock. I was tired, he was jet-lagged, and tomorrow we'd decided to have Cecilia and Perry over for Christmas dinner.

On Christmas morning I experienced a light case of vertigo again but after getting out of bed it seemed to dissipate. In the back of my mind, though, I'd made myself a promise and knew what I had to do.

Weston fixed breakfast—scrambled eggs and toast and my favorite decaf latte. My appetite had returned since yesterday and I felt fine by mid-morning. But while Weston was on the phone with Perry I ran upstairs to find the pregnancy test kit, followed the directions, set it behind my make-up bag on the countertop in the bathroom, and ran back downstairs.

"That was Perry," he said when I sat down next to him on the couch.

"What did he want? They're still coming for dinner aren't they?"

"Yeah. We were just saying hello. I haven't talked to him much since I left in July. He wanted to know what time dinner was."

"You told him four, right?"

"Yep… Hey, Santa seems to have left you something under the tree. Did you see it?" He pointed to a box underneath the green branches.

I shook my head. "No, I didn't know he'd stopped by." I laughed. "Should I open it now?"

He gestured toward the ten-foot spruce. "I think you'll like it."

"How would you know?" I looked at him seriously. "Did he tell you what it is?"

Leaning over, he gave me a chaste kiss. "He and I are best buds. Go ahead, open it."

I walked over and picked up the small box wrapped in shiny red paper with a curly white bow. Sitting back on the couch, I slipped off the ribbon and discovered a dark blue velvet box. Inside was a delicate gold bracelet.

"Oh my God, West, it's gorgeous," I said under my breath.

"Look at the inside edge," he prodded.

I read it out loud, "I'll love you forever." Turning toward him, I kissed his clean-shaven chin, working my way up to his mouth. He ran his hands up and down my back in a soft caress.

I was melting under the warmth of his hands but my mind was too preoccupied with the pregnancy results. "I'll be right back," I said, pulling away from his embrace. "Your present's in our bedroom."

I ran up the stairs like a flash of lightening, took a deep breath, and pulled the stick out from behind my make-up case—a plus sign. I was pregnant! I had to return to Weston and give him his gift. But which one? The soft leather jacket I'd bought for him while in San Francisco earlier in the week? Or the little box containing the blue plus sign on the stick?

My being pregnant would bring us around full circle, to when I found out I was carrying his child last time. I took the stairs slowly, my mind a whirlwind of disjointed thoughts and feelings about my condition. I sat down next to him and handed him the white pharmacy bag.

He took it tentatively. "You can't afford wrapping paper?"

Cupping his face in my hands, I looked him in the eyes. "This is for both of us, West." He looked confused, his eyebrows drawn down in a deep vee. "Go ahead and open it."

He unfolded the paper bag, shook out the small stick. "You're pregnant?"

"*We're* pregnant, West." I paused. "Are you happy? I'm happy."

"Do you even have to ask?" He took me in a huge hug, lifted me off the couch, and swung me around in a circle then placed me back on my feet. "Of course I'm happy."

"Maybe it's too soon after losing Christine but I think it's a sign, West. We were meant to have a child. This baby brings the two of us back around to each other again, from the bad place where we were after she died."

His smile went from one ear to the other. "I'm happier than I've been in a long time. Should we tell Cecilia and Perry?"

"I don't want them to feel uncomfortable."

He nodded. "You're right. Perry said they've spent thousands of dollars trying in vitro."

"And it didn't work."

"You know Cecilia better than I do. How do you think she'd react?"

I thought about it for a second. "She'd be happy for us. If she thought I didn't tell her because of their experience with IVF she'd be mad."

"Then let's celebrate with them."

We had a great time at dinner and they joined us in a toast to my being pregnant. The food was delicious; we exchanged small gifts, concluding the evening by watching a movie on the Hallmark channel. After they left I remembered to give Weston his leather jacket. He tried it on right away and modeled it for me and he looked terrific. It had been a great Christmas, one I'd remember for the rest of my life.

Chapter 10

I made an appointment with Dr. Farney for early January, after Weston returned to New York. The nurse ushered me into a patient room where she took a blood sample then I dressed in a paper gown.

Dr. Farney came into the room, a smile on her face. "So you think you're pregnant, Brandy?"

I raised my eyebrows. "I'm not?"

She laughed. "As a matter of fact the blood test agrees with your assessment. I'm concerned you didn't make an appointment earlier, though."

"I took a pregnancy test on Christmas Day and made the appointment immediately, doctor."

"Well, I'd say you're four months along already, Brandy. Didn't you realize you'd missed your period?"

I shut my eyes, trying to count back four months. "So I got pregnant when?"

"My best guess is early September sometime."

"Labor Day?"

She looked at the calendar on the back of the door and flipped back the pages. "Yes, I'd say that would be pretty accurate."

I was thinking about my time with Weston over Labor Day weekend. "Yeah…"

She placed her hand on my forearm. "Is this good news, Brandy?"

I looked up sharply. "Oh, sure. It's great news. I was just thinking about Labor Day when Weston came home from New York for the weekend. Wow! I guess we were lucky."

"I'd say so," she agreed. "Now, why don't you get dressed and have my nurse give you the information you'll need regarding vitamins and make another appointment for one month from today."

I slid off the table and got dressed, thinking about my past pregnancy, hoping this one would have a happy ending. That evening when Weston phoned we discussed my appointment, sharing our surprise I'd conceived so quickly. The project in New York was scheduled for completion on January fifteenth. He'd be flying home on January twenty-second. We were counting down the days until his return.

* * * *

Traffic at five p.m. to San Francisco International Airport was worse than I'd expected. I should have listened to Cecilia. She'd told me any flight arriving at SFO after three o'clock in the afternoon would mean driving on the freeway in gridlock traffic. And that's where I found myself at 5:15 on Friday evening. I had planned to park and meet Weston when he disembarked from his flight from New York, scheduled to arrive at 6:15 p.m. Now I wasn't sure I'd be on time.

I'd spent most of the afternoon getting ready for our big night, my dark auburn waves held up on the sides with tortoise shell combs, jaggedly-cut bangs hung just below my eye-brows. I'd applied my makeup with a subtle hand, brown eyes lined in smudged pencil, mascara graced my thick black lashes, a dash of pink lipstick.

I wore a short black dress with a not-too-modest V carved down the front. I was five months pregnant but the weight I'd gained was all baby. Cecilia had told me I looked the same as always if she was looking at me from the back.

The traffic eased up considerably a few miles from the airport and I easily negotiated the Mercedes into the main parking complex, screeching to a stop when I found a space near the elevators. I was familiar with the terminal, and was able to find Weston's arrival gate in minutes. The big clock on the wall said it was 6:11. His plane would not have arrived yet.

I slowed down, took a few deep breaths, and found a comfy chair to sit in, away from the madding crowd hovering in front of the arrival gate. I was anticipating Weston's surprise at my wearing the new dress I'd bought for his homecoming. This was reminiscent of the early days of our relationship, when he'd show up at the door to take me out for dinner.

They announced the arrival of his flight and my heart did a little dance. We hadn't seen each other since his departure after New Year's, and our phone calls were often short, late at night, both of us exhausted and sleepy. I looked forward to cuddling up next to his big warm body, an experience I'd gradually begun to miss during the months he'd been away. I couldn't wait until we could be alone together. There were so many things I'd taken for granted and I wanted to prove to him how much I wanted him home for good.

Passengers streamed off the jet way, making their way toward family and friends waiting for them in the lobby area. Most looked tired from the long flight from New York, along with the fact they were functioning on East Coast time. After a large group hooked up with those waiting for them, moving down the escalators to the baggage claim area, the flow of people slowed to a trickle. Then I noticed the captain and co-captain laughing and power-walking toward the crowd, probably scheduled for another flight, and thought I'd written the information incorrectly.

I checked my notes in my purse. This was the right flight. Weston had to be on it or he would have phoned and told me his change in plans. I grabbed my cell phone. No missed calls. I was about to call home to see if he'd left me a message, when I noticed a gorgeous blonde woman walking behind a man in a wheelchair, swishing her waist-length hair with all the grace of a runway model. Not dressed in the uniform for this airline, I surmised she must be one of the passengers.

Weston exited the jet way behind her and slowed his pace, his gaze traveling left and right, until our eyes met. At once, he began a quick jog over to where I was waiting for him, picked me up and twirled me around, before placing me back down. He pressed his body into mine, kissing me, weaving his fingers through my hair. I could feel the bulge in his slacks hard and full against my abdomen and couldn't wait to get him to the car!

Then I heard someone clearing their throat. Weston turned around sharply and I dropped my hands from where they were draped around his shoulders. The striking blonde I'd seen exit the plane in front of Weston was standing a few feet away from us.

"Brandy, this is my secretary, Carol Smith. She'll be working on our project in San Francisco. Carol, this is my wife, Brandy."

Chapter 11

"Hi, Brandy! It's nice to finally meet you. Weston's talked a lot about you."

When I noticed Carol's hand sticking out in mid-air, I grasped it and gave it a firm shake. "Nice to meet you, too. I didn't know Weston was flying in with anyone."

He put his arm around my shoulders, giving me a light squeeze. "Carol got bumped onto this flight but I was in first class. I was seated first and didn't even know she was on the plane until we landed."

She nodded. "I was supposed to leave much earlier but the flight was cancelled. I hate flying coach, but the company wouldn't pay for my flight otherwise." She laughed. "I just wish Weston could have gotten me a seat in first class."

He shrugged. "Sorry, Carol. No can do." He looked at me and rolled his eyes.

I wouldn't make more out of this than necessary though I hadn't forgotten the one conversation she and I had had several months back. Carol looked like a model on the front of *Vogue* magazine. But I'd be my normal generous self and welcome her to California. "Do you need a ride somewhere, Carol?"

She smiled, showing full lips glistening with red gloss. "Thank you but I've already arranged for a private driver to take me to Alameda."

"You'll be *living* in Alameda?" I tried to keep the surprise out of my tone but knew my face had already given me away.

She glanced over at Weston. "West told me how beautiful your little city is."

I noticed she'd referred to him in the more "familiar" form. Calling him West seemed to flow easily from her hyper-glossed lips. "Will you be living in an apartment?"

She shook her head, her blonde hair falling like a sheet of water over her shoulders. "I'll be renting a fabulous house on Santa Clara. I've seen pictures of it on the internet."

"We should go to the baggage claim area," Weston interrupted.

She turned around and began walking ahead of us, stepping onto the escalator. Every male head turned in her direction. I hadn't exaggerated her beauty. She had a thousand-watt smile that would shake the socks off most men and she knew it. But I tried not to be catty, grabbed onto Weston's solid left arm, and snuggled my ample breasts next to him for support.

He looked down at me and whispered, "I've missed you, Brandy."

I smiled.

We stopped in front of the baggage carousel, and Carol turned toward me while we waited for the suitcases to begin pouring out the chute.

"So, Brandy. Weston tells me you're pregnant. When's your due date?"

"Sometime in early June. Do you have children?"

She shook her head. "Nope. Don't want to be tied down. It's just not my style."

Nodding, I said, "Well, it's not for everybody. It's a good thing you realize that now. Being a parent is a real sacrifice."

We were interrupted when Weston said, "Here come our bags. Which one's yours, Carol?"

"The hunter green one over there." She pointed toward a Coach suitcase spilling down the chute. "I'll get it, West."

"No, don't worry. I've got it."

I stood next to Carol, watching Weston lean over the edge of the carousel and grab a dark green suitcase, along with two of his own pieces of luggage. He brought them over to where we were waiting, dropping hers at her feet.

He let out a deep breath. "Geez, what have you got in there?"

She laughed, poking him in the ribs with one of her perfectly manicured nails. "You mean you don't know?"

He shook his head, frowning, his face tinged a deep shade of red. Walking toward the turnstile, he shoved the claim tickets into the hands of the nearest security person and moved out toward the elevators leading to the parking lot.

Traffic had died down by then, and the drive to Alameda took only thirty minutes. I was preoccupied thinking about Carol Smith. She was drop-dead gorgeous and suddenly the arguments Weston and I had had when he arrived in New York stood out as possible evidence something could have been going on between him and this woman.

I recalled the conversation I'd had with her when I'd phoned and Weston's defensive attitude when he and I discussed it afterward. Would she continue to be his secretary here too? A small cloud had been hovering over me since she'd arrived at the airport.

Wending our way through traffic, Weston laid his hand on mine, squeezing my fingers in his large grasp.

"I've missed you so much, Brandy. Have you missed me?"

I looked over at his profile, noting how handsome he was, realizing it wouldn't be surprising at all that other women were attracted to him. "I'm going crazy living in such a big house all by myself."

He smiled. "God, it's good to see you. I've waited for this day for a long time."

"Are you sure about that?"

He pulled the Mercedes into the fast lane and we flew across the Bay Bridge. "What do you mean?" he asked, taking a quick glance at me.

I hesitated, not wanting to start an argument. "Can we talk more when we get home? I'm so tired I could go to sleep right now."

He paused, his brow furrowed. "This pregnancy seems to be taking its toll on you."

"It' worse than last time. I'm just exhausted." I glanced out the side window, seeing Alcatraz Island in the distance over his shoulder, recalling the evening our first baby was conceived. "Hopefully that's not a bad sign."

"What does Dr. Farney say?"

"That I'm fine, the baby's fine, and to quit worrying."

"Stressing yourself out won't do you or the baby one bit of good." Bringing my hand to his lips, he grazed my knuckles with a light kiss. "The same thing isn't going to happen again, you know?"

"How do you know that?" My voice quivered with emotion.

"Because I trust Dr. Farney. If she said you'll be fine, I believe her. Brandy, what happened with Christine was terrible but not typical. This is a new pregnancy, a new baby. You'll get through this just fine. And I'll be right there with you."

I turned to look out my window, watching the sailboats tacking back and forth across the bay, contemplating the past. "I know you will."

Within moments, he pulled the car into our driveway and shut off the engine. Turning toward me, he placed his hands on my shoulders. "Wanna go inside?"

I nodded, staring into his deep brown eyes.

He leaned over the console and gently placed his hand under my chin, bringing my face closer to his. He lightly traced the edges of my lips with his tongue then deepened the kiss. Pulling away, he grabbed the door handle, jumped out, and came around to help me out of the car.

I noticed him looking around the neighborhood. "Did you miss this place?"

"Yeah, I did. Alameda's a quiet little town. I didn't like falling asleep to the sounds of traffic… alone in bed without you next to me."

He took my hand and we walked to the front door then he led me through the foyer up to our bedroom. Pulling me gently toward him, he guided me down beside him on the comforter, then slid my dress off my shoulders, past my breasts, over my hips, and threw it onto the floor, leaving me with nothing but my black lace underpants.

"You are so damn beautiful, Brandy," he whispered, slowly inching his way on top of me. He straddled my hips and unzipped his jeans, revealing his already engorged member, glistening with anticipation of our coupling. His hands splayed across my belly, his fingers drawing my panties down past my knees, inching them along my ankles and feet, where I kicked them off to the side.

I took him in my hand and guided him inside me, wrapped my legs around his back, squeezing his body tightly against mine. Rocking in tune to our own sweet music, we rode the waves of our mutual orgasms, whispering "I love yous" until exhaustion overtook our sweat-drenched bodies.

He heaved himself to the side of me, his arm draped across my waist, cradling my back against his chest. Suddenly, images of having sex with Edward sliced through my half-slumber. This hadn't happened to me over Labor Day when West and I had last made love. It seemed strange they should appear now, so much later after my transgression. When should I tell him? It was too late tonight. I could already hear his deep breathing, jet lag overtaking him within moments.

"Tomorrow," I whispered to no one…

Chapter 12

I awoke to Weston placing a breakfast tray at the bottom of the bed. I could smell Columbian roast coffee, and when I looked down large buttery croissants lay on white china plates, with linen napkins on the side.

"Where'd you get the pastries, West?"

"Merritt Bakery in Oakland, right through the Posey Tube. Took me fifteen minutes round trip. I knew you'd still be in bed."

"Thanks, I'm starving. I don't remember being this ravenous…" I reached for one, but Weston was faster and grabbed me by the wrist, slowly pushing me back onto the bed.

"Not so fast. I'm hungry too but not for breakfast."

"Oh, I see how it is." I giggled. "You thought you'd start my juices flowing when I smelled the coffee, then swoop down for the kill." I placed the back of my hand against my forehead. "I feel faint from lack of nutrition. I am with child, you know."

He grinned, kissed me full on the mouth and let me sit up. I grabbed the sheet to cover my ever-growing breasts, and stuffed one end of the croissant into my mouth. He stirred cream into my coffee and brought the cup to my lips. I moaned in appreciation.

"You spoil me, you know? That's why I love you so much," I cooed.

"Not for my infectious laugh? My smashing personality?" He dabbed at my lips with the napkin. "You're so beautiful when you're pregnant. There's something about your body that just makes me want to eat you up."

"Awww. That's so sweet, West. I know some guys wouldn't be turned on seeing their wife pregnant. I guess you're one of the special ones."

His kisses started at my neck, moving down my stomach to my

inner thighs, then my knees. He worked his way back up again, stopping at my breasts. I tilted my head back, enjoying every moment of his loving me.

An unwanted glimpse of Edward and me on the couch cut sharply through my mind and my body flinched.

"Brandy?" He hesitated and sat up, a worried look on his face. "Is it the baby?"

I couldn't do this again without telling him. The guilt overwhelmed me. "Can we talk?"

He moved to the foot of the bed, letting out an exasperated sigh. "We're just getting a chance to spend time together, I'm about to make mad and passionate love to you, and you want to have a discussion?"

I closed my eyes, knowing I couldn't go on like this, knowing there'd never be a good time to tell him the truth. It wasn't right to keep him ignorant of what I'd done.

The bed dipped down, I could feel him next to me. "I didn't mean to be harsh, babe. What's wrong?" He put his arm around my shoulders and gave me a squeeze.

What was that expression about time not waiting for anyone? This was it. I had to confess. "I was so messed up last year after I lost Christine—"

"Let's not go there, Brandy," he interrupted. "That was back in June and you've come such a long way. We're going to have a baby. You should be happy."

I looked down at my hands, then up at him. One tear dripped down my right cheek. "Let me get this out, okay? I need to say this and get it off my chest."

He tipped his head, looking unsure. "I won't interrupt again."

Letting out a breath, I looked away. I felt like such a traitor. "Right after you left for New York I met an old classmate of mine from high school. He invited me to his house for dinner." I paused, took another deep breath. "We had sex. Once. I never saw him again." I turned to look at him, gauge his reaction.

He didn't move for several seconds and I kept quiet, waiting for him to say something, anything. He stood up in slow motion, bent down to pick up his jeans still lying in a heap on the rug from our night of passion, and roughly jammed his legs into the pants.

"What are you doing? Where are you going? Please, Weston, let's talk about this."

"I work my ass off in New York while you're at home screwing other dudes?"

I pulled the sheet around me, ran over and grabbed his arm. "I wasn't screwing other dudes." He ripped his arm out of my grasp. "*I* was the one who was all screwed up. Then you went to New York and all we ever did was argue on the phone. You don't tell your secretary you're married and she treats me like shit on the phone…"

By now, he was fully dressed, shoes and jacket on, wallet grabbed off the bureau. His hand hovered above the doorknob. His face looked void of emotion, wiped clean of all expression. "I can't do this," he mumbled.

I sobbed, knowing I'd hurt him and betrayed his trust. I felt like a slut. "I'm sorry," I cried. "I made a mistake. But I love you, Weston."

He stood near the door, shaking his head, tears dripping from his chin.

"I know I've hurt you and that wasn't my intention. I wasn't thinking straight." My legs shook. My stomach cramped. I *had* to make him understand. "I'll regret it forever. You don't deserve this but I'm asking you to forgive me."

His eyes swam with tears, his chin quivered with emotion. "I had sex with Carol Smith."

I drew in a sharp breath and clamped my hand over my mouth.

"But only once," he continued. "I was so damn drunk and out of my mind, worrying about you and how depressed you were. I couldn't help you, you'd rejected me, wouldn't make love to me. I guess I was feeling sorry for myself." He paused and took a deep breath. "And it never happened again. I woke up the next morning in my hotel room—alone."

Granted, I'd wondered whether Weston had had a fling with his secretary; but going over the scenario in my head, I never imagined my telling him about Edward would lead to his revealing his own tale about Carol.

"Both of us?" my voice came out in a whisper. I wasn't sure he'd heard me.

"Both of us screwed up," he answered, his voice shaky.

Our eyes locked in a stare. Silence pounded in my ears. This was surreal.

"What do we do now? I still love you, West."

"And I love you," he murmured.

I walked over to the bed, covered myself with the comforter, and hid my face in the pillow and cried. What was I supposed to do? Both of us had to forgive the other but then what? I was five months pregnant. We were expecting a baby in June. We needed to make plans for our future, *if* there was going to be one.

* * * *

The sun's rays edged their way through the white lace curtains covering the bedroom windows. Six o'clock in the morning, and I'd slept through the night. Weston was lying beside me, his warm body curled against mine. I turned toward him, feeling exhausted from our argument but needing to know we could somehow get through this problem together. His eyes were wide open.

"Brandy, I'm so sorry," he said softly. He fingered a stray tendril of my hair, tucking it behind my ear. "Do you love this guy?"

Tears dripped from the corners of my eyes onto the pillow, never dreaming we'd be in this situation. "I never had feelings for him. We probably spent a total of fifty minutes together. I was so depressed, I couldn't get past my grief over losing our baby. Then when you and I couldn't do anything but fight—"

"We were both hurting, Brandy. I thought you didn't love me anymore. When I got so drunk and Carol came onto me like a bitch in heat, I—"

I interrupted him. "I don't need to hear it."

He placed his mouth on my lips, deepened the kiss, and pressed his lower body toward mine. I gave in to my desire for him. We'd been apart for too long, and I needed to feel the closeness we'd always shared.

Our lovemaking felt frantic. Like two boats in danger of capsizing, we both were paddling madly to stay afloat. We lay there afterward trying to catch our breath, silent, the bedside clock ticking off the minutes. Thinking about our relationship, I believed we were stronger than our individual moments of misguided passion with strangers.

Lying on my back, staring at the ceiling, I whispered, "Can we get past this? Move on and forget this ever happened?"

Placing his hand on my waist, he turned me toward him, looked me in the eyes, his cheeks wet with tears. "That's what I want, Brandy. I'll do anything to keep you. I wish I'd never met Carol Smith. First thing Monday morning she'll be transferred to another department. I don't want you to feel suspicious of what I'm doing while I'm at work. I'll make sure you never doubt me." He was crying softly, his head lying on the side of my pillow.

I cradled his face in both my hands. "I believe you. My old classmate moved to Washington. Let's start over from here. No more lies. No more secrets. We have to trust each other, or this marriage can't last another day."

"We can do this, Brandy. We've been through a lot together, losing our baby last year, and now this."

I couldn't stop the tears. "Let's focus on our baby, West. Our summer baby. We have so much to be grateful for. I'm healthy, Dr. Farney says the baby's healthy. Let's be happy."

Our lives together had endured incredible challenges in a short amount of time. We could look beyond a one-night stand and overcome anything Carol or Edward could do to us.

Chapter 13

My birthday was February fifth and Weston and I decided to celebrate it quietly at home. He'd been gone for so long and we wanted to spend as much time together as we could cram into his short vacation. Plus, I'd been feeling ill, something that hadn't happened when I was pregnant with Christine.

But Dr. Farney continued to allay my fears, explaining some women had morning sickness both day and night and I needn't worry. The queasiness seemed to occur mainly when I hadn't had enough sleep or was stressed out so it didn't come as a surprise given what Weston and I had just been through.

After his first few days back at the job, he arrived home early one evening unexpectedly. Coming up behind me in the kitchen where I was fixing a salad, he wrapped his arms around my waist, nuzzling my neck.

"Wow! You're home early," I said. "Playing hooky?" I continued slicing carrots, resting my head alongside his.

His roving hands inched up toward my breasts and he pressed against me from behind where I stood at the counter.

"I wanted to take you out to dinner tonight."

His kisses warmed the side of my face. I leaned my head back, arching my chest, enjoying his attentive hands. "Are we celebrating something special?"

His breathing escalated, his chest expanding against my back. I turned my head to the side, stretching to reach his waiting mouth. Our kisses deepened, mouths wide, tongues searching. I curved my body around to face him, needing to feel him needing me.

"Carol Smith quit her job."

I opened my eyes, searching his, trying to gauge his feelings. "I thought she was here for the duration."

His tongue found my earlobe. Chills slid the length of my spine as he licked his way down my neck toward my breasts pouting over the top of my shirt. "She admitted she came to San Francisco hoping I'd leave you for her."

I was on the edge, too aroused to respond to his words. One syllable escaped, "And?"

He gently glided me to the kitchen floor, grabbing a towel to place under my head. Massaging my swollen breasts with one hand, pulling down my panties with the other, his tongue danced around my navel toward the patch of hair on my pubic bone. When he reached my sweet spot, I was beyond listening to his explanation. My hands grasped his head, running my fingers through his thick hair. I was all sensations. My orgasm was wonderful, freeing, intense.

My breathing slowed, my mind cleared. "You didn't answer me."

Covering me with his body, he stared down at me. "I told her I'd never leave you."

I could feel his unfulfilled need nudging against my leg. Wrapping my hand around him, I caressed him firmly, enjoying the feel of his hard swelling within my grasp.

Unzipping his pants, he pulled out his swollen shaft, ready to enter me. I wrapped my legs around him, edging my body down, sliding him snugly inside. His rhythm escalated until the moment of his release, his body shivering to a halt, leaving me breathless under his weight, pressing me into the floor. It was a fantastic exercise to help me forget about Carol Smith.

* * * *

I called Cecilia the following week and invited her over for coffee. Though we lived next door to each other, we respected each other's privacy, and talked on the phone more often than we saw each other. She was excited we were getting together. We hadn't seen much of each other since Weston's return, and I wanted to have "girl time," talk with her about what had happened between Weston and me.

It had been a long time since I'd had a close girlfriend. After we'd moved to Alameda the previous year, I spent a majority of my time alone, writing my second novel and promoting the first book online. I hadn't had many opportunities to cultivate friendships. Having Cecilia as my next-door neighbor was a gift, especially during this stressful time in my life.

I'd always been able to count on her to be there for me but I couldn't be sure how she'd react to my having had extra-marital sex and I was anxious to find out. I was in the kitchen baking muffins when the doorbell chimed and I ran to answer it.

"Cecilia, come in!" We hugged each other, and I guided her into the kitchen.

"How have you been? I miss our talks."

"Since Weston got back from New York, it's been a bit stressful around here." I opened the cupboard and took out two plates, placed a muffin on each of them, set them on the table, then took a seat across from her.

"Perry told me what happened. I'm so sorry, Brandy."

Our conversation skidded to a stop. "What did you say?"

Her eyebrows knitted in concern. "I said I'm sorry about what happened between you and Weston. What's wrong Brandy?"

I shook my head. Unbelievable. "Weston told Perry?" She nodded. "About both of us having an affair?" She nodded again. "Well, at least I won't have to bore you with the details."

"Oh, Brandy. I'm not here to judge you. I'd be the last person on earth to do that anyway, what with my jaded past."

I stared at her, unblinking. "What do you mean? You and Perry are the most solid couple I've ever known."

"We've had our rough times." She sighed, leaning back in her chair. "You know how we've been trying for years to have a baby? At one point, oh I'd say about three years ago, I was so depressed about the in vitro not working. I met a man at the Alameda Athletic Club. Anyway, I was this close"—she gestured with her thumb and forefinger—"to having an affair with this Adonis look-alike."

"You're not serious!" My eyes widened in disbelief. "I don't picture it. You and Perry seem like the perfect couple." Noticing her staring down at her muffin, I added, "And you know what? The baby thing will happen for you guys when you least expect it."

She looked up at me, smiled, and her eyes lit up. After taking a bite of muffin, she wiped her mouth with a napkin. "Well... one of the reasons I've missed you so much is because you're one of the few people who knows anything about the in vitro process. And you were so sympathetic when we talked about it." She paused and took hold of my hand across the kitchen table. "I wanted you to be one of the first to know. I'm pregnant, Brandy. I'm due in November!"

I let out a loud "whoop," ran around to her side of the table and gave her a big hug. I was so happy for her. It had been difficult for the two of them since they'd been trying to have a child. "I don't believe it, Cece. Congratulations! We're going to have our babies within a few months of each other! Fate must be intervening for us."

"I knew you'd be happy for us. And I'm so sorry about what's happening with you and Weston. But don't feel like you're alone. I'm here for you if you ever need to talk."

"I know, Cece. And that means a lot to me. You know, Weston and I are still committed to our marriage, but it was so shocking. First I told him about Edward then he told me about Carol. Totally bizarre."

"You two give a deeper meaning to the word forgiveness."

"After losing the baby I was a mess. You remember the talk you and I had."

"Yeah. But I'm surprised to hear about… what was his name again?"

"Edward. I met him at Peet's. He was an old friend of mine from high school. He asked if he could fix me dinner at his house. It had seemed totally innocent—just two old friends getting together again. I never dreamed I'd have sex with him. But once we were alone, I needed… I don't know. Something was missing. Weston was gone, and he and I were arguing every time we talked on the phone and—"

"It just doesn't sound like you, Brandy. When Perry told me, I couldn't believe it."

"Looking back, neither can I. I keep asking myself, 'Who was that woman?'"

"And Weston? What were his reasons for sleeping with his secretary?"

"I didn't want to have sex with him, remember?" She nodded. "He thought I didn't love him anymore. He was drunk. She was there. You can imagine the rest."

"And now?"

"I love Weston. He loves me. We'll work through this. I know we will."

"I know you will too," she agreed, smiling.

I reached out and grabbed her hand. "Are you going to find out whether it's a girl or a boy?"

She shook her head. "We want to be surprised."

"The technician who performed the ultrasound asked me if I wanted to know. I told him I wanted to be surprised this time." I looked wistfully out the window, remembering my last pregnancy.

"Brandy?"

I shook my head, the memories like cobwebs in my brain. "Uh, yeah. I was just thinking about the past and—"

"Don't go there. This baby is just the gift you and Weston deserve for all you two have been through." She shoved her chair back. "I've gotta go."

I got up and gave her another big hug. "Thanks for listening."

"And thank you for the muffins."

"My pleasure. Anything for my best friend."

Chapter 14

Spring was approaching and March in Alameda was a beautiful time of year with mild temperatures and soft breezy afternoons. The yard was filled with trees bearing bright green leaves. Rose bushes along the pathways bloomed with pink, red, and yellow petals. The grass was thick and lush from the rainy season.

During the cold weather, my daily running routine, fighting the wind and rain, was anything but enjoyable. And now that I was going into my seventh month, I looked forward to walking briskly down my favorite lanes and avenues of this quaint city, the sights and scents of spring lifting my spirits. I was happy being pregnant.

One weekend Weston and I decided to take a walk along the beachfront. We both needed the exercise and enjoyed the fresh air and salty breeze so we stopped to play along the shore. I loved the feel of the tide between my toes along the water's edge.

Half-way down Shoreline Drive, the street that runs the length of the beach, stands the Alameda Towne Center, a small shopping mall, newly-renovated, with a Starbuck's, a Safeway, a few clothing stores, and a Mexican restaurant. We agreed having something to drink would be a good idea before our journey back home and veered off the boardwalk to have an iced coffee.

I found a table for two while Weston ordered our drinks. He'd just brought them over and was settling in his chair, when we were interrupted before taking our first sips.

"Brandy? Is that you?"

I looked up into the same-as-ever, gorgeous smiling face of Edward Barnes, dressed in faded blue jeans that hugged his body in all the right places, and a short-sleeved white polo shirt that set off his tanned arms and well-formed biceps. His dark mustache was neatly trimmed and those blue eyes of his latched onto mine, leaving me speechless. He was a man who could turn the head of any female within glancing distance.

I stared, mesmerized, completely taken back, my mouth half-open. Realizing I must look like a fish out of water, I cleared my throat and blinked several times. "Nice to see you again." My mind whirled. I had to think of something to say before this blossomed into an ugly scene. Turning toward Weston I said, "Edward is a friend of Cecilia's. She and I were having coffee at Peet's and she introduced us."

Edward turned his gaze in my direction and squinted. I gave him a fake smile, hoping he'd get the hint.

Weston looked up at Edward and thrust out his hand. "I'm Weston Chambers, Brandy's husband." He grasped Edward's hand in a firm shake. "I just got back from the East Coast a few months ago. I haven't been to Peet's yet. Where's it located?"

Edward shot a quick glance my way. "Over on Park Street. My law office was just down the street, then I moved to Washington State for a while. I just transferred back here… hated the rain."

Weston laughed. "I hear ya'. So you're back for good now?"

"Yes, thank God, I'm here to stay. Lucky for me, I rented out my house while I was away and didn't sell it, so I didn't have to go through the hassle of finding a new place to live when I returned."

"Good for you… Brandy, you all right? You look a little weird, honey."

Reeling from this surreal situation, shocked to be in the same room with Edward and my husband, I didn't know what I could say that would sound normal. I mentally gave myself a shake. "I'm okay, West," I answered, placing a proprietary hand on his forearm with a smile.

"You're looking well," Edward said. "How's Cecilia?" he asked, with a tiny smirk on his face.

I felt like I'd swallowed a rubber ball. I could hardly breathe, putting words together was a feat beyond my capabilities. But this was not the time to freak out. I cleared my throat again, which seemed to have clamped shut, unclenched my teeth and forced another smile. "She's doing fine."

Weston jumped in quickly, grinning, "Brandy's almost seven months pregnant, we're expecting in June. Congratulations are in order for my beautiful wife here."

Edward looked over at me and I noticed his eyes move downward toward the table. However, my purse was lying on top of my belly and he couldn't see below my breasts. "Well, congratulations to both of you." His expression was anything but happy. He frowned, his eyes riveted on mine.

"Thank you," I managed to squeak out.

I kept my attention aimed at Weston, anything to keep me from having to look at Edward. "Honey, suddenly I'm not feeling too well. It must have been all the walking. I think we should go." If I could have, I would have run as fast as my legs would carry me out the door toward home.

Weston took hold of my arm, helping me to my feet. "Sure." He gathered up the cups and napkins, while I raced to the door. Edward pushed it open for me to exit ahead of him.

When I reached the edge of the sidewalk he gently took hold of my arm and turned me toward him. "Whose baby is it, Brandy? Mine or Weston's?"

What was he talking about? Dr. Farney had confirmed I got pregnant over the Labor Day weekend, hadn't she? My mind raced, seconds ticked by. I wouldn't do this. Not now. Not ever. He had no right to confront me like this.

Weston was just pushing the door open and rushed over to me. He could tell by my expression I wasn't happy, though he'd naturally attribute it to my not feeling well. "I don't mean to impose but could you drive us home, Edward? Brandy doesn't look well—"

"No! I'll be fine!" Embarrassed from my sudden outburst, I managed a small smile. "I just need some fresh air. The walk home will do me good. I already feel better now that I'm outside."

Weston, ever the gentleman, just *had* to intervene. "Are you sure? It's probably no big deal for him to give us a lift." He turned toward Edward.

"It would be my pleasure, Weston." He gestured toward the parking lot. "I'm parked right over there."

"Thank you." Weston smiled at him. "Come on, Brandy, it'll only take a few minutes."

I didn't want Edward to know where I lived. A huge sign appeared in my mind's eye: Stop right there, don't go any further. Granted, I wasn't thinking straight. He could obviously look up my name in the phone book to see exactly where I lived. And Alameda was not a big place.

Somehow it seemed wrong or just plain weird to allow him to drop us off at our home, like inviting a criminal to your house. But I was outnumbered. Weston guided me across the parking lot to Edward's SUV, assuring me we'd be home soon enough, where I could lie down and rest.

I could do this for the few minutes it would take to get to our house on Lauren Drive. During the five-minute drive from South Shore Center, Weston told Edward about working on the Bay Bridge project which segued into Edward's telling a story of his first ride in a car across the bridge when he was young.

We pulled up to our house and it took everything in me not to shove the car door open and run to the house. I needed to get away from Edward, especially now that he'd had the audacity to confront me about the paternity of my unborn child!

"Thanks so much for the ride, Edward. That was very kind of you. Brandy hasn't been feeling up to par lately and we appreciate it. Would you like to come in?"

"Not this time," he said. Relief washed over me like a cool shower on a hot day. "Thanks for inviting me, though. I've got work to do at the office. Doesn't matter that it's the weekend in my line of work."

Weston shook Edward's hand. "Maybe some other time then. Thanks again for the ride."

We walked up the pathway to the front door. I felt indescribably relieved entering the safety of our home. I ran up the stairs and shut the bathroom door, turned the lock, and sat down on the side of the tub, cradling my head in my hands. Breathe, I kept telling myself, you've got to get hold of yourself, calm down for the baby growing inside of you.

I never thought I'd come face to face with Edward Barnes ever again. He'd moved to Washington, to their new satellite office. He wasn't supposed to be in Alameda. Plus, I'd never entertained the idea he could be my child's father. Granted, predictions of when a baby is conceived aren't exact, but when Dr. Farney confirmed I was pregnant, she and I both talked about the Labor Day weekend as the likely date of conception.

And I hadn't marked the calendar with the day Edward and I had had sex!

I heard a light tapping on the bathroom door and assumed Weston wanted to see if I was feeling better.

"Brandy, honey? You okay in there?"

I stood and unlocked the door, then sat back down on the side of the tub. "Yeah, I'm fine. Just taking a moment."

He sat next to me and took my hands from my face where I was cradling my head. "What's wrong? Talk to me."

"It's nothing. I just felt light-headed and a bit queasy. I need to sit here for a few minutes. Maybe I got too much sun today. I'll be fine. Stop worrying, West."

He stood up to leave. "Why don't I get you something to drink. 7UP?"

"Thanks. That sounds great. I'll be right down."

I splashed cool water on my face then slowly walked down the stairs to where he was waiting for me in the front room. We both were aware of what could happen if I lost another child. Any time I didn't feel a hundred percent, both of us became alarmed. We were marking the days off the calendar hanging on the back of our bedroom door, counting down to early June.

That evening, we had dinner outside at the redwood picnic table. Weston had barbecued chicken and I, being a vegetarian, had fixed my favorite meal—a cheese quesadilla and a salad. Pregnant or not, I always took good care of myself.

Later that evening, we settled down in front of the television, and I leaned my head on his shoulder. We planned to watch one of our favorite movies, *The Last Samurai* and I'd just put the DVD in when the phone rang.

Weston reached over to answer it with a quick, "Hello." He paused for a few seconds and I guessed whoever was on the other end of the line must be talking. "Hello? Hello?" He pressed the 'End' button and placed the phone back in its cradle. "I guess they didn't want to talk to me. Geez, my feelings are hurt."

We both laughed and I pushed 'Play'. The movie was one of my top choices to watch again and again. I loved Tom Cruise and Ken Watanabe and those pink-blossomed cherry trees always made me feel mellow when they appeared on the screen.

By the time the ending credits were rolling, both of us were nodding off. The phone rang again. This time, I reached across Weston's chest. He was snoring lightly and the ringer was on low. He didn't stir when I said "Hello" into the receiver.

"Brandy? It's Edward. Can you talk?"

He was kidding, right? Calling me at home? Had he been the one who phoned a while ago and then hung up when Weston answered?

"What the hell do you think you're doing?" I whispered. "You can't call me. *Ever*. What are you thinking?" I stood up, tiptoed into the kitchen, and closed the door.

"What am I thinking? You *know* what I'm thinking, Brandy. Am I the child's father?"

"Don't you dare ask me such a question!" I hissed between gritted teeth. "Of course the baby's not yours! What would make you think such a thing?"

"I can do the math, Brandy. If you're almost seven months pregnant then the baby could be mine and you know it!"

I shut my eyes, trying to think straight. "You're saying you know the exact date we—"

"August twenty-fourth," he interrupted.

I opened my eyes, feeling frantic. Could this be true? "How did you get this number?"

"I'm an attorney. I have connections. It was easy."

"Oh, that's just great. I guess that's small town favoritism for you."

"Don't make it out to be some big deal. It's not hard to find anyone in Alameda. Back to the subject. When can I see you?"

"You're not. I have no intention of seeing you again. Ever."

"I'd be careful what you say, Brandy. I could just as easily have talked to Weston when he answered the phone before."

"Oh, so it *was* you. I thought so. Please don't do this. Leave me alone."

"I want to meet with you. I have a right to know if I'm the father. Just tell me when and where, and I'll stop calling you."

"All right. All right." I was so afraid Weston would wake up and hear me on the phone. "Tomorrow. At Peet's. Three o'clock." And I hung up the phone.

I was shaking, livid. I was so damn mad. Why would a young single guy with a great career want to be tied down with a child? It didn't make sense to me. What did he want? Did he plan to take my baby away from me and raise it? Did he want to give me money to help support the child or to start a college fund? He *had* to have a reason. What did he have to gain by doing this?

And why now? Why the hell was this happening to me now? Everything in our lives was going along so smoothly, and now this had to happen? It took every fiber of my being not to walk outside and scream at the top of my lungs at the unfairness of life. Just when Weston and I were enjoying our renewed relationship. It wasn't fair.

Chapter 15

It was easy to slip away the next afternoon. Weston wanted to take it easy, just hang out in the yard and putter around the house. I told him I wanted to go for a walk in the fresh air. I often needed quiet time when I was writing a book and running had always been my method of choice for thinking over ideas, enabling me to get through my own particular form of "writer's block." At this point in my pregnancy walking as fast as I comfortably could helped me gather my thoughts.

I left the house at two-thirty, wanting to give myself enough time to do deep breathing exercises and power walk my way to Peet's. When I opened the front door to the coffee house, there sat Edward at one of the tables overlooking Park Street. In all his handsome glory!

No doubt about it, he was one of the most virile men I'd ever met. His movie star looks were like a magnet, of which I'm sure he was aware. No man could look in the mirror every day and not see it. He couldn't be that oblivious. But I loved my husband. And I wouldn't let Edward ruin the relationship Weston and I had tried so hard to put back together.

I approached the table and he stood then leaned over to give me a kiss on the cheek. I pulled away as if I'd been slapped. It just seemed such a lie, his reaching out to me for some sort of affection.

"You're mad, aren't you?" he asked, a tiny grin on his lips.

"What did you expect? You're trying to blackmail me and you want me to be happy about it?"

He flopped down in his chair, glanced out the window then looked up at me. "I'm not trying to blackmail you, Brandy," he said in a low tone. "I just want to know if I'm the father of the baby you're carrying. I have that right."

I slowly lowered myself into the seat across from his then

squinted at him, filled with rage. "You have *no* right, Edward. You can't prove we've ever had *any* type of relationship outside of being friends when we were in high school."

He shook his head from side to side then engaged my eyes in a serious stare-down. "I can and I will. I know people. The owner of this place? He'll testify he saw us here. Talking. Having coffee together. It's the truth, Brandy. We sat at this table, remember? He'll testify in front of the Alameda Superior Court judge. Who just so happens to be a good friend of mine, who I play racquetball with every weekend." He leaned back in his chair, holding the mug of coffee in his hands. "Brandy, you'll lose this fight if you try to go up against me on this. I guarantee it."

It was fairly obvious, I had no choice. I didn't know much about the present day Edward but I was quickly finding out. He was an Alameda home boy. With connections. I had nothing to bargain with.

"What do you want me to do?" I muttered.

He slid a white business card across the table toward me. "Here's the name of a close friend of mine, Dr. Emily Rogers. She's in San Francisco. An ob/gyn. I've already talked with her about this. I have an appointment to see her on Monday so she can get a sample of my DNA. She's waiting to hear from you so she can get a sample of the fetal DNA." He paused. "I put my home phone and cell number on the bottom. Call me with the results of your test."

"You're pretty damn sure of yourself, aren't you?" I asked with more than a little sarcasm in my voice. "You went ahead and did all this before talking to me?"

"You gave me no choice, Brandy. Do this or I go to Weston. It's the right thing to do."

"The right thing to do? Are you kidding me?" Realizing I'd raised my voice, I looked around at the other tables but no one seemed to be watching us. I whispered through gritted teeth, "You want to ruin my marriage? Trample all over my life, my husband's life, my future child's life? You don't give a damn about doing the right thing. You're a hypocrite!"

"No, *you're* the hypocrite. I'm not the one who's married. *You* are. You're the one who had an affair behind your husband's back, not me. I'm not married, remember?" He scraped a hand through his hair then let out a deep sigh. "Look, I never seriously thought about what I'd do if I fathered a child but if I *am* this baby's daddy, I want to know because I'd feel responsible."

"And it doesn't bother you that you could be ruining my marriage, my family life—"

"Brandy, listen to me, will you?" He laid his hand on my wrist, looked down at the table, then up at me. "You don't really know me anymore. High school was *years* ago. I get that. What you don't know is this. Remember I told everyone my father passed away when I was a little kid? Well, that was a lie. He walked out on my mom and me when I was ten years old. I never saw him again. I loved my father. And I don't know why he deserted me. I'll never know. And I won't abandon any child of mine."

Wrenching my hand from underneath his, I stood up to leave. I'd heard enough of his sorry story. "I'll call your doctor friend tomorrow. I'll be in touch."

I swung around and walked out the door, walking as fast as I could down Central Avenue toward our house. I had to clear my head, although it wouldn't do any good even if I ran all the way across the country. I was cornered and had to do what he wanted. Or else.

I walked into the house and acted as if everything was fine. What else could I do? I'd have to call Dr. Rogers and make an appointment for the DNA test. I had no other option. We had a quiet Sunday dinner, watched television, then went to bed.

The next morning, after taking a short walk around the neighborhood and a light breakfast, I found Dr. Rogers' business card where I'd hidden it in one of the cubby holes of my desk. Her assistant seemed to recognize my name, giving me an appointment for that afternoon at one o'clock.

The procedure went quicker and easier than I'd expected, much like an amniocentesis. She explained there was a slight risk of bleeding or upset to the fetus, though a small one. I had to have it done, so I put my mind at rest, knowing the probability of anything going wrong was small. I was in and out of her office, and back on the freeway by two o'clock. Weston would never find out.

It would take a week before I received the results in the mail. The longest seven days of my life. Physically, I was feeling pretty good. Mentally, I was trying not to lose it and felt like climbing the walls. So I continued my deep breathing exercises, as well as my yoga each morning.

The weather was mild, in the mid-seventies, and I was enjoying being outdoors, continuing my writing each day while sitting in the back yard at the redwood picnic table shaded by the umbrella. I'd almost finished the revisions and was taking one long last look through the manuscript before sending it back to my agent. It kept my mind occupied with something other than the letter I'd be receiving soon.

The following Monday, one week after seeing Dr. Rogers, I went to the mailbox and there it was—with her name and address in the upper left-hand corner. My hands were shaking. Though a fairly warm day, I felt cold all over. I sat down on the couch in the front room, took several deep breaths, then slipped my finger under the glued edge of the envelope, sliding it across.

With trembling hands, I pulled out the single sheet of folded white paper. I shut my eyes, unfolded the letter, and read the few short sentences which graced the page: thanking me for visiting their facility, the name of the laboratory that performed the DNA testing, the ninety-nine point nine-nine percent match with Edward J. Barnes.

Weston was indeed "not the baby's daddy." A part of me was expecting this and the other part was stunned that Fate had been so cruel. What I'd been refusing to deal with had to be faced head-on, soon. I hadn't thought this far ahead, believing there was no need to "go there" without solid proof Edward was the father.

Now that I was aware of the truth, I couldn't dodge what needed to be done. Weston first, then Edward. I'd deal with it in that order. As soon as possible. I didn't have much time. Edward would begin calling me soon. That meant I'd have to confront Weston immediately.

I felt doomed. I couldn't begin to predict what he'd do. I had no clue.

Chapter 16

That evening I got ready for bed and had just leaned back against the down pillows when Weston came out of the bathroom, just showered, looking so handsome. He sat down on the comforter and leaned over to kiss the tip of my nose. I smiled at him, feeling so much like the traitor I was.

"What's wrong, babe? You look like you're in another world."

"I need to talk to you about something."

"Sure, what's up?"

I could feel my palms sweating and my tongue stuck to the top of my mouth. After swallowing, I took a deep breath and looked down at my folded hands, then up at him.

"Remember that man we saw in Starbucks the other day?"

"Yeah. Nice guy. Seemed like an interesting person."

"I lied to you. He's not Cecilia's friend. He's the man I slept with, the one I told you about."

His face fell, devoid of expression. "Oh-kay," he strung out the word for several seconds.

"When he found out I was pregnant, he asked if he was the baby's father. He said if I didn't have a fetal DNA test, he'd take me to court and force me to be tested. I found out today he's the baby's father."

I didn't know what to expect. I figured it could go either way—he'd go ballistic or he'd be hurt and emotional. His stare frightened me. He leaned toward me without blinking, without talking, and I pressed myself back against the headboard.

"When did you have sex with him?" he whispered between gritted teeth.

I slid sideways away from him but his arm was propped up against my left side and I couldn't escape. I dropped my gaze to the edge of the sheet and squeezed my eyes shut, horrified by this blossoming nightmare.

"I didn't remember the exact date… But *he* said it was August twenty-fourth."

I could feel his breath on my face, hot and dry. I waited for him to say something, anything, utter words to make this all go away, change what was happening into a bad dream we'd never have to face.

"Right before I came home for Labor Day?" he shouted, startling me. I covered my face with my hands, squinching my eyes shut, wishing with my whole heart this wasn't happening.

I could feel the side of the bed rise up, heard him walking away. My hands fell to my sides and I opened my eyes. He grabbed his jeans and shirt and walked out the door. I'd never seen him look that way before. I wanted him to argue or shout or do something to show how he felt about what I'd told him. But perhaps this was the proverbial "straw that broke the camel's back."

I wasn't surprised when he didn't return that night. I slept fitfully, tossing and turning. When the first rays of dawn sprinkled through the edges of the curtains I resolved to put my best foot forward, go about my daily routine, and wait to hear from him.

At six-thirty a.m. someone knocked at the front door. I couldn't guess who would be visiting this early and was completely surprised when I found Michael, Weston's co-worker, standing on the front porch.

"Hi, Brandy! How're you doing?"

"I'm feeling good these days. Would you like to come in?"

"Sure. Thanks." He walked into the foyer and glanced down at the rug, then up at me, with an odd look on his face. I didn't know why he'd come by and could only guess it might have something to do with Weston's leaving.

"What brings you here so early in the morning? Shouldn't you be at the job site?"

"I'm kind of embarrassed. Weston asked if I'd come by and pick up some clothes for him and other small things. I don't want to be caught in the middle or anything, so I'll understand if you send me packing."

I covered my mouth with my hand, tears edging toward my lashes. Did Weston want to move out before we had an opportunity to discuss what happened last night? Had he already made the decision to leave me? If so, he wasn't thinking straight. And he certainly wasn't being fair to us, to our marriage, by acting rashly. But he obviously didn't want to talk to me. Instead he'd sent his lackey to do the job for him.

"No, Michael. It's okay. I'll make up a suitcase for him. I'll be right back."

I ran upstairs and pulled Weston's travel case out of the closet. Tears clouded my vision while I packed enough clothes for a week, along with his bath toiletries. For a second I entertained the thought of sticking a note inside; but I didn't want that to be misconstrued as some sort of cutesy gesture, so I decided against it. I didn't know what I would have said in a note to touch his heart anyway. I felt totally lost and didn't know what to do next.

I swiped the tears from my cheeks then brought the bag downstairs where Michael paced in the foyer, looking anxious to leave. I could imagine how awkward he must feel and had no idea how much Weston had told him, which made me even more embarrassed.

"Here you go." I thrust the suitcase toward him and opened the front door. "I apologize if this made you feel uncomfortable, Michael." We said our goodbyes and he rushed to his car.

My body felt like a five hundred pound weight. Lying down on the couch, I shut my eyes, hoping to steal a few moments of rest, but awakened with a start when my cell began playing its distinctive ring tone. Someone not on my contact list must be phoning me.

"Hello?"

"Brandy, it's Edward. Did you get the DNA results yet?"

"I just got them in the mail yesterday. I had to talk with Weston first, so I wasn't going to phone you until today."

"And?"

"You're the father. Are you happy now?"

Silence answered my statement. Several seconds passed before I heard a deep sigh. "Wow," he whispered then paused. "I'm a father for the first time in my life."

"So now what?" I asked, irritation in my voice.

"Now I have certain responsibilities, Brandy. I guess we should talk."

"About what?"

"Do you have to make this any harder than it already is? You know, it takes two to make a baby. I wasn't the only one on my couch that night, so stop blaming me for this entire thing."

I let out a deep breath. He was right. "I've been doing a lot of thinking. Of course it's not your fault this happened. It's just… It's *my* life that's going be ruined, not yours. I'm the one with the husband. You don't have a partner you have to answer to, you know what I mean?"

"I understand. Unfortunately for you, that doesn't change anything. I'm the father of your baby, and I'm determined to do the right thing. I have parental rights that I plan to exercise in whatever way I can, with or without your cooperation. If I were you, I'd cooperate. It'll make this whole thing go a lot easier on both of us."

I felt beaten and wanted to crouch in the corner in a fetal position to hide from the reality raining down around me. "What do you want from me?"

"I guess a judge will determine that," he said, in a matter-of-fact way. "It has to go to court. There's no way you can hide this."

"It's too late for me to hide *anything*, Edward," I explained in a nasty tone. "I've already told Weston. I'm just not familiar with the law as you are. I guess I'll get an attorney and we can go from there."

"How did Weston take it?"

"That's none of your business," I shouted. "And I certainly wouldn't feel comfortable discussing that with you. I'll retain an attorney, and he or she will be in touch with you. Are we done now?"

"I guess so. For now. I'll talk to you soon. Thank you for doing all this, Brandy."

"Oh, no, Edward. Thank *you*." I slammed the phone down.

I stared out the window, numb. What a nightmare. My life was slowly deteriorating, unraveling day by day. What was I supposed to do now? Maybe Cecilia or Perry knew of a good attorney. Who else could I ask?

My knee-jerk response was to phone Weston and ask for help, but of course, I couldn't do that. I didn't know where he was staying anyway, and I wasn't sure when I'd next hear from him Maybe I'd have to look for a divorce attorney, too.

Would he be willing to work this out? Could we stay together, and get through this? I loved him, and I knew he loved me. Nothing had changed except finding out I wasn't carrying his child which was a surprise to *both* of us. But I believed if we were willing to work on our relationship after both having had an affair, we were strong enough to withstand a custody trial.

Chapter 17

I waited several days before calling Cecilia, overwhelmed by the enormity of what was happening. When able to talk about it, I picked up the phone. "I have a small favor I'd like to ask you. Do you have an attorney you could recommend for a paternity case?"

"Umm, I could ask around. What's this about?"

"Maybe you should come over."

Within moments, she arrived at my front door carrying a small plate of muffins and her personal coffee mug. "What's goin' on?"

She followed me into the kitchen, pulled out a chair at the table, pushing her mug toward me. I grabbed the pot of freshly brewed coffee and filled her cup.

I sat down across from her and breathed in the strong scent of Columbian French roast, then took a sip. "My baby's father is Edward Barnes."

Her mug slipped from her hands and dropped onto the kitchen table with a thud, brown liquid streaming over the sides of the table onto the floor. I pushed back my chair, stood up quickly and grabbed a towel, throwing it on the table to soak up the mess. After wiping everything down with a sponge, I refilled her mug and sat down again.

"You could have warned me," she said. "Maybe give me the news after a prologue or something. How in the hell do you know this anyway?"

"Edward saw Weston and me at Starbucks and demanded to know whether the baby was his or not."

"The guy's got a lot of nerve."

"As he so aptly said, he could do the math. Weston told him I was almost seven months pregnant. Edward simply counted backwards."

"But how do you know he's the—"

"He insisted I have the baby's DNA tested or he'd approach Weston."

"Pretty determined guy, huh?"

"He said he'd take me to court, do whatever he needed to get the truth."

"So he's the father?" she whispered.

"Yeah, he is. And Weston left me the night I told him."

She shook her head, looking confused. "God, I never asked you *when* you had sex with Edward. I just figured you missed your period and Dr. Farney determined the date of conception."

I stared out the window, wondering why I'd never seriously thought of the possibility that Edward could be my baby's father. What had I been thinking? I guess I *hadn't* been thinking at all.

Her hand covered mine and I turned toward her sympathetic gaze. "I don't know what the hell is wrong with me, Cece. I never… I didn't mark the date I had sex with Edward on the damn calendar!" I shouted, bursting into tears.

I could hear her chair slide across the floor then felt her arm around my shoulders. I leaned in toward her and she hugged me while I cried deep gulping sobs, the dam of my heart bursting from holding in all my regret and sorrow.

"Have you and Weston talked about what you're going to do?"

I pulled out of her embrace and she grabbed a napkin off the table and handed it to me.

"This is such a mess," I said, patting my cheeks dry. "I've cried so much since the night Weston left, I didn't think I had any tears left to shed." I smiled at her, though it was obviously more of a sickening grimace. "I don't know what to do. I haven't heard from him in days. He won't take my calls. The switchboard routes me to the secretary and it goes to voice mail. I haven't been able to reach him."

She leaned over and took my hands in hers. "Look at me." Her understanding eyes locked on mine. "You'll make it through this. I don't know what will happen with you and Weston but I *do* know you've been through a lot—losing your baby, Weston working in New York, both of you admitting to having an affair." She squeezed both my hands. "You lived through all of that, honey. You're an extraordinary woman. Whatever happens, you'll be fine. We'll find you a good attorney, and you'll go to court about Edward's parental rights. I'm sure you and Weston will work something out."

I nodded. I wanted to believe her. At the very least, I could handle myself better than I had after losing Christine. I had to give myself credit for how well I held onto my sanity, practicing the coping skills I'd learned. I wasn't walking around in a daze, no scattered thoughts.

I had to be strong for the child I was carrying, no matter who the father was. Whatever happened now with Weston, I'd handle it. And whatever happened with Edward, well, I felt a strength in me I hadn't known existed. Cecilia's words resonated with truth. I'd be fine.

Chapter 18

Saturday arrived. Weston didn't work on the weekends, and I needed to talk to him. Every time I called his cell phone, it immediately went to voice mail. I'd left numerous messages, asking him to phone me, but he wouldn't return my calls.

Determined to communicate with him somehow, I decided to send him a confidential letter and mail it to him at work. What recourse did I have at this point? I felt helpless and unsettled, everything out of my control. If I could do nothing to mend fences, at least sending a letter to his office might make me feel less impotent.

While sitting on the couch, trying to come up with the right words to express what was in my heart, I looked up and saw the mailman stuffing letters and magazines into our red mailbox near the front gate. I walked out to retrieve them, waving to him as he made his way down the block. There were two magazines, my *Vogue* and Weston's *House Renovation*, and a few envelopes.

I brought the stack of mail into the house, to add to the other days' arrivals I still hadn't sorted through. Nothing seemed more important than saving my marriage, and I couldn't concentrate on mundane chores. Sticking out the side of today's pile I noted a legal-size envelope from the Law Offices of Lance Cook and Sons. I slid my finger under the flap and extracted a document several pages long titled "Official Request for Divorce Proceedings" initiated by the first party, Weston Chambers.

Unbelievable. I felt light-headed, my stomach queasy. Weston and I hadn't spoken to each other since the night I'd revealed Edward was the father of my baby, and I assumed we'd get together to discuss what we wanted to do. I *assumed* he'd at least want to give us an opportunity to work things out.

Talk about blindsided! In my opinion, this was a knee-jerk

reaction. He couldn't possibly have thought this through. He needed time to mull things over then get in touch with me when he was less emotional. This was just wrong.

I was about to lose my husband.

I was about to become a divorcee.

Immediately I phoned Cecilia and asked if she could come over right away. I left the front door ajar and went into the kitchen to brew fresh coffee—*not* decaffeinated. The front door slammed shut, and I turned to see her rushing into the kitchen, hair sopping wet, wearing sweatpants and an oversized t-shirt.

"What the hell's going on?" She pulled out a chair and plopped down on the seat with a huge sigh. "I'd just gotten out of the shower when you called. You sounded frantic."

I poured two cups of the dark brew into mugs and brought them over to the table. My hands were shaking as I set them carefully on the place mats then sank down in the chair across from her.

"Are you ready for this?" She nodded, her brows clutched together in a frown. "Weston filed for divorce."

She sat back in her chair, her face void of expression, and looked out the window overlooking our yard.

"You knew about this, didn't you?" I felt betrayed before I even heard her response.

"Perry told me this morning while we were still in bed. But he said you probably wouldn't receive the papers for a couple of days."

I tapped her on the hand lying next to her mug. She looked over at me. "Would you have told me?"

She paused, but her gaze never wavered from mine. "Yes, I would have told you. I swear to God, Brandy, I would never have kept this from you. I just hadn't had time yet to think of how to do it."

"Really?" It felt awkward knowing someone else was aware of my impending divorce before *I* knew about it, as if she held a secret that should have been mine to tell and not her.

She grabbed my hand and squeezed it, hard. "Yes, I was going to tell you… even though Perry made me promise I wouldn't. To me, it felt wrong for Perry and me to know and you not having a clue."

I nodded. It still hadn't sunk in—the reality that in the immediate future, I would no longer be Weston's wife.

She cleared her throat, looked down into her mug of coffee. "I have a friend, a woman friend, who's a divorce attorney," she said meekly, in a half-whisper.

My lips curved up in a small smile. "What's her name?"

"Claudette Delacroix. I've known her for years. We met at the athletic club way back when. Very French, and extremely good at her job from everything I hear."

I stared into the bottom of my mug, which I'd drained in a couple of minutes, the caffeine kicking me into high gear, a buzz churning through my veins.

"Are you gonna be okay, hon? Should I stay for a while? What can I do?"

My head swirled with questions. What if Weston tried to take the house from me? Where would I live? Could he prove me an unfit mother because I was carrying another man's child? This was a Weston I didn't recognize, so I couldn't venture to guess his intentions.

"Not to be rude, Cece, but do you think we could talk later? I want to call your friend." I grabbed a pad and pen from the countertop and scribbled her name. "Claudette Delacroix, right?" She nodded. "I'd like to set up an appointment soon."

She stood and put her arm around my waist as we walked to the foyer where she gave me a tight hug. I slowly closed the door behind her, gritting my teeth, edging toward the gaping maw of depression. But I had to stop this type of thinking. I could not go down that road again, giving up on life. I had to fight this with everything in me.

I'd raise my child in this city, in this house, send him or her to the best schools and I'd do it with financial help from the father of my baby. We'd work out that part during a court hearing. And if Weston didn't want to be married to me any longer and refused to be a parent to this baby, I'd have to accept that, too.

I made an appointment to see Ms. Delacroix for Wednesday, anxious to find out my options and what Weston's attorney would reveal concerning his wishes. I'd yet to find a lawyer to handle the paternity issue but surmised Ms. Delacroix would be helpful in that regard.

On Wednesday, I drove the few minutes to her office located in a beautifully restored Victorian house on Grand Street. After her secretary announced my arrival, Ms. Delacroix opened the door to her office with a smile.

"Mrs. Chambers, come in." She gestured me into her office where I took a seat facing her desk. "Since we'll be working together on your divorce, please call me Claudette," she said in a heavy French accent.

I nodded. "Call me Brandy."

"All right, Brandy. Do you have the papers from your husband's attorney with you?"

I removed the documents from my purse and handed them to her. "I received these a few days ago. Somewhat of a surprise, I have to admit."

Perusing them, she glanced up at me. "Sometimes that happens... Nothing premeditated such an action on your husband's part?"

I took a deep breath, looked down at my folded hands. "Yes, something definitely happened, but I thought he and I would work through it. I've been trying to get in touch with him for weeks, then suddenly I received these in the mail—"

"May I ask what happened, Brandy?"

A hot blush crept up my neck. I'd only told my story to Weston and Cecilia and felt embarrassed to have to explain it to a total stranger. However, she was my attorney, bound by complete confidentiality. "While my husband worked temporarily in New York, I had an affair. The man moved to Washington state but then he returned to Alameda, found out I was pregnant, and insisted I have the child's DNA tested. He's the father."

She nodded, finished looking through the papers I'd given her, and tilted her head. "You were forced to admit to your husband you'd been unfaithful, no?"

"Yes. And after I told him about my affair, he admitted to having had an affair too. But when I revealed I was pregnant with another man's child..." I shrugged. "He left me."

She opened a side drawer, pulled out several sets of stapled documents. "I'll need you to fill out these standard informational forms, which will explain your personal and financial status. Take them with you and mail them back to me. In the meantime, I'll contact your husband's attorney, Lance Cook, and find out what he wants to do with regard to alimony, your unborn child, any other concerns he may have.

"Depending on whether you and he agree on the details will determine how long it will take to finalize your divorce. It can be completed in six months if there are no disagreements. Or it could take much longer, depending on what I find out. I'll contact you soon." She leaned back in her chair, placed her reading glasses on her desktop and frowned. "Do you want this divorce from your husband?"

My eyes blurred, the tears imminent. I was so embarrassed. I never cried in front of strangers, and especially now. I didn't want to appear like the weak and helpless soon-to-be divorcee.

"I must ask the question, no?" she continued. "Your husband is the one filing for divorce, Brandy. What do *you* want?"

Clearing my throat, I blinked several times then replied, "I was hoping Weston and I could work this out. So, no, I don't want the divorce, but he obviously doesn't want anything more to do with me, won't answer my calls… If we don't talk, how can we resolve this?"

She stood, placing both hands flat on top of her desk. "It sounds like you've tried your best to get in contact with him, eh?"

"Yes, I have." I stood and looked her in the eyes. "I surmise he thought about it, made his decision, took the time and effort to acquire an attorney. So I assume he's determined to do this." I paused. "I don't like living in limbo. If my husband doesn't want me in his life, I have to move on."

She came around to the front of her desk and we shook hands. "I'll take it from here."

Before I left, she gave me the name of a gentleman who would handle the paternity issues between Edward and me, Mr. Harvey Denzel, who also had an office in Alameda. I left feeling much better. I tried to "let it go," knowing she'd handle the details. I'd done all I could for the moment.

My life was in a stage of metamorphosis. I'd be a single mother in a few months. Though I would hope Weston and I could have an amicable divorce and Edward's demands would be reasonable, I had to be realistic. I might have to battle it out in court with both men before the divorce and custody issues were final.

When I arrived home, I phoned Mr. Denzel's office and scheduled a meeting with him the next day. I was anxious to go forward with my life, glad I didn't have to wait weeks to meet with either of my attorneys.

I contemplated my upcoming appointment with Mr. Denzel. What if Edward insisted on shared custody? How would I feel about having my child live fifty percent of the time with me and the other half with the biological father? I couldn't imagine having to force my son or daughter to live in two homes for most of his or her life. My stomach clenched at the thought of a potential fight in court over parental rights.

Feeling burdened with these upsetting thoughts, I drove to Mr. Denzel's office the following day, fear roiling up my throat at the prospect of having to acquiesce to Edward's demands. After the secretary announced my arrival over the phone, I looked up when I heard the door open. There stood an older man, over six-feet tall with a thick head of white hair, dressed in a dark suit set off with a bright yellow tie.

"Mrs. Chambers," he declared in a deep baritone voice. "Come right in." He gestured dramatically for me to enter his office.

After taking a seat in front of his desk, I looked around and saw photographs of what appeared to be a younger version of him lining the walls. He was dressed in a baseball uniform, all labeled with the number "12."

"Like baseball?" he asked, a huge smile forming below his full, mostly-white mustache.

"Watching baseball relaxes me. It's not a super-fast sport, and when I'm stressed out I often turn on the television to the Sports Channel to see if I can catch a game. Did you play professional baseball?"

"Angels, 1970 to '75. Pitched four no-hitters in five years."

"But you wanted to be a lawyer."

"Wrist injury. Got my law degree and set up shop here in my hometown. Made a lot of good friends over the years practicing in a small city like this. I'll treat you right, I assure you."

Nodding, I had to grin. He seemed like a real character, unlike any lawyer I'd ever met. Was he giving me a subtle heads up he knew people in high places? Perhaps that would be in my favor. Or just extremely self-confident and boastful? I guessed I'd find out soon enough.

He leaned back so far in his chair I could practically hear it groaning under his weight. "Tell me what's going on, uh..." He looked down at the sheet of paper I'd filled out. "Brandy. I knew a Brandy once in college. Man, oh man, she—but that's water under the bridge. Tell me what you've come to see me about."

I suppressed another grin. He'd succeeded in making me less nervous, his demeanor so relaxed my stomach stopped grinding. "I'm married and had an affair. The other man is my child's biological father and—"

"What's this other man's name?" he interrupted.

"Edward. Edward Barnes."

His bushy slate-grey eyebrows popped up. "Attorney?" I nodded. "You know how to pick 'em."

"What do you mean?" Alameda's a small town and I shouldn't have been surprised Edward and Mr. Denzel knew each other.

"He's a helluva nice guy, Brandy. Doubt he has anything squirrelly up his sleeve if you're worried about him taking your child away from you."

I shook my head. "He's not a horrible person, Mr. Denzel—"

"Call me Justin," he interjected.

"I don't want my child to have to live half of her life with her mother and the other half with her father. I have no idea what Edward's rights are in this matter, and I haven't a clue what he wants either."

"I'll get in touch with whoever's representing him, Brandy, see what he has in mind." He leaned forward in his chair, folded his hands on the leather blotter. "I'll have my secretary call you with the date for the hearing." He stood up and walked around to where I sat. He stuck out his hand and I put my palm in his. He helped me out of the chair with a smile. "Wipe that frown off your forehead. It'll all work out just fine. I guar-an-tee it."

"Thank you, Justin."

"No worries, my dear."

I left with the oddest feeling in my gut everything could work out after all—just as Justin promised. I'd done everything I needed to, turning matters over to those who dealt with the legal issues. And with Claudette and Justin on my side, I didn't feel so alone now.

Chapter 19

April. And I was eight months along in my pregnancy. I met with my ob/gyn once every two weeks, and the baby was apparently right on the mark in weight and size. I was healthy and felt fine, especially considering the emotional upheavals surrounding my life. The weather was warmer and I'd started a vegetable garden in the backyard, just as I'd done in San Francisco. I was planting seeds when the phone rang in the kitchen, and I rushed inside the house to answer it.

"Brandy? Edward here."

The sound of his voice chilled me. "What do you want?" I barked.

"God, do you have to be so hostile? You and I might be seeing each other a lot, Brandy, so we should cultivate some type of friendly relationship."

I sighed. "I haven't heard from my attorney yet and I don't know what to make of that. Is there a problem I'm not aware of?"

"I haven't spoken with my lawyer in a week or so either. He went out of town for a conference. That's probably why you haven't heard from yours. At least, that's my educated guess."

"Yeah, you're probably right."

"Listen, Brandy. Maybe I've seen too many of these situations go sour, so I want to make this whole thing legal. Can you blame me? You've fought me the whole way on this, since the beginning. And I'm not asking for much. I'd like to be able to see my child a couple of weekends a month. I want to help out financially as well, start a college fund along with a monthly stipend."

I let out a deep breath, relief flooding through me. "I have no problem with that. I was afraid you would demand a lot more and I appreciate your being so understanding about this."

"You're welcome," he replied. "So, how are you feeling? Everything going okay with your pregnancy?"

"Yeah. The baby's fine. I feel great. No problems in that area."

There was a pause in the conversation, then he asked, "Does that mean there are problems in other areas?"

I didn't answer right away, not sure whether I should reveal any personal information. But why not? This man would be a part of my life for years and bound to find out about the dissolution of my marriage fairly soon. "Weston filed for divorce."

"Wow. I'm sorry to hear that."

"You know, Edward, we don't know each other well anymore but suffice it to say, Weston had an affair of his own while in New York."

"You're kidding me! That changes things. Did you forgive him his transgression?"

"Yes, I did. We were enjoying a renewed relationship when you showed up and blew everything to pieces."

"I'm sorry. It was never my intention to hurt you or your husband. I only wanted to do what's right." He paused and let out a sigh. "Geez, I don't know why your husband can't see his way past this. I mean, you weren't intentionally trying to get pregnant for God's sake. Doesn't he get that?"

"I guess not. I never had a chance to talk to him about it. He doesn't want anything to do with me."

"What a mess. That night you came over my house, I should never have let things go as far as they did. It's just… you were sitting there looking so pretty and I'd been infatuated with you since high school then when I kissed you—God, I'm sorry. About everything."

He sounded so genuinely remorseful I almost felt sorry for him. "No need to apologize, Edward. I'm a big girl. I made a decision to have sex with you. No one forced me into it. But I never thought the child was yours. The blood test determined the date of conception around Labor Day when Weston came home for vacation." I paused, thinking back to my one night of passion on the couch in Edward's front room. "I hadn't even thought about the date I went to your house. Now I'm reaping the benefits of my foolish act. But I can't blame you. I'm responsible for my own behavior."

"Sounds like you've given it some thought. Actually, you sound like you're doing pretty well with it. Are you going to do the whole natural childbirth thing?"

"Yeah. I'm looking forward to it. You know, the last pregnancy ended in such a disaster, I'm anxious about this one. This child is really special to me. Not that every child isn't, but it's like I've been given a second chance."

"Everything will be just fine, Brandy."

"I hope so. I had a complete meltdown after my first baby died. I blamed myself. I believed I must have done something wrong during my pregnancy that caused her death. And I figured Weston must blame me too. I was so filled with guilt. And shame too, because of the way I'd treated him." I sighed, remembering the past, and regretting it too. "I should never have slept with you."

"You're right. But don't be so hard on yourself. Losing a child is one of the most stressful times in anybody's life. You were obviously acting out of character at the time we got together."

"Yeah. I walked around like a zombie most days. But I'm fine now. I'm happy to be pregnant again. It's not Weston's child, but it's still an exciting time for me."

"I have a question for you. And I don't expect you to answer me right away, but… I'd like to help you out. With the birthing classes. If you need a partner, I'd be happy to be that person."

Caught off-guard, I stumbled to get out the words. "Uh… I'll have to think about it. Discovering I'm pregnant with another man's child is new territory for me. I'm sure you understand."

"Absolutely. I've never gotten anyone pregnant before. Anyway, think about it. I'll understand either way."

"Okay. I've gotta go now. Thanks for calling."

Having such a friendly talk with Edward surprised me, never anticipating we'd be civil to each other. But it felt right. If our futures should end up becoming intertwined because of the baby, better to have an amicable relationship rather than fighting and arguing at every turn. Maybe it wouldn't be so bad after all.

Chapter 20

Claudette Delacroix's secretary phoned and asked me to make an appointment to talk about the divorce proceedings. I was anxious to find out what Weston's demands were regarding the house, alimony, my child. Unfamiliar with California law, I felt uncomfortable not knowing how my life would change once the divorce was final.

When I arrived, Claudette said she'd ask me several questions, give me the list of Weston's requests, and explain the details of what my new life as a divorcee would look like, depending on what I thought was fair.

"Brandy, you and Weston have been married for almost seven years. You own a home in San Francisco which you're currently renting out. You moved to Alameda, purchasing the house at 1716 Lauren Drive. That is correct, no?"

"Yes, that's right. I got pregnant while we were living in the city, then we moved here. Unfortunately, I lost the baby in June of last year."

"I'm sorry to hear that. On the positive side, your husband's making no claims with regard to your future child. It would be almost impossible for him to acquire custody of the child anyway, unless he tried to prove you're an unfit mother, which he has no intention of doing. Additionally, you now have proof the child isn't his. If anything, Mr. Barnes could fight for custody of your baby, but Mr. Denzel is representing you with regard to that case, no?" She glanced up and I nodded.

"Looking at your combined assets, if you sell your house in San Francisco, you could purchase Weston's portion of your home in Alameda, split the remaining assets, and you'd be left with a great deal of money. He has agreed to that. He's unwilling to pay support for your future child but agrees to pay you a reasonable monthly alimony. This seems more than fair to me."

"Wow! I haven't spoken to Weston since the day he walked out of the house, so I had visions of this divorce being anything but amicable. The terms seem more than fair to me too."

With a monthly alimony and money left over to invest for the future, I wouldn't have to worry about my baby's future. I'd received a considerable inheritance when my parents died several years back. Being an only child, I was their sole heir and they'd invested wisely. After selling their house, I'd been able to devote my days to writing, a dream I'd had since graduating college.

"That part's done then, Brandy. I'll take care of all the paperwork and your divorce should be completed in six months, sometime in October."

How easy to dissolve a marriage, to throw away years of loving and caring for each other. I still loved Weston, but he obviously couldn't handle my carrying another man's child. In the end, my deceit and lies helped ruin our marriage, and I couldn't blame anyone but myself.

I picked up my purse, preparing to leave. "By the way, Claudette, do you know where Weston is living now?"

"The address I have on these documents is 2030 Santa Clara Avenue."

I felt like I'd been slapped in the face. When Weston had told me Carol had left the company, I assumed she'd returned to New York. "You're kidding me?"

"Does it matter to you?"

"It's where his old secretary lives. Well, not old, age-wise. She was his secretary in New York, the one he had an affair with when he lived there."

"I'm sorry. It's obviously been quite a year for you. But I'm glad your divorce is turning out to be one of the easier ones, Brandy. They can get quite messy. By the way, your husband wants to pick up his remaining items in the house, shoes, clothes, things like that. I'll have my secretary arrange a date agreeable to both of you. You'll be hearing from me if there's anything I need to ask you."

We both stood, shook hands, and I left her office, disoriented and depressed. Weston living with Carol Smith stuck in my gut like a knife. Why hadn't Carol moved back to New York?

Claudette's secretary phoned the next day and I agreed to Weston coming over Friday to pick up his things. The morning he was scheduled to arrive, I woke up feeling nervous and anxious, knowing he'd be here in a few hours. I hadn't seen or heard from him since March and I missed him. Then again, I resented the fact he hadn't wanted to talk about our marriage before he filed for divorce.

I dressed in my nicest maternity outfit, though it was near impossible to look like anything but an oversized marshmallow in my white capris and stretchy white top. When the bell rang, I took a few deep breaths and reached for the door knob. There he stood, looking handsome in his distressed jeans, black biker boots, hair neatly trimmed, his mustache and goatee dark and sexy. This man always made my heart skip a beat. Some things would never change.

"Brandy." He nodded once. "How're you feeling?"

"Fine, thanks. Come in."

He followed me into the front room where we sat at opposite ends of our favorite couch. It was an awkward situation. I felt as though I should make conversation with someone I didn't know very well.

"You noticed the boxes next to the front door?" He nodded. "Those are your things but feel free to look around and take what you want. I won't be a jerk about this, Weston."

He leaned forward, elbows on his knees, and looked down at the rug. "Thanks, Brandy. I—"

"I would have liked to talk with you about everything before it came to this, West, but you've made it impossible to contact you. However, my attorney did mention you're living on Santa Clara Avenue now. I'm assuming you're with Carol?"

"It's none of your business who I live wi—" He paused, shaking his head. "Shit, I'm not gonna do this. I apologize."

He turned toward me, tears in his eyes. I stood up and knelt in front of him on the rug, taking his hands in mine. "For what it's worth, I'm sorry. Sorry for doing what I did, sorry for getting pregnant, sorry—"

He leaned over and kissed me lightly on the forehead. "Don't, Brandy, don't do this. I'm sorry too. Sorry for sleeping with Carol. Sorry for being so weak. Things went so wrong with us. I don't exactly know why. Maybe just too much bad stuff happened, Christine's death, your depression, my affair with Carol, yours with Edward. Don't get me wrong, I don't blame you for freaking out after Christine died. It was a horrible thing to endure.

"I don't know." He shrugged, squeezing my hands in his warm grasp. "Everything just got so messed up. And when I left for New York, I felt lonely and sad about you, about our baby. I just lost it. My good sense went out the window... But, hey, water under the bridge."

I looked up at him. "Can we still be friends?" I searched his eyes, trying to gauge his response.

"I don't hate you, Brandy."

I paused, not wanting to ask the question, but I had to know. I'd been obsessing about it since finding out he was living with Carol. "Do you love her?"

He glanced toward the front window. "I don't know. She's been there for me since I left you and..." He raked his hand through his hair, then shook his head. "I've gotta go, Brandy. Thanks for packing my stuff."

He stood up, leaning over to help me up off the floor. I followed him as he walked toward the front door. After opening it, he turned toward me, eyes glistening with unshed tears. "I'm sorry... about all of this." He leaned over and picked up a couple of boxes.

I opened my mouth to say—what? This felt like the end. If he loved Carol there wasn't much more I could say. We were both sorry and sad, too. One chapter of our lives was ending. Another was starting for Weston and Carol, and mine was just beginning for me and my child.

"Need help?" But I was talking to his back as he slowly made his way down the path toward his car.

He turned around, our eyes met. "No, I can handle it."

I closed the door softly, my hand lingering on the knob after it shut. He wasn't handling the end of our marriage well at all. He seemed confused and unhappy. How could he throw away all we had so *easily*? Then again, he appeared to be having a difficult time with it so I rephrased my confusion. How could he throw away all we had, period?

Chapter 21

I signed up for three weeks of birthing classes starting in May. There would be six to eight couples, meeting in one of the rooms in the older section of Alameda Hospital. However, I couldn't do it alone. I needed to make a decision about Edward's offer to be my partner.

I'd told Cecilia about Edward's offer, but she and I hadn't had time to talk about that. Granted, I needed someone to take the birthing classes with me, yet she was my only friend in Alameda. Since Weston and I had moved here last year my life had been a roller coaster ride, and I hadn't established any other contacts besides her. And Edward, of course. But was that reason enough to ask him to be my partner?

Cecilia had always been my perfect sounding board since the day we met, so I invited her over for coffee. When the doorbell chimed, I anxiously ran to answer it. "Come in, Cece! You look great. How're you feeling?"

"Queasy in the mornings, but overall, Dr. Farney says everything's going well."

"Good. Don't you love Dr. Farney? She's so friendly, like a girlfriend."

"Yeah. Hey, did you sign up for birthing classes?"

"Every Tuesday at seven o'clock. Will you be taking them too?"

"Yeah. Ours start in October. Perry and I are really looking forward to it. He's so jazzed about this baby, Brandy. What about a partner?"

"I wanted to talk to you about that. Come in and sit down. I'll make us both a decaf latte."

I prepared our coffees while trying to negotiate my stomach around the island in the middle of the kitchen. "I'm on the fence about it. I'll be a single woman in a matter of months. Weston's not coming back. There's really nothing stopping me from accepting Edward's offer, right?"

After taking a sip of her coffee, she gazed out the window overlooking the back yard. "I've been thinking about that." She turned back toward me. "You told me Weston's living with Carol, right?"

I took a deep breath, stuck my finger in the foam at the top of my latte, then licked it off. "The fact she left the company obviously didn't end their relationship. And when he came over to pick up his things, I asked him if he was in love with her. He said he didn't know then he left. Like he was running away. From the feelings he still has for me… That's what *I* think anyway."

She patted my hand, gave me a little smile. "Water under the bridge, Brandy. You said your divorce will be final in October?" I nodded. "Then, I'd go for it. Tell Edward yes."

I grinned. "You're right. Why the hell not?"

It felt so good to share thoughts and feelings with another female, especially someone expecting a baby too. Cecilia had a good head on her shoulders and I took her advice seriously.

"I'll call Edward and tell him I want him to be my birthing coach. Is that weird or what?"

She stood up to leave, giving me a quick hug. "You'll get past the weirdness of it. I gotta go. Paperwork awaits me!" She raced out the door.

I waited until later that night, found Edward's phone number, and went into the front room to put my feet up. It felt awkward phoning him but he *was* the father of my child. Weston had already gone. I was alone, soon to be a single mom, needed someone to lean on. Maybe it would be Edward. He answered the phone immediately.

"Edward. It's Brandy."

"Hey, how're you doing? I've been thinking about you. How did it go with Weston? Last time I spoke with you, you said he'd filed for divorce."

"I retained an attorney, Claudette Delacroix, and the divorce should be final in October. It's an uncontested divorce. He and I agreed to all the terms, the finances, the houses." I paused. This conversation seemed surreal—telling Edward about my divorce?

"Claudette's a good attorney. I've known her a few years, attended several conferences with her. Nice lady. I'm glad everything's going smoothly with Weston. It'll make your lives so much easier that it's uncontested. So, what's up? Why the phone call?"

"I've been considering your offer of being my partner in the birthing classes and, if the offer still stands—"

"Of course it still stands. I'd be honored. When do classes start?"

"On May fifth. I'll send you an e-mail with the days and times. I appreciate your doing this, Edward. I couldn't do it alone."

"No problem. My e-mail is 'edwardbarnes', one word, no caps, 'at gmail dot com'. Just send me the info. I have another call, so I'll talk to you soon. And, thanks, Brandy, for saying yes."

"You're welcome."

I placed the phone back and sat thinking how strange life can be sometimes. Who would have thought I'd be a soon-to-be-divorced woman, expecting a man's baby who I'd known in high school but didn't know much about now, and I planned to attend birthing classes with him! Totally bizarre.

I'd wanted to share this experience with Weston, but that couldn't happen. And, yes, I felt depressed about his leaving me during this eventful time in my life, but Edward appeared excited about being a part of this pregnancy and birth. I resigned myself to the fact I couldn't have what I wanted and would have to accept this altered situation. Life didn't always go the way I planned, and I'd have to change my attitude in order to enjoy this experience. I was happy to be having a child, thrilled I'd soon be a mother, and Edward was happy about being a father. Overall, life was good.

Chapter 22

I planned to spend the entire month of May putting the final touches on my second novel. I'd be entering my ninth month and wanted to finish the majority of the editing before the baby was born. Over the last few months, dealing with the divorce and meeting with my attorneys had made it difficult to concentrate on writing, and soon I'd have an infant needing my attention. I had just sat down with my MacBook and opened the iPages program when the phone rang.

"Hey, Brandy! You busy?" It was Cecilia.

I smiled. It was always a treat to be interrupted by my best friend. She rarely phoned during the day, aware I had a personal schedule I tried to adhere to with my writing, and blogging on my website took an inordinate amount of time.

"Hi to you, too. I'm trying to finish up this book. I don't want Brent to see it before I've gone through it at least a hundred times." I chuckled. "He hates it when I make his job *too* hard."

"When will this one be published?"

"Oh, I don't even have a contract yet. Brent's a real stickler for perfection. He knows what he wants and won't take anything less. But if this book gets published, it'll be because of him. He has great contacts and I think it's just a matter of time."

"Lucky you—I don't want to take up anymore of your time. I just wanted to ask if you'd be interested in co-hosting our summer block party in a few weeks. Perry and I will organize the whole thing. Your due date is coming up in early June, and we don't want you to stress out over this. We just wanted to know if we could have it at your place. Ours isn't big enough and your back yard is huge."

"Sure, I'd love to. Will you know ahead of time how many people will be coming?"

"Yeah. I'll go door-to-door and get a fairly accurate head count.

But usually there are quite a few people who show up unannounced, you know—people's friends or family. You can invite anyone you want since the party's at your house."

"Sounds fun."

"Will you ask Edward?"

"I haven't had time to think about it." I chuckled. "But, yeah, why not? Our birthing classes start on May fifth. He and I really don't know each other well. I mean, it's been many years since we were in high school and now he's going to be my birthing coach? It's a little embarrassing, if you know what I mean."

"I understand the classes can be pretty touchy-feely, so I see what you're saying." She paused. "Just so you know, Perry's inviting Weston, but you probably already figured that out."

"Now you mention it, of course he'd be invited. Perry and Weston are best friends. But there shouldn't be a problem. We're all adults. Weston's the one who wanted the divorce. I'll be polite and friendly. If Edward decides to join us, he'd be the perfect gentleman, I'm sure. I'm not worried about it." I paused, thinking of the elephant in the middle of the room. "Is Weston bringing Carol?"

"Perry told me he isn't but he didn't tell me why Weston's not asking her to come. Anyway, I just wanted to keep you apprised of the situation. Hey, I'll let you get back to work. We'll talk about particulars later. See ya'."

I opened my laptop again and stared out the front room window, thinking about the block party, when the phone rang again. I shook my head, trying to break out of my reverie, then answered it.

"Brandy, it's Edward. How's it going?"

"Fine. I knew you'd be calling. At least, I hoped you would. Are you still up for doing this?"

"Of course I am. I'm not one to change my mind once I decide to do something. Would you like to go out to dinner before class starts, say five-thirty or so? Class begins at seven, so we won't be late."

"I'd like that."

He said he'd be by around five o'clock. Like deja vu, I remembered back in August, the second time we saw each other at Peet's, when he'd asked me to come to his house for dinner. I hadn't spent a moment thinking about my answer. It was as if someone else was speaking for me. And that's how I felt now. I blurted out I'd go to dinner with him without thinking twice. Was this a wise idea? Did he consider it a date? And, if so, what in the hell was I doing?

I e-mailed the final draft of my second book to Brent. He and I were hoping Harper Collins would pick it up for publication. In the meantime, having written two books already, I knew after typing "The End" on the last page of your novel, beginning the next one was the only way to improve one's craft, so I'd already started writing my third book. It always felt good at the end of the day, seeing how my writing had improved after all my hard work.

On the night of the first birthing class, Edward arrived a few minutes before five. When we walked out the door, I noticed an expensive Porsche, a two-seater, shiny hunter green parked at the curb. I remembered when he'd driven Weston and me home from South Shore he had an SUV. This car had "bachelor" written all over it. A twinge of jealousy ran through my veins, though I couldn't explain why. Perhaps it was the fact I was in my ninth month and felt like an oversized meatball.

And here was Edward, looking as delicious as an Italian meatball, single, no obligations other than work every day, rushing to my side of the car to open it for the fat pregnant lady. I felt so unattractive and frumpy. After packing myself in the passenger seat like a sardine in a tin can, I tried to put my seatbelt on, not realizing it would be an impossible feat to do alone.

"Hey, let me help you with that," he interrupted my frustrated grapplings with the end of the belt. "This car's kind of small. I apologize but the Yukon's on its last breath and this is all I've got." He leaned over me toward the window to get hold of the metal clip. He was having a hard time finding it, lying across my big belly, struggling to grab the clip with his left hand. I could smell his cologne—Abercrombie & Fitch's *Fierce*. I breathed in the scent as he pulled the belt over me and plugged it into the holder on my left side. Everything about him exuded maleness. He was sexy looking as hell but he didn't act as if he knew it.

"Thanks. I feel like a ninety-year-old lady, needing help with everything."

He seemed to take it in stride, grinning. "Comes with the territory, eh? We're going to L'Orangerie, off Park Street. Ever heard of it?"

"No, but it must be French. That much I can figure out."

"Nice place, great service. I love it."

"Then you've been there before?"

"Two or three times. Usually for lunch though. Partner meetings. Pretty boring. It'll be nice to eat there without having to talk business, believe me. So, hey, Brandy, do you realize we know almost nothing about each other's lives before we met in high school?"

"I don't know what happened with you after high school either. You know, I can picture your mom, but that's about all I remember about your family."

"Where did you live before you moved to Alameda? I know you didn't have any brothers or sisters, right?"

We pulled up to the L'Orangerie restaurant where a valet drove the car away and parked it for us. Edward had made a reservation, so we were shown to our table next to a window overlooking a lovely little garden at the back, in the middle of which stood a cascading fountain. After placing menus in front of us, the waiter discreetly left us alone and stood off to the side, waiting for a sign we were ready to order.

"I was born in Oakland," I said. "Grew up in San Leandro. Middle-class parents. You remember my dad, Bill?"

He nodded. "How could I forget him? He was a fireman, wasn't he?"

"In Oakland. For thirty-five years. My mom stayed home and took care of me. I went to St. Felicitas Grammar School in San Leandro and we moved to Alameda when I was ten years old. You and I met during freshman orientation, remember?"

Grinning, he said, "How could I forget? You were eating a chocolate chip cookie from the refreshment table and I was watching you—"

I put my hand up, palm facing outward. "No," I interrupted. "Don't remind me."

He laughed in a deep, low chuckle. "Your eyes got all wide and you were looking around like a madwoman, ran over to the garbage can, and spit out a big gob of something..."

"And when I looked around you were standing there watching me..."

"I started laughing so hard. I thought you were puking your guts out."

"Those were the worst cookies I'd ever tasted in my life!"

"So I brought you a cup of water and asked if you were sick—"

"And I told you I wasn't sick but the cookies were enough to make anyone hurl."

"So I offered to bake you the best chocolate chip cookies you'd ever taste in your entire life."

"And that was the beginning of our friendship for four years."

I couldn't stop giggling over the memory. Edward reached across the table and squeezed my hand. Looking up, our eyes locked. He held my gaze until I gently pulled my hand away from his.

"We lost touch after high school," he continued. "Didn't you go to Cal?"

I nodded, took a sip of water. "Where I got my master's degree in Creative Writing."

"What did you want to do with your degree?"

"At the time, I thought I might teach. But, I couldn't picture myself standing in front of a classroom, lecturing behind a podium. I started writing my first novel when I was working part-time as a teaching assistant at Alameda Junior College."

"Did you get published?"

Smiling at the memory of receiving "the call," I answered, "Yeah, I did. *Passing Through Brandiss* hit the shelves about two years ago. I'm working on my third book now while waiting to see whether this editor at Harper Collins is interested in my second novel."

He sat back, eyebrows arched. "Wow! So you're a real live author. I'm impressed. When did you and Weston meet?"

"About ten years ago. I met him at a wedding in the Oakland hills. A friend of mine introduced us. We hit it off and were together about two years before we got married. We lived in San Francisco for a few years. I got pregnant and we moved to Alameda. After our baby died, I had a meltdown. Then you and I met again at Peet's—"

"Wow! Your life sounds like a book."

"As long as I get to have my HEA."

He looked confused. "What's an HEA?"

I smiled and explained, "It stands for happily ever after. I learned the phrase after writing my first book. It didn't have a happy ending and I quickly found out it wouldn't sell without one."

"Does it look like you'll have your own personal HEA, as you put it?"

I shrugged. "I don't know yet, but I hope so." It felt cathartic, sharing my life in synopsis form. And he seemed truly interested in what I was saying. "What about you?"

He gestured to our waiter who briskly came to our table and took our orders. After refilling our water glasses, he left us alone and Edward sat back in his chair, glanced up at the ceiling then looked across the table at me.

"I grew up in Salinas, east of Carmel and Monterey. Not even close to middle class. I was an only child too, but like I told you before, my dad split when I was ten years old and I haven't heard from him since. Mom and I moved to Alameda when I was thirteen. She was a nurse, got a job at Alameda Hospital. After I graduated from Hastings Law School in San Francisco, I worked at a small firm here in Alameda, made partner early, and here I am. Much less drama in my life than yours, Brandy. In comparison, quite boring. No one would want to read about *my* life, that's for sure."

"And you've never been married?" He shook his head. "Have you ever come close?"

"Not even. I think I may be a commitment-phobe! I mean, I've had a few serious relationships, but the women all had visions of walking down the aisle in their white wedding gown with hundreds of people celebrating at a black-tie reception. It just didn't feel right. I couldn't picture myself with any of them for the long term—you know, sitting across the kitchen table, growing old together, that sort of thing. So, I'd make my excuses, take a permanent hike, until the next woman came along."

"We sure have lived different lives, huh?" I wiped a few breadcrumbs from the tablecloth, focused on the silver spoon next to my plate. "People intrigue me. Everyone's so unique. It's what makes the world so interesting I guess. The stuff books are made of."

Again Edward reached for my hand and ran his thumb over my knuckles. "That's why we have authors like you, Brandy. Maybe I can get an autographed copy of one of your books?"

I looked up at him and grinned. "I'd be delighted," I said, suddenly realizing I was having a good time.

The waiter brought our dinners, and the food tasted delicious, just as Edward had promised. We were planning to have coffee afterward but, noting the hour, I suggested we get to class. Edward gave a short wave to the waiter who brought him the check, and soon we were tucked back inside the Porsche on the way to our first birthing class.

Chapter 23

After negotiating our way through the maze of hallways, doors, and turns within the old part of the hospital, we finally found our way to the classroom. We'd been seated for only a few seconds when our instructor, who introduced herself as Becky, began the class. She gave a detailed overview of what we would be learning for the next three weeks and sent us home with a ton of literature to read before the next class.

Though all the information felt a bit overwhelming, once back on the road headed home, Edward told me he was excited about helping me out when my time came. I would have thought he'd find his role boring and had pegged him as the consummate bachelor, not the least bit interested in babies, or any kids for that matter.

It amazed me he'd want to be in the company of a fat pregnant woman. I had to admit, I didn't know him well, though after having dinner together, I had a much better idea of the type of man he was. However, our time together had been too short to get a good idea of what made Edward Barnes tick.

At the next class, our instructor, Becky, had us introduce ourselves. Edward and I were the only two people who weren't married. That didn't seem to bother him, though it made me feel out of place. I'd never pictured myself as a single mom, and I surely never thought I'd be in a birthing class with Edward Barnes, learning the basics of breathing during labor!

When it came time to practice the exercises in mock preparation for giving birth, we all sat on floor mats with our partners. She instructed Edward to straddle me from behind, wrap his arms around my belly, and massage my hugely protruding abdomen. He jumped right to the task.

I could feel his biceps rubbing against my breasts. I'd always been well-endowed and just as it had been during my first pregnancy, I was bigger now. They were a highly sensitive area and I could feel my nipples growing hard while he practiced belly massage.

His head lay right next to my cheek as he looked downward, concentrating on performing the exercise correctly. Becky walked up and down between the couples, giving guidance when necessary. However, when she came next to Edward and me, she explained to the rest of the class they should watch because he performed it exactly as it should be done.

I turned beet red, my face blazing hot. I didn't relish being the focus of everyone's attention; however Edward just smiled and continued massaging me until Becky announced it was time for class to end.

We walked back to the car, and he opened the passenger door. "Would you like to go for coffee? My treat."

I was starving and didn't feel like going home right then anyway. "A hot latte sounds great." I situated myself in the deep seat of the Porsche and waited for him to get in the car.

"May I?" A cute little smirk graced his lips.

I leaned my head back on the headrest, turning to look at him. "One of these days the seatbelt won't fit around this kid. I guess if you don't want a traffic ticket I'll need you to buckle me in."

He leaned across my abdomen to grab the buckle next to the door, but had a tough time pulling it out. I tried not to breathe too deeply which would press my breasts into the side of his head. The whole situation embarrassed me, especially given the exercises we'd just practiced in class.

Struggling to grasp the buckle, his head nudged the front of my shirt. I looked down and noticed my nipples protruding through the material of my shirt. The interior lights of the car were still on and when he finally got hold of the buckle, he turned his head in my direction, his nose accidentally bumping into my nipple.

His eyes immediately shifted up at the same time I looked down. My face flushed hot and I heard his sharp intake of breath. He quickly sat up after plugging in the seat buckle and fumbled with the key as he tried to turn on the ignition. Silence hung like a heavy curtain between us. I didn't know what had just happened but was sure he'd felt it too.

He cleared his throat and turned on the radio. "Is Peet's okay?"

I nodded, then realized he couldn't see my reaction, so I mumbled, "That's fine."

The coffee house was located a few blocks from the hospital and we listened to the radio without talking. At last he turned his gaze in my direction, and his eyebrows drew together. "You all right, Brandy?"

It was my turn to clear my throat. "I'm fine," I replied, then pointed. "There's a spot right in front."

We found a window table in the coffee house, the scene of our first meeting almost a year ago, back in August. Was he thinking the same thing but didn't mention it? It was near impossible to recall that day without taking it further—to the night I went to his house and had frenzied sex on his front room couch.

I felt embarrassed reminiscing about it now, perhaps because I didn't feel like the same person as when I saw Edward in Peet's last year. I remembered being so spaced out, my head clouded with the ever-invasive depression that had plagued me since my baby's death. I recalled the second time I saw him, accepting his dinner invitation—the beginning of the end of my marriage.

"Brandy? You all right?" Edward asked again.

"Yeah. Fine. Just daydreaming." I smiled over at him.

We sipped our coffees, watching the parade of people pass on their way to dinner, the theatre, or shopping. Sitting across from Edward struck me as nothing short of, well, amazing.

"Do you ever think what it would be like if I hadn't run into you and Weston at Starbucks?"

Had he been thinking along the same lines as I had, recalling how we first met? "I wouldn't be here drinking coffee with you, that's for sure!"

"I know *that*. I mean, if you were still married to Weston you'd be carrying my baby and neither of you would have known the difference. Doesn't that make you feel weird?"

I glanced at him, then out the window across the street at the unending line of people walking along Park Street. "You know what? You're the one who told me you and I had sex one week before Weston came home for the Labor Day weekend. I didn't recall the exact date, though obviously you had." I turned my head away from the window to look at him. "The baby could just as easily have been Weston's child. I had no idea I was carrying your baby, Edward. But what if something were to happen to the baby and he or she needed blood? The truth would have come out. We would have discovered our child's father wasn't Weston. My entire life would have blown up in my face. Weston would have left me sooner or later. It was just a matter of time. In retrospect, I'm happy the truth came out when it did. It saved all of us from further heartache down the road."

He placed his hand over mine and gave it a comforting squeeze. "I agree with you about the truth. For most of my life my mother lied to me about my father—why he left, where he went. I always had the feeling she knew exactly what happened to him but she'd never tell me."

"Why do you think your mom was hiding something? I mean, did you ever ask her about your father?"

"I was around sixteen years old, searching in my mom's closet, looking for something to put a birthday present in. Way up in the back next to some sweaters I found a shoe box. It fell on the closet floor, and these letters just spewed out all over the place. I was trying to put them back when I realized each one of them had the same return address. The same name on every single one of them— Matthew Barnes."

"Were you able to see the postmark, the city where the letters were sent from?"

"I don't remember the exact address, but it was somewhere in California, but the city didn't ring a bell at the time."

I shook my head. It seemed such a cruel thing to do to a child, allowing him to believe his father didn't want anything to do with him. "So your father had been sending letters to your house for years?"

"Well, I thought my mom had lied to me about not knowing where my dad lived. But when I asked her about it, she said they were old letters she'd received from my father's dad, my grandfather, right? They both had the same name—Matthew- so I believed her. She said my grandfather had passed away years ago and she'd never gotten around to throwing them away. I believed her but the next time I was in the house alone, I went back to her closet. The box?" He shook his head, looked up at the ceiling for a moment. "Vanished!

She'd been lying to me. Those letters had been written by my father. But she stuck to her story until she died. Lying always ends up hurting someone."

I interlaced my fingers with his and nodded. For some reason, Edward's story was a turning point. I'd put him in a pigeon-hole, clumped him together with the other attorneys I'd heard bad stories about. I thought he'd turn out to be an inveterate liar, someone I'd never be able to trust. And he'd proven me wrong. His tale was a sad one—not knowing what happened to his father, finding out his mother had lied to him for most of his young life. And since she had already passed away, the truth still evaded him.

"It's getting late," I said, stifling a yawn. "I'm exhausted."

We stood up and got back in the car for the short ride home. We said our goodbyes and we'd see each other next week. This was my ninth month and I had less energy with each passing day. But today had been a good one. I'd learned a great deal about the father of my baby, and he'd turned out to be one of the good guys.

Chapter 24

I discovered several of Weston's shirts and a couple pairs of pants when I went to the dry cleaners. I didn't plan to send them to him in the mail and decided to call Carol's number which I'd found in the Alameda phone book.

It rang eight times before a female answered. "Hello." It was Carol, and she sounded like she was already in bed, her voice throaty with sleep.

I made an effort to be friendly and polite. "Hi! Is Weston home?"

"He can't come to the phone. Who's calling?"

Unless he had other women phoning him at night, Carol knew exactly who was on the other end of the line. "This is Brandy. Could you tell him I phoned please?"

"Sure."

The next thing I heard was a dial tone.

I was so angry, I wanted to spit! How dare she treat me like that? I wasn't the one who'd stolen her husband. *I* was the injured party. *I* was the loser. No reason for her to be angry with *me*.

She wouldn't get away with this. I didn't deserve to be treated rudely by the likes of Carol Smith. I pressed the redial button and once again, the phone rang and rang. After the twentieth ring, I hung up and again pressed the redial button. This time, however, after two rings someone picked up.

"Hello." It was Weston.

"Hi, it's Brandy. Sorry to call so late. I went to the dry cleaners the other day and a few of the items were yours, some shirts and pants."

"Did you phone a few minutes ago?"

"Yes, but Carol hung up on me before I had the chance to explain the reason for my call."

"What do you mean, she hung up on you?"

"Well, I asked to speak with you, she said you were indisposed at the moment, so I asked if she'd tell you I called. She said 'sure' then hung up the phone. To be honest, it pissed me off because I don't see any reason for her to be mad at *me*. So I phoned back."

"I see your point. And I'll deal with her later. Would Friday at four o'clock be okay for me to drop by? I don't want to disturb your writing."

"Friday at four is fine. I'll see you then." I started to hang up the phone, when I heard him say my name. "Yes?"

"Thank you. Nice hearing your voice, Brandy."

It didn't sound to me like everything was hunky dory in Weston's household. Carol appeared to be the jealous type, and he wasn't happy about her attitude toward me. Oh, well, none of my business. I put it at the back of my mind. He and I were on our way to having an amicable divorce. I sure wouldn't want to be on the receiving end of *his* wrath.

Promptly at four o'clock Friday afternoon, the doorbell chimed. When I answered it, Weston stood on the doorstep, wearing a pair of low-slung jeans, a tight-fitting T-shirt, and biker boots. My mouth went dry. The guy would look macho wearing a muumuu!

"Come in. Can I fix you a latte?" We were still friends and we'd be officially divorced in a few months. We could share a cup of coffee, right?

"I'd love one." He followed me into the kitchen, where I started the espresso machine, just as I'd done so many times in the past. "I want to apologize for Carol's behavior toward you the other night. It's been kind of a rocky time for us. She doesn't like other women very much. She has no girlfriends. I don't care for the way she treated you when you called… I'm thinking of moving out."

Wow! He and I had never been hit by the "green monster," neither of us being the jealous type. Until we discovered each of us had had an affair, of course. He'd feel uncomfortable with Carol's clingy and possessive behavior.

"I'm sorry to hear that. From the little interaction I had with her at the airport, she didn't strike me as your type."

"Uh, no. In fact, she doesn't want kids and… Things just aren't working out the way I thought they would."

I was in the middle of foaming the milk when the doorbell rang so Weston said he'd answer it. While stirring the foam into the coffees, I heard the sound of raised voices in the foyer, quickly unplugged the espresso machine, and ran out of the kitchen. Edward's foot was jammed against the front door, not allowing Weston to close it.

"What's going on?" I couldn't believe what I was seeing—my soon-to-be ex-husband trying to push my birthing partner (and the father of my baby) out the front door onto his butt!

Edward spoke first. "Brandy, your ex won't let me come inside your house."

"I'm not her ex. Not yet, anyway. I asked you what the hell you're doing here."

Oh, this did not look good. I hadn't told Weston about Edward and me having any type of relationship. It was none of his business, just as he'd told me Carol Smith was none of mine.

"Weston, please. Edward has as much right to come inside as you do. Would you mind removing your hand from the door and please let him in."

"What right does this asshole have coming here? Is he harassing you, Brandy? Because if he is, I'll put a stop to it right now."

"Weston, please. Stop this."

His face had turned purple with rage. I'd never seen him act jealous. This wasn't the man I'd known for years, his voice rough and loud. He turned and looked at me. "Stop what, Brandy? I'm trying to help you out. I'm not the bad guy here."

There was no way I could avoid telling the truth. But that was a good thing. I had to come clean or someone would get hurt.

"Edward is my birthing coach, Weston. He and I have been attending classes at Alameda Hospital."

The look on his face? Pure incredulity. Or was it hurt? I couldn't tell. Truthfully, it surprised me he was acting this way. I had assumed he was over me. Before I'd spoken with him today, I figured he and Carol would get engaged and be married soon. I hadn't been aware there were problems in paradise.

His jaw went slack for a few seconds. He glared at Edward and opened the door extra wide to accommodate his entrance, allowing him a wide berth. "I'll see you later, Brandy. Thanks for picking up my things." He grabbed his clothes hanging on the hat stand and strode off toward his truck.

Edward stood next to me, watching as Weston pulled away from the curb. "That went well… You didn't tell him about me being your birthing coach, did you?"

I shook my head. "I didn't see any reason to. When I asked him about his girlfriend Carol, he told me to mind my own business. I didn't feel obligated to reveal anything about you and me."

"That's fair then. He was royally ticked off when he saw *me* standing there. I thought he'd rip my head off."

"Sorry. I'm sure it won't happen again. Come in. I wasn't expecting you."

"I picked up some groceries from Safeway and thought I'd make you dinner. You up for it?"

I paused and thought, what the heck! "That would be great. As a matter of fact, my feet are killing me. My lower back too. I'd enjoy sitting around for a while, letting someone else do the cooking."

"Sit down, relax, put your feet up, and leave it all to me." He gestured with his hand. "Go on, get outta here, will ya?"

I laughed. It still seemed ludicrous to me, seeing Edward in my kitchen cooking dinner while I sank down on the couch with my feet up, looking at a *Vogue* magazine. How things had changed!

Chapter 25

"You are a culinary genius, Edward! Or maybe I was just starving." I'd taken my last bite of a beautifully grilled cheddar cheese quesadilla with sliced tomatoes on the side, and a fresh salad. Edward had grilled chicken and we'd just finished our dinners, relaxing at the kitchen table.

"You ate enough for four people, Brandy, so I take it you enjoyed dinner!"

I slapped him gently on the wrist. "You aren't nine months pregnant. Are you familiar with the expression 'eating for two'?"

He gave me a sideways glance. "An old wives' tale."

We both laughed. I picked up our plates to put them in the dishwasher and he placed his hand on my shoulder, pressing me back into my chair. "I'll do everything tonight. As Bob Marley once said, 'Don't worry, be happy.' Just sit and keep me company."

I wouldn't fight him on this. I was exhausted. My soon-to-be ex-husband and Edward had almost come to blows in front of my eyes a few hours ago, and it still upset me.

Edward rinsed off the dishes, put them in the dishwasher and wiped down the table and counters. He was good at it—a sexist idea, but I hadn't known many men who cleaned up so thoroughly. He turned around, unwound the dishtowel he'd tied around his waist, and sat down next to me.

"You're still as sexy as any model I've seen on a *Victoria's Secret* catalogue."

"Get outta here, Edward. No man would look at me twice in my condition. Unless he was legally blind, that is."

He remained serious, unsmiling. "You look exactly the same as the day I saw you in Peet's. Same curves, full breasts, beautiful wavy hair. The only thing that's changed is some added waistline, and that'll be gone soon anyway."

"Oh Edward, Edward, Edward. You're such a bullshitter."

"I am not bullshitting you, Brandy. I don't know why you think you look so different from back then. You're pregnant. It's not like you've turned into the Wicked Witch of the West."

I smiled. He was so cute. And always sexy. He was staring at me which made me feel uncomfortable. And we were sitting too close to each other so I scooted my chair over a couple of inches.

Just as it had been when we were at his house the first time, he placed a finger under my chin and brought his face inches from mine then brushed his thumb gently across my half-opened lips. Closing the gap between us, he covered my lips with his, gently inserting his tongue, widening the kiss, until I wanted to scream with wanting him.

His hands covered my breasts, full with milk at this time in my pregnancy, and desire whipped through me like an electric current. He massaged my nipples, lightly squeezing them and for the first time in months, I wanted to make love.

Dropping one of his hands, he slid his fingers under my skirt, inching his way past the edge of my panties, until he found my sweet spot with his thumb and rubbed ever so gently. Then I heard a moan, and didn't know if it came from him or me.

I couldn't stop him. I didn't want him to stop. I found the front of his pants bursting with his erection and placed my hand over the bulge waiting for my caress then frantically ripped down the zipper, brought out his swollen member and rubbed hard and fast, up and down his slippery shaft. I could feel my orgasm coming, the pulsing a wonderful release of tension built up inside me for months and increased the rhythm of my hands until he throbbed between my grasping fingers, his body shuddering.

I could hardly catch my breath, and felt like I'd run a marathon. I sat still, knowing my heart rate would eventually slow.

I smiled. "That was the best sex I've ever had—sitting in a kitchen chair with all my clothes on!"

"We're lucky your neighbors can't see inside the windows," he whispered, his chest heaving.

"I don't understand what you do to me, Edward."

"Best hand job I've ever experienced."

I pulled back as if I'd been struck. "You're crude, Edward." He grinned. "We both had an orgasm, didn't we?"

"Technically, that's correct. But next time, I'd like to do it without any clothes on."

I paused, looked him straight in the eyes. "I don't know if there *should* be a next time. I mean, what are we thinking, Edward? You're my birthing coach, not my boyfriend."

"Once again, technically, you're correct, I'm not your boyfriend. But, Brandy, I—"

"You're what? You want to be my lover?" I said, my voice filled with irritation.

"No, I was going to say—"

"I don't want you to be my lover, Edward. I don't need a lover. I'll be a mother in a few months and—"

"And I don't want to be your lover either," he said in a stern tone.

"Good. Because as I said, I have to think of my child. Fooling around in my kitchen, for God's sake! I'm not a teenager!"

His eyebrows shot up. "I'm not a teenager either."

I sighed. "What do you want from me?"

His voice came out in a whisper. "I think I'm falling in love with you, Brandy."

My mind screeched to a halt. "You're joking, right? You, Edward Barnes, the, to quote your words, 'commitment-phobe,' expects me to believe he's falling in love with me?" I chuckled. "Come on now. Don't insult my intelligence. That's no way to get me into bed with you. Go find one of your 'women', as you call them, and tell *them* you're in love with them. Maybe they'll fall for that bullshit, because I don't!"

He leaned over, grasped my upper arms, bringing his face inches from mine. I could feel his breath, smell his cologne, and see every blue fleck in his gorgeous eyes.

"Brandy, I love you. And we don't have to sleep with each other again until you're ready. I don't want another *woman*, as you call it. I want you, dammit. Take me seriously, will you, because I'm not kidding." He paused. I didn't reply. "We'll continue this discussion later."

He released his grip on my arms, letting his hands fall to his sides. I didn't move, didn't speak, didn't know what to say to him. This couldn't be real. I didn't want to get hurt again. A few months ago Weston walked out on me. I believed he was a "keeper" who'd fight before giving up on his marriage. Man, had I been wrong. And I could be wrong now if I believed Edward. Could I take that chance?

The phone rang and I took the opportunity to answer it in the front room.

"Hey, Brandy!" It was Cecilia. "Did you talk to Edward about the block party? I'm trying to get a count of how many people will be there."

"No, I haven't yet, but I'll ask him now. We just finished dinner."

"You did? You go, girl! Call me back tomorrow."

Edward came up behind me, eating a cookie, a big grin on his face. "What are you going to ask me?"

I pretended to be appalled. "You listened to my phone conversation?"

He looked down at the floor. "Sorry. I couldn't help it. Your voice carried all the way into the kitchen."

I grinned. "My next-door neighbor, Cecilia and her husband Perry, and I are co-hosting the annual block party this Saturday. Here at my house. Would you like to come?"

A wide smile enhanced his beautiful white teeth. "What time should I be here?"

"Any time after five. Cecilia and Perry are handling the organization. All I have to do is get my house in order so people can roam around inside and outside. I've hired a gardener and a housekeeper to get the place ready before the big bash."

"Sounds good. I'll see you this Saturday then. Gotta go."

I walked him to the front door, where he turned and kissed me goodbye. I hadn't been expecting it, so I didn't have time to turn my head or move out of the way. He placed his hands on my butt and pressed me close to his obvious erection, then deepened the kiss, leaving me breathless.

Not only was he good looking, he had a killer smile, a great personality, a super job. Quite the package. But could he be trusted with my heart? And my child's heart? Time would tell, if I chose to give him a chance to show me he was serious.

Chapter 26

Saturday turned out to be a glorious day for the block party—weather in the mid-seventies, little puffy clouds scooting across the blue-blue sky. Thanks to Susannah, my house looked immaculate. She took care of several houses on Lauren Drive, and I knew right away I'd hire her permanently. Dave the gardener came highly recommended and the lawn looked lush and trimmed, the rose bushes pruned. He'd also hung little lanterns amongst the branches of the trees, making the atmosphere both romantic and festive.

Cecilia had hired a small band to play music and every neighbor had a specific job. The barbecue was smoking, the corn cooking, and a variety of cold salads lined the tables in the street, blocked off for the event. Couples were dancing in the backyard, everyone having a great time.

Perry and I were dancing to a Beatles' song when I felt a tap on my shoulder. I turned to find Edward standing behind me, smile flashing, muscles bulging in a tight t-shirt, Levi's hung off his perfectly-formed butt. He looked in his early twenties, but he was my age—thirty or thirty-one years old.

Perry backed up and shook Edward's hand, introducing himself, then walked away to find Cecilia.

Edward took me in his arms and wrapped his hands behind my back. "You look good enough to eat, Brandy. Are you the dessert?"

I chuckled under my breath. "You could sweet talk the President, Edward."

He looked at me, brows knitted. "You offend me with your blatantly erroneous statements. Why would you say such a thing anyway?"

"Because of what you've told me yourself. You know, all those women who wanted to marry you, so you moved on?"

He nodded. "You're right. But I didn't lead them on. Brandy. When I found out they were on a different track, I let them down easily, no hard feelings. I'm still friends with all of them, believe it or not."

"Oh, really? So they left amicably, no fighting, no arguments, and you still talk to all these women?"

"Talk being the operative word. I don't date them anymore. I told you, I don't whisper sweet nothings in their ears so I can get them in bed."

I pulled back further and squinted at him. "And what about us?" I teased. "I never heard from you after you and I—"

"You can say it, Brandy. You and I had sex. I forgot your married name, I didn't know where you lived. I'd given you my home and work numbers, and when I didn't hear from you and never saw you again at Peet's, I figured you weren't interested. Then I transferred to Washington."

"Are you saying you were interested in me back then?"

He nodded and grinned. "I've had a crush on you since high school for God's sake. But I don't pursue a woman if I don't feel she's interested."

By now, the music had stopped, but we were both still moving from side to side to a beat no one else could hear, eyes latched, in our own little world. Suddenly Edward pulled away from me and whirled around, putting his back to me. Weston's hand was clamped down on his shoulder, and they were glaring at each other. This did not look good.

"Good I dance with muhwife, pleeze?" He was drunk. I *so* hoped Edward would read the situation, acquiesce, and not make a fool of all of us at my neighborhood party.

"Sure, buddy. She's all yours." He backed away, arms outstretched, bowed low to the ground, and exited through the back gate. Thank God!

Weston grabbed me by the arm, pulled me forcefully against the front of him, my belly blocking him from getting too close. He leaned down to place a sloppy kiss on my lips.

I pulled back, slapping his face with my open hand.

"Ow!" he yelled. Placing his hand on the side of his face, he stared at me, looking shattered. "What didja do that for?"

I don't think I'd ever seen him this intoxicated and he'd never been forceful. This public display of pushy affection and possessiveness was totally out of character, not to mention inappropriate. Arms crossed below my breasts, I stared at him with the sternest look I could manage. "You and I are no longer a couple, Weston. You filed for divorce, remember?"

"Iz jure fault we split up, Brandy…"

"No, Weston, it's both our faults. You had an affair. I had an affair. Fortunately for you, you can't get pregnant. But *I* can. And I *did*. We've already been over this, okay? Let's not retrace our steps."

I gently grasped his arm and walked him toward the back gate. Luckily, most people were out front eating dessert and drinking coffee, so we hadn't been seen by but a few couples.

Weston allowed me to lead him out to the front yard. He was having a hard time explaining just exactly where he'd put his vehicle, but I noticed it parked at the corner and picked up the pace.

"Sorry, sorry, sorry. I'm drunk. I diddun mean to break up your pawty."

I grabbed the keys from him and opened the passenger door. He crawled up into the seat and I shut the door then walked slowly around to the driver's side. I remembered exactly where Carol and Weston lived. When I pulled up in front of their house on Santa Clara Avenue a few minutes later he was snoring so loudly I couldn't hear the radio that had been on when I started the engine.

After parking in the driveway, I maneuvered myself out of the truck. I had no choice. I had to see whether Carol was home to help me out. Weston weighed over two-hundred pounds, and I couldn't help him out of this big truck.

I rang the doorbell, hearing the *My Country Tis of Thee* tune echoing throughout the house. I had to stifle a laugh. That had to be Carol's choice because Weston would never have wanted to listen to it in a million years.

Footsteps clicked on the floor, coming closer to the front door. It flew open, and there stood the beautiful and luscious Carol Smith.

"What do *you* want?" Her tone would stop most men cold, but she didn't intimidate me.

"Your man, Carol, is drunk, in his truck, and I need help getting him into the house." I wouldn't try to make small talk with her.

Before today, it was obvious she had it in for me and she surely wouldn't want to stand on the porch chatting with her lover's not-yet ex-wife.

She looked down at my belly and smirked. "You're going to help him out of the truck? Who are you kidding? You look like a small rhinoceros." She leaned her head back and laughed.

I was not in the mood for this. I was so pissed off that Weston had come to our block party skunk drunk, interrupting my dance with Edward. And now I found myself pleading with my husband's whore to help me get him into *her* bed! How weird was that?

"Carol, why don't I leave him in the truck and you can deal with him? I'll walk home." I flung the keys in her direction. "Later."

I turned on my heel as quickly as my fat body would allow, and walked down the driveway, crossed the street, and headed for home. The look on her face had been priceless. No way could she get him out of the truck on her own. But hey, he wasn't my problem any longer.

Chapter 27

June fifteenth—and the baby's arrival was delayed. Dr. Farney had told me the due date was early June and I was anxious beyond measure and *very* uncomfortable. Flashbacks of giving birth to Christine plagued me every day, and I tried to tamp down the scary feelings popping up in my head.

The day before our last class, Edward called and asked me out to dinner again, saying it would be the perfect time to continue our unfinished discussion from the previous night. No way could I get out of it, so I acquiesced and agreed to his picking me up at five o'clock.

Sitting on the couch, my favorite decaf latte in hand, I tried to imagine having a relationship with him. It seemed inordinately risky, given what he'd told me about his checkered past. Savoring the rich taste of the espresso mixed with foamy milk, I mentally tossed around the "cons" of becoming emotionally close to him when suddenly a gush of warm liquid seeped out from between my legs. My water had broken. It was time!

I called Edward at his office and, lucky for me, he was at his desk with a client. He took my call immediately and said calmly that he'd notify Dr. Farney I was heading to Alameda Hospital then he'd ask Cecilia to come over and stay with me until he arrived.

I had already packed my overnight bag and placed it in the hall closet. Nothing needed to be done but wait for Edward to drive from his office near Park Street to my house. Within minutes, Cecilia walked through the front door and ran into the front room where I was working on deep breathing exercises according to Becky's instructions.

You could barely tell Cecilia was pregnant. Only a small bump showed underneath her silk shirt. She'd never been overweight, and her skin looked pink and glowing. She ran over and knelt down beside the couch.

"Oh my goodness." She let out a deep whoosh of breath, and laid her hand on her chest. "I ran over here as fast as I could. How are you doing? Can I get you anything?"

I inhaled deeply through my nose, my eyes tightly shut, then exhaled loudly through my mouth. "Make the pain go away, will ya'?"

She grabbed my hand, squeezing it tightly. "Can you grip my hand?"

I tightened my grasp, grimacing.

"Is the pain bad?"

"Only when I breathe." I tried to smile but had a helluva time pulling it off.

"Let me get you some dry clothes." She ran up the stairs and returned with a fresh pair of underwear and capri pants.

She'd just finished helping me put them on when Edward knocked on the front door and let himself inside. He took one look at me, smiled hugely, and in his best Jack Nicholson imitation, he opened his arms wide and said, "It's tiiiiiiiiiime!" I tried to laugh through the pain. He grabbed my suitcase, put his arm around my waist, and I waddled out the door toward the car.

We'd just pulled away from the curb when his relentless questioning began. "Is this your way of getting out of our discussion—because it won't work. We'll have to talk about us sometime, the sooner the better."

"Edward, I… ohhhhhhh God, here it comes again." I didn't look forward to hours of contractions, but tried not to "anticipate." Becky had warned us that could make the experience worse. "Feel in the present," she'd counseled—logical but at this moment almost impossible.

He reached over and grabbed my hand, telling me to squeeze as hard as I could. So far, he'd done everything right, and I had faith in his calm ability to guide me through this. The hospital was located only six blocks from our house. When we arrived a nurse met us at the front entrance with a wheelchair. They immediately took me to the maternity ward where Edward helped me put on a pink cotton gown and booties.

No one else was in the room, and the nurse explained it had been a slow day with only a few admissions to this ward. Framed prints of paintings by Monet hung on the walls, and the room had been painted a lovely mix of blue, pink, and yellow. Huge windows faced the beach. From this floor you could see the San Francisco Bay, the light blue sky, and marshmallow clouds. Dr. Farney walked in soon after I settled in bed. After checking me, she gave us the good news—I had already dilated to eight centimeters and they'd be moving me to the birthing room down the hall.

Edward joked with her, seeming at home in this environment. He appeared relaxed, rubbing my shoulders, holding my hands while I squeezed his in a vise grip with each contraction. They were coming much stronger and more often now, and felt entirely different than I remembered when Christine had been born. This time I could breathe normally, not needing an oxygen mask to help me through the last birthing phase.

Edward spoke to me in a soft voice, telling me about the people walking past the doorway, the client he'd been talking to when I'd phoned him my water had broken. He kept my mind occupied on everything but the relentless contractions. When I almost screamed from the pain, he coerced me into deep breathing exercises, along with gripping both his hands in mine. I believed I'd make it through this with his help.

Dr. Farney returned and encouraged me to bear down with the next contraction. I felt a swoosh of baby and fluid.

"Here's your little girl," she announced.

I fell back onto the pillows, exhausted and relieved.

"We'll need to clean her up first and perform the Apgar tests then she's all yours."

Within moments I heard a high-pitched cry. Our baby was alive.

The head nurse turned toward us carrying a wrapped bundle in her arms and placed the baby on my chest. Edward leaned over and pulled the corner of the blanket back to take his first look. I watched him, wondering how he would react to seeing his first child.

Tears hung from his long black eyelashes, and he mouthed, "Oh my God" then looked over at me. Bending down, he placed a soft kiss on my lips then pulled away and whispered, "I love you, Brandy."

Time stood still. We gazed into each other's eyes, his face inches from mine. It was written all over his face—the sincerity, the seriousness, the love. He didn't move, but leaned over me, his eyes piercing, steady. Oh my God, he's waiting for my answer!

My heart was full, bursting with love for this man who had tried so hard over the last several months to prove to me he cared about me and our baby. I didn't know where this relationship was heading or where it would go, but right now, at this moment, I knew.

"I love you too," I whispered.

Chapter 28

Within minutes, they moved me back to my room. While Edward held the baby, I fell into a deep sleep for a couple of hours, and awoke with the oddest sense of deja vu. It was dark outside, no one lay in the bed next to mine, just as it had been after I'd given birth to Christine. I was afraid to turn my head toward where the plastic bassinet should be. Last time, nothing was there. My baby had died and the room was empty save for Weston, sitting in a chair next to my bed.

I squeezed my eyes shut as hard as I could, hoping when I re-opened them, the bassinet would be next to my bed with my baby in it. Turning my head slowly, I opened my eyelids. Edward was leaning over in a chair, holding our child in his arms, eyes riveted on her tiny face.

"Edward?"

He picked his head up to look at me. "How are you feeling?"

"Much better now that I've slept. How's she doing?"

"She's fine, scored high on all levels of the Apgar, and Dr. Farney says she's good to go! She weighs nine pounds six ounces."

"No wonder I felt like I was about to burst!" I pushed up on my elbows. "Have you been here the whole time?"

He looked at me askance. "Where else would I be? I wouldn't leave you. And I certainly wouldn't leave our baby." He paused, looking down at her. "And we can't keep calling her our baby. I guess we forgot about picking out a name."

I began to laugh then winced. My stomach muscles felt as if I'd been doing crunches all day. I laid my head back on the pillow. "It's not funny, but yeah, we *did* forget. How stupid are we?"

He looked over at me, "Do you have a name in mind?"

"I've had the precious opportunity to name one child in my life.

She didn't make it, but she'll always live in my heart. I think it's your turn, Edward."

His mouth hung halfway open, eyes wide. "Are you serious?" I nodded. "I have a favorite name that carries a lot of meaning for me."

"As long as it isn't something like Matilda or Hildegard, I'll be okay with it."

"My mother's name was Jessica."

I raised my eyebrows.

"I know, I know. She hid my father's letters from me and lied about it. But in my heart I've forgiven her—a long time ago. Brandy, she raised me. All alone. And she did a good job. I'll always love her."

"It's a beautiful and feminine name," I said, smiling. "It fits her… Our baby," I whispered.

"Yeah, our baby. Yours and mine, Brandy. And I love both of you. So very much."

"Oh, Edward. Do you really?" I asked, frowning.

"I've never lied to you, Brandy."

I paused, took a deep breath. "I don't know when it happened, but I love you too, Edward. And it scares the hell out of me."

His eyes squinted and he shook his head. "Why would you say something like that? I've never done anything to hurt you. As a matter of fact, it was you who treated me badly after we made love on my couch. You're the one who walked out on me."

"Let's please not revisit history." I sighed. "That night is etched like a tattoo on my brain."

His eyebrows shot up. "That awful, huh? I enjoyed it. One of the highlights of my year."

"Oh, stop it. Always the jokester. It was the best sex I've ever had."

"Now that's what I like to hear. A satisfied customer!"

I rolled my eyes, looked up at the ceiling. He could be so exasperating! "You're so not funny today!"

He smiled. "Then why do you laugh at my jokes, huh?… Will you marry me?"

I closed my eyes in frustration. "Will you stop it! I just gave birth and it hurts to laugh."

"I'm not joking," he said. "I want to marry you. We have a child together. I love you. So let's get married."

I shook my head and pleaded, "Don't do this. I'm exhausted from pushing out a nine-pound baby, and this discussion is wearing me out. I can't take you seriously right now. You've just been through a very emotional event. It's all new to you. You're confused and overwhelmed. Can we puh-leeeze table this discussion until later?"

"For now, I'll acquiesce to your demands. But not for long. The next time I decide to bring it up, do you promise you'll discuss it?"

"I promise. Now, you're not spending the night here, so when are you leaving me in peace?"

He stood up, holding Jessica. "You're right, I'm tired. I'll be back tomorrow. Early in the morning." He bent down and gave me an extremely thorough kiss. "I love you." He kept staring at me with a funny look on his face, his eyebrows raised.

"I love you too, Edward," I whispered.

He smiled and laid Jessica on my stomach. What a day it had been! And what a happy ending.

Chapter 29

Dr. Farney allowed me to go home the next day. My milk was flowing freely, and it was easy to nurse Jessica. She was one hungry little girl and took to suckling right away. When we arrived home, after helping settle me in bed with her, Edward headed downstairs.

He was talking with Cecilia, and I laid my head back on the pillows he'd placed behind me, and took a moment to gather my thoughts. My body melted into the pillow top bedding and I pulled the down comforter over me. Exhaustion was slowly creeping into every muscle and I was so tired. I'd spent a good portion of the night awake nursing the baby and had woken early this morning when one of the staff came in to take my vitals.

The front door shut, followed by footsteps coming up the stairs, and I thought it might be Cecilia. When the edge of the bed dipped down, I opened my eyes and saw Edward.

"How're you feeling?"

"Tired. I nursed your daughter most of last night. Where's Cecilia?"

"She went home. When we drove up she ran over to ask me how you and the baby were doing. She said her back hurt and she can't get in a comfortable position. You women should get an award for all those months being pregnant then giving birth. I could never do it."

"An award? Can it wait until I can stand up without hurting? I just need to close my eyes for a few minutes." I snuggled against the fluffy down pillows while the baby suckled heartily. "I thought Cecilia was sleeping here tonight in case I need anything."

"She planned to, but I told her not to worry about it. I'll stay. I've taken some time off work. You have nothing to worry about." Resting his hand on my outstretched leg, he added, "Rest at ease, Edward Barnes at your service."

"But you can't just leave your practice to take care of me!" I argued, raising my voice. "You never mentioned you'd be taking time off work."

"Maybe because I knew you'd put up a fight about it. Just like you're doing right now."

"Well, wh-what about your law practice? You're a partner."

"Which is why I can do whatever the hell I want. Just for a few days." He gestured toward the front of the house. "I have my briefcase and paperwork in the car. I'll do some work tonight. Don't worry about me. Now, stop arguing, all right? I'm staying here until you get back on your feet." He stood up and straightened the comforter. "What would you like to drink? Dr. Farney told me you have to replenish the fluids you're losing from nursing Jessica."

I couldn't stop staring at him. "I suppose you got your nursing degree along with your J.D."

"You're so funny." He grinned. "I just want to take care of you and our baby. I want to and I *can*. That's what's so great about being a partner. Anyway, I haven't taken any sick leave or vacation in years."

"Okay. You win. I'd love some sparkling water." I smirked. "And you can run my bath later."

We burst out laughing. It felt good to have someone at my beck and call, running to get me whatever I wanted, when I wanted. I was so accustomed to taking care of myself and Weston, having Edward coddling me was a treat!

That evening he brought dinner to me in bed, placing a tray over my lap, on top of which stood a tiny vase with a red rose. He'd grilled my quesadilla to perfection, carved the tomatoes to look like open flowers, and laid baby radishes on the side, each having a tiny face cut in the middle. He endeared himself to me every minute he was around, snuggling his way into my heart like a Labrador puppy.

That evening I could hear him shuffling papers around on the dining room table downstairs, and I assumed he was working. He had a busy practice in criminal law, and taking time away from his job was a sacrifice. It was ten o'clock when he entered my bedroom, looking beat. He sat on the side of the bed, arranged my pillows, then smiled at me.

"Thank you for coming to my rescue, Edward, and for helping me out like this. I should be up and about by tomorrow."

"I'm not worried about it, Brandy, so you shouldn't be either. Now why don't I put Jessica in her cradle then run you a nice hot bath?"

"Sounds luxurious."

He carefully lifted the baby out of my arms and placed her in the handmade cradle he'd purchased several weeks ago. It had an electrical box on the underside with a cord that plugged into the wall, making it rock back and forth after switching it on. I could already tell it would be a godsend.

Afterward he made his way into the bathroom and started the water running in the tub. Déjà vu . I recalled Weston's helping me out of bed into the bath after I lost Christine, making today feel sadly reminiscent of that time in my life.

I shook my head to clear out the cobwebs. That was then. This was now. Everything had changed. This was Jessica lying in the cradle. Edward was the one drawing my bath. Different day, different people. This was a happy time for us. How things had changed! I smiled, laid my head back on the pillows and must have fallen asleep.

Next thing I knew, Edward's arms reached beneath my legs and back, and he carried me into the bathroom, set me down on the thick rug next to the tub and undressed me, then gently took my hand and guided me into the soothing hot water. I didn't recognize the aroma, but when I looked at the shelf near the foot of the tub, I noticed a new bottle of lavender aromatherapy foaming bath. Millions of scented bubbles surrounded me, and I lay my head on the bath pillow hung over the side of the tub. He'd lit several candles and had placed them along the tiled edge, allowing just enough light so we could see each other.

"You look gorgeous lying there in all those bubbles—like an angel." He knelt down and reached for the bar of lavender soap, rubbing it in his hands until they dripped with foamy lather. He began washing my breasts, up my neck, back down over my stomach, then around and around my nipples. It was an extraordinarily sensuous experience.

Bending over the tub, he kissed me tenderly, wending his tongue around the outside of my lips, down my neck, nibbling my ear, while rubbing his soapy hands over my breasts and nipples. I never realized my body could feel such heightened sexuality while lying in a bath tub!

If I hadn't just given birth, I knew where this would have ended; however, we both knew it was not the time and all my important places were sore right now. He didn't say a word. He washed my hair, rinsed it with glassfuls of water from the tub faucet then let me lie there quietly. He left the room, and I could hear him preparing the bed, fluffing up the pillows and straightening the sheets and comforter.

Returning to the bathroom, he took my hand and helped me out of the tub, then wrapped me in an oversized fluffy towel. When he finished drying me off and patting the water from my hair, he led me into the bedroom and helped me dress in a nursing gown Cecilia had bought for me.

Jessica whimpered, so he gathered her up in his arms, kissed her on the forehead, then placed her on my stomach to nurse. As he walked out of the room, I whispered "Thank you," and he turned around and smiled. I had just been given a gift, an unselfish act of love, from a man I never thought would be a part of my life. I could picture my mother's voice saying, "Oh, Brandy, wonders never cease!"

Chapter 30

I nestled into the pillows to take a short nap until Jessica's next feeding. It was still dark outside when I awoke and found Edward curled up next to me in bed asleep. I hadn't heard him come in, but I didn't mind he'd joined me under the covers. I turned toward him.

He was so beautiful. His features were perfect—nicely shaped nose, full lips under a dark mustache, long dark eyelashes I knew covered the most gorgeous blue eyes ever. His physique was muscular and his chest and legs were covered in thick dark hair. He'd told me he went to the same gym as Cecilia and worked out with weights at least four times a week. He was in very good shape. I could lie here and watch him for hours.

His eyelids fluttered open. "Hi," he whispered.

"Did you get any sleep?"

"A little. I hope I didn't waken you. I had so much paper work to do."

"Why don't you go back to sleep. Jessica should be waking up soon and I'll try to keep her quiet. As long as she's nursing, she doesn't make any noise."

"Wanna cuddle?"

"I'd love to."

I turned toward the windows and he put his arm around my waist, spooning me from behind. It was so comforting having someone in bed with me again. It had been months, and I missed it. I fell asleep within seconds but woke up when Jessica whimpered. I picked her up immediately and sat up in bed in the dark, relishing the quiet time with my baby, listening to Edward's steady breathing while Jessica sucked and swallowed. When she finished, I laid her back in her cradle and turned on the rocking mechanism so she could be lulled through the night.

The next morning she slept longer than usual so I picked her up to nurse. She was ravenous and it took half an hour until she was satisfied and sleepy again. Edward had already gotten out of bed, and I assumed he was fixing breakfast. After I placed Jess in her cradle, I heard him coming up the stairs.

"How are you feeling, oh Princess of Lauren Drive?" he asked with a mischievous grin.

"Much better, thank you."

"You didn't wake up when Jessica cried last night at three a.m."

I furrowed my brows. "You're kidding me."

He put both hands up, palms facing outward. "I kid you not."

"Why was she crying? She'd already been fed."

"Her diaper needed changing. I figured out how to do it without waking you up to ask." He motioned toward the bedroom door. "Did you want to come downstairs and eat?"

"I think it's about time I did, yes," I said, looking around for my bathrobe. "I'm feeling strong as ever and I need to start walking again. I'm not sick, Edward, just postpartum. I'll be fine. And I'm ravenous."

He walked over to the closet where he took my bathrobe off the hanger then brought it to me. "Soft-boiled eggs, whole wheat toast, butter, jam, and Peet's decaf coffee—all waiting for you in the kitchen. How does that sound?"

"Great! What are you up to today?"

"Depends," he said, helping me put on my robe. "If you're ready to return to your normal routine, I'll go home to my place."

"Sounds like a plan." After slipping my arms in the sleeves of my bathrobe, I turned toward him. "I really appreciate you helping me out like this. You don't know how much it means to me—that you took time off work, helped out with the baby. You're really good at this whole 'daddy thing'."

He nodded and smiled. "I hope to be. When she stops nursing, I can feed her bottles, too. I'm a man of many talents." Pausing, he looked serious. "Maybe now's the time, Brandy… to talk about marriage?"

I took hold of his hands and gave them a light shake. "I still think you need to go home, rest, think about this with a clear head, away from me and Jessica."

"I don't need to think about it," he said then grasped me by the shoulders and looked me straight in the eyes. "Do you honestly believe a man of my age—by the way, I'll be thirty-two, February first—anyway, that I need to *think* about it? I've lived my life meeting women who wanted to get married. I told you that. And it was never the right time, or the right woman. But I know what I want, Brandy, and I want you."

"You know what the best thing is?"

"What?" His eyebrows dipped downward.

"My birthday's February fifth, so we can celebrate them together."

"Oh, nice answer." He dropped his arms to his sides and squinted. "Will you please be serious."

"If I felt you were one hundred percent sure about this, I'd give it my complete undivided consideration." I sat back down on the side of the bed. "But you told me yourself—you're a commitment-phobe. That wasn't something I guessed about you. It's something you told me about yourself."

"And I also told you why." Nestling next to me, he put his arm around my shoulders. "I've never met anyone who made me want to give up being a single guy. But you do. I love you, Brandy. And I love Jessica. Will you give it some thought?"

I turned to face him. "I'll think about it. Honestly, I will. I promise." Then I stood up and tied the robe's belt around my waist. "And I'm getting up today and getting on with life. You go home or to work or wherever, okay? Cecilia's right next door if I need something so don't worry so much. Go, shoo," I gestured with my hands.

"I'm going, I'm going," he said then stood up.

I walked downstairs with him and he rushed into the dining room to grab his briefcase. I pushed him out the door, and he turned toward me. "I'll be back, you know? You can't get rid of me that easily." He leaned in and gave me a chaste kiss on the lips.

"I'm not trying to get rid of you, Edward. You need to get back to work. Now, why don't you call me later and I'll let Jessica talk to you on the phone."

"Oh, you're so funny! Talk to you later." And he headed off to his car.

Chapter 31

Nursing Jessica was a dream fulfilled. Watching her tiny pink lips latched onto my nipple, her hand lying on my breast, gave me a feeling like nothing I'd ever expected. I never thought I could love another human being as much as I loved her. All the books I'd read in preparation for the birth of my baby should have helped me deal with the emotional side of having a child. However, I realized words could never describe it.

Until I purchased a jogging stroller, I was determined to get outside and move. So I walked every day, carrying Jessica in a baby pack slung over my chest, the rhythm of my pace lulling her to sleep.

One morning after returning from our walk I was nursing the baby when the doorbell rang. I laid Jess in the cradle Edward had purchased for the front room, and went to see who was at the door, surmising it was Cecilia. She dropped by almost every day to ask if I needed anything. She'd pop in, give me a hug and the baby a kiss, then go back home to work.

When I opened the door, Weston was standing on the doorstep, dressed in his signature distressed jeans, a hunter green polo shirt, and black biker boots—handsome as always, never seeming to age, always in good shape.

He smiled at me over the top of a huge bouquet of pink rosebuds. "Perry told me you had a little girl. Congratulations!"

It took me a few seconds to find my voice. "Uh… thank you." I hadn't heard from him since the fiasco at our block party and didn't feel completely comfortable inviting him in.

He looked down at his feet and cleared his throat. "I want to apologize for my behavior at your party. I was drunk, and humiliated myself and embarrassed you in front of all your friends. Carol and I hadn't been getting along and I—"

I gestured toward the front room. "Why don't you come inside."

"Thanks." He wiped his feet on the door mat and walked in, following close at my heels.

I picked the baby up and turned around. "This is Jessica."

He placed the roses on the coffee table and turned toward me. "May I hold her?"

"Sure. I'll get a vase for the flowers."

He nestled down on the couch, and I laid the baby in his arms then went into the kitchen. When I returned, I sat on the other end of the sofa, put the vase on the table in front of me and fiddled with the flower arrangement.

"She's beautiful. Perry told me everything went well at the hospital."

I nodded. "No complications. I haven't had a single problem. How are you doing? How's Carol?"

He stood up, laid Jessica in my arms then sat back down. "I moved out."

A story lay behind this newest development in their relationship, but I didn't want to talk about it with him. Last time I'd asked about his relationship with Carol he hadn't been open to sharing, and the subject seemed too personal now. "Where are you living?"

"I'm in a house on the lagoon. I'm renting for now until I figure out what I'm doing."

I lifted my eyebrows. "I would think you'd look for a house to buy. The divorce should be final soon. Have you heard from your attorney recently?"

He fidgeted with his watchband. "That's what I wanted to talk with you about."

I laid the baby in the cradle then settled back in my corner of the couch. "What's up? Have you changed your mind about the financial agreement or something?"

"No, nothing like that, Brandy. I…" He looked up at me, his eyes glassy with what looked like unshed tears.

I had this horrible thought something was wrong with him, maybe he was sick. "Is something wrong?"

"No, no." He pursed his lips then opened his mouth as if he was about to speak. Then he took a deep breath. "I want to come back home. Moving out wasn't a good idea. I… I love you. I never stopped loving you. But my pride, my ego, call it whatever you want, got in the way I guess. I miss you so much it's killing me."

Covering my mouth with my hand, I shook my head. This was unbelievable. "What about you and Carol?" My voice came out in a whisper.

"She and I could never have a future together. She doesn't like kids, and I want children. And she's *so* jealous. She gets angry if I speak to any woman. It creeps me out, she's so needy. And she's a bitch." He paused. Maybe he was waiting for me to say something. Then he blurted out, "She's not you."

My mind whirled. "I'm sorry… but a lot has happened since you left me."

"I'm not asking for an answer now. Just think about it. Please. I told my attorney to put a hold on filing the papers." His Adam's apple bobbed up and down, and he looked very uncomfortable. "Do you still love me?"

"It's not that simple. *You* left *me*. I slept with Edward. You slept with Carol. We're both to blame for our marital problems. I wanted to work on our marriage, but you dropped out of my life completely. You couldn't handle the fact I was carrying another man's child. The only difference between our situations is *you* can't get pregnant."

"I know. I couldn't accept your being pregnant by another man. But that was my ego talking. I've had time to think about it. We were good together and hopefully we learned from our mistakes. We could make it work again, I know we could."

I shook my head. "I can't."

"You can't?" His voice shifted from pleading to stern. "What do you mean you can't?"

I looked him straight in the eyes, my voice unwavering. "I can't just let you move back in here and start where we left off. I was devastated when you walked out on me, West. You destroyed all the faith I had in you as my partner. You didn't love me enough to work on our marriage." My determination to say what I had to say without crying dissolved, tears edging their way down my cheeks. "I don't trust you anymore… with my heart, with our relationship." I stood up and pointed my finger in his face. "I have so much resentment toward you for not sticking it out, for leaving me when I hadn't done anything worse than what you'd done."

He stood up and reached out to grasp my hand. I shook it off and took a step backward.

"I know this is unexpected, Brandy. I've shocked you. And I'm sorry for how I handled this whole thing. I screwed up. Big time. But please, can't you at least think about it?"

I turned away and looked out the front room window, shaking my head. He had a lot of nerve coming here begging for forgiveness.

His footsteps clattered on the hardwood floor as he walked away then the front door opened. "Call me if you want to talk, Brandy. I love you, no matter what." The door clicked shut. I covered my face with my hands and wept.

Chapter 32

Promoting my first book on the Internet and blogging on my website took a lot of time, and recently I'd visited our local Borders, trying to set up a book signing. Now I needed to line up someone to take care of the baby. I'd asked around the neighborhood, searching for a teenager who might be interested and qualified.

It was a warm night in July, the front windows open to let in the mild coastal breeze, when I heard car tires screeching, then silence. I ran to the window to see what had happened but could only detect a car's headlights near our driveway. I rushed outside and noticed a man bending over a young girl lying in the street next to a bicycle.

"Should I call 9-1-1?"

He glanced up at me, eyes wide. "Yes… please… quickly."

I sprinted back into the house and after phoning, I grabbed a blanket and a bottle of water.

Kneeling down on the asphalt, I placed the blanket over the young girl. "Are you hurt?" I couldn't see any obvious bleeding or scrapes on her face or arms.

She struggled to sit up. "I think I'm okay."

I put my hand on her shoulder. "Stay still until the paramedics arrive." I unscrewed the cap to the water bottle and placed it in her hands.

Within minutes, we heard the screaming wail of the ambulance, along with the fire truck's siren, followed by a police car. Altogether, there were two policemen, three paramedics and four firemen at the scene. I backed away, knowing she needed to be examined for injuries.

Her bicycle appeared untouched, though that was the least of anyone's worries. Apparently she had no lacerations or internal bleeding, and I could hear the paramedic advise she call her personal physician the following day. The police took statements from her and the driver then departed.

The man whose car had hit her didn't make a move to get back into his vehicle, but came over to where I stood next to the young girl. "My name's Michael Lorin. I'm so sorry, I'm not familiar with the area and was looking for a certain address. Luckily I was already slowing down when I saw the blinking light on your bicycle."

The girl smiled broadly at him, showing a full set of braces wrapped around perfectly straightened teeth. "Hey, it's all good, Mr. Lorin. It obviously could have been way worse, right?"

He gave her a weak smile. "You're lucky no bones were broken." He handed her a business card. "Here's my auto insurance information. You'll want to give them a call as soon as possible to file a claim."

She nodded. "I'll give this to my mom and dad. My name's Stephanie Palmer, by the way. I live around the corner, on Bay Street, next to the bed and breakfast. I better get home. They'll be worried about me."

Mr. Lorin and Stephanie shook hands. I stood off to the side, trying to give them some private time. I didn't want to leave until she could walk home safely on her own.

"My name's Brandy Chambers." I pointed to my house. "I live right there. Are you okay to walk home?"

"I'm just a little sore on my left knee where I fell on the ground. No biggee. Thanks for calling 9-1-1. I don't have my cell phone with me."

"Let me go inside the house and get my little girl. I can put her in the stroller, you grab your bike, and I'll walk home with you."

Her eyebrows shot up. "You have a baby?"

"Jessica. She's five weeks old. I'll be right back." I ran inside and put Jess in the stroller and was out of the house within minutes.

She bent down and took a look at Jess, still sound asleep. "She's so tiny," she whispered. "I love kids."

"Do you ever babysit?" I mentally crossed my fingers.

"I took care of my little sister all the time when she was a baby. And my parents made me take the American Red Cross baby sitter's course. I learned CPR and even have a Red Cross notebook filled with references from friends of my parents when I babysit their kids."

I started walking, noticed she was hobbling, with a slight

grimace on her face, and slowed my pace. "Do you go to school around here?"

"I graduated from Encinal High School and I'm taking classes at Alameda Junior College. I plan to apply to the university. I'm living with my mom and dad so I can save money."

"Sounds like a good idea." I paused, hoping my hunch was correct. "If I ever feel like getting out of the house, would you be interested in babysitting?"

She beamed. "I'd love to. I'll loan you my notebook so you can check out my references. I'm not planning on job hunting just yet. I want to concentrate on my studies. But I could use some extra cash."

She stopped in front of a huge Craftsman style home, next door to Alameda's only bed and breakfast. "I'll go inside and grab the notebook."

I followed her toward the front door. Half-way up the walkway, the door opened and a woman who looked not much older than I stepped outside. "Where have you been, honey? Your dad and I have been so worried about you."

Stephanie exhaled a deep breath then smiled. "Brandy, this is my mom, Patricia Palmer. Mom, this is Brandy Chambers. She lives around the corner on Lauren Drive."

She reached out her hand for me to shake. "Nice to meet you, Brandy. Oh, Stephanie, you're limping! What in God's name happened to you?"

"She was hit by a car in front of my house, Mrs. Palmer. But the paramedics said she's fine. I wanted to walk her home, just to make sure she got here okay."

She instantly turned toward her daughter, her eyebrows knitted in worry. "Oh, my God, Steph. Are you okay, honey?" She took her daughter by the shoulders and looked her up and down, inspecting every inch of her from head to toe.

Stephanie smiled and pulled her mother in for a hug, patting her back. "I'm fine, Mom. I got the man's insurance information right here." She handed her mother the business card. "We can take care of this tomorrow or whatever. I'm going to get that information for Brandy, okay?"

Mrs. Palmer pulled away from Stephanie's embrace. "I'm so glad you're all right, sweetie."

"Mrs. Palmer?" I interrupted.

"Please. Call me Patricia."

"Patricia… I've asked Stephanie if she's interested in babysitting for me." I pointed toward the stroller. "I have a five-week-old baby. Stephanie said she'd loan me her notebook of references to read, if that's okay."

She smiled. "I think that's a great idea. We don't want Stephie working much while she's studying. She needs to get good grades if she's applying to the university. But she could use a few extra dollars for fun. Very kind of you to offer."

Stephanie had already gone inside the house and was walking out, hand outstretched, holding a notebook with an American Red Cross emblem stamped on the front. "Here, Brandy. My home and cell numbers are inside too. Call me anytime."

We said our goodbyes and I turned to go home, the notebook tucked under my arm. I wanted to speak with a few of the people she'd worked for. If I felt comfortable with what they told me, Stephanie's misfortune would be my good luck. Maybe I'd finally found someone to take care of Jess!

Chapter 33

Edward came over several times a week to see Jessica. He'd often bring gifts, a new toy, or an item of clothing. He'd enter the house, give me a peck on the cheek then hold the baby while I took a relaxing bath or lay down for a short nap, maybe pop over to the store for a few minutes. He'd often arrive bearing a present for me as well—chocolates from See's Candies or a knickknack from a quaint store on Park Street.

We hadn't had an evening together alone since Jessica was born, so I wasn't surprised when he asked if I felt comfortable leaving the baby with Stephanie and we could go on a date. I'd phoned every person listed as a reference for Stephanie and they'd all given her glowing recommendations. She was smart, well-liked, educated in crisis situations, and she had a lot of experience taking care of children and infants.

Adult time with Edward sounded like heaven, and I phoned Stephanie right away. She was available for the following Saturday night.

On the evening of our date, I took a shower, washed and dried my hair, and applied my make-up with extra care. I dressed in one of my favorite silk dresses, a red clingy number with a deep-v in the front. After spraying Nicole Miller perfume behind my ears and at my throat, I was ready to go. The doorbell chimed then I heard Stephanie and Edward chatting. I took one last look in the mirror then walked down the stairs.

"Wow, do you look great, Brandy! Good enough to eat!" He covered his mouth with his hand and added, "Excuse me, I didn't mean that literally."

Stephanie was the first to make light of his faux pas. "That's all right, Mr. Barnes. I think we know what you meant."

We all three laughed. I kissed Jessica good-bye and we walked outside to the Porsche. It felt so good heading out to a restaurant, all dressed up. Instead of wearing sweatpants with my favorite basketball shoes, I felt sexy for the first time in months.

The Porsche hummed down the street, and Edward glanced over at me. "I made reservations at your favorite restaurant, L'Orangerie. That okay?"

I smiled. "Perfect. This is so much fun! I'm out of the house, all dressed up, and I get to talk to someone my age!"

His laugh was low and sexy. "We should do this more often, especially now that you've found such a reliable sitter."

"I'd love to and I don't worry much since we're only a few minutes from home."

"By the way, how's Cecilia?" he asked while negotiating a particularly windy street, one hand on the steering wheel, one on the gearshift.

"We had coffee yesterday. She's fine. They're so excited about the baby. Her due date's in November but she doesn't even look like she's expecting."

"I'm happy for her and… Perry, isn't it? Is he the Perry who's Weston's best friend?"

"Yes, they're close buddies. Cecilia and Perry are such a fun couple. I love spending time with them. But since Weston left, I've felt funny around Perry. I can understand his allegiance to Weston, and maybe the awkwardness is all in my mind, but it's how I feel. Cecilia and I are best friends, though. I love her and she's been so good to me since I moved here."

We arrived at the restaurant, were quickly seated, and ordered within moments. It was early, and there were only a few other tables occupied. I loved the quiet atmosphere, and we could talk without shouting above other voices.

After toasting our glasses of Coke and white wine, we sat back and listened to the tinkling sound of the outdoor fountain.

"When will your divorce be final? In October, right?"

I hadn't thought Edward was aware of the time frame for my divorce, and I could feel a hot flush creep up my neck. I hated it when I blushed.

"I've been meaning to talk to you about that." I mentally groped for the right words. "Weston came to see me the other day. He was very upset, said he made a huge mistake when he left me. He and his girlfriend aren't living together any longer and—" I paused, took a deep breath. "He wants to move back home, and try to work it out."

His jaw clenched and he gazed out the window toward the fountain, looking like he was trying to control himself. Or perhaps he was searching for the right words in answer to the bombshell I'd just thrown out.

After several seconds of silence, he turned his head in my direction. "Is he moving back in?"

"No, he's not. I'm still angry with him over leaving me when he found out I was carrying your child. He never gave me any indication he wanted to try to work things out before now. After he left, he refused to speak to me, wouldn't take my phone calls, then he filed for divorce. I found out he was living with his past lover, Carol, so I believed he was serious, that he wanted out of our marriage. And when he came over to the house to pick up his things, he didn't say the actual words, but I got the distinct impression he was in love with her. I never thought he'd want to come back home."

"What are you going to do?"

"I don't know if I could ever trust him again, whether he'd be willing to work on the problems that inevitably arise in any marriage. It reminded me of the phrase, 'When the going gets tough, the tough get going'. In his case, he got going alright." I reached across the table and grasped his hand. "You've been so wonderful to me since you came into my life. You're honest and kind and good and I enjoy spending time with you. You make me laugh. You're intelligent. We can talk for hours about anything."

I paused, thinking. One thing stood out in my mind, glaringly obvious. The thought had been lingering on the periphery of my consciousness ever since Weston had asked to come home. "You're the father of my baby."

"As I said, what are you going to do?" His tone was flat, unemotional.

"I love you, Edward. But I'm torn. I can't give you an answer right now." I searched his eyes for some glint of understanding. "He's the first man I ever loved. He and I have been through a lot together. Until now he'd always been there for me—when my mom and dad died, when I lost Christine. He stuck by me while I spiraled into such a deep depression I didn't know if I'd ever come out of it." I paused, trying to decide how much to tell him without making this situation worse. "When he left me, I was devastated. But I never stopped loving him. I can't see my way to either side of the question. Do I take him back or not?"

I felt uncomfortable sitting in a public restaurant, crying, my tears dripping onto the tablecloth as I searched in my purse for a tissue. He reached over and gave me the white handkerchief he always carried in his pocket.

He stood up, pulled out his wallet and brought out his credit card. "Let me pay for the meal then I'll take you home. You're upset. I'm upset. I think I need to give you your space, let you have as much time as you need to figure this out on your own."

I nodded in agreement and we left the restaurant.

When he pulled up in front of my house, he left the Porsche idling, reached across the console and took my face in his hands. He kissed me lightly on the mouth.

"I love you, Brandy. You're the first and only woman I've ever wanted to marry. I'm not in any position to fight for you against an enemy who had your heart before I entered the picture. You and I don't have any real history, but… we have a connection. Jessica. And she'll always be here. Which means we'll be seeing each other for many years to come. I don't know how that'll go down because watching you with another man is gonna kill me."

Tears seeped from beneath my eyelids, dripping onto his hands still gently holding my face, his gaze penetrating, unflinching. "And every time you see me, you'll know I'm the man who wants to make love to you every night for the rest of our lives. My feelings won't change, Brandy. I want to marry you, have more kids with you. I love you so much. Just keep all this in mind while you're trying to figure things out."

I nodded, unable to speak, my heart breaking. I opened the car door and stepped out, and walked up the pathway to the front door. I could hear his car gliding down Lauren Drive and wondered if I'd ever kiss him again.

Chapter 34

Several weeks passed and I welcomed the warmer days of August, my favorite month of summer. I hadn't seen Cecilia since my last date with Edward. She and Perry had taken a vacation to Montana to see his family, and I was dying to talk to her about my dilemma, hoping she'd guide me down the right road, wherever it might lead me. I had invited her over to visit and was waiting for her to arrive. She had always been such a great sounding board for my personal issues when I needed someone to listen and I had faith she'd come through for me this time too.

There was a knock on my front door, and I made sure Jessica's cradle was rocking and she was still asleep, then ran to answer it.

"Cecilia, hi! I've missed you sooo much." We hugged tightly. "How are you feeling? How was your vacation?"

"We had a great time. Perry's mom is a great cook. I ate so much I think both the baby and I gained ten pounds each."

Laughing, I said, "Have you seen Dr. Farney since you've been back?"

"Yesterday. She said I'm doing fine. but she's moved up my due date. Now she thinks I'm due at the end of October. So Perry and I plan to take the childbirth classes next month, in September."

"You'll love them. It really helped me. And Edward, of course."

She grabbed onto my arm and smiled. "Speaking of which…"

"Come into the kitchen. Let's sit down and have a decaf latte. I've got the espresso already made. I just have to steam the milk."

She followed behind me and sat at the kitchen table while I finished preparing our coffees.

"We'll have plenty of time to talk baby later, Brandy. I want to talk about Weston, and Edward, of course. Tell me what's going on with you three."

I glanced over my shoulder and gave her a withering look. "We three? Oh, that's cute." When the milk reached one hundred and sixty degrees I turned off the valve and began pouring the milk into mugs. "You're right, though, it *is* a love triangle. I already told you Weston wants to come back home. But I've been dying to talk to you about Edward. The other night he took me out on a date and we went to L'Orangerie, right? And he asked me when the divorce would be final. I couldn't lie to him, so I explained Weston wants to get back together."

"Did he go ballistic or what?"

I brought our mugs to the table and sat down. "At first he looked really angry, but I think he was hurt. He told me he loves me and wants to marry me and it will be hell for him seeing me if Weston's living here when he visits the baby. He wants to give me my space to think about it and make my decision." I took a sip of my latte and leaned back in the chair. "Oh, Cecilia, I don't know what I'm going to do. I feel like I'm being pulled in two different directions and I'm going nowhere."

She shook her head. "I don't envy being in your position. I mean, it's great you have two of the most handsome men on the planet fighting over you, but I don't know what I'd do either."

"Don't say that, Cecilia!" I shouted. Placing my hand on her arm, I added, "I'm sorry, I'm upset. And I'm counting on you to help me make a decision."

She looked out the window for a few seconds then turned her eyes in my direction. "Brandy, I'm a firm believer everything happens for a reason. I know that may sound a little 'out there' to you, but I believe Edward came into your life for a reason. You lost Christine then met Edward and got pregnant with Jessica." She shrugged. "I don't know. And I think Carol came into Weston's life for a reason too. And now she's out of his life—for a reason. I don't know how this will all play out, but maybe Weston wanting to come back is just the incentive you need to make a decision. Who do you want to spend your life with, Brandy?"

"You're right, Cece. No one can make this decision for me. And I can't sit on the fence about this. But it's so hard. I don't want to hurt either of them."

She tilted her head. "Are you leaning in any particular direction?"

Our eyes locked. "When Weston asked if he could come back home, expecting me to accept him with open arms after the way he treated me, I—"

"You don't trust him, do you?"

"West?" She nodded. "No, I guess I don't."

"You guess?" She frowned. "What about Edward? How do you feel about *him*?"

"I love him, Cece." I noticed her smile. "What?"

"Anything else?"

"He's the father of my child," I whispered.

"I wouldn't worry too much about this, Bran. It seems to me you're well on your way to making a decision." She patted my forearm. "Believe in yourself."

It had been so good to talk to her about my predicament. I couldn't be indecisive about this. My future and Jessica's future were weighing in the balance and the scales were already tipping in Edward's direction.

Chapter 35

September—and I hadn't contacted Edward for several weeks. Both men were waiting for me to make a decision. To my surprise, Weston showed up on my doorstep two days before the custody hearing.

"May I come in? I wanted to ask you something. Am I interrupting?"

It was understood I would be the one to contact him, so what was going on? "I was in the front room, writing. Come in," I gestured.

I sat down on the couch, and he settled in one of the armchairs across from me.

He bent forward, legs spread apart, his hands clasped between his knees. "I'll make this short. I know we had an understanding. You'd be in touch with me after you had time to think about our conversation." He looked down at his hands, then up at me. "But I want us to spend time together, Brandy. We haven't been together, alone, since March and…"

I interrupted, "When you walked out. And wouldn't return my phone calls. Then you come here to pick up your things and tell me it's none of my business what's happening with you and Carol—"

"I didn't say—"

I held up my hand. "Then you show up at the block party drunker than I've ever seen you and completely humiliate me in front of all the neighbors. After that you ask if you can move back in because Carol's a bitch. Have I gotten the sequence of events correct here?"

He hung his head, looking like a kicked puppy. "I know, I know. But remember how messed up you were after Christine died? You were *so* on the edge you slept with Edward. Well, I know what it's like to be on the edge too, Brandy. You don't hold a patent on that. When I found out you were pregnant with his baby I went ballistic." He tapped the middle of his chest with his fingers. "My heart broke into a million pieces. I was shattered. Then Carol started phoning me, and she and I got together. I'm not asking you to condone my actions. I just want you to understand why I went to an attorney and wanted a divorce. And why I acted the way I did at your party. Both were inexcusable. But give me another chance. Give *us* another chance."

He was right. He wasn't the only one whose behavior was inexcusable. I'd been an emotional wreck when I'd slept with Edward. I had to acknowledge the fact he, too, was devastated when our baby died and he'd slept with Carol. Finding out I was carrying another man's child had been the last straw for him, a blast to his ego and his heart. But that was no excuse for leaving me. It wasn't fair to blame me for being a woman, able to conceive a child.

"What did you have in mind?" I asked, skepticism in my voice.

He shook his head. "You, me, and Jessica. We could have a picnic in the Oakland hills. I want us to spend time together, Brandy. Everything happened so abruptly at the end."

"There was never any closure, West. We never had a chance to talk. I didn't have a say before it ended."

"I'm not looking for closure, Brandy. I want this to be the start of something new."

"I'm not sure there's anything to talk about."

"Maybe not, but I'd like to see how it goes. Don't let today be goodbye, Bran."

My heart wasn't completely empty of feelings for him. Perhaps this was our one chance to see if we could work things out. And that was a big *if.* "All right."

He smiled, a look of relief on his face. "Great! How about ten o'clock Friday morning?"

I nodded. "Okay."

I'd be seeing Edward in two days at the custody hearing and planned to tell him about it then. As Cecilia said, everything happens for a reason. Maybe this time together was just what Weston and I needed to help me make my final decision.

* * * *

Edward and I met in court so our attorneys could work out the specifics of his visiting rights with Jessica. He and I had already discussed what he wanted and agreed to his taking Jessica every other weekend, with his visits open to change as she grew older. The judge was amenable to what our lawyers had drawn up, and the entire process took less than a half hour.

We exited the courthouse and Edward approached me as we headed toward our cars in the parking lot. "That went well."

Smiling, I replied, "I'm glad you and I agree because it makes it much easier. She's your daughter. You should be able to see her whenever you want."

"I appreciate your being so liberal about my visits with her. And, you're right, it'll be much less difficult because we agree on what's best for Jess."

We reached my car and I leaned against the driver's side door. "Edward, I have to tell you something." He nodded and smiled. "Weston came over the other day. He wants to go on a picnic with me and Jessica. To talk. Everything's happened so fast since he left. He and I never had the chance to discuss things."

His mouth clamped shut, his jaw clenched. He looked sternly at me. "You're spending a day with your ex-husband? So, you've made your decision."

I unlocked the car and threw my purse inside. "He's not my ex yet, Edward. And I haven't made any decision. I knew you'd make this out to be something it's not. That's not what's going on here. We'll use the time to talk about him and me." I took a deep breath. "In fact, I had a long talk with Cecilia. She believes everything happens for a reason, and I'm beginning to agree with her. I lost my baby then slept with you and got pregnant with Jessica. Weston slept with Carol and left me after he found out I was having your child. Then he realized Carol wasn't right for him and he came crawling back to me." I laid my hand on his forearm. "I need closure, Edward. I'm hoping this get-together with Weston will give me that. And him too. I have to do this."

He took both my hands in his and looked me straight in the eyes. "Okay. I see where you're coming. But I have a bad feeling about this, Brandy, knowing you'll be alone with *him*."

Wrenching my hands from his, I said, "Look, if you can't understand what I'm doing, just forget it. I'll be spending a few hours with him. He and Jess and I are driving to the Oakland hills for a picnic. I wanted to be honest with you, Edward. I didn't have to tell you about this, you know. I'm going because it's the right thing to do. There's no way I can make plans for my future without discussing my past relationship with Weston."

He nodded, but he looked sad. "All right. I guess I don't have a choice. It's just… you took me by surprise. But I understand you have to do what you believe is right. You go, work this thing out with him. I'll be here when you get back, waiting."

I got into the car and looked up at him, trying my best to smile. "I'll call you."

He leaned down and gave me a kiss. "I'll wait for you to phone," he said, shutting the car door for me.

Chapter 36

On Friday, I sat with Jessica in the front room waiting for Weston to arrive. Historically, September in Alameda had the best weather of the year and today looked to be no exception. They predicted it would reach seventy-five degrees with a slight breeze. When the doorbell chimed, I put the baby in the stroller, grabbed my purse, and answered it.

"Good morning." Weston bent down and put his finger near Jessica's hand. She instantly grabbed onto it and smiled. "She's a happy little thing, isn't she?" He grinned.

"She rarely cries unless she's hungry and she loves to sit in her baby seat and look out the window while I'm writing, happy as a little bug."

Straightening up, he asked, "Ready to go?"

I picked up my purse and handed him the diaper bag then pushed the stroller out the door, locking it behind me. I reached the truck and realized I'd forgotten to bring the car seat.

"I'll be right back. Her car seat is in the garage and—"

"I have one in the back seat, all set and ready to go," he interrupted.

I glanced in the back seat of his truck and frowned. "Why do you have a kid's car seat in your truck?"

He smiled and explained. "I invited both of you today and it's the law so I went out and bought one. It's approved by the Department of Transportation so you don't have to be concerned."

I gave him a confused look. "But—"

"It's no big deal, Brandy. Don't overanalyze it," he said, his tone testy.

I decided to table this particular discussion. It was presumptuous on his part if he'd already planned future road trips for the three of us, and it made me feel uncomfortable. But I didn't want to spoil our day together so I dropped it.

He drove the back route to the park instead of taking the more direct way via Highway 880, which was always congested and packed with eighteen-wheelers. It was a leisurely drive through the back roads of the hills of Oakland, dense with dark green foliage, the evergreen trees forming canopies above the two-lane road. The twists and turns meandered for miles, and we encountered few other vehicles along the way.

We reached Tilden Park and found a shaded picnic table near a creek. Weston took Jessica out of her car seat and held her while I laid a red-checkered cloth over the weathered wood and arranged the lunch basket at the end for easy access. Then he placed her in the baby seat in the middle of the table and I sat down. He straddled the bench next to me then leaned over and fixed the tie on one of the baby's booties.

"Remember when we went horseback riding at Anthony Chabot Equestrian Center, West?"

He grinned at me then laughed. "I got stuck with the old white mare with a back so concave I felt like I was sitting in a hole."

"But it was a blast riding through Bort Meadow," I countered.

"Well, yeah. You got to ride that beautiful dark brown horse, the one with the funny way of running—"

"It's called a gaited horse, Weston," I interrupted. "And he didn't run funny," I argued with a smile. "Those horses naturally have many gaits. You sit there as if you're in a Barcalounger and the horse does all the work."

"We should go back there sometime. Maybe you could get a babysitter, and you and I could take the day off, just the two of us." He leaned over and gave me a quick peck on the lips.

I wasn't expecting it and pulled back instantly. "What was that for?"

He grinned. "Do I have to have a reason to kiss my wife?"

"Uh, actually, yes. Yes, you do. Or did you forget you wanted to divorce your wife?"

"I explained that to you already, Brandy. I made a mistake leaving you."

"I didn't know I was carrying Edward's child."

He placed a hand on my forearm and I looked over at him.

"Why'd you sleep with him, Brandy?"

"Oh, Weston," I sighed. "We've gone over this before. Did losing our baby excuse my behavior? No, but I understand why I acted that way. And I never told you this but… I blamed myself for her death. And I thought you did too but you'd never admit it. A part of me hated myself back then."

Shaking his head, his brows dipped together in a frown. "What the hell are you talking about? It wasn't your fault she died, Brandy."

"I know that *now*, but at the time I believed I'd done something when I was pregnant that caused her death. I'd killed our child, a child we never got a chance to know, never would see grow up, never be able to love. I know it sounds all screwed up, but I wasn't thinking straight. I didn't want to make love to you because I had terrifying visions every time you touched me. They were so graphic, I'd feel physically sick every time they'd come into my mind, I… But I couldn't tell you how I felt. Truthfully, back then, a part of me knew it sounded crazy."

"You never told me *any* of this, Brandy. How could I know you felt that way? You never talked to me about your feelings, not after the first few days you were back from the hospital. Afterward you just clammed up, and I guessed it was your way of dealing with it, so I left you alone. I didn't want to constantly bring up a subject already causing you so much grief."

I stared at him. "It's what anyone would have done in your place, Weston. Unfortunately, a person as depressed as I was isn't thinking correctly. My head wasn't on straight. Like an insane person living in a sane world, nothing made sense to me."

"Wow." He let out a deep breath. "I had no idea. I wish you'd told me how you were feeling. Maybe I could have helped you make sense of it all. Hell, I don't know. I should have known."

I shook my head. "There's no way you could have known what I was going through, Weston. I was good at covering up my depression. When you left for New York and I was on my own… I'm not blaming you, but maybe being alone was the worst thing for me at the time. While you were away I met Edward, and that was the beginning of the end of you and me. I did an insane thing—I slept with another man." I shrugged my shoulders. "I look back and wonder, 'Was that really me?'"

"You look so sad, Brandy."

"So much has happened in our relationship," I said then paused. "I don't feel the same about anything."

"How do you mean?" His forehead wrinkled.

"When you walked out in March, I was certain it would be for a couple of days, you'd come back and we'd talk. Everything would return to normal. But I didn't hear from you and you wouldn't return my calls then I received the divorce papers. You obviously didn't want anything more to do with me and didn't want to try to work it out. And you all but admitted to being in love with Carol." I looked up at the dark green trees towering above us then down at my hands. "So, I guess I gave up on us too. I was pregnant with another man's child, and you couldn't handle that. It must have been a huge blow to your ego, your manhood. But as I said before, that's not playing fair. Just because I got pregnant didn't make what I did any worse than what happened with you and Carol. So I let it go, Weston. And I moved on."

Jessica whimpered and I stood up to grab her bottle out of the diaper bag. When I returned to the table to feed her I noticed she'd fallen asleep so I sat down on the bench.

"You said you moved on," he continued. "You're talking about Edward, aren't you?"

"Edward was a surprise. I didn't turn to him for comfort if that's what you're implying. It wasn't like that at all."

"What was it like then?"

I stood up again to stretch my legs and gather my thoughts then turned toward him. "At first I was so mad, I hated him. He was the enemy. He'd ruined my marriage by demanding the DNA test, and I didn't want to be in the same room with him. But I realized I was blaming him for *my* indiscretion. He wasn't the one who was married and had sex with someone else. I blamed him for wanting to discover the truth. And that's no reason to hate or blame someone.

"The truth about Jessica's real father would have come to light eventually, due to a medical procedure or something. In hindsight, I'm glad it all came out now rather than later. You and I would have been living a lie and perhaps not known it for years."

"So what do you mean when you say you've 'moved on'?"

"Well, when I stopped blaming him for what I'd done, I had to come to terms with the fact he would be a part of my life, maybe forever. When he insisted on his parental rights, I realized he was here for the long term. He was no longer a one-night stand. He'd be around me and Jess for years.

"He wanted to be a real parent to her. I hadn't known his father had walked out on him and his mother when he was ten years old. He was determined to be a father to his child. I got to know him better, then he asked to be my birthing coach, one thing led to another and—"

"You fell in love with him, didn't you?"

I hesitated. Weston and I had always been good friends. Sharing and caring was a big part of who we were together. I'd learned from the past what lies could do to a relationship. Telling the truth was always the better option.

Reaching for my hand, he whispered, "I still love you, Brandy. I never stopped."

I shook my head. "I'm not saying I fell out of love for you. It's just—a lot has happened in the past year. I'm not the same person I was when you walked out. Hell, who doesn't change, right? I've grown up, learned things along the way. I don't want to go on as we were before. I'm not the same woman you were married to back then."

"Do we have to start all over, act like we're dating? You want me to court you?"

I pulled my hand from his grasp. "No. You didn't expect me to spend a few hours with you and suddenly know exactly what I want to do about our relationship, did you?"

"No," he answered, looking like a scared puppy.

"But that's how you're acting," I said between gritted teeth.

"I'm sorry." He sighed. "I didn't mean to pressure you."

"But that's exactly what you're doing," I shouted then remembered the baby was asleep and lowered my voice. "You know something? I didn't want to divorce you, Weston. Edward wasn't waiting in the wings for me to return to him because he was in love with me. You, on the other hand, turned *again* to Carol who obviously was lurking on the sidelines and was still in love with you… and you fell in love with her. Then you dumped her and now you want me back."

I swiped at the tears as they fell. "I don't trust you anymore. When we hit rock bottom I turned to you so we could work it out. I didn't turn to Edward. It was *you* I needed. But you deserted me and chose Carol to give you what you needed." I pounded my fist on my chest, sobbing. "I was your wife damn it… and you turned your back on me." The burden I'd been carrying inside lifted with every word I said, each sentence a revelation for me and I suppose, for him too. I never realized how resentful and angry I felt over the way he'd ended our marriage.

He stared down at his hands and I noticed tear drops had landed on his knuckles. I sat down on the bench again, facing him, and waited for him to speak. I'd said everything I needed to say. My feelings about him and our relationship had finally coalesced and explaining them gave me an odd sense of freedom.

After several minutes, he looked up at me, his eyes red and watery from crying. "So this is it? We're finished?"

"I'm saying I have some serious thinking to do." I paused. "Would you mind taking me home?"

"But we haven't even eaten, Brandy. And Jessica's still napping. Couldn't we at least straighten this out between us," he pleaded.

I picked up Jessica and put her in the car seat then returned to the table and began gathering up the picnic basket. He stood up and placed a hand on my arm. I stopped and looked over at him. "I need to be alone, West. Can we please just go?" I grabbed my purse and got into the truck. He folded the tablecloth, hopped in, and started the engine. We drove home in silence.

He took the freeway instead of the back roads, and we reached Alameda in a half hour. I was anxious for him to drop me off. A part of me would always resent his walking out on me when we should have been coming together as a couple, seeking solace from each other. And now *he* decided it was time to work on our relationship? I wasn't sure I wanted to do that. And that made *me* the bad guy?

When he pulled up to the house I jumped out of the truck, opened the back door, and took Jessica out of the car seat. He came over to my side of the truck and handed me my purse and diaper bag.

"Bye," I said, not looking him in the face. I turned to walk away.

He touched my hand and I glanced over at him. "Will you call me?" He paused. "When you've made up your mind?"

I nodded, turned, and walked up the path to the front door. His truck pulled away from the curb and I felt relieved he wasn't with me.

Chapter 37

A week later Edward called and left a message he'd like to take Jessica for the day. I hadn't heard from him since our court date and was anxious to see him. When he arrived at the front door, I could tell from the look on his face something was awry. He was dressed in sharp looking khaki pants with a white Izod shirt; however, the good looks stopped with the clothes. His face had a pinched quality, as if he'd been reading too much. And his stance wasn't the casual, self-assured one I was accustomed to seeing. Maybe he'd been hunched over a table writing on a legal pad for days.

"Hi. I'm here to pick up my little girl."

I motioned for him to come inside. "Not to be mean, but you don't look too good. You have circles under your eyes. Late nights?"

"Yeah. Hanging around the office until midnight. Sometimes I don't leave until two, three in the morning."

"What's up with that? Big case or gorgeous secretary?"

He gave me a dirty look. "My secretary is sixty-four years old and wears a chain around her neck to hold up her bifocals. She and I aren't really into each other, if you get my drift."

"Then it must be work." I gestured toward the front room where I took a seat at one end of the couch and he plopped down on the other end.

"Oh, yeah. Being a criminal lawyer is tough sometimes. One of my clients is a guy who looks like Wally Cleaver but he's more like Ted Bundy. He says he's innocent and the prosecution has only circumstantial evidence tying him to the crime. But I know the guy did it and that's really hard on me."

"It's your job to prove he's innocent, right? What makes this case so special?"

He leaned back into the pillows and took a deep breath. "He's accused of murdering his next door neighbor's five-year-old daughter. DNA evidence proves he's been in the house, but the parents were friends with him, so that's not incriminating evidence. He actually babysat the little girl sometimes. But somebody murdered their daughter and the couple believes it's my client." He shook his head, pulled at the lobe of his ear. "I've got this niggling little thing in the back of my mind. I know he's guilty. But I'm his attorney and it's my job to prove his innocence. It's the prosecutor's job to prove he's guilty. And there's no way they can do it. I know it and they know it. So the guy's gonna walk. And I just can't wrap my brain around this one. It's tearing me up. But I believe in the law and I believe in my job so I'm doing my best to get him set free. I'm good at what I do and I'm betting he'll walk."

"How terrible," I said, feeling sad for him, for the murdered child, for her parents. "The couple must be devastated, losing their little girl like that. I can't imagine their grief."

"I know what you mean. Now I have a kid of my own, and this kind of case hits me right in the gut." He paused, looking deep in thought. "There could be quite a public backlash if I prove him innocent. He'll have to have police protection until he decides to move out of Alameda."

"What about you? You'll be considered the bad guy who got him acquitted," I said, feeling scared for him. "What about *your* safety?"

He sat up straight, folding his hands between his knees. "Don't worry about me. I'll be fine… How was your time with Weston?"

"We talked. Or I should say, I talked. I tried to explain where my head was at when I saw you again after all those years, that sort of thing."

"You didn't tell him he could come back home, did you?"

"I told you I wouldn't do that. I need time to think things over. And I promised you I wouldn't make my decision before seeing you. In fact, I'd like us to spend some time together when you're next free. When does your case go to trial?"

"December."

"You look tired, Edward. You're working too hard. Can't you take time off, perhaps on the weekends? Rest, relax—remember what that's like?"

"Can't recall that I do. Seriously, I'm hoping this trial will be over by my birthday. February first, remember? Then I'll take a few weeks off, go somewhere sunny. Or not. I wouldn't want to go alone." He gave me one of his killer smiles, which always made my insides feel like JELL-O.

I reached for his hand and pulled him down onto the couch then I moved to sit on the armrest, turning him away from me so I could massage his neck muscles. He was tense, and for good reason.

This case was taking its toll on him both mentally and physically. I didn't know how I could help besides just being there for him if he needed to talk. Or if he wanted a good neck rub. He leaned back against my lower legs and bent his head forward while I performed deep tissue massage on his neck, then down his back.

After several minutes, I could feel his muscles relax, the tension dissipating with my kneading hands and fingers. He sat up and turned toward me, pulling me down toward the cushions of the couch, then covered me with his body and began kissing me as if today was the last time we'd ever see each other. He seemed ravenous, as if he couldn't get enough of me. His tongue explored my mouth, his kisses flowed down my neck, moving to my breasts, biting my nipples through my shirt. Working his way back up to my lips, he suddenly stopped, looked me in the eyes, and said, "Do you know how much I've missed you, Brandy? I've wanted to call you, come and see you, every single day. I miss our talks. I miss just being with you."

"And I've missed you."

"Multiply that by a thousand and you'll know how I've felt for weeks. I've wanted to make love to you since I saw you in Starbucks last March… It's almost October."

"How about we go out on a date in a few weeks?" I suggested.

He raised his eyebrows. "L'Orangerie? We could have a nice quiet meal."

I nodded. "Sounds perfect."

He stood up and was out the door before I got up off the couch. I was anxious to see him again—already.

Chapter 38

On October twenty-first Cecilia gave birth to Amylynn who weighed eight pounds five ounces. She and Perry were two of the happiest people on the planet. I talked to her on the phone several times when she was in the hospital and again after she arrived home. We agreed on a day and time when she'd come by for a visit.

The oven timer had just beeped for the blueberry muffins I was baking when the phone rang. I snatched the pot holders off the table to take the muffins out to cool then reached for the phone.

"Brandy? You sitting down?" Brent's voice echoed over the phone line and I surmised he was talking on his blue-tooth, on his way to another meeting.

I cringed inside, not knowing whether this would be good news or bad. "Why do you ask? Should I get out my box of Kleenex?"

He made several "tsk-tsk" sounds, then chuckled. "Oh, ye of little faith," he said then paused.

"Do you enjoy torturing me, Brent?" My legs were twitching in anticipation of the news.

"Nooooo," he answered, drawing out his reply.

I remained silent, waiting for him to end this insufferable mind game.

"I pitched your book to my editor friend at Harper Collins—"

"I knew you'd already done that, Brent. What did he say?"

"Verrrry interested," he answered, lengthening his response. "I'm not saying it's a done deal but I've worked with him before—Mark Stefano. He loved it. We both agree the market is on the upswing for the women's fiction you write, Brandy." I could hear his smile through the phone line.

"Thank you *so* much," I yelled, realizing too late I'd probably hurt his eardrums. I lowered my voice, reining in what I termed my "yippee yappee and yahooee" factor. "Do you have any idea about the time frame—when you'll hear back from him?"

He laughed. I already knew what his answer would be.

"You've been through this before, Brandy. It's a waiting game. No one enjoys it, least of all the author. I'd say we should know something within the next three months. After being in this business for twenty years, the one sure thing is you have to be patient. But I was surprised to hear from Mark so quickly. I almost fell down the stairs when he called me."

"Fell down the stairs?" His ability to shock me with his stories never ceased. I always enjoyed his tales of working in the Big Apple.

"I was late for a lunch date with an editor I'd been schmoozing for months when Mark called me on my cell. I was waving down a taxi and slipped on the last few stairs before I reached the curb. Practically fell flat on my face when I looked at the caller i.d. Multi-tasking can be a bitch!"

I could hear a car horn honking in the background, then Brent's voice shouting, "That's my taxi, you jackass!" then dead silence. I figured our call had been dropped and surmised he'd call back if he had anything important to add to our conversation. Though I'd wanted to share with him my scheduled book signing at our local Borders after the New Year, that could wait until later. I still actively promoted my first novel, *Passing Through Brandiss*, and he was always interested in anything I did on a promotional basis.

He'd told me everything I needed to know for right now and it was good news. I understood the slow process of getting a book accepted by a publisher, especially one of the "big" ones like Harper Collins. I'd just keep writing my third book—the anecdote to any worries about the future of my second novel.

There was a knock on the front door and I ran to answer it, making sure the oven was turned off and Jessica's cradle was still rocking in the front room.

"Cecilia, hi! I've missed you sooo much." We hugged tightly. Looking to the side, I saw the baby stroller holding Amylynn. She had beautiful thick dark hair, long eyelashes, and long arms and legs. "She's going to be a ballerina, Cecilia, I can tell already."

"That's what Perry said too. Isn't she beautiful? Of course, what else would I say, right? But I can't keep my eyes off her. We waited so long to finally have her, Brandy, it seems like a miracle."

"I know what you mean. Amylynn *is* a miracle baby." I leaned over to get a better look. Her dark hair, button nose, and high cheek bones were total Cecilia. "She's gorgeous, Cece. Come in and I'll see if Jessica's awake. The two of them can meet, since they'll be best friends."

I picked up Jess from her cradle and Cecilia and I sat on the couch, ready to relax and have girl time.

"Let me get us some coffee and muffins." I placed Jessica in Cecilia's arms, ran into the kitchen, and was back in moments.

Placing the coffee cups and a plate of muffins on the table, I took Jessica and sat in a chair across from Cecilia. "How's Amylynn doing? Perry told me she nursed right away. You're so lucky!"

"The nurses told me that as well. Oh, Brandy, she's such a good baby. She wakes up twice during the night to nurse, eats ravenously for maybe five to ten minutes then falls asleep in her cradle next to my side of the bed. We bought one just like yours, the kind that rocks on its own. I love it."

I paused to take a bite of muffin and a sip of coffee. "Have you made plans for the holidays?"

"Perry and I were just talking about that. We'd like to have a Christmas party but our house isn't—"

"Let's have it here," I interrupted.

"Really?" She smiled, then picked up Amylynn. "Time for her feeding." She picked up the bottom of her shirt, nestling her daughter against her breast. "Perry insists on inviting Weston," she added, reaching across and snagging a muffin, then taking a bite.

"Fine with me. The two guys *are* best friends."

"What about Edward? Are you planning to invite him?"

"Seems sort of childish not to. I think we can put aside our feelings for one night of holiday cheer."

"You'll ask him then?" She snuggled back against the pillows with her coffee cup in her hand.

"We're going on a date tomorrow night. I'll tell him about it and let him make up his own mind whether he wants to come to the party or not."

"Call me and tell me what he says, okay?"

I looked across at her and grinned. Sitting in the front room with my best friend while she nursed her baby, sharing stories about Jessica's father—I felt content. My life was full. I had my health, my child was healthy, I had an editor at Harper Collins who might be interested in my second book, and tomorrow night I had a date. Life was good.

Chapter 39

The following evening I paid particular attention to my make-up and hair, which was longer and fuller than it had been in years, falling to the middle of my back, the soft auburn waves lustrous and shiny. I dressed in a short hunter-green velvet dress, its bodice cut low in the front, paired with five-inch black open-toed heels, and a black velvet purse.

Turning to the side to look in the mirror before Edward arrived, I patted my stomach. I had lost the weight I'd gained during my pregnancy and was down to my normal one hundred and twenty-five pounds. The doorbell rang and I hurried to splash my favorite perfume behind my ears and along my wrists. He'd made reservations and I didn't want to be late.

He stood at the bottom of the stairs, talking with Stephanie who was holding Jessica. When he looked up and saw me carefully negotiating the steps, he gave a low whistle of praise. "You look gorgeous, Brandy. And it's only been, what, five months since you had Jessica? Man, oh man, you are a beauty."

I faked a Southern accent and replied, "Why, Edward, I do dee-claruh, you're making me blush, dahlin!"

He laughed, Stephanie laughed, and then so did I. I was unaccustomed to all this attention, though it felt good to be dressed up, wearing make-up, and a pretty outfit with heels. We got in the Porsche and drove toward L'Orangerie; however, he didn't turn at Park Street. Instead he sped down several extra blocks to San Antonio Boulevard.

I glanced over at him, confused.

"You recognize this place don't you?" he asked.

"What's going on? I thought we were eating at L'Orangerie?"

"We were. But yesterday I thought, Hey, I'm a great cook, I'll fix you dinner at my place. We'll have a quiet evening alone, no distractions. And we'll be able to talk. No interruptions from other people or waiters or anything. Are you okay with that?"

I paused, thinking. "That sounds wonderful."

We walked up the pathway leading to the front door and, just as I stepped over the threshold, I noticed candles glowing on the dining room table, set with crystal glasses, china plates, cloth napkins, and a vase at the end filled with yellow roses. No restaurant could have looked so romantic and inviting.

Guiding me gently toward the table, he pulled out a chair. "Dinner's ready. I'll be back in a moment."

When he returned, he placed a wooden bowl on the table filled with mixed lettuce, tomatoes, cucumbers, and radishes, accompanied by heated sourdough bread and butter, thin slices of chicken for him, various sliced cheeses for me, white wine for him, a Coke for me.

"This looks delicious," I said. "I'm still nursing Jessica and I get ravenous at dinner time."

"Good. I'm glad you aren't disappointed I brought you home with me instead of eating at the restaurant."

I looked up in surprise. "You've never disappointed me, Edward. You continually amaze me with the things you say and do."

He looked down at his plate and I caught a glimpse of a grin on his face. "Aw, shucks, Mrs. Chambers, you're embarrassing me."

"Can you ever be serious? I'm trying to give you a compliment and you joke around."

He placed a hand on my forearm and our eyes met. "Sorry, Brandy. I guess my automatic response is to crack a joke, make people laugh. Forgive me for being insensitive."

"You're forgiven. Now, can I eat?"

He nodded. "Of course. In fact, let me serve you."

He stood and dished up an array of fresh greenery onto my plate along with thin slices of cheese, placed a piece of steaming French bread on the side dish, then poured my Coke over chunks of ice in a crystal goblet.

I waited for him to serve himself, savoring the sight of a meal I didn't have to prepare. Relaxed, I let the quiet and silence of his home envelop me. There weren't a lot of cars in Alameda, the population being around seventy thousand people, so the typical traffic of a big city was pleasantly absent.

"How's the murder case coming? I know you're working long hours."

He let out a big sigh. "Man, this one's big. There hasn't been a case like it in Alameda since 1972. Selecting a jury was a bitch. Initially I requested a change of venue, to L.A., but the judge would have none of it. So my client will be tried in Alameda by Alamedans and people from the surrounding area. Everyone for miles around has heard about it. But, as I told you before, the prosecution doesn't have anything to hang their hats on anyway. They're gonna lose and they know it."

"What makes you think he's guilty?" I asked, anxious to know how someone could figure out the mind of a murderer.

"I don't *think* he's guilty. I *know* he's guilty." He patted his midsection with the palm of his hand. "I can feel it in my gut. Some of the things he's told me, the way he acts when we talk about the day of the murder. I can't reveal any more, but suffice it to say, the guy's guilty of murdering the little girl. He knows it and he knows I know it." Then he shrugged. "My job's still the same, to prove he's innocent."

"This must be horrible for you, knowing he killed that child," I said, shaking my head.

"I believe in the law. For years I've dedicated my life to learning the law, studying the law. It's in my blood, in my soul. It's what makes this country what it is today. The guy's innocent until they prove him guilty and unfortunately that's not gonna happen in this case."

After dinner, he led me to the front room while he cleaned up and made us fresh cups of coffee. When he returned, he lit a fire in the fireplace and we sat on the couch together, watching the flames flicker and sputter behind the fire screen.

"You said you wouldn't make up your mind about Weston moving back home until you and I could spend time together. Dumb question number one—are you leaning more toward him or me?"

I shifted toward him. "Edward, this is our time together, just you and me. It's not about Weston and me. I don't feel comfortable answering that question right now." I turned to face the fireplace, leaning back into the pillows, and he placed his arm around my shoulders.

"Can you at least answer me one question?" I glanced over at him. "Am I still in the running?"

"Do me a favor, will you?"

"What's that?" he whispered.

"Shut up and make love to me."

Chapter 40

The look on his face was priceless. I saw surprise, disbelief, quickly replaced with a huge smile. "You do recognize where we're sitting right now, don't you?" he asked.

"It's our couch," I replied. "The one we were lying on when you impregnated me."

"Oh, that's sooo romantic, Brandy. Why don't we change venues? Or do you prefer the memories attached to this piece of furniture?"

I patted the cushion. "I'm kind of fond of this thing." I lay back on the pillows and opened my arms, inviting him to join me. "Come here," I said sweetly.

Holding up a finger indicating 'just a second', he said, "I've got a better idea."

He turned around and shut off the lights, leaving us with only the tranquil glow of the embers in the fireplace. The rest of the house was steeped in darkness, giving me the feeling we were in our own little world. We could do whatever we wanted, we had no one to answer to—no children, no phone calls, no one but us.

He walked back to the couch, leaned over, and tucked me in his arms then laid me down carefully on the thick Persian rug in front of the fire place. Slowly, he began removing his shirt, then shoes, socks, and finally his pants. I'd never seen a man undress in the glow of firelight—like having a private viewing of a male stripper.

His body was perfectly sculpted, all the muscles flexed and firm in all the right places. After kneeling next to me, he slid my dress off my shoulders, down my thighs and calves, and threw it aside, leaving me with my black thong, thigh-high nylons and heels. He leaned back, taking in every inch of my body, his eyes roaming from my feet up to my thong, to my breasts.

I sat up slowly, tucking my fingers over the sides of his briefs, pulling them gently down over his hardened member. I lay back, awaiting his touch, anticipating the feel of his hands on my body, needing his mouth to cover my lips with kisses, desire welling in my groin at the thought this man would give me the orgasm I wanted so badly.

He straddled me, one knee on each side of me. "What's wrong, Brandy? Are you afraid you're doing the wrong thing here, being with me?"

"That's not it at all. I'm doing exactly what I want, right here, right now, with you. It's just… it's been a while since we've, you know, had sex, and you—"

"We'll go slow, Brandy. Very, very slow. By the time I'm through with you, you won't feel anything but good, I promise. God, I love you."

Hearing his words, seeing him hovering over me in all his muscular beauty, I trusted him to take care of me, not only my body but my mind. He always made me feel so wanted, so needed, so intelligent, such a good mother and person. I closed my eyes and let him transport me to all the places he wanted, opening my body to his ministrations.

He was right. By the time he entered me, I was begging him to end my wanting him so badly. Placing my hands on each side of his waist, I pushed him deeper inside me. With each thrust I forced him in further, until he groaned, pleading me to stop, so I ceased urging him on, wanting us to have our orgasms at the same time. I finally gave in to my own pulsing waves of sweetness, signaling Edward it was his turn. Bucking and moaning, I could feel the surge of his ejaculation inside me.

Saturated with sweat, my skin glistened in the firelight. With Edward lying on top of me, I felt sated, pleasure seeping from every pore of my body. Sweat dripped from his chin onto my neck, and he turned on his side, allowing my body the freedom to bask in the firelight.

"That was more than great sex, Brandy."

"There are no words to describe how you make me feel. I felt like I travelled to another place, another time. I love you so much, Edward."

He sat up, gazing down at me lying in front of the fireplace. "Are those the same words you said to your husband?"

"Actually, no, I didn't. And tonight's been so special for me." I turned away from him, facing the flaming logs, watching them flicker and burn.

"I'm sorry. It's just my jealousy rearing its ugly head, I guess."

He gently rolled me over to face him and kissed me generously and slowly. By the time he leaned back, I was out of breath. He rested his head on his hand and gazed intently into the flames.

"What are you thinking?" she said.

"Do you really want to know?" I nodded. "About how much I love Jessica. Everything about her makes me feel, I don't know what you'd call it—awed, thankful, in love? I look at her and I can't believe she's my daughter. Is that how you feel?"

"Yeah. There's something humbling or just plain unbelievable about giving birth, bringing a new life into the world. It was a miracle. One minute my child's inside my body moving around, the next minute, she's in *our* world. And she wouldn't be here without you."

His eyes focused intently on the flames, still spinning and leaping toward the chimney. "Blows my mind. If anything ever happened to her, I'd feel like killing myself. Is that weird?"

"No, it's not. There's a force inside me that's so strong, if she's sick and I'm worried about her, something just takes over me, like a bolt of electricity running through every vein in my body. They talk about being a mother bear with her cubs?" I laughed. "It's true."

Edward leaned down, pressing his lips over mine, prying them open with his tongue, searching for mine. I gave back as good as I got, matching his intensity, until we found ourselves once again making love in the light of the burning embers.

It was late and I had to get home so Edward drove the few minutes to my house, where he pulled into the driveway. I turned to face him before opening the car door. "I forgot to ask you something. Cecilia, Perry and I are hosting a Christmas party on December twenty-third. I'd like you to come, but Weston will be there. I didn't want to keep this from you. I'm through with ever being deceitful. But I don't expect you to be there, so don't feel obligated. It could be an uncomfortable situation for you."

"Don't worry about me, Brandy. I can handle myself, and I'm sure Weston will be civil to me. I don't expect him to be my newest BFF." He grinned.

"I knew you'd inject your own personal brand of humor into the situation. I'll talk to you before the party." I leaned over and kissed him goodbye then jumped out of the car and ran into the house.

It was past midnight, and Stephanie was studying at the dining room table. I quickly paid her and sent her off to hitch a ride home from Edward. I had a lot to think about after tonight.

Chapter 41

The next day I phoned Weston at work, expecting to leave a message on his voice mail, and was surprised when he answered after the first ring.

"Brandy, it's good to hear from you. I hope you called to tell me… something."

"Actually, I'm phoning about the Christmas party. I know Perry already told you about it. He said you're coming, right?"

"I wouldn't miss it. Are you free for dinner before then?"

I paused for a few seconds and took a deep breath. "I'll be completely up front with you, West. I need more time to think about you and me, and about Edward and his involvement in Jessica's life and my life. Right now, I need to be alone. I'm trusting you'll support me in this and not be upset about it."

"Of course I support you. And I understand. I won't bug you about it. When you're ready to talk, can I trust that you'll discuss your decision with me?" His tone seemed friendly and upbeat and I was relieved I wouldn't have to argue with him about my decision to be left alone.

"Yes, I promise. And Weston? It's only fair you know Edward's coming to the party."

A beat of silence ensued. "I wasn't expecting that."

"I'll understand if you don't want to attend. I told him the same thing and he still wants to come."

"If he's okay with it, I'm okay with it."

Weston had manifested a "macho" side of his personality a few times since I'd known him, but I'd never been in a situation in which two men were vying for my attention—one of them my husband, the other the father of my child. And I wasn't sure how Weston would react given this particular scenario. However, he'd agreed to come to the Christmas party anyway, and I'd just have to deal with my feeling uncomfortable about it.

"All right. I've gotta go, Weston. Take care of yourself." And we said our goodbyes. This could be the most unusual Christmas party ever.

Cecilia and I talked on the phone almost every day. She was enjoying motherhood and Amylynn was a healthy, happy baby. I'd explained everything that had happened between Weston and me, and Edward and me too. She enjoyed hearing about my personal drama. It reminded her of the soap operas she watched while nursing Amylynn! I didn't know whether to take it as a compliment or not. At times, it seemed I was living the life of one of those characters too.

All the hustle and bustle preparing for our party didn't leave me much free time to think about my predicament. But I'd made myself a promise, my own personal deadline. I'd make a decision by my birthday, February fifth: Weston or Edward. I couldn't continue to see them both. It was like riding an emotional roller coaster. I had a husband I still loved but when I needed him and the chips were down he'd run away. At a time of marital crisis he'd let me down and now I couldn't trust him. And I also loved Edward, the father of my child, who'd been there when I had no one else to turn to and had stuck by me ever since.

As the days went by the murky curtain inside my brain became more transparent, my thoughts and feelings distinct. My head began to clear.

The night of our party, the weather was crisp and clear, no rain in sight. Our neighbors, Angeline and Roger Morris, and their two children, Erik and Lauren, were the first to arrive. They were a great family, always waved to me when I saw them, helped me out numerous times when my faucet leaked or my heater malfunctioned.

Then there was Michael, the only single guy on our street, who arrived with his girlfriend, Lani. Our most talkative neighbor, Michael was constantly on the lookout when I stepped into the front yard. He'd rush across the street and tell me about his newest job endeavor which would invariably not pan out. His intentions were well meaning, but he didn't have the drive needed to stick it out to the end, always searching for the next new opportunity.

Nicole and Jamie came over right after Michael and Lani. They were a cute couple, just married, in their early twenties, whose only child, Sidney, was a golden retriever on whom they lavished all their attention. They could always be seen either on a walk to the dog park, or washing Sidney on their front lawn with a bucket of soapy water and a hose.

Cecilia and Perry Saxton were just walking up to the front door, Amylynn in her stroller, when I heard Edward's Porsche round the corner. He was parking in one of the few spots left on the block when I noticed Weston's truck coming down the street. Wouldn't you know they'd arrive at the same time! I'd hoped to keep them separated, but I guess that wouldn't happen now.

After hugging Cecilia and Perry, and nuzzling little Amylynn, I noticed Edward coming up behind them. He gave me a quick kiss on the mouth before coming inside then Weston strode up the pathway a few feet away. He might have seen Edward kissing me, but I made a concerted effort to act nonchalant, greeting him warmly with a hug.

His facial expression said a thousand words. He wasn't happy, but I told him Cecilia and Perry and a few of the neighbors he knew were in the front room, grabbed his hand, and brought him along with me. Guiding him to where Perry sat with Cecilia, I left him to chat with them.

If I could make it to the end of this party without Weston and Edward getting too close to each other, everything would be fine. Truthfully, I didn't believe Edward would say or do anything impolite or inappropriate. Given his career as a criminal attorney, having to speak in front of a courtroom filled with jurors and a judge, he was accustomed to holding his emotions in check, not giving away what lurked behind his attorney facade.

Weston, I'd learned from experience at the last party, could be overprotective of what he thought of as "his." And that would be me. I'd seen him angry several times in the past, when he talked about couples, love, and infidelity. I recalled him getting pretty hot under the collar when he told me the story of a friend of his whose wife had been having an affair. He definitely had hot spots when it came to the women he loved and I hoped everything would go smoothly tonight. However, I had no clue what lay ahead.

Chapter 42

I was in the kitchen pulling a baked Alaska out of the freezer to thaw, when Edward came into the room and grabbed me from behind. Nuzzling my neck, whispering how much he missed me, I suddenly heard Weston's boots clunking on the kitchen floor. He'd worn those boots since I'd met him years ago, and the sound they made was indelibly etched on my brain.

Both Edward and I glanced up at the same time, caught in a position no explanation could possibly change. I knew exactly what it looked like—a lover's embrace. Edward stood behind me, his arms wrapped around my body with his hands splayed beneath my navel, his head buried deep in the side of my neck. Oh, did this look bad!

Edward quickly backed away from me, sticking his hands in his pants' pockets and walked toward the back door. It all happened so suddenly it was hard for me to explain later to Cecilia, when she asked me about it. Weston took two long strides around the island in the middle of the kitchen, fists clenched at his sides. Before Edward could react, Weston's right arm shot out and he punched him in the face, knocking him backwards into the screen door. Edward rolled head over heels, slamming the door into the railing, flying down the back steps.

I stood rooted to the floor, fingers covering my mouth. "Oh my God, what have you done?" I whispered. Rushing past Weston, I ran down the stairs to find Edward lying on his back at the bottom near the lawn, unconscious.

I had no idea how badly he'd been injured—a concussion, broken neck or back? I'd never been this angry with Weston. He was standing at the top of the stairs, looking down at me. I leaned over Edward, knowing I shouldn't move him.

"Call 9-1-1!" I yelled, glancing up at Weston, tears coursing down my cheeks. "Call an ambulance!"

I picked up one of Edward's hands, bringing it to my lips where I laid a kiss on his palm, glaring at Weston, challenging him to act. He squinted at me, his lips set in a tight grimace, hesitated a few seconds, then turned and walked back into the kitchen.

Cecilia and Perry rushed past him down to where I knelt sobbing, holding Edward's hand, calling to him over and over, hoping he'd wake up. He wasn't moving, his eyelids weren't fluttering—nothing.

Cecilia's voice broke me out of my stunned state. "Brandy, he has a pulse. It's slow but I can feel it. Listen, I hear the ambulance. It'll only be a few seconds before they're here. Don't worry, honey. Come on, be strong."

I had to gather my thoughts, get a grip on my emotions. I had a houseful of guests, some of them children, forming a ring around Edward and me, looking terrified, not understanding what was going on.

"Cecilia, can you and Perry herd everyone away from here?"

Cecilia stood up and ushered the children and adults into the front yard while Perry ran up the stairs to explain what was happening to any guests who were still inside. At the periphery of my mind lurked the knowledge the police would ask me what had happened. If I told the truth my house would turn into a crime scene, all of my neighbors would be questioned, statements taken. No one but Weston and me had been privy to what had gone on in the kitchen.

Three paramedics and four firemen jogged around the corner. I immediately stood and backed away, letting them take charge of the situation. I heard murmurings as if in the distance while I watched the paramedics listen to Edward's heart with a stethoscope.

A voice interrupted my scrambled thoughts. "Mrs. Chambers?"

I turned to face a young looking policeman, holding a small notepad, pencil poised above the blank sheet of paper. "Yes, I'm Brandy Chambers."

"Could you tell me what went on here?" he said politely.

They placed a brace behind Edward's neck then carefully moved him onto a gurney. "This man," I pointed over at Edward. "His name is Edward Barnes." I paused. I had to make a decision, truth or tale? "I don't know what happened. You'll have to ask Mr. Barnes." I figured if Edward wanted to press charges that would be his decision, not mine.

The paramedics unfolded the gurney to a standing position then rolled it away toward the back gate.

"Was anyone around to see what happened, Mrs. Chambers?"

I shook my head. "I don't know. Maybe. Listen, I'm sorry but I have to check on my baby upstairs. Would you excuse me?"

He nodded, and I sprinted up the back stairs, frantically searching for Stephanie or Cecilia. I met Cecilia in the hallway and pulled her aside.

"Could you take care of Jessica for me or find Stephanie and ask her if she—"

She took me by the shoulders and gave me a quick shake. "Don't worry about a thing, Brandy. Go be with Edward. Stephanie and I will take care of the baby. I'll stay here."

I ran to the front of the house and found the paramedics about to shut the doors to the back of the ambulance. I asked if I could ride in the back with him and they readily agreed.

The ambulance pulled up to the Emergency Room at Alameda Hospital in less than three minutes, only six blocks away. I walked alongside the stretcher as the paramedics guided it through the automatic doors leading to the E.R. That was as far as they allowed me inside. The triage nurse told me she would return and inform me of his status as soon as possible.

I sat down in a hard plastic chair in the far corner of the waiting room, worried to death he'd either be paralyzed or fall into a coma or die, and felt sick to my stomach. Taking several deep breaths to fight the nausea, I tried to think positive thoughts: he'd be all right, he'd make it through this, people didn't always die because they fell down a few stairs.

It happened in the movies all the time—people stood up, brushed themselves off, and walked away from this type of thing. I had to believe that would happen to Edward. He'd probably been knocked unconscious and would be awakening soon. I tried to feel it, *really* believe it, but a corner of my consciousness kept repeating, "He's going to die. He's going to die."

Inhaling deep breaths, I placed all negative thoughts in my little box and mentally laid it aside. I focused on my folded hands lying in my lap and began an internal mantra, "He's going to live, he'll be all right, he'll make it through this, he's going to live," over and over.

I didn't know how long I sat whispering to myself, taking deep breaths, concentrating on filling my mind with positive thoughts, picturing Edward alive, walking toward me, healthy and strong. I forced myself to believe it, willed myself into thinking it was reality, when someone called my name. I looked up and noticed a young woman dressed in light blue scrubs holding open the oversized metal door to the E.R., motioning for me to come over.

"Brandy Chambers?" When I nodded, she continued. "You can see Mr. Barnes now."

"You mean he's alive?" I ran over to her, my hands and legs shaking so badly, I was afraid I'd collapse. She nodded her assent. I bent my head toward the floor and sobbed.

She put her arm around my shoulders and gave me a quick squeeze. "It's okay. The doctor says he has a mild concussion. We'll keep him here overnight. If he's doing well tomorrow morning, he'll be released. He's asking for you, so go on in. Let him see a smile on your face, though, will you?" She grinned and motioned me toward a room at the end of the hall.

I straightened up, standing erect and tall, tousled my hair with my two hands, wiped the tears from my cheeks, and shook my head several times to perk myself up. After taking one huge breath, I walked into the room she'd indicated. He was lying on a bed in the middle of a small room with his eyes closed, a serene look on his face. I stood by the side of his bed and picked up his hand. Tears poured down my cheeks.

"Edward? Oh, God, Edward." I laid my head on his chest and cried, saying his name over and over, feeling the steady beating of his heart through the thin hospital gown. Fingers reached through the back of my hair and gently massaged my scalp.

"Brandy?"

I looked up, and he smiled that gorgeous smile of his, that devastatingly killer smile that reached all the way to his unbelievably blue-blue eyes.

"I thought you were going to die. I never thought I'd talk to you again. God, I love you. Please don't leave me."

"Is this an inappropriate time to ask you to marry me again?" He grinned, flashing ultra-white teeth.

"My God, you can never, ever talk without making a joke, you're incorrigible. My divorce isn't even final yet."

"Doesn't mean you can't answer me 'yes' or 'no'. I could

probably expedite your divorce proceedings for you. I know people in high places."

"You goofball. I think the damage to your brain has seriously impaired your thinking. How about dealing with the crisis of the moment before anything else?"

"Did the police question you about what happened?"

I could feel my face start to flush and turned aside then Edward's hand gently tilted my head toward him. "Brandy?"

"I didn't know what to say. I couldn't think straight. I didn't know if you were going to live or die or be paralyzed. I was worried about your reputation, the time you'd want to spend pursuing this if you wanted to press charges. I wasn't sure what you'd want to do so I… I sort of implied I hadn't seen what happened."

He cupped the side of my face in his hand and smiled. "It's okay, Brandy. Maybe Weston and I can work out a deal. He files the final divorce papers, I don't press charges. Sounds like a win-win situation to me. What do you think?"

I shook my head, a smile on my face. He could make me laugh at the most inappropriate times. I placed a light kiss on his lips, not wanting to upset his concussed head. Keeping his hand behind my head, his fingers tangled through the waves of my hair, and he pulled me down gently for a kiss, this one deeper and more thorough than the one before. This was an "I want to make love to you" kind of kiss, and I groaned, not only with pleasure, but with relief he was alive.

I felt so lucky to have him in my life, luckier now because he'd be in my future. I'd already decided to call Claudette the following day and ask her to contact Weston's attorney. I wanted a divorce. This was the last straw. I hadn't led Weston to believe he and I would get back together. His proprietary attitude upset me and taking out his anger and jealousy on Edward was completely inappropriate.

They asked me to leave so Edward could be transferred to his own room, so I kissed him goodbye and walked home, needing to clear my head. When I reached the house I found Cecilia and Stephanie sitting together on the front room couch, sipping coffee and talking.

"How's Edward?" they asked in unison.

I slumped down on the nearest armchair and let out a whoosh of air. "He'll be all right. It wasn't as bad as it looked. He has a concussion, and they'll keep him overnight for observation. They plan to let him go home tomorrow."

"Thank goodness," Stephanie said. "I thought he might be, well… dead."

"You aren't the only one." I smiled at her, unbelievably relieved.

"What in God's name happened Brandy?" Cecilia asked.

I leaned my head back and closed my eyes. "Weston saw Edward and me in the kitchen." I looked over at the two women who were privy to the drama in my life. "Edward was kissing me on the neck." Cecilia's eyes widened. Stephanie leaned forward in her seat. "Weston went ballistic, socked Edward in the face and he fell out the back door and down the stairs."

They turned toward each other then back at me.

"Is Edward going to press charges?" Stephanie asked.

I shook my head. "He told me he'd make a deal with Weston. He won't press charges if Weston files the final divorce papers."

Cecilia's eyebrows shot up. "Edward must really be in love with you, Brandy."

I nodded.

"Do you love him?" Stephanie whispered.

Tears sprang to my eyes. I'd been in an emotional tailspin and felt drained from all that had happened. I looked down at the floor, thinking about Weston and Edward and Jessica and me. One thought stuck out prominently over all others. "Yes," I replied quietly. I'd meant it when I told Edward in the hospital that I loved him. I glanced up quickly. "*Yes!*" I shouted.

I could hardly see through the blur of tears. Both women popped up off the couch and came over to where I sat. Cecilia plopped down on one side of me, Stephanie on the other. They each put an arm around my shoulders and gave me a hug.

"I told you you'd know when the time was right," Cecilia said, squeezing me close to her side. "Didn't I?"

I nodded then looked over at her. "You sure did."

Chapter 43

Edward was released from the hospital the next morning, Christmas Eve, and he agreed to come to my house to recuperate. I could tell he was antsy and he didn't want to be pampered or rest in a bed. The murder case he'd been working on for months was scheduled to begin the day after Christmas. I didn't want him to push himself too hard, but he was extraordinarily stubborn when it came to his work and anxious to be fully prepared for trial.

We'd only been home a few hours when the doorbell rang. A young man holding a brown envelope stood on the front step.

"Are you Mrs. Brandy Chambers?"

"Yes, I am."

He extended his arm with the envelope and said, "You've been legally served." He turned and walked away.

I undid the clasp, pulled out several sheets of paper, and was confronted with three words in big bold letters: Dissolution of Marriage. Weston had obviously talked with his attorney that morning and gone ahead with the divorce.

Now I wouldn't have to phone Claudette—one less call to make, one less item on my to-do list. I physically and mentally let out a sigh of relief. Though I'd already made the decision to go ahead with the divorce, the fact Weston had initiated the final proceedings was a validation for me. He must have known his behavior at the Christmas party would be the final nail in his coffin, and decided not to fight the inevitability of our final separation.

I played nurse to Edward all day, wanting him to recuperate quickly so he could go back to work. The murder trial weighed heavily on his mind and he was anxious to have it behind him. I couldn't imagine how he did it—knowing his client had killed a five-year-old girl, yet believing his job was to prove him innocent.

He'd explained the time it might take for witnesses to testify and the jury to deliberate. It could be a day or it could take weeks then the verdict would be read and it would be over. He was confident his client would be found innocent and after the verdict came in, he'd literally and mentally close the file and focus on his other clients.

After fixing dinner, I went up to my bedroom and found him sleeping, sprawled across the bed, legs tangled in the sheets. I knelt down next to the bed and watched him, grateful he'd only received a mild concussion and nothing more severe after his fall.

"Edward," I whispered, knowing he'd sleep through the night and miss dinner if I didn't wake him up.

His eyes fluttered open, and he smiled. "Hey," he mumbled.

"You've been asleep for hours. I made dinner. Would you like me to bring it to you in bed?"

He sat up, leaning back against the pillows. "No, thanks. I'd like to get out of bed and shower, walk around."

I grinned. "You don't know how to do nothing, do you?"

He shook his head. "Tomorrow's Christmas, Brandy. I have a few errands I need to take care of."

I sat on the side of the bed and took hold of his hand. "You can't act like nothing happened to you. You have a concussion. You're supposed to take it easy."

"I feel fine. I won't go jogging or to the gym to lift weights. I'll come downstairs and eat dinner with you after I take a shower." He leaned over and kissed me lightly on the lips. "Then I have to go out for a short while."

I shook my head and let out a sigh. "Okay. I'll be in the kitchen. Take your time. There are clean towels and shampoo and everything you need in the bathroom."

I could hear the shower running as I set the table and took the vegetable casserole out of the oven. I'd also made a salad and was pouring a couple of glasses of sparkling water when he walked in. His hair was slicked back and he had a two-day stubble covering his cheeks. I'd brought him a change of clothes from his house and his jeans hung low on his hips, a white t-shirt setting off his dark hair and mustache. He looked sexy as hell.

I set a plate in front of him and he waited for me to be seated before taking his first bite.

"This is delicious. I'm glad I didn't have to spend Christmas Eve eating hospital food."

Laughing, I agreed with him. "Me too. I guess you're stuck spending Christmas day with me and Jessica."

A grin graced his gorgeous face. "I consider that a Christmas gift, Brandy, so you don't have to give me another present."

"Sorry, I already have something special for you. It's under the Christmas tree."

"And I have to go out for just a few minutes." I opened my mouth to protest. He placed a finger over my lips. "Stop. I'll be gone for less than a half hour, I swear. The stores are open until at least nine o'clock and I know exactly what I want so it won't take me any time at all."

I raised my eyebrows. "You promise you won't go to the office to work on the murder case?"

Putting up his right hand, palm facing me, he said, "I promise. I'll be home in thirty minutes, Mom."

"God, you're exasperating. But you've got to take it easy. And tomorrow as well. You were just discharged from the hospital for God's sake."

"And I feel fine, Brandy. I'll rest up tomorrow and be ready to go to trial the day after."

There was no shaking his resolve. He was a very determined man. I couldn't tie him down and force him to stay in bed, his body would tell him if he was overdoing it anyway. He left shortly after dinner, and I fed Jessica and rocked her to sleep.

When he entered the front door thirty minutes later, his face lit up when he crossed into the front room. "I always love Christmas time and your place feels so homey."

A wealth of ornaments hung on the Christmas tree, tiny glittering lights throughout its branches. Stockings were strung on the mantel above the fireplace and the scent of evergreen permeated the front room.

"Thank you. I had fun getting the house ready for the party but I couldn't have done it without Cecilia and Perry. We worked for hours the night before so it would really have that holiday feeling."

"Why don't I build a fire?" he asked. "I notice you have logs right here. Then we can cuddle on the sofa and wait for Santa."

Taking his hand, I led him to the couch and pushed him down onto the cushions. "*I'll* build the fire. You sit here and watch me. You have to take it easy, Edward. You're so stubborn."

Grabbing me around the waist, he pulled me down on top of him. "I can be stubborn about a lot of things. And one of them is you. How many times do I have to ask you to marry me?"

I wriggled out of his grasp and rolled onto the rug. "I have to put these logs on the grate and light newspaper under them. I promise to discuss this with you tomorrow. We've both had a trying two days, Edward. You just got out of the hospital. Let's enjoy the peace and quiet of our first Christmas Eve together."

"Agreed," he said, grabbing the quilt off the back of the couch. He settled into the couch and watched as the flames licked the edges of the paper and the wood crackled and spit.

I sat down next to him and he pulled the blanket over my legs, wrapping his arm around my shoulders. "I love you, Brandy. I don't know what I can do to prove it to you."

I kissed him then leaned my head on the back of the couch. "You don't have to do anything to prove it to me. I see it in everything you say to me, how you treat me, the way you are when we're together. I just want to be with you right now, Edward—no heavy discussions, no mention of Weston. I want to watch the flames and let them lull me to sleep. I'm mentally drained."

He pulled me in closer and I laid my head on his chest, snuggling against his firm muscles, reveling in his manly scent.

"Me too. It feels so good having you here in my arms. I'll enjoy this time we have together, no pressure. Merry Christmas, by the way."

My eyes were closed and I could feel myself drifting asleep, listening to his voice, feeling the warmth of the fire's blaze. "Merry Christmas," I whispered.

Chapter 44

I woke up the next morning still lying on the couch, Edward's arm draped over my back, my head on his chest. Gently lowering myself onto the rug, I tiptoed into the kitchen to make us coffee. I brought in a tray filled with fresh croissants, butter, strawberry jam, and two latte's, and set it on the coffee table.

Leaning over, I placed my lips softly over his then gently pried them open with my tongue, deepening the kiss. His eyes fluttered open and he wrapped his arms around me, pulling me on top of him.

"Did Santa come last night?" he whispered.

"Let me check." I sat up then walked over to the tree, kneeling down beside it. "Well, I'll be darned, this one has your name on it." Bringing the tiny box over to where he sat on the couch, I placed it on the cushion next to him.

"Merry Christmas, Edward. I hope you'll like your gift."

He smiled and picked up the box. After pushing aside the red curlicue bow, he tore off the wrapping and slowly opened the lid. Pulling aside the white tissue, he looked down to find a small white card with my writing scrawled across the front. He mouthed the words, "Yes, I will." He paused then looked up at me. "It says, 'Yes, I wi—' Oh, Jesus, do you mean, yes, you'll marry me?"

I smiled a Cheshire cat grin. "Yes."

He pushed me back onto the couch, kissing me deeply and completely, his hand digging between the cushions. Sitting up, I asked, "What are you doing?"

Pulling out a small gold-wrapped box with a red velvet bow tied around it, he placed it in my lap. "Merry Christmas, Brandy."

I untied the bow then gently unwrapped the box, revealing a small blue velvet jewelry case—the perfect size for a pair of earrings. But, when I flipped open the lid, there lay a huge diamond ring.

"Will you marry me, Brandy?"

Tears welled up in my eyes then rolled down my cheeks. "It would make me the happiest woman on the planet."

He knelt down and took the ring out of the box. Placing it on my left hand, he leaned in and kissed me. "On my birthday?"

I nodded. "On your birthday. February first. Do you think the trial will be over by then?"

"It starts tomorrow, and I'd bet it doesn't last more than a month. But if it goes beyond that, I'll ask for a motion to delay for a couple of days so we can get married. I want you to be my wife, Brandy." He paused. "What about the divorce?"

"I received the final divorce papers yesterday. Weston must have talked with his attorney immediately." I raised my left hand, turning it left and right in front of us, admiring the diamond's sparkling facets. "Dennis's Designs on Park Street, right?"

He grinned. "How'd you know?"

"Because I've walked by the place a hundred times and always stop to admire their jewelry. He creates all his own rings, you know."

"Which is why I knew exactly where to go. I'm an Alameda homeboy, Brandy. Come on now."

"You know what? I don't want to talk. I just want to sit here with you under the blanket and make out. Are you up for it?"

He reached over and took my hand, placing it in his lap. "Did you ask me if I was up for it?"

I could feel what he was getting at and burst out laughing. "You are too funny. I love that about you. Life is serious enough without making all our moments together solemn, right?"

His face suddenly turned thoughtful. He lay sideways on the couch, bringing me beside him. "I don't want to talk either, no jokes—nothing. I want to simply look at you. Then I want to make love to you. Just like we did at my house in front of the fire last time, remember?"

"You think I'd forget? That was the most out of body experience I've ever had with a man. I—"

He placed his index finger on my lips. "Shhh. Don't say another word."

Then, so slowly, like watching a movie on slow speed, he undid the buttons on my shirt, revealing the thin silk camisole beneath. He slid his tongue in and around my navel, pulled the camisole over my head, then massaged my breasts. Walking tiny kisses up and down my stomach, he squeezed my nipples, turning them round and round with his fingers. I arched my back, whispering his name. He replaced his hands with his mouth on first one breast, then the other.

I needed the release burning in my groin. Reaching for the zipper of his pants, I ripped it down, feeling inside for his full and erect member, stiff as steel beneath his briefs. I remembered the pleasure he'd brought me the last time we'd made love and I couldn't wait to experience it again.

He quickly untied the bow on the waistline of my sweatpants, shoving them past my knees along with my bikini underwear. I didn't waste a second on foreplay. Edward appeared more than ready, and I didn't have the patience to wait. I placed him between my legs and he glided inside me. After the first careful thrust, he began a frenzied pattern of entry, then partial exit, driving me crazy with needing him, wanting every inch of him inside me.

I didn't want him to stop his relentless thrusts, moving me toward the waves of my orgasm. He could feel my squeezing undulations surrounding him and I knew he'd soon experience his own heady release. Looking down at me with those blue eyes, he mouthed, "I love you," as he continued pushing faster, his breathing labored, his chest heaving with exertion. I hoped he'd never stop, wishing this would never end.

I cupped my hands over his back side, pushing him deeper, until he arched his back, head toward the ceiling, and groaned my name. His body shuddered, then stilled, and he slumped back onto his side.

This time differed from the last. It felt as though he was trying to crawl inside me with his body. And I needed him to fill me up completely with his. I was wonderfully satisfied. If I could do this every day of my life until I died, I would know I'd been given a special gift. Making love with this man was otherworldly, transporting me to a place close to nirvana.

His breathing slowed and his hand moved up and down the side of my arm. He reached up and circled my lips with his thumb and whispered, "What just happened?"

I stared unblinking into his eyes. "I'm not sure. I've never been there before. With anyone."

"It was scary. I don't remember what was going through my mind. I couldn't think about anything except how much I wanted you, how good you felt, how much I loved making you come. I was here, but not here."

I didn't have anything I could add. Making love with Edward was something I had no words for, the most right I'd felt with any man.

He was right for me. He was the one. I knew it now. I had my answer.

Chapter 45

Edward was engrossed 24/7 in the murder trial, and I was deeply involved in my third book. I hadn't heard from Brent about whether his editor friend, Mark Stefano, had any news about Harper Collins' interest in my second novel. However, since it could likely take three or more months I tried to put it on my mental back burner and engage my mind in writing. Jessica stayed awake longer, and I enjoyed my time with her. I found it comforting when she sat in her baby seat next to me while I worked on my MacBook.

When New Year's Eve rolled around and Edward looked as tired as I felt, we decided to postpone any celebrating until our wedding. We made a huge bowl of popcorn and settled in front of the television to watch *Activities Around the Globe*. We found it fascinating, the footage skipping from the U.S. to Jerusalem, to London, New York, and Chicago, hundreds of people dancing in the streets, bands playing, kids running wild—an eye-opening experience, learning how other cultures and countries brought in the New Year.

At eleven p.m., I looked over at him, his head on my shoulder. He'd already fallen asleep, and I smiled to myself. What a lively pair we made! In our thirties and already acting like an old married couple. After the ball dropped in Times Square, I gently slipped my shoulder out from under his head, replaced it with a pillow, and went to bed. Jessica had been asleep since seven o'clock and the house lay silent.

At nine a.m. I got up and realized she hadn't wakened for her regular six a.m. feeding. She gurgled in her crib, and I picked her up and crept downstairs. Edward was still asleep. I made sure not to make any noise as I brewed coffee, warmed up a croissant in the microwave for breakfast, and heated up a bottle for Jess. He'd already told me he was going into the office though it was New Year's Day. I had no specific plans of my own other than watching the parade, taking a nap, playing with Jess, or reading a book.

We'd agreed to have a small wedding at my house with a group of close friends. So far the only people who were aware of our engagement were those working in Edward's law office. I planned to phone Cecilia and a few others today, guessing most people would be hanging out at home, tired from a big night out or just taking their last free day before returning to work.

Tomorrow my intentions were to tackle the logistics of the wedding—a Justice of the Peace, flowers, the caterer, and lastly, my dress. I wanted to go into the city with Cecilia to select my gown. The wedding would be in a month, and I didn't have a lot of time left.

I was writing a to-do list when Edward's hands encircled my waist from behind, his face nuzzling my neck.

"Good morning, beautiful. Your couch is more comfortable than your bed."

I turned around, wrapping my arms around his neck. "You said you'd be moving back to your house tonight. Do you still plan on doing that?"

Pulling back, he asked, "Why? You have someone coming to take my place when I leave?"

"Stop kidding around," I laughed. "Seriously, I have to make a few phone calls. There are people I want to invite to the wedding. I'd like to sit on the couch and do nothing, but I have a lot left to do."

He began nibbling my ear and whispered, "Then I won't feel so jealous 'cause I have to work all day. And I mean *all* day, into the night, and then some."

He sat down at the kitchen table, and I poured him a cup of coffee.

"When do you think you'll do your summation?"

He picked up his mug, breathed in the strong scent then sipped the dark brew. "Thanks for the coffee." He smiled. "Probably in a week. Then the jury will deliberate, we'll have our verdict, and I can take time off—to get married."

Sitting down across from him, I sighed. "You're so romantic. I hope it all goes according to your plan, babe, otherwise we'll have a slam dunk ceremony and you'll return to work the next day."

He patted my hand and shook his head. "Not to worry. I've done this more times than I can count. Like I told you, I can always file for a motion to delay for a few days, which would give us enough time to have our wedding and slip away for a short honeymoon. We're getting married on my birthday, Brandy. I promise."

He left after finishing his coffee, and I took a few moments to look over my list again. I decided to call Cecilia and invite her to the wedding. She picked up immediately but didn't sound like her normal happy self.

"Hey, it's Brandy. What's going on? You sound weird."

"Amylynn's sick. She has a 104.5 temperature and I'm waiting for the advice nurse to call us back. I'm so worried about her, it's making me sick."

Now I understood why she'd sounded funny. She must be distraught. "Have you given her anything for the fever?"

"No. I wasn't sure what the best thing would be, whether to let her body fight it off naturally or give her some aspirin. I just can't think straight. She's our first child, Brandy, and—"

"Look, Cece," I interrupted. "You've got to keep a cool head, all right?" I said calmly. "I'm not a doctor but Jessica's gotten sick a few times, so I'll tell you what to do, right now, while you're waiting for the nurse to call. Do you have any baby Tylenol, not aspirin, but acetaminophen for infants?"

"I could send Perry to the drug store to pick some up—"

"No," I interjected. "I have some right here."

"Perry's on his way over right now," she said, sounding anxious. "I had you on speakerphone."

"Great. Just follow the dosage on the bottle. I'm not trying to alarm you, but a temperature that high is nothing to mess around with. You have to get it down at least a few degrees then she'll feel much better. Does she have any other symptoms, a cough, runny nose?"

"No, it's so scary. I don't know what's wrong with her."

"Don't freak out. I've been there, honey, and felt the same way you do. Amylynn will be fine. You just have to reduce the fever. It's your number one priority. The advice nurse can take over from there."

"Thanks, Brandy."

There was a knock on the door. "Perry's here." I opened the front door then rushed to get the Tylenol while holding the phone to my ear.

"Did you call to tell me something?" she asked.

"No, just to chat. Call me if you need *anything*."

Grabbing the bottle I raced back to the foyer and placed it in Perry's outstretched hand. He looked like he hadn't slept—his eyes were red and his clothes rumpled. I gave him a pat on the back and he ran next door.

I could relate to the fear they were feeling, and it felt good to be able to help out with their sick child. Inviting them to the wedding right now was inappropriate. I also wanted to set up a date to look for a wedding dress and ask Cecilia to be my maid of honor, but I'd leave that for another day too.

The clock was ticking on my to-do list, and I was anxious to cross off at least one item. But then I caught myself thinking this and guilt overwhelmed me. Here they were dealing with a very sick infant, and I was worried about when she'd be free to help me select my wedding dress? I took a mental step back and counted my blessings. Did I have a reason to be worried about my upcoming wedding? I didn't think so. I poured myself another cup of java and went into the front room where I planned to hold Jessica and watch the parade.

Chapter 46

I arranged for Stephanie to come by one morning a week so I could jog around the streets of Alameda and have some much needed "alone time." Since she was available, I took advantage of her willingness to babysit whenever she didn't have a class.

I'd slacked off during the holidays, and my New Year's resolution was a personal promise to exercise every day no matter what was happening around me. If I wanted to stay healthy I had to get out there and raise my heart rate. And using the jogging stroller was a godsend, allowing Jessica to get out in the fresh air and sunshine, and me to think about my book.

Edward had made a similar promise—to return to the gym, working with weights, and running on the treadmill. He was under so much stress, exercising was the only reliable way to maintain his sanity during the trial. When he called me on Friday, he sounded upbeat and happy.

"My summation is next week. The jury will begin their deliberations after that. So far we're on track with my plan for a February first wedding. My predictions are turning out to be right."

"You are such a conceited brat," I teased. "Of course you're right. What would *I* know about the law? I'm a simple *housefrau*, with nothing to do but wait for her man to come home and tell me what to do. And how would you like your shirts ironed, creases down both sides of the sleeves?"

"I assume you're joking," he laughed. "You're a complicated woman, Brandy, and I don't pretend to have you figured out yet."

"I'm kidding. Now you know how it feels when you're trying to be serious and someone is always making a joke."

"All right, all right. I'll try not to kid around so much," he said seriously.

"Oh, come on now. I wouldn't want to change a thing about you.

You're perfect just the way you are. If you were any different you wouldn't be the man I fell in love with."

"So by process of deduction, you wouldn't love me as much if I wasn't such a wise-ass."

"God, you're incorrigible! Stop with the attorney jargon. Can I come listen to your summation next week?"

"It's a public trial. If you have the free time it wouldn't bother me to have you there. And if we break early maybe you and I can have a quickie in the back seat of my Porsche."

"Geez. Could I coerce you into having a serious conversation?"

"You could coerce me into doing more than having a serious conversation."

"Okay, I'm done," I sighed then chuckled. "I have to get off the phone. I'd like to hear your summation and if my being there won't distract you I'll see you in court."

He'd be working through the weekend so we said our goodbyes. I looked forward to seeing him in his element, having never witnessed an honest-to-goodness trial before. The closest I'd come was watching Judge Judy on the television.

I'd called Cecilia two days ago to see how Amylynn was doing. She'd told me her fever had gone down to one hundred degrees and they'd taken her to the doctor who diagnosed her as having a virus. She'd probably be better in a few days. I phoned her, and the answering machine picked up so I left a message for her to call me back.

Later that evening, after having put Jessica to bed, I sat down to relax and watch a Hallmark movie. The moment I turned on the television the phone rang. I contemplated letting the message machine pick up, feeling too lazy to get off the couch, but it could be Edward or Cecilia, so I answered it and heard Cecilia's voice. I surmised she must have a terrible cold because she sounded congested along with a deep scratchy voice.

"Amylynn's really sick." Her voice quivered and I could hear her crying.

"What's going on?" I asked, remembering how helpless I felt whenever Jessica was ill.

"We're at Alameda Hospital and they just admitted her through the E.R. They don't know what's wrong with her. Perry is beside himself, I've never seen him this upset. And I feel like I'm coming apart."

"But you told me she was getting better. When I spoke with you two days ago, her fever had gone down and you said she had a virus."

"I know. That's what the doctor told us. Then today her fever spiked again, it was 105.2 and we rushed her to the E.R. This all just happened so I've gotta go. I just wanted you to know."

"I could come over, keep you company for a while, Cece. Stephanie would be happy to babysit Jess. But I don't want to intrude—"

"No, you stay with Jessica. Perry is here and we're taking care of each other, though it's kind of like the blind leading the blind. There's nothing you can do, Brandy, and I know how much you hate hospitals because of Christine. Seriously, I'll call you when I know more."

"Okay, honey. Call me whenever you can." And we hung up.

Life could sure turn on a dime. One minute everything's fine, the next you find yourself wondering what the hell happened. I was so worried about Amylynn. And Cecilia and Perry, too. This was their first child, they were newcomers to the land of childhood illnesses. And it was a minefield of worry. Though I was a first-time parent myself, I'd bet it never ceased being a gut-wrenching event no matter what age—infant, toddler, kindergartner… teenager. It would probably never get any easier.

* * * *

The weekend before his summation, Edward and I talked on the phone several times. He'd be living at the office for the next few days working on the murder case.

By Sunday I hadn't heard from Cecilia so I called Stephanie to ask her to babysit and drove to Alameda Hospital. The receptionist told me Amylynn Saxton was in the Intensive Care Unit.

I rode the elevator to the third floor while my stomach clenched and my heart fluttered. The elevator pinged when it reached the ICU, and like an automaton my feet took me to the nurse's station, memories of the deaths of my parents and Christine flooding my brain. I asked the nurse if Cecilia or Perry was in their daughter's room and she informed the Saxtons of my arrival.

Several minutes later Cecilia walked down the hallway, looking like she hadn't slept in days, her black hair pulled up into a straggly pony tail, face devoid of make-up. She ran up to me, and I wrapped her in my arms.

"How is she?" I asked, hugging her.

She pulled away and swiped the tears from her cheeks. "She had a febrile seizure after we arrived at the hospital but the doctor said it's fairly common in babies if the fever's high. They had to pack her in ice to bring her temperature down but she's responding. It's down to one hundred degrees now. The doctor wants to keep her overnight just to make sure she's out of the woods."

I wrapped my arm around her shoulders and walked over to the nearest chairs. We sat down next to each other and I turned toward her. "I can't imagine how frightened you and Perry must have been. What did the doctor say caused such a high fever? Can they treat her with medication?"

She shook her head and sighed. "He said it was probably some sort of virus so giving her antibiotics wouldn't do her any good. She does have a runny nose but her chest is clear, no sign of pneumonia or an ear infection or anything."

"Jessica's doctor explained to me an infant's immune system is still developing at this stage and they often can't fight off some of the viruses going around." She nodded and gave me a half-smile. "I won't ask to see her, Cecilia. Just call me if you need anything, okay?"

She stood up and we hugged again. "I'm sorry. I know coming into this hospital brings back every awful thing about Christine's dying. Thank you for coming, Brandy."

I gave her shoulders a little shake. "Don't you dare apologize. You helped me after Christine died, you talked to me, called me every day to check on me. I want to be here for you the same way. I can handle it. You're my best friend, and I love you like a sister." I gave her a small smile and another big hug and left.

Cecilia and Perry were good, kind, and loving people and I was relieved Amylynn was recovering. They'd gone through so much to finally have her in their lives and I was glad this episode would have a happy ending for the three of them.

Chapter 47

The following day, Monday, I planned to watch Edward's summation and was excited about seeing him in action. Cell phones had to be turned off while in the courtroom, lending me a sense of being away from it all, free for just a few hours from the outside world.

I arrived early and found a seat at the front. When Edward walked in just before nine a.m. he squeezed my right shoulder as he passed by. This would be such a treat for me, I had butterflies in my stomach.

We stood when the judge entered the courtroom, the bailiff calling the court to order. The judge asked if Mr. Barnes was ready to give his summation to the jury. Edward replied, "Yes, your Honor," stood up, walked to where the jury were seated, and folded his hands behind his back.

He smiled and opened his arms wide. "Ladies and gentlemen of the jury," he said, then drew his eyebrows together and wiped the smile from his lips. "The prosecution's job is to prove my client William Carper guilty of the murder of Heidi Bailey. You may cast a vote of 'guilty' only if the prosecution has proven beyond a reasonable doubt my client committed the crime."

He turned to the side and pointed to the table nearest to him. "The prosecution states my client broke into the Bailey residence and brutally murdered Heidi Bailey with a kitchen knife." Turning back to face the jury again, he continued, "But they have not been able to prove it. There isn't a shred of evidence pointing to my client being in the Bailey house at the time Heidi Bailey was killed."

He shook his head from side to side and pointed his index finger toward the ceiling, wafting it from left to right. "My client's fingerprints were not on the murder weapon. There was no hair or clothing from my client found at the scene." He dropped his hand and put it behind his back again, still shaking his head. "There is nothing, ladies and gentlemen, *nothing* to prove my client was there at the time the crime was committed. The DNA found where the crime was committed in the Bailey house does not match my client's DNA. In fact," he pointed toward the parents of Heidi Bailey seated behind the prosecutor's table. "The DNA at the crime scene belongs to Pat and Jeff Bailey. It does not match that of William Carper." A rustling noise came from the spectator's area and I noticed Pat and Jeff Bailey being comforted by those sitting near them.

Edward walked over to where he'd been sitting, reached into his briefcase, and took out a stack of papers, waving them in front of his chest. "The evidence the prosecution has presented is completely circumstantial. The coroner has determined Heidi Bailey was killed sometime between midnight and two a.m. A neighbor claims to have seen my client walking across the lawn of the victim's house sometime on the night of the murder but doesn't recall the exact time." He fingered through several sheets of paper, looking through them, then folded them back and pointed at the top sheet and read, "In fact, the neighbor only remembers seeing someone 'looking sort of like' William Carper walking toward the victim's house." Then he looked up and stared at the jurors. "Once again, flimsy and circumstantial evidence, ladies and gentlemen."

He put the papers back in his briefcase then leisurely ambled over toward the jury box, all the while turning his head slowly from one side of the jury box to the other. "My client does not deny he went to the victim's home on the night the murder was committed. He admits to being at the door of the victim's house at ten o'clock the evening of the murder." He shrugged. "Mr. Carper went there to borrow some coffee for the next morning, for him and his girlfriend, Carmella Anthony. My client states he walked up to the door, noticed there were no lights on in the house, looked at his watch, noted it was ten p.m., and realized it was too late to be bothering the Baileys. He then returned to his home. He was gone for no more than three minutes. He states he then went to bed around eleven p.m."

Placing his hands on top of the railing in front of the jury box, he glanced from one juror to the next as he raised his voice. "William Carper was a friend of the Baileys. He babysat Heidi Bailey several times at the request of her parents, Pat and Jeff Bailey." He slapped once lightly on the top of the railing. "Yes, he'd been in their home, but only when asked. Did he enter their home on the night of the murder? No, he did not."

He gestured toward one side of the courtroom. "His girlfriend, Carmella Anthony—" He glanced in her direction for a second, returning his gaze to the jury box. "—testified Mr. Carper stepped out for a couple of minutes to go next door to borrow some coffee. She swears he was gone for only a couple of minutes." He brought up his left hand and ticked off four fingers, one at a time with his right hand, counting with each point he made. "That did not give my client enough time to break into the Bailey house, find the knife in the kitchen in the dark, walk down the hallway into Heidi Bailey's bedroom, and murder her. Ms. Anthony states she and my client went to bed at eleven p.m. and he never left her side. They were both awakened the following morning when the police arrived to question them."

Walking back to the middle of the courtroom he stood in front of the judge's raised desk and turned back toward the jury. "Neither my client nor Carmella Anthony heard anything during the time the coroner's office said Heidi Bailey was murdered. They were in bed from eleven p.m. on the night of the murder until the police knocked on their door the next morning at six a.m. Ms. Anthony testified she's a light sleeper and she swears my client, quote, 'Sleeps like a log and snores like a bear' which is why she knew he never left her side after they went to bed that night. In fact, she swears he kept her awake the entire night of the murder because of his snoring."

He walked slowly to the jury box, eyes facing downwards, and stopped in front of the railing and looked up, lowering his voice. "My client has no history of violence. He's never even had a parking ticket. Neighbors have testified to his behavior before and after the murder of Heidi Bailey and every one of their testimonies states my client is incapable of committing such a crime."

He pointed to the prosecutor's table with his right hand, never shifting his gaze from the jurors. "The prosecution has no evidence proving my client murdered Heidi Bailey, members of the jury, and it is your job to listen to their lack of evidence and judge my client innocent of the crime of murdering Heidi Bailey."

He grabbed onto the top of the railing with both hands and leaned toward the jurors seated in the first row, looking at each of them, left to right and back again. "You cannot judge my client guilty beyond a shadow of a doubt. The prosecution's entire case is filled with dubious and doubtful circumstantial evidence." He switched his glance upward to the next row of jurors and perused each of them left to right and back again. "That is not enough to convict my client of the murder of Heidi Bailey. They know it and you know it. It is your duty as jurors of this courtroom to find my client, William Carper, innocent of the murder of Heidi Bailey."

He turned around, showing the jurors his back, walked several paces then turned back around to face them. "It's the right thing to do, ladies and gentlemen." He nodded and pointed his finger over at William Carper while still staring at the jurors. "If you judge my client guilty of this crime, it would be an abomination of the legal system. You must not only do the right thing, you must do the legal thing. Find my client, William Carper, innocent of any wrongdoing." He dropped his arm that had been lifted in his client's direction. "I rest my case, Your Honor." He nodded once then smiled. "Thank you, ladies and gentlemen."

Edward walked quietly to where his assistant sat behind their two opened brief cases and took his seat at the table. He'd spoken succinctly and with total confidence. Granted, I hadn't listened to the witnesses' testimony or heard what the prosecution had said about his client, but based on what Edward had told me, it appeared his client would be set free. And I understood how that made Edward feel. He was doing his job to the best of his abilities, yet he was setting a murderer free. He was carrying his own personal weight of sorrow for the murder victim and her family. However, he also would walk away from this trial knowing he'd upheld the law and done his job well.

Chapter 48

I left the courtroom after hearing Edward's summation. I wanted to run by the hospital to check on Amylynn, but when I arrived at the ICU, the nurses must have been involved with patients because there was no one at the main station. I walked over to Amylynn's room. Empty. Looking around to find someone to ask what was going on, I saw one of the other patients in the ICU surrounded with doctors and nurses and knew I shouldn't interrupt.

I took the elevator to the first floor waiting area, hoping Amylynn had been released. Upon approaching the receptionist's desk, I stood at the counter while she finished speaking with someone on the phone.

"Is Amylynn Saxton still a patient?"

She typed the name on her computer and her eyes roved left to right as she read the information on the screen. "She was released from the hospital today."

"Thank you so much." My smile was so wide it hurt the sides of my mouth. I rushed to my car, jumped in, and searched through my purse for my cell phone with one hand while I started the engine with the other. I pressed in Cecilia's home number as I backed out of the parking space, headed for home.

After a few rings, she answered. The sound of her 'hello' told me everything I hoped to hear.

"Hey," I said, grinning to myself. "I just left the hospital. How's Amylynn doing?"

She sighed. "Her temperature's finally normal and the doctor told us to keep a close eye on her but she should be fine within a week." I could hear her sniffle. "I don't know what I would have done if something had happened to her, Brandy, I—"

"Don't even go there, Cece," I interrupted. "Be thankful she's okay now. And you sound so relieved, I feel like crying too."

"Thanks for being such a good friend. It means a lot to me. And to Perry, too."

"Hey. Good things happen to good people, Cecilia. You guys waited a long time for Amylynn. You deserve all the happiness she's bringing to your lives."

"Want to have coffee together this week?"

"Just give me a call. I'll bake the muffins."

By that time, I'd reached my house and parked in the driveway. After explaining to Stephanie what had happened, I asked if she could babysit a while longer. I wanted to see if I could find Edward and tell him the good news. Perhaps he'd have time to talk when court recessed for lunch. I drove the few blocks to the courthouse. It was almost noon so there was a good chance I might run into him.

After pulling around to the back lot, I noticed his Porsche was still parked there. I maneuvered the Mercedes next to his car, shut off the engine, and leaned back, trying to collect my thoughts. The courthouse was located on Shoreline Drive, across from the beach. Reclining the seat, I laid my head back, rolled the window down a few inches, and listened to the calls of the seagulls. The next thing I heard was a light tapping on the car window.

Edward's face peered through my side window. I sat up and stared at him, momentarily disoriented. "Oh my God! What time is it?" I opened my car door and he bent down to where I was seated.

"How long have you been out here, Brandy?"

I shook my head and blinked several times, my brain muddled. "You're kidding me! I got here right before noon."

"Did you drive over here for a reason? Were you planning to come inside or just sleep in your car overnight? Where's Jessica?"

"I came here to see you, hoping you'd have a break for lunch. I closed my eyes to take a little rest and I must have fallen asleep. Stephanie's at home babysitting Jess."

"What did you want to talk about? Is there something wrong?"

"Just the opposite." I smiled.

"Wait a minute." He closed the car door, walked around to the passenger side, and got in. "Talk to me," he said, taking hold of my hand.

I twisted in my seat to face him. "I told you about Amylynn being sick." He nodded. "But she was getting better. Then her fever spiked again, over one hundred and five degrees, and after they admitted her to Alameda Hospital she had a febrile seizure. I guess she was fighting some sort of virus. But anyway, she's fine. Her temperature's back to normal and she's home now."

He pulled me in toward his chest, wrapping me in his arms. "Wow. I bet she and Perry are relieved."

I leaned back and rested against the car door. "Oh my God. Cecilia was so upset, she was crying on the phone. If anything had happened to Amylynn she'd be devastated." My bottom lip quivered and he took both my hands in his.

"It brings up bad memories."

I nodded. "Yeah. But at the same time, I'm so grateful to have Jessica in my life. And you." I smiled and dabbed at my eyes with the tips of my fingers.

The sun's rays were dwindling and twilight over the bay cast yellow and orange light inside the car.

Edward leaned toward me and kissed my forehead then pulled back to look at me. "I saw you in court today."

I cradled his face in both my hands and smiled. "You were brilliant," I said then grasped his hands in mine. "I understand what you meant now. It looks like your client will go free."

"The jury's out deliberating." He looked down at his wristwatch. "Scratch that. It's four-thirty so they've been released for the day. Would you like to go out somewhere quiet to eat? I'm starving. I missed lunch today."

"How about we pick up a pizza at Demarco's then go to your house? I just have to call Steph, explain about my falling asleep, and make sure she can stay with the baby awhile longer."

He gave me a gentle kiss. "I'll follow you in my car."

I called Stephanie from my cell phone and she said she'd be happy to stay. She had plenty of studying to do and enjoyed the quiet of my house. We stopped and picked up a garden pizza to go, then drove to Edward's house. While I sat in the dining room he lit a fire in the front room fireplace, and I could hear the logs crackling and spitting. He placed several lighted candles on the windowsills, creating a soothing atmosphere. We ate in silence for a few moments, comfortable just being together.

"You know, this episode with Amylynn brings up some personal issues I've been dealing with. Since Christine died, I've had a helluva time coming to terms with the death of any child. I just can't believe an all-loving God would let this happen. I've been questioning the foundation of my beliefs, everything the nuns taught me in Catholic school.

"I understand my mom and dad dying. They'd both been ill and were relatively old. But Christine and all the children who die every day? Sometimes I turn on the television and Marlowe Thomas is speaking about St. Jude's Children's Hospital, all those kids dying with cancer. I swear, it just doesn't make sense."

He placed his hand over mine and held it tightly. "Have you talked with Cecilia about this? Does she feel the same way?"

"She and I spoke about it once. She believes in karma. She explained how bad things will inevitably happen to everyone, but if a person has tried to live a decent life, good things will come back to them. I agree with her. It happened to me. Christine died then I gave birth to Jessica. Makes more sense than some entity controlling what goes on in our lives, letting children die before they've had a chance to experience life. I could go on but you get what I'm trying to say, don't you?"

We'd never had a dialogue about religion, or God, or the church. For all I knew, this had the potential to cause problems for us in our relationship, but I hoped not.

"I don't blame you for feeling that way. You carried Christine for nine months then she died at birth. I can understand why you'd doubt the existence of God."

He leaned his elbows on the table and looked intently into his glass of wine. "I've always thought of God as more in terms of energy. Like a spirit or force of goodness. I believe everything good comes from that energy, and if you do good, it adds to that energy." Looking up at me, he continued, "I'm not trying to be all 'Star Wars' or anything. You can call this force or energy any name you want— God, karma, whatever. That's just semantics.

"I wasn't raised Catholic, so I don't have this vision of a big guy with a long beard wearing a white robe up in the sky, orchestrating what goes on in the world. I find it easier to accept there's a living non-physical goodness, and we all contribute to it, as well as receive from it." He paused. "Have I lost you?"

I shook my head. "No, I like the way you explained. And, you're right, call it karma or label it whatever you want, it's all the same thing. I went to parochial schools all my life. And I don't want to drop out of the whole religious scene just because I don't buy into the belief system I had when I was eight years old. My perspective's changed but that's okay, right? My new way of thinking isn't messed up, it's just different than when I was a little girl."

He nodded and gave my hand a squeeze. He did understand. He got me.

We'd both finished eating and were relaxing, sipping our drinks. I felt a little better after having eaten, and the peace and quiet helped me feel less stressed. He stood, took my hand, and guided me toward the couch in front of the fireplace, where we cuddled under the blanket, warm and full from our dinner.

We both fell asleep. I felt emotionally exhausted, and Edward had been burning the candle at both ends. When I woke up it was nine o'clock, and I realized I had to get home; I hadn't told Stephanie I'd be gone this long. Edward drove me home then dropped Stephanie at her house. He was returning to the office for a few hours to work on other cases and tomorrow morning he had a meeting with his assistant. He was wound tight as a clock and hadn't been sleeping well, so we planned to get together after the verdict came in.

I climbed into bed, thinking of Cecilia and Perry and what they'd just been through. I was so glad there had been a happy ending for them. They were a solid couple with a deep faith in the goodness in the world—Cecilia's karma, Edward's energy. What goes round, comes round. It had happened for me, and now it had happened for them too.

Chapter 49

The second week of January—and our wedding was just around the corner. I hadn't completed my list of things-to-do yet. Then again, a lot had been going on. What with Edward's trial, Amylynn being in the hospital, and now waiting for the jury's final verdict, my mind was focused on everything but the wedding.

If the jury reached a decision soon, as Edward predicted, he and I would have about two and a half weeks to finish up what needed to be done, leaving us time to slow down and take a breather.

They hadn't reached a verdict by Tuesday and Edward called to tell me he was heading to the gym to work out then have a quick dinner and try to catch a few hours of sleep at his house. He explained he felt this way whenever he was awaiting a verdict and I shouldn't take it personally.

I couldn't relate to the pressure and stress he must be under being a criminal attorney, speaking in front of a judge, jury, and courtroom. It seemed an unbelievably daunting job. I'd never be able to perform in front of so many people. It took a helluva lot of self-confidence to pull it off. But it came with a price—sleepless nights and wound-up days.

The following day I had the television turned low, listening to a daytime soap opera while paying bills, when the newscaster's voice announced "breaking news." Looking over at the television, I turned up the volume on the remote, assuming the verdict had come in on William Carper.

"We've just learned Mr. Edward Barnes, attorney for William Carper, the man on trial for the murder of little Heidi Bailey, has been shot on the courthouse steps. The jury announced their verdict of 'not guilty' and Mr. Barnes was leaving the courthouse when one shot was fired. Just a moment. We're receiving live video from in front of the

Alameda Superior Courthouse. Lacy Beerjin is covering this breaking news. Lacy?"

I dropped the remote and stood, eyes riveted on the television, watched in horror while the picture on the screen switched to the courthouse steps where dozens of people formed a large circle around what I assumed was Edward's body. Paramedics and police were trying to keep people away; however, the media with their zoom lenses were able to get close-up video of the scene.

I knelt in front of the television and touched the screen with my fingertips, not believing the scene unfolding in front of my eyes. I forced myself to listen as the newscaster gave a blow-by-blow account of what had led up to the shooting, her words painting a horrifying picture in my mind—a gun, Edward dropping onto the steps, a man running away, the police capturing the shooter.

I stared at the picture on the screen, my mouth half-open, heart pounding so hard I could feel the "thrump-thrump" beating wildly in my chest. Two paramedics were wheeling away my fiancé, my Edward, the father of my child, on a gurney toward the back of an ambulance. One of them held up an IV next to Edward as they loaded him inside. That meant he was still alive, didn't it? Oh, God, please... please... please. The rear doors swung shut and the vehicle sped away from the courthouse.

I ran to the phone and called Stephanie. She'd seen the news too and was already looking for her purse so she could come over to my house. She had babysat for me so many times, I didn't have to give her instructions. I was getting into my car as she jogged around the corner. She waved to me, held up the house key I'd given her, and let herself inside.

I arrived at Alameda Hospital in less than three minutes. I stood back as the paramedics slid the gurney out of the back of the ambulance and wheeled it toward the doors to the Emergency Room. His face was covered with an oxygen mask, his hair disheveled, his skin the color and sheen of a grey porpoise. His white dress shirt was drenched in reddish-purple blood from his belt to his collar.

Not being related to Edward yet, I wouldn't be allowed to accompany him. One paramedic was talking to someone on a two-way radio, detailing Edward's vital information to whoever was on the other end of the line. They raced through the doors into the hospital and several words cut through my consciousness: extremely low blood pressure, not responding, heart rate rapid—all signs pointing to someone in very bad shape. I watched, numb, as they disappeared beyond the inner sanctum of the Emergency Room doors.

I ran over to the reception desk where a woman sat in front of a computer, typing information from a sheet propped up on the desk. She didn't acknowledge I was standing there so I tapped on the window separating her from the rest of us in the waiting area and when she didn't look up, I knocked on the glass with the palm of my hand.

"Excuse me? Could you tell me where they've taken Edward Barnes? He was just brought into the E.R."

She looked up from her keyboard and glanced down at a piece of paper on her desk. "Are you related to Mr. Barnes?"

I tried to look confident, straightened my shoulders and placed my hands firmly on the countertop. "I'm his fiancé. We're getting married in a few weeks. I just want to know if he's been admitted," I answered, my voice quivering with held-in emotion.

She looked up at me then down at the paper then up again. I thought she might know Edward, the attorney for the accused murderer of the five-year-old girl. Perhaps she was aware he'd been shot on the courthouse steps. But something in her eyes showed she felt sorry for him or for me. "Your name?"

"Brandy Chambers. Someone shot him on the steps of the courthouse. I just want to know what's happening to him. I'm his fiancé and I know I don't have any rights yet because we aren't married but—"

Realizing I'd raised my voice, I began whispering. "If you could just tell me if he's been admitted to the hospital or if he... didn't make it?" I couldn't make myself say the word 'dead', and I couldn't pretend to be strong much longer.

"He's been admitted," she whispered. "He's in the ICU now. If you go around to the front of the building and enter the hospital from the main floor, take the elevator to the third floor. That's where the ICU is and you can try, and I mean try, to talk your way into seeing him, but I'm not promising anything. I don't know the nurses who work there, so I'm not sure what they'll tell you. But you can give it your best shot. I'm sorry."

It seemed I'd been holding my breath since walking into the building. I let out a sigh of relief, thanked her, and ran out the E.R. doors to the front of the hospital. When the elevator reached the third floor I felt a sickening wave of déjà vu, memories of Christine and Amylynn and my parents hit me like a slap in the face. I couldn't move. My feet seemed incapable of exiting the elevator. The doors began to close, and I stuck out my arm to stop them from shutting.

I had to do this. I had to go to him, tell him how much I loved him in case he didn't make it. I stepped out and the elevator doors shut behind me. I was dreading what I'd learn, hating what I most feared—that Edward was dying and I'd lose him forever.

But I wanted to know the truth, even though a part of me felt more comfortable being ignorant of it. However my need to know won out. I walked as if maneuvering through quicksand until I came to the hub of the ICU—the nurses' station.

A woman dressed in green scrubs looked up from her computer screen. "Can I help you?"

"I'm Edward Barnes's fiancé. My name is Brandy Chambers. I was told he's here in the ICU. Someone in the Emergency Room told me I might speak with you about his condition. Could you tell me how he's doing? I'd really appreciate it."

She stood up and leaned toward me, taking both my hands in hers, squeezing them. "He's in the ICU because his condition is serious, Ms. Chambers," she whispered. "I can't tell you much more. The doctors are examining him to determine how extensive his injuries are and whether he needs to have surgery. I would guess we'll know within the hour exactly what their plan of action will be. Does Mr. Barnes have any relatives? Do you know if he has a will or living trust with a medical directive?"

I shook my head. "His mother's dead, he doesn't know where his father is, he hasn't any brothers or sisters, and he's never told me about any relatives. As far as a will or living trust, you can call his law office. I'll give you the number. They should be able to tell you something. Can I wait here? I mean, is there a waiting room?"

She nodded, pointing behind me. "There's a special waiting room for relatives of ICU patients just over there, to the right of the elevators. As soon as I phone Mr. Barnes's law office and get the medical information, I'll know more about his situation, if he has any relatives or not and verify your identity as his fiancé. I'm sure you understand our position."

"I do. And I appreciate your help." I took one of Edward's business cards from my wallet and placed it on the counter then wrote my cell phone number at the bottom. "The people at his office should be able to answer your questions. I wrote my cell phone number here too." Slipping it toward her, I added, "I appreciate your being so understanding."

"I'll call you when I know anything. We have a cafeteria on the first floor, if you're interested."

I thanked her again and walked around the corner to the waiting room. Several chairs lined both walls. At the far end, a window overlooked the parking lot, letting in substantial sunlight, making the room appear bright and somewhat eerily cheerful. I sat down and put my head in my hands. I could feel my heart twisting inside me, clenching in my chest.

This couldn't be happening. I had no one to talk to. Cecilia was taking care of Amylynn. Stephanie was babysitting Jessica and I couldn't call her and talk about my feelings; we didn't have that type of relationship. Truthfully, I had no one to commiserate with, to discuss how helpless I felt. I decided to go to the cafeteria, get something to drink then return to see if there was an update on Edward's condition.

Chapter 50

The cafeteria was large and airy, windows lined the walls. I purchased a latte from the in-house Starbucks and was looking for an empty table when I heard the Fergie ringtone coming from my cell phone.

"Brandy, I heard about Edward." It was Cecilia. "How's he doing?"

"I don't know yet. I saw it on TV and came to the hospital right away, but when I got to the ICU they still hadn't finished examining him. I'm in the cafeteria. I gave the nurse my cell number. Cecilia, I can't believe this is happening. I think I'm in shock. Who shot him?"

"Heidi Bailey's father, Jeff Bailey. They arrested him. I doubt he'll make bail if they allow him to be released on bail anyway. The man's spent a ton of money already on an attorney for his daughter's murder. They keep showing the video of the shooting over and over again so don't turn on the television when you get home."

"I won't. Then again, I probably won't be going home. At least not until I find out what's happening with Edward."

"I could meet you at the hospital, stay with you for a while."

"I appreciate your wanting to come here but, no, you shouldn't. You need to be with Amylynn. She just got out of the hospital and she's still recovering."

"Hey, Perry's taking a mental health day today. I could come sit with you, unless you don't want me to then of course I'll understand."

I tried not to cry. Cecilia had been through her own emotional upheaval with Amylynn having been in the hospital. But now Amylynn was getting better and Perry was home. Deep down I was scared and having Cecilia with me was exactly what I needed. "I'd love it if you could meet me here. I feel so alone. I—"

"I'll be right there. Should I meet you in the ICU or the cafeteria?"

"I'm going back up to the ICU waiting room on the third floor. And Cecilia, thank you for doing this. I love you."

"See you in a few minutes."

Exiting the elevator on the third floor, I walked straight to the nurses' station, hoping they'd know something by now. I was so worried about him. One of the nurses turned and saw me. I could tell she recognized me or maybe she'd been told who I was.

She hurried over. "Brandy Chambers, right?" I nodded. "Dr. McBride said she'd like to talk with you. If you want to follow me, I'll tell her you're here."

I took a seat in the conference room that faced the beach, though the windows on the third floor were so high I gazed into a bright blue sky studded with marshmallow clouds. A few seconds later, a young female doctor, thin, attractive, with short, curly black hair, entered the room and took a seat across from me. She put her elbows on the table and looked me straight in the eyes.

"Ms. Chambers, I'm Dr. McBride. I've spoken with Mr. Barnes's law office and confirmed you're his fiancé. Mr. Barnes informed them you were the person to contact in a medical emergency. He has a living trust but the attorney at his law office who took care of it is on vacation. They're trying to get in touch with him now. I've decided to share with you all information concerning his condition."

"Is he going to die?"

She leaned back in her chair, twisted a pen between her hands. "Ms. Chambers, let me tell you what we know so far. He's suffered an extenuating cervical spinal trauma from the bullet along with internal injuries. It was a hollow core bullet and it shattered. One of the pieces must have nicked the spinal cord. He's in a coma, which is a good thing. It's his body's way of dealing with the physical trauma.

"We're not sure yet whether he'll have use of his limbs, and until he comes out of the coma, which he may not, we won't be able to tell if he's sustained any brain damage. So, in a nutshell, it's a waiting game and it's too early to give a prognosis. But I wanted to keep you apprised of his current condition. We'll know more as time goes on." She stood to leave.

I thanked her and remained seated. She walked quickly out the door into the hallway of the ICU. I didn't have the energy to get out of the chair. My legs felt rubbery, numb, my head cluttered with worry, my body exhausted from the tension of not knowing what would happen to him. He was in a scary state of limbo—in a coma, perhaps quadriplegic, internal injuries. Would he ever wake up? Would he ever speak to me again? Would we get married as planned? I highly doubted that. It all sounded terribly frightening and uncertain.

Placing both my hands flat on the conference table, I tried to push myself up, gathering a strength I wasn't sure I had, hoping it was hiding somewhere inside me. Little stars clouded my vision and I shut my eyes until I felt less dizzy, waited a few seconds then reopened them. After taking a deep breath, I walked unsteadily to the ICU waiting room, assuming Cecilia would be there by now.

She was standing in the waiting room, gazing out the window, and walked over to me when I entered. "How are you doing? How's Edward? Did you talk to the doctor?"

I collapsed in the nearest chair, placing my head in my hands. "I talked to Dr. McBride. He's in a coma, with internal injuries." I turned toward her, leaning the side of my face in my hand. "At this point it's a waiting game. I guess Edward told someone in his office to contact me in case of a medical emergency."

She sat in the chair next to me, putting her arm around my shoulders. "Well, that's a good thing, Brandy. You won't be kept in the dark about how he's doing. Is there someone he authorized to make medical decisions for him, you know, if he can't do it himself?"

Looking down at the floor, I shook my head. "I don't know. He never mentioned any relatives to me. Hopefully, it won't come to that."

"I'm sorry you have to go through this. It's all so sad."

I turned toward her. "You know, just the other day Edward and I were talking about karma. And he gets it, Cecilia. All the good in the world comes from us and it also comes back to us. He's a good person and he deserves to live."

She gave me a small smile and kissed me on the cheek. "Of course he does. You need to be strong now, Brandy. He's alive and you have to believe he'll pull through."

"I want to see him."

She took hold of my arm. "Then let's ask if that's possible, maybe for just a few minutes."

We walked to the main station in the ICU and waited until I noticed the first woman I'd spoken with walking out of one of the patient's rooms.

"I'm Brandy Chambers. I spoke with Dr. McBride a while ago. I want to see Edward Barnes. May I visit him?"

She looked at the computer behind her, scrolled down through what I surmised was Edward's medical file. "Dr. McBride notes here that you're authorized to visit Mr. Barnes, but only for five minutes each hour, Ms. Chambers." I raised my eyebrows in surprise. "For the first seventy-two hours," she added. "Hospital rules."

I nodded. "I understand. Cecilia, why don't you wait for me in the other room, or down in the cafeteria."

"I'll go get a cup of coffee then come back up here. Take your time, Brandy. I'll be in the waiting room when you're finished."

Chapter 51

He was in room 310—a number I was sure would be etched on my brain forever. I walked to within a few feet of the door's entrance and stopped. Was I ready for this? Inside my head, I was already repeating over and over, "Please don't let him die." I closed my eyes, gathered whatever remnants of inner strength I could muster and walked forward.

A breathing tube snaked out of his mouth, and his dark mustache looked like a caterpillar draped over the clear plastic hose. An IV was connected to his left arm, a bag of life-giving solution hanging from a pole next to the bed. He looked like he was asleep, his face appeared normal, there wasn't any bruising. He was as handsome as when I'd last seen him. He seemed serene, at peace. Then again, he looked like someone lying in a casket before being lowered into the ground.

I quickly let go of that thought and stepped to the side of the bed free of medical paraphernalia, and picked up his hand. I turned his palm upward and kissed it then stared at the tiny faint lines running up, down, and sideways. His life line was extra long—perhaps a good omen—and I recalled my teenage years when we used to read palms whenever we had slumber parties, giggling and scaring each other until three or four in the morning. I wasn't giggling now but I sure as hell was scared. Would he wake up from the coma? Would we be able to get married some day?

Pushing those thoughts aside, I took another deep breath and turned my eyes again toward his face. He seemed so content. Had he been awake and aware of anything right after he'd been shot? I hoped not. I wouldn't want to be cognizant of my surroundings, people crowding around trying to help, the sounds of a dozen voices shouting out directions, the wail of the ambulance, the fire engine's siren, the burning agony of a bullet lodged in my body. I'd rather be incoherent than have to experience such a thing and hoped Edward hadn't known what was going on.

I leaned over the side rail and kissed him gently on his cheek then whispered how much I loved him, and I was here for him whenever he woke up. There were a million different opinions, both medical and personal, concerning whether or not a person in a coma can hear what's being said to them. I'd read medical articles and true-life accounts in which people talked to individuals in a coma, read books to them, and generally treated them as if they were awake and listening to everything they were saying.

Several people who woke up related stories of hearing what had been said to them, validating the opinion that speaking to comatose patients was not some ridiculous hocus-pocus.

A nurse came in and told me my five minutes were up. How ludicrous—five minutes for each hour? That wasn't enough time to help Edward in any significant way. How could I have time to read to him and talk to him if I only had five minutes an hour?

Glaringly obvious was the fact I had a seven-month-old baby who needed me and hospital rules didn't allow infants in the ICU. I couldn't ask Stephanie to play mommy 24/7. She'd be taking additional classes soon and wouldn't be available as often. If I had been single, with no child, I could stay by Edward's side around the clock, but I quickly realized that wouldn't work.

It was terribly frustrating knowing I could help him by being there most of the day, but I had responsibilities I couldn't hand over to someone else—a husband, or a friend, or Stephanie. I couldn't ask Cecilia. She was taking care of Amylynn who was just a few months younger than Jessica. I had to triage my life, and my child came first.

I walked back to the waiting room and found Cecilia on her cell phone. I gathered she was talking to Perry because she ended the call by saying, "I love you."

"Was that Perry?"

"Yeah. There's some kind of emergency. He has to get back to work. I hope you understand."

"Of course. In fact, I can't stay either. I have a baby who needs me and I've got to go home. I'll visit when I can, but they'll only let me see him for five minutes each hour—for the first seventy-two hours, that is. Then I don't know what the rules will be."

She looked at me, pensive, then patted me on the back. "You can only do so much, Brandy. I know you love him. But the hospital has rules for patients in a coma and it's what they believe is best for their recovery. Like you said, you can't sit here 24/7, even if you wanted to. Jessica needs you. You mustn't feel guilty about putting her first. You'll probably be able to visit him every day for a little while. And maybe later you can visit for longer periods of time. Stephanie could come over after classes and babysit. Just do what you can, accept it, and let the rest go."

I nodded, relieved she understood. "You're right. I just feel bad, or maybe I feel guilty, for not being able to do what I think would help him. It's so damn hard, putting him at the bottom of the totem pole. He won't have anyone here with him. He's all alone."

"He has *you*, Brandy. Do what you can, love him deeply, and let it go. Try to be positive, think good thoughts, believe he'll get better. You can make a difference in your own way even though you can't be by his side all day. For all you know he'll come out of the coma and you'll be setting a date for your wedding."

I smiled at her, thinking again how lucky I was to have her as my best friend. "Thanks, Cece. What would I do without you?"

"You'll be fine. Why don't you come over to our house and have something to eat before you go home?"

"I can't, but thanks for the invite. Stephanie's been babysitting all day and I have to get home. We'll make it some other time."

We parted ways in the parking lot. When I arrived home, I was exhausted. I needed to go to bed. I'd given my home number to the nursing staff, knowing they'd keep me updated on Edward's condition. I could go to sleep knowing he was in good hands. If he took a turn for the worse, I'd be there in a few minutes.

Chapter 52

The next morning I phoned the hospital to see how Edward was doing. Nothing had changed. They were planning to operate to remove those bullet fragments that could potentially move and hit vital organs. Other bits and pieces could be taken out at a later date. They were scheduled to operate that afternoon, and the nurse promised to phone me as soon as he came out of surgery. I couldn't bring Jessica with me and Stephanie couldn't babysit. She'd be in classes most of the day and had tests she was studying for.

I planned to go about my normal routine and carried my cell phone with me whenever I left the house. I decided to take Jessica in the stroller I'd purchased and jog along the beach front. I needed to exercise if I wanted to keep healthy and stress-free. The only way I'd make it through this most recent trauma would be to ramp up those endorphins while exercising, and keep a positive attitude as Cecilia suggested.

When I returned, I put Jess down for a nap and decided I could use one too. I was exhausted, having slept fitfully throughout the night. Obviously the mental stress was affecting my body. I tried to think positively, believing Edward would make it through surgery and wake up from the coma.

The insistent ringing of the phone woke me and I noticed the clock read 4:15 p.m. I'd slept for three hours! The house was so quiet and I'd been tired after my morning run. I fumbled for the handset next to the bed.

"This is Hannah Greathouse from Alameda Hospital. Is this Brandy Chambers?"

"This is she. I remember you, Hannah. We spoke in the ICU."

"Dr. McBride asked me to phone you. Mr. Barnes's surgery went reasonably well. They were able to remove several of the bullet fragments, however he's still in a coma. You're aware the first seventy-two hours are the most critical."

"Yes, I am. Dr. McBride told me if he doesn't wake up within that time frame, the prognosis for a full recovery lessens considerably. It's been twenty-four hours since he was shot."

"Yes, it has. I just wanted to keep you apprised of the situation."

"I'll be there soon." I slowly replaced the phone on its base, and stared fixedly at the wall.

Thirty-six hours to go.

Stephanie said she'd come over for an hour between classes while Jessica was napping. I planned to visit Edward during that time—a routine I hoped would not continue for long.

When I'd explained my situation to the doctor, she said she'd allow me to see him for an hour if I stayed quietly by his bedside. I guessed she felt sorry for me and was willing to bend the rules a bit. Whatever the reason, I was grateful.

When I arrived at the hospital at five o'clock, the head nurse at the ICU said she had news concerning Edward's living trust. They'd finally contacted the lawyer Edward had retained who was on vacation. A month ago Edward had made a change, designating me the person in charge of medical decisions for him in the event he was incapable of doing so. I was sickeningly surprised.

In my gut, I didn't want the responsibility. If his condition worsened, I would have to decide whether or not to pull him off life support and I didn't want to be put in that position.

I left feeling more depressed than before. Of course I wanted Edward to come out of the coma and one day be his old self again. But if his condition took a turn for the worse, which the doctors had explained was statistically probable, I didn't want to be the one to decide to let him die. Now my hope for his recovery was coupled with my wish not to have to ever make a decision about his life.

That evening I sat in the front room trying my best to relax for a moment when Cecilia called.

"Hi, Brandy. Any change in Edward's condition?"

"None. If he shows no signs of improvement within the next twenty-four hours, the chance for even a partial recovery are pretty slim."

"I'm so sorry."

"Plus, I just found out he put me in charge of making medical decisions for him if he's incapable of doing so." The tears started again and my voice quivered, "My God, Cecilia, I don't want to be the one to tell them to pull the plug!"

"Brandy, listen to me," she said firmly. "There is absolutely no reason to anticipate the worst case scenario. Not right now. You're anxious enough dealing with the situation as it is. You don't need to think about the 'what ifs'."

I tried to stem the tears, but was so overwhelmed and depressed I could hardly talk. "I want to believe he'll get better. You know I hope that'll happen. But the doctor said—"

"Stop this," she interrupted. "You and I both know, no matter *what* the statistics say and *what* the doctors predict, that does *not* mean that's what will happen to Edward. There are hundreds of cases where the pros gave a person little or no chance of living more than a few months, or living through an illness or some kind of awful injury. And the next thing you know the person's walking around, talking about the latest Giants game, and eating at Burger King."

She made me laugh, and the sound was like music to my ears. "Okay. I agree with you. I guess I just needed a pep talk."

She sighed. "Look. I know this is an impossible situation to deal with. No one can tell you what's up because they just don't know. So why go down the path of the worst case scenario. Try walking down the other road—the road where you see Edward hopping out of that damn hospital bed with that shit-eating grin on his face, his booty hanging out of the back of his hospital gown. And smile, Brandy. Visit him with a grin on your face, not a frown. What have you got to lose? And you might have a whole lot to gain if your positive attitude makes a difference to him."

"You're the best friend I've ever had, Cece."

"And I can say the same about you, Bran. Now I've got to feed Amylynn. Keep your chin up."

* * * *

Seventy-two hours and Edward was still in a coma.

Hours turned into days, then a week, and still no change. Dr. McBride explained to me that after two weeks, if his condition stabilized and he could breathe on his own, they'd have to move him to a care facility—where he'd stay until he came out of the coma at which time they would assess whether he'd need rehabilitation therapy.

If he remained in a coma, he'd likely never regain consciousness. Listening to Dr. McBride say those words gave me goose bumps, imagining Edward in a convalescent home in a coma until he died.

The worst part was, no one could predict what would happen. He'd already been pulled off life support and was breathing on his own. And visiting him was difficult. Ironically, he looked completely normal and his coloring appeared natural. But he never moved. He looked like a handsome prince, lying so still and serene.

If he awakened, the doctors didn't know if he'd ever move his limbs again. Each day a therapist exercised his arms and legs to maintain blood flow, moving him from side to side to keep bed sores from forming. During my hour visit, I would tell him what I'd done that day, sometimes I'd read him the newspaper headlines. I'd tell him how much I loved him, beg him to wake up, try to open his eyes. Each day he never twitched, moved, or opened his eyes to indicate he'd heard my voice or felt me holding his hand and kissing his lips.

Unfortunately, the nearest facility with an opening for a patient needing the level of care Edward required was located in Pleasanton—a good thirty-five minutes away with no traffic. I had assumed he'd be in a facility much closer, perhaps in Alameda, and this new twist in his future felt like a knife in my chest.

If I wasn't allowed to bring Jessica, and Stephanie was busy with college courses, I wouldn't be able to visit him as often. I already felt guilty I was neglecting him by visiting once a day, seven days a week. Relocating him to Pleasanton would drastically reduce my visits, and if Stephanie wasn't available, I wouldn't see him at all. And the two week deadline before moving him out of the hospital was the next day.

Stephanie babysat Jessica the following day while I drove to Alameda Hospital to fill out the paperwork for Edward's transfer. I followed the ambulance to Pleasanton to the new facility where I filled out another set of papers for his arrival at his current home. I was so upset seeing him there I wanted to cry but held the tears in check.

The facility was pleasant looking, painted in bright colors, plants on every window sill, windows shiny, allowing in generous amounts of light. They wheeled him into the room where he would, hopefully, not be staying for long. But watching him lying there expressionless and still, I cried when I kissed him goodbye on the cheek. What if he died here and no one was sitting with him when he took his last breath?

I drove home, tears coursing down my cheeks, blurring my vision. I drove in the slow lane, not wanting to get in an accident, and when I arrived home, Stephanie took one look at me, gave me a big hug, and told me to call her if I needed anything. When I shut the door behind her, it hit me like a hammer to the chest—today was Edward's birthday, February first. We were supposed to be standing in front of a Justice of the Peace, exchanging promises to love each other for the rest of our lives.

Chapter 53

February fifth was my birthday and all I could do was cry, recalling how it felt to leave Edward only four days ago on his birthday, abandoning him to strangers at the care facility. Jessica was still asleep when I got out of bed at my usual six a.m. I didn't relish this quiet time.

I was more depressed now because Edward no longer resided in Alameda and his prognosis was grim. The reality of his situation, coupled with the feeling I'd abandoned him, made celebrating my birthday seem so wrong. I wished the hours would pass quickly until bedtime then I could hide in the cave of my slumber and stop thinking about him… about us.

The weight of his absence weighed me down, my body and mind falling deeper into depression. However, I couldn't do this again. I refused to revisit the horrible place I'd been after Christine's death, living on the edge for months afterward, neglecting myself, Weston, our relationship.

Now I had sole responsibility for Jessica, and she needed me to be the best mom I could be, every day. I couldn't turn her care over to my husband. I had no husband. And I couldn't let Stephanie raise my child. She was a young college student, busy with pre-med classes, not a surrogate mother.

The probability Edward would be my next husband seemed more remote with each passing day.

I took a hot aromatherapy bath and listened to the silence of the morning, washed my hair, and put on my make-up. I dressed in one of my favorite outfits—Abercrombie & Fitch pink sweats and a white ribbed t-shirt—stuck my feet into Jordan basketball shoes, sprayed Avril Lavigne cologne on my wrists, and headed downstairs to wait for Jess to wake up.

While sitting at the kitchen table looking out the window at the trees and rose bushes, sipping a latte, there was a knock on the front door. I made a mental tally of who it could *not* be—Cecilia would be working at home, Stephanie was studying for tests, and my neighbors would think it rude to come over at eight o'clock in the morning. I turned the door knob and could see a figure on the other side of the lace curtains covering the beveled glass. It was Weston.

"Happy birthday, Brandy." Something was different about him. He seemed… happy.

"What are you doing here?"

"I remembered it was your birthday. I saw what happened to Edward on the television. No matter what you think, I'm sorry about his being shot. And I'm sorry about losing my temper and punching him in the face at your Christmas party. I was jealous and I never intended for him to fall down the stairs. My behavior was inexcusable, and I felt terrible about what happened. I never took the opportunity to tell you, or him, how sorry I am about what I did."

I let out a sigh. "In the grand scheme of things, Weston, it's no big deal. I forgive you. I know you weren't yourself at the time. You've never been a violent man, and I know it was an accident. With Edward being in a coma, what happened with you two in the past is just that—the past. It's the least of my worries."

Tears flowed down my cheeks, coursing their way along my chin onto my shirt. Weston gently smoothed them aside with his fingertips, then cupped the side of my face with his hand.

"I'm sorry you have to go through this, Brandy. No matter how jealous I may be, I'd never wish this on anyone. I'd be the first person to understand why Edward's in love with you, and I don't blame him for anything. Our marriage went sour before he came along. Your having his child wasn't the only thing breaking us apart. I played my part in it too. I just hate to see you so unhappy. You've had more than your share of sadness. I wish I could help you, take some of the pain away."

I closed my eyes, feeling the warmth of his hand on my cheek. My tears continued to flow, the sadness overwhelming me in his presence. Before our problems began he'd always been there for me, bending over backward to lift my spirits after Christine's death. But back then, I was beyond anyone's consolation.

Since that time, I'd learned a lot, both about acceptance of the bad things that happened in my life, and my new-found way of looking at life in a positive way. Yes, I had to accept what happened to Edward, but I believed something good would come along later.

I opened my eyes and found myself looking straight into Weston's eyes, his expression unreadable. I couldn't tell whether he was sad, remembering our past together, or if he was about to say something to make me feel better. I was wrong on both counts. Instead, he leaned forward and placed a gentle kiss on my lips, at the same time dropping his hand from my cheek, placing it on my hip, drawing me toward him.

With both hands on his chest, I pushed myself away from him with all the strength I could muster, stumbling backward. "What the… what the hell is wrong with you? I thought you were being noble telling me you were sorry about Edward, but that's not why you're here—"

"I'm sorry, Brandy," he interjected. "I didn't come here to do that. I wasn't trying to take advantage of you."

I squinted at him and stepped closer. "Get the hell out of my house," I screamed. "My fiancé is in a coma, he could die, and you're here trying to seduce me?"

"No! I wanted to tell you how sorry I am about—"

"Go tell it to someone who cares, all right? You make me sick," I said and pushed him out the front door.

He grasped the edge of the doorjamb to keep from falling and sneered at me. "The best thing I ever did was divorce you."

"I hope you told Carol that. I'm sure she'd want to know," I replied then slammed the door in his face.

What a creep. If Edward wasn't in a coma, would Weston have come over here and tried to take advantage of me like that?

Edward was going to wake up. I was still his fiancé and I was willing to wait however long it took for him to come back to me. My relationship with Edward, such as it was at the moment, was not over. And I certainly didn't need to fill the void in my life with another man. Weston had offered himself to me on a silver platter, but too much water had flowed under *that* bridge. We couldn't just pick up where we'd left off. It would never work out. I couldn't trust him to be there when the going got rough.

And I'd be fooling myself if I thought he'd accept Jessica as his daughter. My being pregnant was the reason he'd walked out on me to begin with, and I couldn't take the chance he might heap his resentment on her in some way. That would be irresponsible and stupid.

My subconscious had already been dealing with the possibility my waiting for Edward could be a protracted experience, going on for years with no end in sight. But this was the man I loved with all my heart. I'd wanted to marry him before he'd been shot, and I *still* wanted to marry him. Though it was depressing to think of him living out his life in a care facility, I'd be there when he woke up.

And I planned to tell him that. Just in case he could hear me.

Chapter 54

Now that Edward was in Pleasanton, I needed at least forty minutes driving time each way if I wanted to visit him, which meant Stephanie had to babysit for two hours. I reached for the phone to call her.

"Hi, Steph. Do you have time today to watch Jess for a few hours?"

"Sure. She's an easy baby to take care of. She likes to sit in her seat and watch me study," she answered.

"How are your classes coming? You still loving your courses in pre-med?" It seemed our previous conversations had centered on *my* life, *my* problems with Weston, or the drama surrounding *my* fiancé Edward. And I wanted to get to know her better.

She groaned. "Another year and a half at Alameda J.C., then I'm outta here."

"Have you selected a favorite university yet?"

"I'd kill to get into Stanford. My parents can afford it, but I've gotta ace every single class if I want to get accepted there."

"I admire your career choice, Steph. How many years are you looking at before you graduate?"

"Man, oh, man… I'd say about eight to ten years, depending on the specialty I select. You know, like, if I decide to be a neurosurgeon or something, it could take longer. It's too early for me to know just yet."

I was at least ten years her senior, and she was more mature than I'd been at her age. "I don't envy you. But you're lucky your parents can afford to send you to a private university. When you graduate you'll have your pick of places to practice. Do you want to stay in California?"

Lowering her voice to a whisper, she said, "I haven't told my parents this, so don't say anything, all right?"

"Of course. What's the secret?"

"I'm interested in joining Doctors Without Borders. My dream is to travel all over the world. If I'm with DWB, I'd be able to do both, practice medicine *and* travel."

"And your parents wouldn't like that?"

She laughed out loud. "*Not.* They don't want me to go to school out of California, and they sure as hell don't want me to practice medicine in Africa or somewhere like that."

"I had no idea. But I guess if they're paying, what, around forty thousand a year if you go to Stanford for six or more years, they probably believe they have a say in where you go afterward."

"Uh, yeah, that's about what they said when I expressed an interest in going overseas after I graduate."

"I wouldn't worry about it right now, Steph. They might feel completely different by then."

"You're right… Hey, what time do you want me to come over?"

"Anytime. Now, later, it doesn't matter. I want to visit Edward, so I'll be gone for about two hours."

"I'll be over right away. I have a ton of studying to do, so take your time. My next class is tomorrow morning."

I felt better after talking with her, especially after the marathon conversation we'd had the other day about my life. Whether the subject was Edward, Weston, or whatever came up, she was always interested. And she'd been privy to a lot of our family drama by now. She was invaluable both as Jessica's babysitter and a friend to commiserate with in good times and bad.

Visiting Edward felt different this time. Yes, the prognosis was grim, and at times my visits appeared useless. And it was hard seeing a loved one in such a bleak condition. But the situation was not hopeless.

I was constantly reminded of how ever-changing life is, turning this way and that, always surprising you when you found yourself going down a path you never expected to walk. But I had to let go of my need to know exactly where I was headed, put the worries in my imaginary box, and just be happy. Attitude was everything, Cecilia had counseled me. And though Edward's situation seemed out of my control, I *could* control how I reacted to it.

Life had veered in a different direction than where he and I had planned—standing in front of a Justice of the Peace with our friends looking on, partying afterwards, cutting a wedding cake, honeymooning in Kauai. But I had to keep those hopes inside my heart, carrying them with me as I lived this "altered" life I'd found myself living.

I stopped at the shopping center on my way to Pleasanton and bought a bouquet of colorful flowers along with a stuffed animal of a Friesian horse. I wanted to liven up his room and lift the spirits of his caregivers.

I wasn't sure whether anyone besides me had been visiting him. He had no immediate family, and all his friends were co-workers. A few had come by when he was in the hospital, but I doubted anyone would be visiting now that he'd been moved to Pleasanton. It saddened me to think of him spending his life in this environment, but he was alive, I told myself, which was better than the alternative. And I wanted to help him on his way back to me.

After parking in the lot behind the facility, I closed my eyes, took several deep cleansing breaths, and braced myself to enter the building. I was in good spirits when I entered his room, believing one day he'd awaken. I stopped by the nurses' station to ask how he was doing, and they told me he was the same, nothing new to report.

He looked less pale than when I'd seen him last and the physical therapist explained to me they exercised his arms and legs twice a day, along with electrical nerve stimulation and massage therapy. His hair had been cut and his mustache trimmed. The personnel were a caring and diligent group of people, going the extra mile in an effort to make the patient and family feel reassured their loved one was being looked after with great care.

One of the staff doctors stopped by soon after I arrived. "Are you Brandy Chambers?" she asked, glancing down at the chart she held in her hands.

"Yes. I'm Edward's fiancé. Has there been any change, doctor?"

Perusing the pages of Edward's medical paperwork, she sighed. "I'm afraid not. I spoke with Dr. McBride this morning. Given Edward's last neurological test results, there's still brain activity. He's breathing on his own. His condition hasn't deteriorated since he arrived here. I concur with her prognosis. On the GCS scale, we'd rate his condition a nine."

"What's the GCS scale, doctor?"

"Oh, I'm sorry. It stands for Glasgow Coma Scale which runs from one to fifteen. The higher the score, the better the recovery."

"So he's right there in the middle," I said, hoping that was a good sign.

"Ms. Chambers, we know less about comas than we do about a lot of medical conditions. Mr. Barnes is in a coma because we believe a bullet fragment nicked his spinal cord. Eleven thousand Americans a year sustain spinal cord injuries, leaving fifty-two percent of them paraplegic and forty-seven percent quadriplegic. However, each SCI patient—" She paused when she noticed me frowning. "SCI stands for spinal cord injury. Each SCI patient's situation is different, and it's almost impossible for us to make a clear prognosis."

This was the first time anyone had rated Edward's future status. There was no way to know whether he'd remain comatose for the rest of his life, and the stark reality of the statistical evidence for his recovery wasn't impressive.

"You never really know, though, do you? He could suddenly wake up."

She looked me straight in the eyes, sympathy written all over her face. "You can torture yourself not knowing, Ms. Chambers, hoping someday we'll tell you something different." She shrugged. "And you may be right. Miracles do happen."

It hadn't happened *yet*, but the glimmer of hope flickered brightly inside my soul, refusing to be extinguished. "Yes, they *do* happen, doctor," I replied, giving her a wide smile.

She nodded once and left the room. I followed behind her and gently closed the door. I wanted to be alone to talk with Edward without any disruptions from passersby or staff.

I rose up on tiptoe to sit next to him on the bed and wriggled up close to his side then took hold of his hand in my lap, enjoying the warmth of his palm.

I slid my fingers through the sides of his hair then bent down and kissed him lightly on the lips. Every facet of his face was unflawed by the shooting. He was so handsome. My insides twisted, seeing him lying so placid and still. I yearned to gaze into those gorgeous blue eyes, to see his smile, or that grin after he made one of his silly jokes.

"Maybe you can hear me, Edward, and when you wake up you'll repeat every word I said. I hope so anyway." I paused and glanced out the window at the cirrus clouds threading through a light blue sky. "You wouldn't think I'd ever be at a loss for words, would you?" I chuckled. "Hell, I was on the debate team in college."

Looking back at his unchanged expression, tears clouded my vision and I dabbed at my eyes with the edge of my shirt. "I love you, honey. More than life itself. I want you to come back to me. And it doesn't matter to me if you can walk or wave your arms or crack those stupid jokes. I don't care." I took in a shuddering breath. "I just need to be with you."

Tears streamed down my cheeks onto the folded-over sheet. "Please, please wake up. I miss you so much, I feel empty inside and I'm lonely without you. I feel as though I've been cut in half. I'm no longer whole without you by my side." I laid my head on his chest, heard his steady breathing. His chest rose and fell just as it had after we'd made love on the couch on Christmas Day.

"I'll wait for you, Edward," I whispered. "Forever if I have to." I sat up, and laid my palm on the side of his cheek, memorizing every nuance of his face. "When you wake up we're going to get married. I promise it'll be the most beautiful wedding ever. I'll be wearing a dress that will knock your socks off." I laughed out loud.

"Then you and Jessica and I will go somewhere by the ocean, maybe Kauai, where the beaches have really white sand and the water's greenish-blue like in the pictures. You and I will make love under the stars on the lanai and fall asleep to the sound of the waves lapping outside our cottage on the beach.

"We'll take Jess into the warm water, and she can tiptoe along the edge of the surf between us, her tiny toes digging into the sand, and she'll squeal and laugh every time the water rushes up to grab her feet."

I closed my eyes, leaned my head up toward the ceiling and took a deep breath then looked back at his gorgeous face. "I swear to God, Edward, I know in my heart you can hear me. You might not be able to answer but the words are getting into your head anyway. I just know it." I held his face in both my hands, kissed his lips then pulled back a few inches. "I'm waiting, sweetie. I promise you, I won't leave you. Ever. I love you so much. I need you. Jessica needs you.

"When you wake up I'll get here as soon as I can, okay? I swear this to you—you and I will grow old together, dammit. We'll watch our daughter grow up and go to college, move out, get married. And you and I will sit in our rockers on the front porch talking about the first thing you did after you woke up."

I kissed his forehead, both his cheeks, then a lingering kiss on his soft lips. "No matter where I am I'll be thinking about you, knowing you'll come out of this. Remember, I'll always love you. And I'm waiting."

I slid off the side of the bed, walked to the door, and turned toward him. "Until then, my love," I whispered, kissed my fingertips then blew the kiss his way.

Chapter 55

During the drive home, I thought about Jessica, almost eight months old now, and her future relationship with her father. I decided to phone Dr. McBride to talk with her about my idea. I didn't know how long I'd be playing both mommy *and* daddy but I didn't think Jessica should be separated from her father for who knew how long. When Edward awoke from the coma, I wouldn't want him to be a complete stranger to her. I was determined not to allow a hollow core bullet dash Edward's plans to be a father to his child.

I decided to turn the time I had spent with Edward in the past into writing the best book I could possibly create, poring my emotional intensity into making my third novel the publishable success I believed it could be. I'd prepare for the book signing Borders had scheduled in March and revise my website to include enticing snippets of my second novel.

Life had been so busy since Edward came into my life and having a child was such an engrossing experience albeit a happy one for me. Now that Jess was crawling, and walking was on the horizon, Cecilia and I had talked about having the two babies play together while she and I visited.

Jessica's world was slowly opening up as she grew older therefore opening up mine to the outside world too. Writing was such a solitary endeavor. Sometimes weeks would pass before I realized I'd been sequestered in my personal bubble inside the house on the MacBook, not having interacted with anyone but Jessica.

When I got home, the baby was napping. I paid Stephanie, thanked her for all her help, and sent her on her way then called Cecilia to see if she'd like to get together. After a few rings, she picked up and we made a date to meet at Peet's the next day for coffee, both anxious to hook up again, getting reacquainted after everything we'd been through.

The following day I put Jess in the jogging stroller and made it to Peet's by ten o'clock. Cecilia had taken Amylynn for a doctor's appointment and was already standing in line to order. The moment I saw her I realized how much I'd missed our talks. Since Amylynn had been in the hospital and Edward had been shot we hadn't spent any time together.

I wrapped my arms around her and gave her a big hug. "I've missed you so much, Cece. You look great."

She smiled. "Thanks, Bran. I started running a few weeks ago, one of my New Year's resolutions. And I feel better than I have in a long time. How about you? How's Edward doing?"

"It's been too long since we've talked." We picked up our coffees and snagged a window table. "I'm visiting him as often as I can in Pleasanton. It's so weird. He looks like he could wake up at any moment. He's not on a ventilator, he has no bandages around his head or anything. I come into the room and it's the oddest sensation. I expect him to open his eyes and crack a joke or something."

I took Jess out of the stroller and set her on my lap. Cecilia did the same with Amylynn and we glanced at each other and laughed. I handed each of the babies a biscotti and nodded toward Amylynn. "She's all better?"

Cecilia's wide smile lit up her face. "She's just fine. And I want to thank you for all your support when she was sick. I know I can always call you no matter what. You never make me feel stupid when I'm freaking out."

I wiped Jessica's face with a napkin and handed one to Cecilia who did the same. It was like watching a mirror image of myself, sitting across from her with her baby in her lap. She and I now shared an extra bond that tightened our relationship more than before the girls were born.

"I feel guilty I haven't been out to visit Edward in Pleasanton yet," she said. "Amylynn was sick and took a few weeks to completely recover then the doctor advised me to keep her away from any health facility just in case her immune system wasn't strong enough to fight off another virus. Then Perry started working a bunch of overtime so—"

"Alameda Hospital didn't allow infants in the ICU anyway, Cece. And now that he's all the way out in Pleasanton, I don't expect you to visit him."

"I know, but I'd like to see him."

"Well, you know what?" She raised her eyebrows. "I talked to Dr. McBride and she's allowed me to bring the baby to see Edward. I'm so jazzed."

She grabbed my forearm and smiled. "What a great idea! Maybe having his daughter in the same room with him will make a difference."

I nodded. "I was thinking the same thing."

"When are you going?"

"This afternoon. I have the perfect outfit picked out for her to wear. It's that little pink dress you bought her after she was born."

"The one with the pink cowgirl boots to go with it?"

I took a sip of my latte and turned the biscotti around for Jessica to chew on the dry end. "Don't you think she'll look so cute with her auburn curls against the pink?"

She reached out and fingered one of Jessica's corkscrew strands of hair. "Did your hair look like this when you were little too?"

"I have several pictures I found when I went through my mother's things after she died. Jess is my clone, I swear."

She patted my hand. "Lucky little girl."

"Wanna switch?" I asked, pointing at Amylynn.

I reached over for Amylynn and Cecilia stood up and lifted Jessica off my lap. We both proceeded to wipe biscuit crumbs from their faces.

"How's the accounting work coming along for Saxton Inc.?"

"Perry's doing extremely well. He's thinking about hiring an assistant to take my place so I can devote myself entirely to the baby."

"Good for you," I said, smiling. "It's hard to get much done when you're constantly getting up and down, isn't it? It's more work than I imagined."

"How's your third book coming along?"

"I get enough written when she's napping and then late at night after she goes to bed. I'm looking forward to my book signing at Borders."

She put down her mug, her mouth half-open. "You have a book signing at South Shore?"

Grinning, I said, "March fifteenth. Will you be there?"

She gave me a withering look. "As if I'd miss it." She paused and smiled. "This is so much fun. We should start jogging together. Then we'd see each other every day."

I laughed. "You're on. You have a jogging stroller too, right?" She nodded. "Then we should start tomorrow."

We spent the next hour people-watching, talking about our neighbors, new movies, and generally just being girlfriends again. I couldn't wait to take Jessica to visit her father that afternoon. I hoped it wouldn't scare her, seeing him lying in bed, unresponsive, but if I approached this experience with a positive upbeat attitude, perhaps she'd see it as an adventure and not be afraid of him.

Chapter 56

After Jessica woke from her nap, I dressed her in a white blouse with short sleeves, a pink vest and skirt, and slipped a tiny pair of pink cowgirl boots on her feet. Her auburn curls framed her perfect little face, she looked like a living doll. Then I took several pictures with my digital camera, planning to print them up and pin them to the wall over Edward's bed.

The drive to Pleasanton went by quickly. My anticipation escalated as the freeway exits I knew by heart whizzed by. Hopyard Road came into view. After parking in the back lot of the facility, I carried the baby in with me, wanting her to feel secure in an environment she was unaccustomed to.

I stepped up to the front desk and the receptionist's face lit up with a broad smile. She recognized me, but I'd always come alone before today. "Who do we have here?" she asked, standing and leaning on the counter. She gazed into Jessica's unsmiling face.

"She's a little shy," I answered. "This is Edward's daughter, Jessica. Dr. McBride said I could bring her to visit him."

She nodded then tapped the toe of one of Jessica's pink boots. "What a great idea. Your daddy's gonna love your boots, Jessica." She sat down and looked up at me. "I think it's so cool, bringing her to see her father." She lowered her voice to a whisper. "So much of the time our coma patients are completely forgotten by their families." She looked from side to side then added, "Personally I believe they can hear everything we say to them even if they *are* in a coma. My girlfriend's boyfriend was in a motorcycle accident and in a coma for six months. When he woke up he repeated every single thing she'd told him about how she seduced him the night they met."

I laughed and shook my head. "I believe Edward will remember his daughter visiting him, too. And I want her to get used to seeing her daddy even though he's not living at home with us right now."

The intercom chirped and she smiled at Jessica. "Give your daddy a big kiss, Jessica," she said then waved goodbye to her.

I walked slowly down the hall, stopping along the way to show Jess the framed prints on the walls.

"We're almost at your daddy's room, Jess," I whispered. "He's in this room right here." I stopped next to the open doorway and gave her a kiss on the cheek. She hadn't smiled since we'd arrived. I'd been telling her during the drive here that we were coming to visit her daddy but she was only nine months old and she didn't understand what was happening. She'd recognize Edward but she wouldn't know why he was here or why he wouldn't talk to her.

I crossed the threshold and rounded the corner, all the while patting her on the back and kissing her cheek to allay any fears she might have. Edward looked the same, freshly groomed and serene. The blinds were pulled up and the windows were open, a warm breeze filtered through the lace curtains. I was hoping Jessica's serious expression wouldn't turn into an open-mouthed wail.

Turning my body so she could see him I said, "That's your daddy, Jess. He's asleep right now so we have to be quiet. We don't want to wake him up."

She gazed over at him then leaned toward the bed away from my chest, thrusting her arms out to Edward. I gently placed her next to his side, moving his hand and putting it on her lap. I walked to the head of his bedside and observed her expression. She twisted her body, tried to crawl up next to his face, then sat on his chest and looked down at him.

Her arms reached out and she patted his lips with her fingers. "Dah," she said, tapping his face with her chubby hands.

"Yes, your daddy, honey. He's asleep."

"Dah," she repeated then straightened her legs out behind her and laid her head down just below his neck. "Dah," she said again.

Tears edged toward the rims of my eyes but I didn't want her to see me cry. Instead, I gave her a wide smile. "Daddy loves you, sweetheart."

She looked over at me than sat up and reached her arms out. I picked her up then bent over to give Edward a kiss on the lips. "Wave goodbye to Daddy, Jessica," I told her. "We'll come another day so you can see him, okay?"

She smiled and waved bye-bye, still looking down at Edward's face. I kissed her on the cheek and turned toward the door, hoping one day I'd be able to tell her that her father was no longer sleeping but had woken up and wanted to play with her.

Chapter 57

March—and spring was in the air. The grass was lush and green in the backyard, the roses were blooming, and the trees were putting on their bright green jackets. I loved this time of year in the Bay Area. The weather was mild, the afternoons sunny.

It was Saturday and I'd just showered and dressed after my morning run with Cecilia, Jessica was playing in her bouncy seat in the front room when the doorbell chimed. Opening it, I saw… a very different-looking Weston. His mustache was fuller and grew down the sides of his mouth, connecting with the goatee on his chin. His hair was long and blown back off his face, reaching the nape of his neck where it curled up a little above his shirt collar. His cheeks were covered in a dark five o'clock shadow.

He wore tattered old jeans, the holes and tears held together by frayed white threads. He had on his old scuffed biker boots, the tops slouched and wrinkled with wear.

After taking this mental photograph during the few seconds after opening the door, my peripheral vision caught sight of a huge Harley Davidson motorcycle leaning on its kickstand in the driveway.

"Hi, Brandy," he said, smiling.

My mouth hung half-open while I tried to incorporate this new image of my ex-husband with the one I was familiar with. This new package didn't fit the picture I had of him the previous time I'd seen him. Then again, the last time we'd spoken I'd slammed the door in his wide-eyed face.

"You look so different." I glanced behind him at the Harley. "Do you own that? I mean, do you ride it?"

He chuckled. "Of course I ride it. It's new. I bought it yesterday."

I took a deep breath. "What are you doing here?"

"To tell you the truth, I was driving down your street and stopped. I wanted to see how you're doing. How's Edward?"

I blew out a puff of air. "Like you're really interested, Weston?"

"Please, Brandy. I'm trying my best here." He glanced down for a second then looked up at me. "I really need to talk to you."

I opened the door and gestured him inside. "I have just a few minutes."

He nodded and answered with a smile then followed me into the front room where we each took a seat at opposite ends of the couch.

"How's Jessica doing?"

"She's fine." I paused and squinted at him. "Weston, what are you doing here? I mean, really? Why did you come by?"

He placed his right boot on top of his left knee and leaned back. "I moved out of Carol's place and rented a house on the lagoon."

"You told me months ago you'd moved out of Carol's place, don't you remember?"

"You're right. I did. But after you kicked me out the front door on your birthday I ran into her, we got to talking… I thought I'd give it one last try. She was still in love with me. I was lonely without you—"

"It didn't work *again* with Carol so you thought you'd come here begging me to take you back," I replied, my tone sarcastic.

"I love you, Brandy. Don't you understand? I never stopped loving you. I can't make it work with anyone else because I don't want anyone but you." He raked his fingers through his hair and sighed. "I'll do anything to get you back. You name it, I'll do it. What do I have to do to make you give me another chance, Bran?"

I shook my head in frustration. "Weston, I knew you were stubborn but this is ridiculous."

"What's ridiculous? Me loving you or you waiting for your boyfriend to wake up from a coma?"

I stood up slowly and gave him a pitying look. "If I was the one in a coma, I'm sure you would have left me months ago, Weston. You know, when the chips are down you run the other way. I've learned that much." I pointed at the front door and whispered, "Now get out of my house, and I don't want you to ever come here again." I paused and stared at him, my gaze unwavering. "Do you understand me this time?"

He stood up and walked toward me but I refused to be intimidated by his size or the look of anger on his face. "When he never wakes up and you find yourself alone with his baby, don't come crawling back to me, begging me to take your lonely ass back into my bed."

I closed my eyes and kept my fisted hands next to my sides, refusing to give him the satisfaction of my anger. I heard his boots clomp across the hardwood floor then the front door slammed. The Harley's engine growled to life. He gunned the motorcycle and sped down the street.

And I breathed a sigh of relief. What a jerk!

Chapter 58

I'd gotten into a routine visiting Edward—three times a week with Jessica and twice by myself. Stephanie took care of Jess while I zipped out to Pleasanton and it allowed me extra time to spend with him talking about my book or telling him about the neighbors, or reading to him from law books his colleagues had suggested which I'd picked up from his office. I'd also kept him up-to-date on the more noteworthy information concerning Alameda by reading aloud from the *Times Star* or *Alameda Magazine*.

Jessica was now completely comfortable visiting the care facility. She'd sit on top of the bed next to Edward and play with the toys I always brought with us. She liked to pretend to read to him from her touchy-feely books. She'd grasp Edward's fingers and place them on the soft fur representing an animal in the book, rubbing his hand along the material so he could feel it too.

I took pictures of the two of them together each time we visited, making sure to document their time together while he was still in a coma. She too would enjoy seeing the photographs when she was older, and be grateful she was able to spend time with him during the formative time of her life.

Jessica had just begun to grasp the edges of tables around the house, pulling herself up to a standing position, and walking without my help was just around the corner. I videotaped her daily so Edward would have the visual history of her growing up. I imagined it was similar to couples where the wife or husband was overseas fighting a war. When they returned they wouldn't feel so sad having missed all the important times in their children's lives if they had photos to treasure.

The signing at Borders had been changed to April since the shipment of my first book had been delayed until the end of March. I hadn't participated in a book signing in at least three years but the store manager was excited about having a local author living in a small city willing to do a book signing, luring people from the immediate area to purchase books at his store.

My big day approached. I was working with a woman whom Brent had referred. She was helping me update and revise my website, and run a readers' contest. We were talking on the phone when there was a knock on the door.

"Can I call you back, Pam?" I asked. "It shouldn't be long. Just think about what the winner would want and I'll phone you within the hour." I put the phone down and went to the front door.

"Cecilia, hey! Sorry but I was on the phone. What's up?" I gestured her inside.

She shook her head. "I can't visit. I just wanted to make sure of the date for the signing. It was changed to April what?"

"The sixteenth, the day after you file your taxes."

"The day we're *supposed* to file our taxes you mean," she said then rolled her eyes.

"Uh-oh. Didn't Perry hire someone to take your place to do the accounting?"

She nodded. "Yeah, but it turns out she's, well, not as meticulous as some of us. If you know what I mean." I shook my head and grimaced. "I'll have to file an extension and clean up the mess. Which brings me to why I came over. Could you babysit Amylynn this afternoon while I go over the books with Perry? I'll be forever in your debt."

"Of course. Just let me call Pam back and I'll give you a ring afterward and we can talk details." She smiled and sighed with relief. "And you're not indebted to me for anything, Cece. Remember you said you'd take care of Jessica while I'm at the book signing."

"You got it. But remember I'll be there too. I can use a friend's twin stroller. It'll be a piece of cake." She backed away from the door. "Call me," she said, waving goodbye.

An hour later when I finally said good-bye to Pam, I was exhausted though elated with the progress we'd made on my website. It looked classy, yet business-like, colorful, eye-catching, easy to navigate and she'd added a link for entering a contest for which the prize was a personal meeting with me this summer to talk about my career and how I'd found an agent.

I was busier than I'd ever been in my life. What with having a ten-month-old child who was learning to walk, visiting Edward five times a week, writing my third book, and jogging every day with Cecilia—there wasn't extra time to fit in much else.

I'd already planned to buy a wedding dress for when Edward woke up. I'd never been the type of person to get strong irrational feelings about things—those gut-level emotions you knew were right, all the way to the core of your being. But when it came to Edward's coming out of the coma, I absolutely *knew* it would happen someday—a knowledge that suffused my heart and soul like red dye in a glass of water.

He was coming back to me, and I'd be fully prepared. I promised him a dress that would knock his socks off, and that was exactly what I'd do. I spoke with Cecilia about it and, knowing her as I did, her reaction was everything I expected. She was game anytime I gave her the word. So I planned on taking an entire day after the signing at Borders to have lunch and shop for a wedding dress in San Francisco.

On the day of the signing I brought Jessica to Cecilia's house at ten in the morning. The signing was scheduled for eleven a.m. and I wanted to make sure everything was set up and ready for customers when they announced over the intercom that Brandy Chambers was signing copies on the second floor of her novel *Passing Through Brandiss*. Coffee and pastries were on me.

When I arrived at Borders in South Shore there was already a line upstairs near the lounge area next to the indoor Starbucks, and the manager informed me they were *not* waiting to purchase a cup of coffee. Apparently an author living in Alameda was a treat for the locals, and the queue went from one end of the back of the second floor near the cookbook section, wended past the chairs and tables for Starbucks customers, all the way to the table and one chair located in front of the balcony that looked out over the beach—where I'd be sitting.

I couldn't have been happier. Everything was set up and ready to go and it was only 10:15! Just as the manager pointed out where I'd be signing books for what looked like two or more hours, my phone vibrated in my jacket pocket. It was Brent.

"It's a twofer," he announced.

"What do you mean by a twofer?" I asked, smiling. I was already in a good mood about this signing and he always made me laugh no matter what.

"When you get two things on one day."

I shook my head, knowing he was being purposely obtuse. But no one could spoil one second of this day for me and I tamped down my minor frustration and laughed out loud. "I don't get it. Would you mind explaining, Brent? I have a book signing in less than forty-five minutes or did you forget?"

I heard his exaggerated sigh. "Of course I didn't forget. The book signing was the first thing you got today. Now I want to tell you about the second thing."

"So what's the second part of the twofer?" I asked. I could never forget he was pitching my second book, but I'd been so busy, it wasn't at the forefront of my mind. "Did you talk to Mark Stefano?"

"He'll probably make you call him Stefano from now on. I swear he gets off on people thinking he belongs to the New York Mafia or something."

"Do you mean he and I will have a working relationship?" I mentally crossed my fingers and toes. A gut feeling this was good news crept up my spine, just like the one I had about Edward waking up.

"Yup," he spit out then laughed.

"Oh my God. You're a genius. I love you." I was practically screaming and looked around for a place to have a more private conversation. I huddled in the corner next to a display of cookbooks and lowered my voice. "So Harper Collins wants to publish my second book?" I whispered.

"Yes, they do," he whispered back. "Hey, what am *I* lowering my voice for?" he yelled into the phone. "Let me call you back tomorrow and we can discuss your contract. Good luck with the book signing." And he hung up.

That was *so* Brent. But wow. I was on the proverbial "Cloud Nine." I turned around to discover the line was longer than before and the manager quickly skittered his way over to me and asked if I could start signing earlier than scheduled. I happily agreed and took a seat at the table near the balcony just as someone made a second announcement about the signing.

Two hours later, at one o'clock, I'd signed over three hundred books and took a moment to talk to Cecilia when she showed up with Amylynn and Jessica in a sleek-looking twin stroller. Both children were chewing on their favorite biscotti and drinking from sippy cups, and I had enough time to kiss them both and say hello to Cecilia before returning to my chair. I noticed the manager had placed new felt-tipped pens and a fresh cup of coffee on the table for me.

My hand was cramping from signing my name so many times yet I was thrilled so many people, mostly women, had come to have me autograph their books. I looked up at the next person in line and thought she looked familiar. Only after she took off her sunglasses and handed me a copy of my book did I realize it was Carol Smith.

"Hello, Brandy. I loved your book."

I noticed she was wearing an oversized smock and it dawned on me. She must be pregnant. "When are you due?" I asked with a forced smile.

"October twenty-third."

"So you're almost four months along?"

She nodded. "Weston's so happy," she smiled, rubbing the small bump underneath her shirt. "He said I must have gotten pregnant on Christmas Day."

I returned her fake smile with one of my own then signed the inside cover of the book and returned it to her.

She opened it then read out loud, "Congratulations to a perfect couple." She glanced down at me, her grin so wide I was sure her face hurt. "Thank you," she gushed, turned and walked away.

How lucky I was to have figured him out before it was too late. He'd obviously been with her right after pushing Edward down the stairs at the Christmas party. And he'd wanted me to take him back knowing Carol was carrying his child? What a schmuck!

Cecilia was waiting for me when I returned to her house at two-thirty. "How'd it go?" she asked with a knowing smile.

I plopped down on the couch, laid my head back and closed my eyes. "Better than I ever anticipated."

"You mentioned you talked with your agent but you didn't have time to elaborate. Gimme the details please."

I looked across at her, lounging on the matching sofa. "Brent called me right before the signing. He wanted to give me some good news."

She quirked one eyebrow upward. "So? What's the good news? Are you going to tell me or not?"

I stood up and pumped my fist in the air. "Harper Collins wants to publish my second book!" I screamed.

She jumped up off the couch, ran over to me and gave me a huge hug. We twirled around several times, both of us laughing.

"Congratulations!" she yelled then lowered her voice. "The kids are both asleep in Amylynn's bedroom."

We returned to our respective couches, smiling at each other.

"I'm so happy, Cece, I'm coming out of my skin." I paused. "Hey, are you still up for going into the city to look for my wedding dress?"

She nodded. "Anytime. Perry says he can take care of both kids. But you still want Stephanie to look after Jessica, right?"

"I think two babies would be too much for Perry. Not that he couldn't handle it, but it's a lot if you're not used to it."

She laughed out loud. "I told him I'd ask you just to make sure you hadn't changed your mind." She lowered her voice though Perry wasn't at home. "He'd go crazy taking care of the two of them. What if they both started crying at the same time? I could just hear it now, both our cell phones ringing while you're in the middle of trying on your wedding dress. And Perry would want us to get home as soon as we could."

I grinned knowingly. "Tell me about it." I paused and glanced out the window.

"What's wrong?"

I looked over at her. "Carol Smith is pregnant with Weston's child," I blurted out.

She leaned forward and stared at me. "You're shitting me."

I shook my head. "I'm perfectly serious. *And*, I signed her book."

"No way! I hope you wrote, 'To Carol. May you rot in hell.'"

I shook my head again. "No. I was the bigger person. I signed 'Congratulations to a perfect couple'."

She tucked herself back into the cushions and smirked. "You are so bad, Brandy."

"Actually, I feel very lucky I didn't take him back, Cece. I guess he was never in it for the long haul. He'd never have stayed with me and Jessica. Someone else besides Carol would have piqued his interest."

"So you're all right with it?" she asked, frowning.

I pursed my lips for a second, thinking. "You know, someone sent me an e-mail the other day. It said something like, 'True love is an acceptance of all that is, has been, will be, and will not be.' It went on to say the happiest people don't necessarily have the best of everything; they just make the best of everything they have."

Chapter 59

After discussing my plan with Stephanie, we agreed to have our shopping day the following weekend. Perry would take care of Amylynn, and Stephanie would babysit Jessica. Cecilia and I had the entire day free to shop and have lunch, knowing the children would be happy and well cared for.

On Saturday I pulled up in front of Cecilia's house at ten in the morning. She rushed out the front door, purse in hand, opened the car door and slid into the passenger seat.

"Man, am I ready for an entire day of girl time," she said with a huge sigh.

I smiled as I backed the car out of the driveway. "Do you have your cell phone? Just in case Perry needs to ask you something."

She gave me a withering look. "For a moment I thought about 'accidentally' leaving it on the counter."

I glanced over at her and raised my eyebrows.

She opened her purse and took out her Blackberry, shaking it from side to side. "Couldn't do it. The guilt would overwhelm me and I wouldn't be able to have any fun." She touched my forearm. "And today is all about having fun."

I shook my head, chuckling. "The bride and maid of honor do San Francisco."

"Brandy and Cece do San Francisco? Somehow that doesn't sound as racy as Debbie does Dallas or whatever that porno flick is."

I burst out laughing. "You never actually saw it, did you?" I asked, merging into the line of cars entering the Posey Tube leading out of Alameda.

"Never. Speaking of which, are you planning to buy any racy underwear to go with your wedding gown?"

I could feel my face fall, the smile disappearing within seconds.

"Brandy, what's wrong? Did I say something to hurt your feelings?"

I could feel her watching me in my peripheral vision and shot a quick glance her way. "No, it's just… Am I being weird going out and looking for a wedding gown when my fiancé is in a coma?"

"No. You believe he's going to wake up, don't you?"

"You know I do."

"Okay. Then what's wrong with buying the dress a little earlier. You'll need it eventually. And unless you plan on gaining a bunch of weight and not fit into your clothes then put the damn dress in the closet and it'll be there when you need it."

A tear escaped down my cheek and dripped off my chin. "I miss him so much."

She put her hand on my shoulder and gave it a squeeze. "Of course you do," she whispered. "And you do an excellent job of holding your emotions in most of the time, too."

I nodded, my lower lip quivering. "Yeah, I do."

"And that's not always a good thing, Bran. You've got to let your hair down sometimes." She paused. "I'm always here for you."

"You're the best friend I've ever had, Cece." I slowed down to pay the bridge toll.

"Which is why I plan to be your maid of honor. And why I just bought the most beautiful dress you'll ever see, except you can't lay eyes on it until your wedding day."

I gunned the engine out of the toll plaza and joined the line of traffic waiting at the metering lights at the base of the bridge span. I turned my head in her direction as she looked out her side window.

"What are you talking about? You already got your dress?"

"Yep. And guess where I bought it?"

"Melanie's Boutique on Park Street."

She slapped the dashboard with her hand. "How the heck would you know that? Did Perry say something to you?"

I shook my head. "No, he did not. Come on now. It's your favorite place to shop whenever you have to buy something really special."

"Anyway, you're not allowed to see it, so don't ask any more questions, okay?"

I ignored her playfully and pointed out the window. "Look at the new span."

"And to think Weston is the lead structural engineer on that project. He must make some bank," she commented.

I nodded. "His alimony payments arrive on time every month. And did I tell you the house sold in San Francisco? After splitting the profit I can buy his share of the house in Alameda and I'll own it free and clear."

"You're really fortunate your divorce was one of the friendly ones."

"Yeah, but after the divorce was final he and I have had a few nasty episodes. He tried to kiss me on my birthday when he knew I was engaged and Edward was in a coma."

"I know. What a shithead." She paused. "He's still in love with you, Brandy."

"Whatever." I glanced out my side window. "Hundreds of sailboats are out. And you can see Alcatraz Island—no fog today."

She looked out her side window then tapped on the glass. "All those prison blocks. Man, the stories they could tell, huh?"

"Forever hidden in stone. Hey, that sounds like a great title for a book."

We turned toward each other at the same time and smiled. Turning my attention back to driving, I took the next exit and made my way to the parking lot behind Nordstrom's. We took the escalator to the third floor and headed toward the bridal section. A Bride's Advisor scurried over to us as we passed under the arched doorway leading to the inner sanctum. I immediately veered off toward a mannequin on a pedestal located in the center of the room.

I could hear Cecilia talking with the Advisor, but I was so entranced with the dress their words didn't register. I knew instantly this was "the one." It was off-white, sleeveless, the bodice covered in hundreds of tiny pearls and sparkly faux diamonds, the waist tapered then flared out slightly in a creamy see-through silk material.

"That's it, isn't it?" Cecilia asked.

"Yeah, it is." I turned to the Bride's Advisor, Kimmee, her name tag read. "The material covering the bottom half of the dress is gorgeous but I can see right through it. Is there something I'd wear underneath?"

Kimmee's smile went from ear to ear, her straight, whitened teeth gleamed beneath the muted lighting. I'd bet she could feel the vibes of a future sale. "Yes, ma'am. That's the beauty of this dress, which is a Versace, but I'm sure you already knew that. We advise you to wear Versace cream tights underneath. I can see you have a beautiful figure. I know you'll look absolutely stunning in this dress. Would you like to try it on?"

Cecilia fingered the price tag hanging from the back zipper. Her eyebrows shot up but I didn't ask her the price. This was "it" for me. I wanted this to be the dress of all dresses, one that would stand out forever in Edward's mind.

Turning to Kimmee, I gave her one of my own gleaming smiles. "I'd love to try it on. And could you bring me a pair of tights. I'd like to get a look at the total picture."

We followed her into a room the size of my front room, every inch of the walls covered in mirrors. I'd never seen myself reflected in so many different angles. I would know right away whether the dress was the size and style for my figure. She left us for a few seconds before returning with a pair of cream silk tights then closed the door behind her.

Cecilia and I looked at each other and burst out laughing. I'd never pictured myself here, with my best friend, about to try on a Versace wedding gown. I knew Cecilia was bursting inside to tell me what it cost.

Standing in the middle of the huge dressing room with nothing on but the tights, I stepped into the gown then she zipped it up the back. It felt like a second skin, hugging my breasts and waist in a comfortable snugness, the deeply cut bodice revealing more cleavage than I'd expected. I stared at myself in the mirrors, turning left and right, then noticed Cecilia's face, where she stood next to me. Tears were coursing down her cheeks.

"What's wrong? Do I look that bad?"

She shook her head. "You look like the only woman who *should* wear that dress. It's lovely. And so are you."

"Thank you." My vision blurred with tears. "I love it, too."

She touched my forearm and I looked at her in the mirror, our reflections surrounding us in every direction. It seemed as if the room was crowded with a dozen people. "Why are you crying?" she asked.

"Right before my mom died she said, 'Brandy,' and her voice had this little quiver to it, you know? She said, 'Promise me you'll spend some of your inheritance on something you really want, just for yourself that'll make you happy. Then I'll be happy too.' We all knew she was dying and it was one of the hardest things for me to look her in the eyes and make that promise." I paused and swiped at my cheeks with my fingertips.

"A promise is a promise, Bran." She bent her head up toward the ceiling and closed her eyes. "This is for you, Mom," she said then looked over at me.

I nodded. "This is for Mom." I turned in a full circle. "Don't you think it's perfect?"

There was a knock at the door and Kimmee popped her head in with a smile. I turned toward her and smiled back. "Can we have a few more minutes? I want to walk around, see how it'll look when I'm going down the aisle."

"Take as much time as you need. I won't bother you again. Just ring the bell over there." She pointed toward a button on the wall near a telephone stand. "Whenever you're ready. I'll be just outside," she added, closing the door.

"I almost forgot." I gestured toward my purse and satchel on a chair. "I grabbed my favorite heels before I left. They're the perfect height."

Cecilia took them out of the bag and brought them over to me. "We can look for shoes to match the dress after lunch."

I heard the Fergie ringtone of my cell phone in my purse. Cecilia rushed over and brought it over to where I stood. I flipped it open, noticing the caller i.d. spelled out "HOME."

"Hi, Steph. Everything okay?"

"He's awake, Brandy."

Confused, I asked, "Who's awake? What are you talking about?"

"Dr. McBride just phoned and thought you'd want to know. Edward came out of the coma."

I closed my cell phone and looked at Cecilia's face in the mirror, my mouth half-open.

She knew before my brain could fully register what I'd just heard. "Edward woke up from his coma, didn't he?"

I nodded and covered my stomach with my hand, feeling nauseous. My head felt as if I'd just taken an elevator to the fortieth floor in less than five seconds. The mirrors surrounding me twirled round and round like a carousel, little black dots blocked my vision and I fell to the floor.

Chapter 60

A cool cloth lay on my forehead. I opened my eyes and glanced up, not recognizing the cream-colored ceiling and antique light fixture. Warm hands held mine and I turned my head. Cecilia was sitting next to where I was lying on the floor.

"What happened?" I whispered.

"You fainted. Right after you talked to Stephanie."

I noticed Kimmee standing next to Cecilia, her brows furrowed. "Should I call nine-one-one?"

"Absolutely not," I answered, struggling to sit up.

"Are you sure?" Cecilia said, grasping my arm to help me.

I glanced at her and smiled. "Absolutely sure. I've got to get home."

I stood up and looked around the room to see if I felt dizzy. "I'm fine. I didn't eat much this morning and with all the excitement, finding this dress, the phone call..."

Kimmee's expression brought a smile to my face. She looked like a lost puppy. "Let me give you my credit card, Kimmee. I'm in a hurry."

Her demeanor quickly changed from serious to overjoyed. This would be quite a commission for her. Cecilia searched in my purse for my wallet, extracted my Visa card and glanced over at me. I nodded and she handed the card to Kimmee.

"I'll be right back with the sales slip," she said, rushing out of the dressing room.

Cecilia unzipped the back of the dress and slid if down off my hips. I carefully stepped out of it while resting my hand on her shoulder so as not to fall. Kimmee scurried back into the room, handed me a pen, and I signed the slip. She pulled the receipt apart, handing me the yellow copy.

"I can have the dress sent to your house this week." She paused and smiled. "No charge."

"Thank you. That would be most convenient."

She exited the room, and I hurried to get dressed while Cecilia grabbed my shoes, stuffed them in the satchel and brought my purse to me.

"Ready to blow this place?" she asked.

Smiling, I said, "Let's jam. You drive."

We raced to the parking lot and I threw her the car keys as we approached the Mercedes. We jumped in the car and she sped down the street. The slate-gray towers of the Bay Bridge soared above us. We headed for home, my mind a whirlwind of thoughts and hopes and questions concerning Edward's condition.

"Do you want to drop me off at your house then you can drive straight to Pleasanton?"

"If you don't mind. Stephanie planned on babysitting most of the day anyway."

"Don't worry. Stay as long as you want. I can always bring Jessica to my house until you get back home."

I touched her arm. "Thank you." I looked out the window at the white caps popping out of the waters of San Francisco Bay, the bright blue sky, the sailboats tacking back and forth. "I'm so scared for him, Cecilia. What if he's paraplegic or quadriplegic? What if he doesn't want to be with me because he'll think I'm staying with him out of pity or something?"

She took hold of my hand and squeezed. "Remember what I told you about not torturing yourself with what-if's. Just wait until you have all the facts. Then deal with it." She gave my hand another squeeze. "You're not a wuss, Brandy. You're a strong-willed woman. You and Edward will make it through whatever gets thrown at you. Stop anticipating the worse. Expect the best."

I turned to face her profile and watched Alcatraz Island disappear from view. "I know you're right. It's just..." My heart pounded in my chest. I felt like I'd come right out of my skin, I was so nervous. "I want to be there right now. I can't wait to see him."

We made it to my house in twenty minutes, and I slid over into the driver's seat and took hold of the steering wheel. Cecilia bent down and gave me a kiss on the cheek. "Now stop worrying. Chin up. Smile on your face. Your fiancé just woke up from being in a coma for almost three months. This is a good day." She gestured toward the street. "Now get outta here."

I grinned and made a u-turn at the end of the street so I could take the tube out of Alameda and make it to Pleasanton as quickly as possible. Every possible scenario played in my head. Would he be able to talk? What about walking, or using his arms? There were so many things that could be non-functioning. And for how long? Forever? A few months?

I drove as fast as traffic would allow and screeched into the back parking lot of the care facility, jumped out of the car, pressed the key fob to lock the car then ran through the front doors, past the receptionist and halted several feet from his room.

Dr. McBride was just exiting his room and looked up from the medical chart she held in her hands. "You got my message," she said.

I gave her a half-smile. "How's he doing?"

She looked me in the eyes. "He's talking but he doesn't recall being shot." She paused. "I don't know whether that's a blessing or not."

"Is he able to move? I mean, is he paraplegic, quadriplegic?"

She gestured for me to join her in the waiting room across the hall. "We plan to take an MRI tomorrow morning but at this moment his mental capacities seem unimpaired though there are still additional tests we'd like to perform this week. His hands, arms, feet, and legs are responding to our standard test stimulation. Again, we'll be able to perform a more thorough evaluation this week. I want to bring in additional specialists to complete our examination."

"May I see him?"

"Of course. Don't stay too long, though. All of our poking and prodding has taken its toll. He appears tired." She touched my forearm and smiled. "I have to tell you, this is a miracle. It just proves we have *less* knowledge about comatose patients than all the medical information we *do* have. We're still flying by the seat of our pants on a lot of these cases. And Edward is only one of many." She paused then added, "He's a lucky man."

I thanked her and walked across the hall, stopping at the threshold. I took a deep breath and stepped into the room.

I wasn't sure what to expect when I pulled aside the curtain. His cheeks were flushed, probably from all the activity and tests they'd put him through in the few short hours he'd been awake. He turned toward me, his face without expression.

"Edward," I whispered then cleared my throat. "How are you feeling?"

He didn't smile or reply to my question. In fact, he revealed no emotion whatsoever. It was as if—

"Who are you?" he asked, interrupting my thoughts.

Chapter 61

Now I understood what the look on his face meant. He didn't recognize me. Then again, he'd always been a jokester, especially at the most inappropriate moments. Perhaps he was trying to be funny.

I tilted my head and smiled. "Edward. It's me." I paused. He remained solemn but I told myself he still might be pulling my leg. I pointed toward my heart and raised my eyebrows in question. "Brandy?"

He shook his head and frowned. "I'm sorry but I don't recall having met you before." He squinted his eyes, staring at my face. "I've only been awake a few hours. I can't place your face but I obviously must have been acquainted with you, right?"

I should have known this could happen. He'd been in a coma for almost three months. Dr. McBride had explained patients often forgot their entire past or arbitrary segments of it, and memories could return suddenly or be lost forever. She'd also mentioned forcing the patient to remember was an ill-advised endeavor, often causing emotional distress that exacerbated their already delicate state of mind.

"We were friends," I said. "From high school," I clarified, not wanting to throw too many emotional memories at him all at one time.

"Here in Alameda?"

"Yes. St. Joseph's Notre Dame High School." I laughed when I saw him smile. "I know, long name, isn't it? Especially for such a small school. There were fifty kids in our senior class."

"And we kept in touch all those years?"

"We'd see each other from time to time. Alameda's a small town." I paused, trying to figure out what to say next so I wouldn't upset him. "Dr. McBride told me they plan on running a battery of tests to assess your physical and mental status."

"That's what she told me as well."

"The nurse advised me I shouldn't visit for long. You've only been awake a short while." I took a few steps backward and smiled. "I should go."

He nodded. "Okay. Thanks for coming by… Brandy, right?"

"Yes. Brandy Chambers. I'm glad you're recovering, Edward. This is wonderful news." I gave a little wave and turned to leave.

"Brandy?" he called out.

I stopped mid-stride and looked back at him, eyebrows raised.

"Will you visit me again sometime?" he said, shyly.

"Uh, sure."

He nodded his head slowly up and down.

I hurried out of the room, passed the receptionist's desk to the front door, slammed my hands against the silver bar across the door and bolted outside. I needed to get out of there. I felt boxed in, nearly claustrophobic.

He didn't remember me. But what about Jessica? And what about our wedding?

When I reached the back parking lot, I was disoriented. I turned left then right, searching for my car. I couldn't remember where I'd parked it.

Jogging toward the end of the lot, I saw the Mercedes and dug my hand in my purse, searching for the key fob. When my fingers finally found it I pressed the button, sighing with relief when I heard the click of the door lock as it opened.

I don't know how long I sat in the car, my head against the steering wheel. I'd never imagined this happening when Edward woke up. I recalled my conversation with the doctor at the care facility when she'd said, "Miracles do happen." Well, one just *had*.

I drove home and Cecilia greeted me at the door. She'd obviously seen my car pull into the driveway from the front room window.

"What happened? How is he?" she asked, grasping my arm, searching my eyes for answers.

I touched my fingers to my mouth, feeling my lips quivering with emotion, knowing I could never get through this conversation without crying.

"Here, sit down," she said, wrapping her arm around my shoulders and guiding me toward the couch.

She gently pushed me down into the cushions, took my purse from my hands, and ran into the kitchen. Within seconds she returned with a glass of sparkling water, pressing it into my hand. "Take a drink, calm down," she urged. "You can talk to me about it. Or not. I'll leave you alone if you want. Just tell me what you need."

I took a huge gulp and leaned back into the cushions then took a few more sips and set the glass down on the coffee table. I closed my eyes, not able to say the words to her face, knowing the pity I'd see there if I looked in her eyes. "He doesn't remember me," I whispered.

Silence greeted my declaration, seconds ticked by. Maybe she hadn't heard me. I opened my eyes and looked at her. Tears ran down her cheeks as she stared out the front room window.

Her head slowly turned toward me and our eyes met. "I'm so sorry, Brandy. And I'm sure you don't have all the answers. Maybe it's temporary… like transient amnesia. Did you tell Dr. McBride?"

I shook my head. "All I could think of was I had to get home, to a safe place, away from that facility… away from him, I—"

"You believed he'd wake up and he did. You need to believe in him again. He'll remember you, Brandy. It's so sad your first encounter turned out that way, but he just woke up. It's been almost three months, for God's sake. Just give him time. And talk with the doctor. You never know, she may be able to allay your fears about his amnesia."

"I'll call her right now," I said, stood up and grabbed the phone from the side table and sat back down on the couch. Dr. McBride's number was stored in the phone's memory. I pressed the Call button. Her receptionist put me on hold for a few moments until the doctor could take my call.

"Ms. Chambers. How can I help you? You talked with Edward?"

"I did; however he doesn't remember me, Dr. McBride." My voice cracked with emotion, "Is that a permanent condition?"

"I know it's upsetting," she answered, her tone unemotional. "And it may be temporary. Statistically speaking, the odds of him waking from the coma were stacked against him, as you know. In *his* case, I wouldn't feel comfortable making any kind of prognosis. He's beat the odds so far, he may continue to beat them. Or not," she added.

"That's what I thought. I just wasn't expecting him to ask me who I was."

"Don't be scared away by this. Keep visiting him. Your presence might jar something in that side of the brain dealing with people and places from his past. My advice to you, Ms. Chambers, is don't give up on him."

"I won't. And thank you for taking my call." I set the phone down next to me on the couch and turned toward Cecilia.

"You were right. She said this may be temporary. Or not. It's the 'or not' that frightens me."

She grasped my hands in hers and shook them. I looked her in the eyes. "Don't give up on him, Brandy," she said sternly.

I smiled then laughed out loud.

"What's so funny?" she asked with a frown.

"Dr. McBride said those exact words."

Her eyes got wide and she grinned. "I told you." She stood up and pulled me up with her. "It's almost dinner time. Why don't we order a pizza and watch a movie. It would probably do you some good."

"What about Amylynn?"

"Perry's at home with her. You and I were supposed to be gone most of the day, remember? He enjoys spending daddy time with her whenever I'm not around. Which isn't very often."

"Then I'll take you up on your offer. Just let me check on Jessica and you order the pizza."

I took the stairs to Jessica's room, feeling a hundred years old. I was emotionally exhausted and slid into the rocking chair next to her crib. Little sucking noises escaped from her tiny lips as she lay on her stomach at the bottom of the crib, her favorite blanket clutched in her hand. She was such a beautiful child. Long dark eyelashes hovered above chubby cheeks, her auburn corkscrew curls were scattered across the sheets.

She was my life, my love, the center of my world. And I wanted to give her father back to her. I was determined to do that. "I swear he'll remember you, Jessica," I whispered. "Even if he doesn't know who I am, I swear to God he's going to know who *you* are."

She turned over and looked up at me with her blue eyes, so like her father's, and smiled. "Maw," she whispered.

I reached down and picked her up, nuzzling her cheek against my neck. "Mama's here, sweetheart," I said through her curls. "And Daddy will be here soon too. I just know it."

Chapter 62

I slept fitfully that night and had the weirdest dream. Edward was using American Sign Language to tell me he loved me; however, since I'd never learned how to sign, it didn't make sense that I understood what he was trying to tell me. At seven a.m. the phone's incessant ringing jarred me out of my slumber. Fumbling for the receiver, I finally grasped it after several rings.

"Hello," I said, trying to clear my voice and sound normal.

"Brandy?" It was Edward.

"Hi, Edward." I struggled to sit up, surprised to hear his voice, wondering why he'd be phoning me. "Is everything okay?"

"I'd like to talk to you. I mean, if you have the time to come here I have a few things I'd like to say to you."

I blinked my eyes then looked around my bedroom. Maybe I hadn't been fully awake when I'd answered the phone. "Did you say you wanted to talk to me?"

"If that would be convenient," he answered.

"Any particular time?" I asked, thinking this conversation felt a bit odd. He didn't sound like the "old" Edward and I didn't know what to make of it.

"They'll be running tests most of the morning; however, I'll be here this afternoon," he said, chuckling.

"Okay," I said. Where else would he be? And had he just cracked a joke?

"I'll see you then?" he asked.

"Right," I replied then placed the phone on the bedside table.

I didn't know what this meant—his calling me like this. Perhaps someone, though I couldn't guess who, had told him about me, that he had a daughter. However, the staff had always conducted themselves with the utmost propriety and were very responsible in the manner in which they dealt with their patients.

My mind was going in all different directions, endeavoring to figure out this puzzle. I phoned Stephanie. If she couldn't babysit then I would call Cecilia. This was not the time to introduce Jessica to her father and I needed to do this alone.

That afternoon when I entered Edward's room I was surprised to see him sitting in a wheelchair, dressed in a bathrobe, holding a cup in his hand. He'd been in a coma for almost three months and he'd lost a good twenty pounds. His face was thinner, his arms and legs had lost the tone he'd acquired at the gym. But he was still a handsome man. Looking at him now brought back all the excitement I'd always felt when I was in the same room with him.

He wasn't quadriplegic since he had use of his arms. Maybe he could move his legs too. If so, I guessed it would take rehabilitative therapy to reach the point where he could stand and walk alone.

"Hello, Brandy," he said, his greeting warm and friendly. "Please sit down," he gestured to a chair across from him.

"Thank you," I replied, taking a seat. I fiddled with the clasp on my purse in my lap, not sure what to say, uncomfortable not knowing what *he* was going to say to *me*.

"I love you, Brandy."

I looked up sharply, my mouth fell partway open.

He held his hand up to forestall anything I might answer after his declaration. "I remember everything—about you and me, what happened between us when you were married to Weston, that Jessica's my daughter, about the plans for our wedding." He shook his head and smiled. "I recall you said something about a stuffed horse you'd brought me."

I clasped my hand across my mouth, trying to hide the quivering of my lips. "This is unbelievable," I whispered. "You heard me talking to you?"

He nodded his head again and grinned. "I swear to God." His expression changed, the smile wiped clean from his face. "Do you still love me?"

Tears edged their way down my cheeks. He leaned toward me and grasped my hands. I stared into those blue eyes that had always made my heart sing.

"Why are you crying?" he whispered.

"I dreamed this. I mean, not this exact scene, but last night I dreamt you told me you loved me. However you said it in sign language. And I understood what you were trying to tell me." I started laughing through my tears. "And I don't even understand sign language." I cradled his face in my hands and smiled. "You remember me. And Jessica. Oh my God, Edward."

He put a hand on each of my shoulders, bringing my face inches from his. "You never answered me, Brandy."

"Answered you?"

"Do you still love me?"

I wrapped my arms around his neck, our lips touched, first in a soft kiss then our tongues slowly entwined in a gentle yet sensuous dance before I pulled away. Our eyes locked. "I never stopped loving you. I always believed you'd come back to me. And now you have."

"Did you ever buy the dress that was going to knock my socks off?" He grinned.

My mouth dropped open—again. I could feel each tear slide its way down my cheek. "You're kidding me."

"I heard you, Brandy."

I couldn't stop crying, the tears were endless. I was so happy I wanted to call everyone I knew and tell them he was awake. Edward had come out of the coma!

He glanced down at his legs. "As soon as I get back on my feet again, I want to get married." He took my left hand in his and looked at my ring finger. "You're still wearing it."

I glanced at the engagement ring he'd surprised me with last Christmas. "I had no intention of ever taking it off."

He raised his eyebrows. "Really?"

"I swear," I said, picking up my other hand, turning my palm outward.

"You'll swear in front of a judge?"

"That I'll love and cherish you for as long as we both shall live, so help me God?" He nodded. I cupped his face in my hands. "I do."

"I do too," he added, smiling that grin of his that always made me melt inside.

We leaned toward each other and sealed our vows with a kiss.

ABOUT THE AUTHOR

Born and raised in the San Francisco Bay Area, Patricia attended St. Mary's College, studied her junior year at the University of Madrid, received a B.A. in Spanish at UC Santa Barbara then went on to get a Master's degree in Education at Oregon State University. She lives with her husband and two teenage children in Alameda, across the bay from San Francisco, along with two very large chocolate labs, Annabella and Jack. Her Friesian horse Maximus lives in the Oakland hills in a stall with a million dollar view.